T0382000

A HARVEST OF HEARTS

A HARVEST OF HEARTS

ANDREA EAMES

HARPER
Voyager

Harper*Voyager*
An imprint of
HarperCollins*Publishers* Ltd
1 London Bridge Street
London SE1 9GF

www.harpercollins.co.uk

HarperCollins*Publishers*
Macken House
39/40 Mayor Street Upper
Dublin 1
DO1 C9W8
Ireland

First published by HarperCollins*Publishers* Ltd 2025

1

Copyright © Andrea Eames 2025

Cover design by Verity Hayhow
Cover illustrations: Shutterstock.com

Andrea Eames asserts the moral right to
be identified as the author of this work.

A catalogue record for this book is available from the British Library.

ISBN: 978-0-00-868716-8 (HB)
ISBN: 978-0-00-868717-5 (TPB)

Printed and bound in the UK using 100% renewable electricity
by CPI Group (UK) Ltd

MIX
Paper | Supporting
responsible forestry
FSC
www.fsc.org
FSC™ C007454

This book contains FSC™ certified paper and other controlled sources
to ensure responsible forest management.

For more information visit: www.harpercollins.co.uk/green

For Lyra, the brightest star.

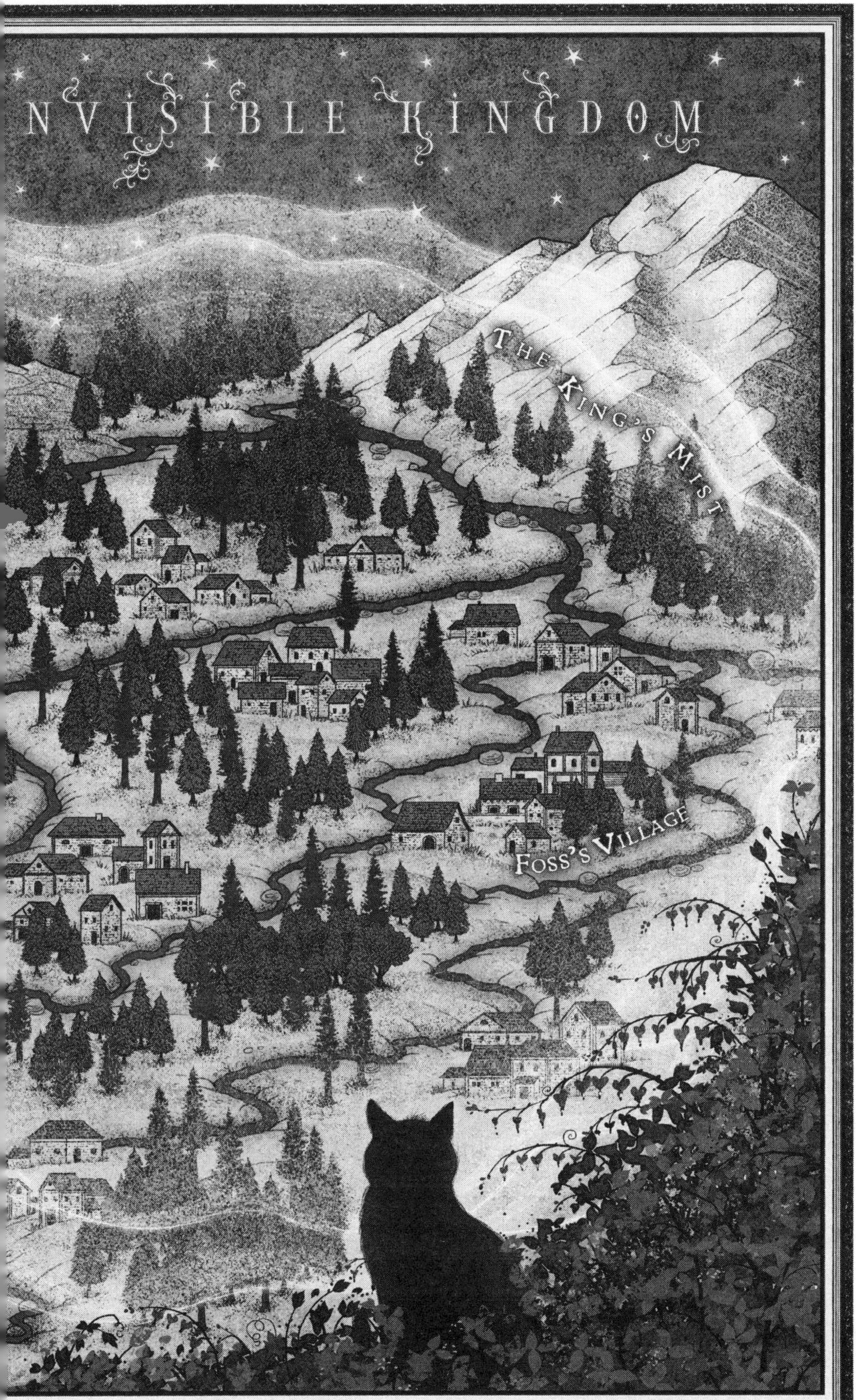
NVISIBLE KINGDOM
THE KING'S MIST
FOSS'S VILLAGE

CHAPTER 1

They said that magic, real magic, not the shite that the hedge-witches peddled with all their little bags of powders and herbs, could only be performed in exchange for a human heart.

That's why all the sorceresses who passed through our village—the ones in the big carriages with the gold scrollwork and velvet curtains—were all so pretty. The sort of pretty that broke hearts, men's and, I'm sure, some women's as well, although, in general, the women seemed to be better at hiding it.

When they visited, the sorceresses made a show of going into the market and buying the herbs we grew, as if they made potions like any old hedge-witch. Really, though, they were sucking bits of heart out of everyone around them, and we all knew it. Yet we gathered around them rather than shutting ourselves away indoors as we should have.

That was their purpose in coming to the villages: gathering bits of heart—second-rate, hayseed hearts, little smears of heart, but enough for small spells. Each smitten man or woman gave a little bit of their heart when they saw one of these ladies, it was said, and she would pocket their devotion to use for a cantrip or a hex.

They rarely took a whole heart, which would involve luring a person away, or so we believed; they seemed to gather enough of what they needed by gradual winnowing during each visit.

I don't know how we knew about the hearts. It was just something we seemed to be born knowing. I suppose our parents told us the story in our cradles, but I do not remember hearing it for the first time.

We knew that hearts were the only source of magic that really worked, although the odd charlatan could get away with tea leaves and herbs for a little while if their luck held; we knew a heart could be taken in bits and pieces, with the victim barely noticing, or all at once, prized from a chest like an oyster from a shell; and we knew the sorceresses got those hearts from us, those who lived in villages far from the city and the king's palace.

And what did they do with all that magic? No one knew for sure, and no one much cared. Whatever they did, they did in the city, and they didn't concern themselves with our affairs, so we didn't concern ourselves with theirs. The ladies probably used their magicks for murdering and all such, we speculated—killing people the king wanted dead. Big, political things.

Our kingdom was never at war and had not been for hundreds of years, as far as anyone knew, and perhaps the ladies and their magicks had something to do with that.

They didn't take enough from us to be a bother, and any inconvenience caused by the gradual stealing of hearts was more than made up for by the excitement of their visits, or so everyone seemed to believe.

That acceptance of what amounted to a slow mutilation seemed strange to me later, but at the time, I was as complacent as the rest of them. So long as they kept to their city most of the time, we could cheerfully ignore them.

Only one man in our village had ever actually been to the city: Goodman Whelk. (Well, one other had gone involuntarily, but more on that in a moment.) But Whelk had visited over thirty years ago, and his mind was almost gone, so he wasn't much help.

None of us traveled away from the village, if we could help it, and certainly never away from the kingdom. Occasionally travelers passed through on their way to Somewhere Else, but more often than not, we would see them again on their way back. They always seemed befuddled at their failure to stay gone. We were remarkably incurious, it seemed to me later, but at the time, we rarely questioned it.

For the most part, in our kingdom, you probably lived out your life and died in the village where you were born. What was the point of leaving? All villages were much like ours; beyond the borders of the kingdom lay nothing but war and danger, from what we heard. And the city held its own horrors besides the sorceresses and their hearts.

We heard stories about children in the city abandoned by their parents—or lost, perhaps—who traveled in gangs of pick-pockets. Or who simply vanished. If we were bad, the adults would threaten us with a cart ride to the city, to join them. Not Da, of course, but other parents.

The wives and sweethearts didn't like it when the sorceresses visited—and some of the husbands, presumably, the ones who saw the longing glances their ladyfolk gave, although, being men, they would never admit it.

The women scowled and glowered and stood with their arms crossed, watching as the beautiful ladies sucked up the hearts that belonged to the womenfolk, by rights. At least, so they believed.

I quite enjoyed seeing the men squirm under the sorceresses' gaze and the womenfolk's fear and anger. The women would come into the shop after one of the ladies had visited and tut their tongues, complaining about the weakness of men, and I would listen stolidly as I wrapped their meat, gleeful on the inside.

I think I liked hearing of their resentment because it meant they knew what it felt like to be me, even for just a moment. Even the prettiest of them couldn't hold a candle to the sorceresses, and I always felt like the plainest girl in the village by a long way.

I knew I would never be one of the young women with a babe on her hip, or even one of the settled matrons in a floury apron. I told myself I was at peace with it, but, as I said, seeing the women's jealousy of the sorceresses gave me a kind of satisfaction. I couldn't find it in myself to feel too sorry for them.

The sorceresses were charming, though. Even I couldn't deny that. I had caught the eye of one once, as she climbed down from her carriage, and she had smiled at me as if I were someone who interested her very much, and whom she might want to learn more about, had she the time. Then I had the inkling of how they might have broken hearts, those ladies.

We had only known one person to be taken by the sorceresses, properly taken. Mostly the ladies just sucked enough heart out of enough idiots to serve their purposes on their rare visits, and then left, like picking the best fruits for the harvest.

Eventually they would run out, I supposed, but perhaps not—the ladies seemed never to age, and maybe they were content to wait till more idiots spawned and grew old enough to leer and yearn after the beautiful city sorceresses. Our village certainly birthed its fair share of idiots.

Perhaps the ladies that visited us were the same ladies who had always visited, back before the memories of even our oldest citizen.

One was taken, though, as I said, to the city. He wasn't anything special—neither handsome nor not-handsome, not young, and not old. Far enough past the usual marrying age for most girls to forget about him, but not so far that they didn't wink at him from time to time.

I could never quite remember his name before that, although I knew it began with a D—Dom? Denys? But after he was taken, everyone knew his name, and it became a name like one in a story, that you whisper, that has its own music to it: *Dav. Dav Mallet.*

A sorceress came to town as usual that day and stepped down from her carriage with a pretty white foot. Some were slim, some ripe and full, but all had faces so fine they could stop your breath; they had skin of all shades, from white to coal dark; and their hair, whatever the texture, was always lustrous, as if lit from within.

You could tell someone had fussed about with it, from all the braids and sparklies hanging off at all angles. They'd stick a jewel wherever a jewel would stick, those ladies, on fingers and wrists and ankles, and some even had their noses pierced.

They wore dresses in all colors, with skirts as big around as four of Goodman Wick's beer barrels, held out with wires to keep them stiff.

Young Sam Stebbin swore he got a look underneath one once, as the lady was stepping up the little ladder into her carriage. He said he was on the ground trying to find something he'd dropped (bollocks), and he looked up and caught a glance of the underskirt, past those jingling ankle bracelets and right up that luscious leg. The lads made him tell this story over and over.

The sorceresses always kept those carriage curtains drawn right till the last moment, keeping everyone on tiptoes and straining to see; the menfolk's trousers bulging out at the seams, no doubt, as if their little fellows could stand on tiptoe as well and get a quiz at the fine city ladies.

Dav worked in the fish market back then. He went out on the river enough days to bring heaps of the stinking things back, dangling from poles. He always smelled a little like fish, did Dav. That was the only memorable thing about him, before that day.

This particular sorceress, the one who took Dav, was golden-haired under her black veil, the gold glinting through the lace like daisies in the grass.

She did not even make the usual pretense of going to the herbalist's that day, but instead stepped her dainty feet in their buttoned boots onto our dirty village ground and looked boldly about her. If she had been a goodwife at the fruit stand, she would have been squeezing melons and measuring the weight of apples; that's the kind of look she had as she eyed the staring crowd with her yellow-green eyes.

She saw Dav standing at his fish stall, with his big tub of brine and his dried fish dangling from his pole like a fringe about him, and pointed one long finger at him.

Dav looked about himself gormlessly, to either side and then behind, then realized to whom she was pointing and poked his eyebrows up so high that they disappeared into his hair.

And then she smiled, and he lurched forward, almost over-tipping his tub of salted water, and made his stumbling way through the silent, watching crowd.

They stepped aside for him as they would step aside for

Goodman Trew, the village drunk, but with none of the laughter and ribald comments. There was just a sense that he should be left to go his way, with no interference.

The sorceress kept her hand outstretched and her finger crooked for all the time he took to wobble up, with nary a tremor in her well-shaped arm. When he reached her, he stood, swaying on his feet, staring into her perfect face. We all stared with him.

She smiled, and all our hearts leaped like Dav's dying fish. Then she opened the door to her carriage and stepped up and inside. He followed, stumbling up the steps, looking like the bumpkin he was. We saw an elegant hand reach from the darkness inside and close the door, and we heard the small *snick* of a lock.

None of us went about our business. None of us spoke. We all waited. Not much time passed—four minutes, maybe five? It was hard to tell. And then the carriage started to rumble, the wheels sucked themselves out of the dirt, and the whole mess of it started to drive back the way it had come.

When it was out of sight, the chatter started. Low-voiced at first, and then louder. Speculation. Lewd suggestions as to what Dav was doing in there with the sorceress. Calls for the guardsmen—she can't just *take* him! Who knows what she's going to do with him? It must be against some law, surely?

And the men looked yearningly after, all wishing it had been them. Maybe they imagined that one day a carriage would stop, and a lady would hold out a hand and take them into the city with her, to be used as she saw fit, and maybe they wouldn't care if she wizened them out like an old fruit. Maybe they imagined the sorceresses were magic all up in their quaints, too. That they had cunnies that glowed, maybe, or shot sparks, or opened up like flowers.

No one called the guardsmen. After all, Dav might have

been taken, but he went willingly. We had all seen it. Besides, the guardsmen were as ineffective as the holy men when it came to sorceresses. Why did we need the law, or even gods, when we lived under the sorceresses' all-powerful protection? Their authority trumped all.

Dav's mother cried. There were half-hearted attempts to contact the city, send letters, but no one knew exactly where to send them.

When Dav came back—must have been a week, maybe ten days later?—he came back alone. They found him lying in his fish stall in the early hours of the morning, when the first market-keepers were trundling in their barrows of produce and flowers.

He was snoring, head on the ground and feet dangling over and into his tin tub of stale, briny water, which no one had bothered to empty. And he was naked with, some said, a great bruise on his chest. I never saw him without a shirt after this, so I can't confirm the truth of it.

They shook him awake, splashed the souring water on his face, slapped him about a bit, and draped him with enough cloth to make him decent. They asked him what had happened. He seemed dazed, looking over their shoulders as if searching for someone else. He looked like a child hunting for his mother in a crowd, on the verge of tears. His great, rough, dry lip wobbled.

Dav's mother kept him out of sight for a while. She kept her curtains closed, too, so none of the village nosy-parkers could peek in.

When he finally emerged, he looked like a man recovering from a long illness. He even walked with a cane, for shite's sake, which I thought was probably for show. After all, his legs weren't what the sorceress had been interested in, presumably.

"Poor fellow," Da said once, shaking his head, as we watched Dav pass by.

"Weak fellow, to be so easily dazzled," I said, blowing a strand of damp hair out of my face. It had been an unusually warm and busy day in the shop, and I was more irritable than usual, and perhaps less generous of spirit. Da shot me a look.

"Don't be so quick to judgment, Foss," he said, but gently. "We don't know what manner of magicks she used on him, nor how we would have behaved in his place."

"I wouldn't have fallen for it, I can tell you that," I said. "No matter how pretty she was."

Da smiled—the same smile he got when he talked about my mam, sad and happy all at once. "We'll see," he said. "You're young yet. There's more than magic that can make a person foolish—or weak, as you call it. Stronger men than Dav have succumbed to it."

I snorted, but I was laughing. He had a way of making me soften up, did Da.

There had been much speculation about Dav's adventures with the sorceress, naturally. Most of it was shouted in the pub or muttered between men on the street and kept away from the womenfolk, but no one really considered me womenfolk, and so I got to hear a lot of it.

It was what you would expect. Talk of dungeons with all kinds of instruments for inducing dark pleasures. Enslavement, Dav in a collar, forced to feed his lady grapes—or, in the gorier versions, little pieces of his own heart, wrapped as elegantly as hors d'oeuvres, perhaps stuffed with pitless olives and silky cream cheeses.

Everyone was eager to hear the musk and moisture of Dav's stories—or, failing that, the blood and horrors. Perhaps a mixture of both.

But Dav said nothing. Whenever he was asked—and he was, subtly at first and then more insistently when he vouchsafed no details—he started to cry like a child, his face open and loose and wet, so that the other men looked away in embarrassment.

He would cry for hours into his ale, himself as free of shame as a baby, but it made everyone else sit at the edges of the room and eye him sideways. After a while, they stopped asking.

Dav never spoke about his time with the sorceress. Nor did he ever marry, nor have a sweetheart. I heard the rumors and saw him often as he passed before the shop window, looking lost and bereft, searching the crowd as if looking for someone.

I didn't think to talk to him myself about the sorceress or ask him about his time under her spell. Back then, I thought I would have nothing to do with the magic ladies besides watching them pass through—more fool me, as it turned out.

CHAPTER 2

Da and I lived right in town, behind our shop, in the mess and bustle of it all. Da was a butcher, and a good one, with arms that looked like legs of lamb themselves, and a way with a cleaver that could make a carcass grateful to be boned.

I worked in the shop with him. It suited me all right. I liked being behind the counter, able to watch the happenings of the village square through the big window while being partly hidden myself, and I liked the work itself.

Most of the running of the place fell to me. Da did the butchering, while I took the orders and the money. Every day, I stood beneath the disapproving portrait of the king that hung on our back wall—every business had to have one, by law—and counted up our coins, doing all the calculating in my head, which I liked, because I took pride in my skill with numbers and the quickness of my mind.

As I've said, our village was pretty much like any other. A few shops, including our butcher shop and the smithy, clustered around a market square where smaller vendors set up stalls once a week, with houses spiraling outward to the farms and the fish market by the river.

For a village where no one really traveled and where few moved away entirely, we were a diverse lot, as the land had been settled and resettled over hundreds of years—by nomads and hunters and farmers first, then by armies in long-past wars.

Despite all the intermarrying that had no doubt occurred, there was still a fair amount of variation in the people. You could look at Goodwife Meg's nut-brown skin, for example, and see that her ancestors had come from somewhere with a good deal more sun, or notice the high cheekbones and near-giant limbs of Big Cully and see that he had some tall warrior race in his family tree—although Cully himself was a gentle man who walked half-bent over to make himself smaller and unthreatening. As for me, my mother had skin that was almost golden, and hair as dark as good tobacco, but somehow Da's paleness had won out in me.

For as long as anyone could remember, though, or their grandparents and great-grandparents, we had lived under the king's and sorceresses' protection, and no invading forces had ventured into our kingdom. The idea of war lingered only in stories of blood and death, seldom told.

I had always been somewhat of an outsider. Mam had been a merchant's daughter, wealthier than most, and surprised everyone—including her own parents, whom I had never met—by marrying a humble butcher. She died giving birth to me, her first and only child, and I couldn't help thinking it had been my fault somehow.

Death in childbirth in our kingdom was almost a curse—not for the mother, but for the child. An old belief, but one that lingered.

One of the benefits of having the sorceresses harvest our hearts, or so we were told, was that mothers survived childbirth, and babies were born healthy. Children, and the offspring of animals, too. It was one of the loudly touted advantages of having the sorceresses' blessing.

Before their magic protected the kingdom, or so the stories went, ewes would regularly lose their babes in lambing season; calves would sometimes be born dead, pulled from their mother encauled and unbreathing.

Under the king's rule, however, hardly any babe was stillborn, and rarely did a mother pass from the strain or exhaustion of birth. Fewer babes were born all round, but that was a small price to pay, even if it meant the elderly in the kingdom outnumbered the young significantly. So many elderly and so few sprouts gave the villages a slightly sleepy, ponderous air—but then, we were a sleepy, ponderous type of people anyway.

My mam was one of the few who lost her life while bringing another into the world. When I was a sprout, the others would taunt me, tell me I belonged with the abandoned children who wandered the streets of the city or who disappeared entirely.

After all, on the rare occasion that a cow or an ewe or a mare died while laboring, there was presumed to be something wrong with the calf or lamb or foal. Rather than waste time and good feed waiting to find out what it was, farmers usually just had the animal's offspring slaughtered right off. Saved trouble later.

The other sprouts' parents didn't agree with them, not outright, but they didn't tell them to stop, either. They never did it where Da could hear. They knew what he was like, how fiercely he loved me. And I never told him; it would only have hurt him.

He had married above his station, and some speculated that my mother had been too delicate for the life of a butcher's wife, our simple life and lodgings.

As I grew to adulthood, I developed strong arms, as suited

a butcher's daughter, a round face, and a figure that could best be described as "solid." My hair was a carroty red, barely long enough to touch my shoulders, no matter how much I combed it through with honey. Because I tucked it under a mobcap while working, however, it was rarely visible.

I wore an apron every day that started out pristinely white when we opened, and ended up crumpled, damp, and blood-stained by the time we closed. It was always hot in the front of the shop, with all that meat and chopping and activity, and I looked a sight, but it didn't matter. Da didn't care, and in the shop, everyone expected sweat and red cheeks, and didn't look at me in any way odd.

It was different when I had to dress to go out, to services or for visits, and squeeze into hose and dress myself up in ribbons and such. In the shop, people knew what to expect, and they expected me, and they got me, as I was, no trussing up. I usually didn't trouble myself with all that nonsense either.

True, sometimes I would see girls, girls with whom I'd gone to the schoolhouse, walking arm in arm with their sweethearts, and I'd feel a twinge.

Sometimes the girls became wives, and then they came into the shop to buy a nice pair of chops or steaks to make a nice dinner for Ned or Niall or whoever was waiting for them at home. And then, usually not much later, they'd be coming in again, this time for practically a whole hog, or the guts to boil up for soup, and I would know they had spawned other little Neds or Nialls.

I had my own Ned or Niall at one point, I'm embarrassed to say. Well, I didn't have him, but I wanted him, and it never occurred to me that women like me—plain, forgettable, *sensible* women—aren't allowed to want things, although that seemed clear as cold water to everyone else.

I thought I was allowed to moon after a boy, as the others did, and to have fantasies of posies dropped on my doorstep and pebbles thrown at my window at night. That was when I was younger, before I realized I was not really a woman but something more like a mule or a laying hen—for use but not for adoration.

It hurts to remember it even now. I had smiled and simpered when he came into the shop for his cuts of meat—the youngest Hodges boy, Aron, with ears that stuck out and chapped lips. Men are allowed to be ugly, you see, and it doesn't make a smack of difference. I had stood and talked to him with my head cocked to one side like I had seen the other girls do.

Now I look back and picture my red, sweaty face under the bloodstained mobcap, staring at Aron like he'd hung the moon, and it's like someone poking me in the ribs with a pointed, malicious finger.

Anyway, I had harbored hopes that Aron was sweet on me. I had certainly dropped enough hints. Every time he came into the shop, I imagined it was to see me. What was worse, so did Da, because he thought the sun shone out of my arse and that I was more beautiful than a thousand sorceresses.

"You'll be giving me grandchildren before I thought, then," he would say. "We'd better make extra space in the pigpen out back for them all to bunk down."

"Da!" I'd say, and I'd swat his arm, but secretly be pleased.

It took me a shamefully long time to realize that not only did Aron not return my affections, but he also had noticed mine, and thought it was all simultaneously humiliating and hilarious.

I know it will sound ridiculous to you, but I did not think to be suspicious when Aron slipped a note under our door. I had lived my whole life with my da, who loved me more than anyone, and despite the childhood taunts and the inauspicious circumstances of my birth, I didn't know yet that I was worth less than shite to any other man.

In his note, Aron had said that I should come to his farm, to help make the wine. That's what his family did, the Hodges: they made wine that they kept in big barrels in the pubs and sent it to the city as well. He told me a day and time. I told my da, and he gave me his blessing. I wore my dress with the yellow sprigs of embroidered flowers and braided my hair into a crown. It was the best I had ever looked.

Aron was there to meet me, on the farm. He had a barrel of grapes, and he was cleaning his feet with rags and water, ready to trample the grapes. He smiled from one sticking-out ear to the other and asked me to take off my boots and do the same. Then he gave me his hand to help me step into the barrel of grapes after I had washed. I remember the green, sweet-sour smell they had, and how they felt bursting between my toes.

He walked me home afterward. I had hoped for a kiss, or at least the holding of a hand, but we merely walked side by side up to the butcher's shop. My feet were still tingling from the grape-crushing, and I could still smell the fruit on me; it was a nice change from the stale butcher's-shop smell of blood.

I have to credit him for the planning of it. It took a while for his scheme to come about, and I just thought he had gone off me when he did not call on me again.

I wet my pillow with tears every night, until the morning I walked out into the market and saw, beside the usual bottles of Hodges wine, one that was called "Toad Wine." Just three bottles of it, with a crudely drawn toad in a butcher's apron on the labels. There stood Aron and his friends, who had been waiting for me to trudge outside the shop, and they were laughing. I turned around and trudged back in.

Da went mad. I'd never seen him like that before. He practically overturned the stall before Aron's father appeared to calm him down. Goodman Hodges had nothing to do with it, after all—only Aron and his friends.

Da smashed the bottles, and a green mush came out, and for a moment I believed the label and thought I had infected the wine with some terrible, ugly disease. Worse, that this green mulch *was* me, somehow, my insides made visible. My wrongness, that had killed my mother and should have killed me too, but for some godsforsaken reason had not.

Of course, it was no such thing. Aron had tipped the grapes we'd squashed directly into the bottles and sealed them up without straining them or turning them into wine, for the sake of the prank.

Still, I kicked sand over all the mess that was left in the square that night, so I wouldn't have to look at it anymore.

I didn't waste time on any boys after that. I had learned my lesson. Perhaps it was all part of the curse I imagined my mother's death had placed on me, that I should be unlovable by anyone but Da. And Da's shine and glow when he looked at me was now as much a mockery and a hurt as my own reflection in the glass.

CHAPTER 3

I had never seen a male sorcerer—no one in the village had, as far as I knew. I hadn't even known they existed. Afterward, folk sounded knowledgeable about it—oh yes, of course, some of the sorcerers were men—but I think it was a load of shite, and they hadn't known either.

We had grown used to seeing the carriages come through once every couple months or so, but they had become more frequent of late, and the sorceresses were more high-cheekboned and lusciously curved than ever.

We'd had an unusually hard year—more sick livestock than usual and poorer crops—so people were looking for entertainment, and we didn't mind the extra visits as much as you'd think. After all, the sorceresses brought our kingdom its prosperity, and surely seeing more of them meant things were looking up.

There was always a bit of a stir whenever one showed up, of course. It was bad manners to crowd around, or stare, but people would find themselves suddenly with urgent business that required them to stand in the middle of the square staring into space, pretending they were remembering their shopping list or some such.

On the day we saw our first male sorcerer, there were even more people milling about than usual, because each recent carriage had been more splendid than the last, and the panting lad who had come running into the square to tell people that a sorceress was coming had said that this carriage would be the most splendid of all.

He wasn't wrong. The carriage was black, but shiny. Not shiny like paint, or like dark wood, but a hard-edged shiny, like stone—although, of course, it couldn't have been stone, because not even the two hulking, great black horses pulling it could have dragged along a stone carriage, however much they showed off with their tossing manes and rolling eyes and the sharp clip of their feathered hooves on the cobbles.

There were black curtains at the windows as well, spangled and hung with beads, and black jewels clustered like frogspawn in the wheel arches and around the doors. Da watched me watch it, the way he did, with his mouth quirked to one side, and then lifted an eyebrow.

"You want to go out, Foss?"

"Nah."

"'S a pretty one."

"I can see it fine from in here."

"Go on. I'll watch the front. We won't get anyone in while the madam's here, anyway."

And I wiped my hands on my apron and untied the cap from my hair, because yes, I did like to go out and look at the sorceresses when they came in, despite all my show of huffing and rolling my eyes.

I knew they took a bit more of us all away every time they left, but I liked to look at them all the same. People like to look at pretty things, me included. I got little enough of prettiness in the shop, and the gods knew I found none of it in the mirror.

I trudged out to stand among those gathering and watched the big coach pull up, with much puffing and stamping of feet from the horses. They didn't need coachmen, the sorceresses, but controlled the beasts from inside the carriage somehow. You never saw them with anyone else, not even a servant or a footman. They came alone.

The only person not in the square that day was Goodwife Tilly, the herbalist. She always got the worst end of it because she had to be in the shop ready to take the sorceresses' orders, such as they were. A snippet of this, a cutting of that. Things they probably didn't need—excuses for their visits, as we all pretended that they were in our village on innocent business.

Even the herb harvest had been sparse lately, and Tilly was glad of the more frequent visits to bolster her meager profits. And the sorceresses paid well.

As I said, almost everyone but Tilly was in the square, pretending not to look, but really agog and about to burst with curiosity, waiting to see that first fall of hair and that first finely turned ankle.

We saw a fall of hair, all right, but shorter than usual, and curlier, without that heavy swing. The foot that popped out was booted—a long, black leather boot with a shine on it like the wet on a dog's nose—and it went all the way up the calf to a muscled thigh that certainly didn't belong to a lady.

No one made a sound, but somehow, we felt a murmur and a muttering pass through the crowd anyway, as it sunk in that the sorceress wasn't an *ess* at all, but an *er*.

When he shook back his black hair, we saw that he was a squarer, harder version of the ladies—the same face, just pushed out in some places and sucked in in others, but with those same fine-bladed cheeks and the same odd, light-filled eyes that they all had.

He didn't look around at us and smile, as the ladies did, but stepped those shining boots down into the dust and shite of the square, and made a beeline for Tilly's shop without speaking a word.

We hovered, the whole countrified swarm of us, fascinated and astonished at once, until he emerged with his brown paper sack of herbs and, again, without a word or a glance, walked back to the carriage.

The horses had been shaking their heads and scratching at the ground like a pair of scrounging chickens while he'd been away, but as soon as his foot hit the ladder again, they quietened right down, necks all arched and proud, standing to attention.

The sorcerer threw his packet onto the seat and then turned round, just once, to cast his chill gray blue gaze over the lot of us, one sweep of it, making everyone shuffle their feet and look elsewhere.

And then he looked at me.

I felt that no one ever had looked at me, not properly. I imagined it was because they could see the whole story of my life stretched out in front of me, like a cart track full of holes, just as I saw it. No marriage, no sprouts. No chance of a sweetheart pressing me against a wall and rucking up my skirts.

It would be easier were I well past the marrying age and an old woman; being young, though, and at the time when the lads should be coming round with flowers and shite, that was different.

But the sorcerer looked at me. Really looked, so that there

needed to be a new word for looking that didn't just mean eyes pointed in a direction.

I could say that it seemed like no one else existed in that moment bar me and him, and I could say that sounds faded, and I felt his stare like something real and sharp going right through me. These things would all be true, but not in the way you hear lovers say them.

The best I can compare it to is when I got a great thorn through my foot, one of the devil thorns that grow by the well, and it poked right through between two of the bones and popped out the other side with its white head all pink with my blood. There was a beat, before the pain, when it felt hot and sharp and almost good, tunneling its way through all that mess of flesh—that's what the sorcerer's look felt like on me, all over, head to toe and right into the dark places, giving them a tug and a twinge.

I saw his face properly, then—a great beak of a nose, mouth curled up at the corners, two black wings of eyebrows and those gray blue eyes beneath, and those swathes of curled hair needing to be pushed back to reveal the sharp bones of his jaw and his long throat, white and smooth, like the throats of the hares Da caught in the woods and sliced open.

When he turned back into the carriage, I felt like someone was yanking out my innards, as if my monthly blood had come. I tried to keep my balance, but I fell, *plop*, down on my bottom, in a puddle, my skirts spreading out around me like a great, ugly lily pad, and I the frog croaking in the center.

"You all right, Foss?"

Hands lifted me up, dusted me off, but there was no saving the dress. I muttered things and shook people off and made my way back inside.

"What the bollocks happened to you?" asked Da.

"I fell."

"Well, you need to get yourself cleaned up."

The only reason Da didn't get an earful for stating the obvious was that I was still reeling from the sorcerer's Look.

"You hit your head?" said Da. I must have looked mazed.

"Maybe," I said. "Maybe I'd better go lie down for a spell."

He huffed and blew through his mustache, but there was nothing to say except, "Fine."

As I dragged myself up the stairs, I heard him call after me. "A sorcerer, eh? Who would have known?"

CHAPTER 4

I lay on my bed, feeling my whole body buzzing and arguing with itself like a hive full of bees. The carriage had gone. I had heard it clattering and rattling off, and it felt like some part of me had been attached to it by a rope and was getting yanked out to follow.

Was this how the men felt when the sorceresses visited? Perhaps I had been too quick to dismiss it as a bulge in the trousers and the memory of a pretty face to summon up when they were having a wrestle under the covers.

I couldn't have been the only one to feel like this, I told myself; he must have done the same to others in the crowd. That was how it worked. I was just the one that fell on her arse in front of everybody. But still, this itching, growling life in all my limbs! I was lying still, but my heart raced as if I had been running.

I slept all through the rest of the day, and all the night, dreaming dreams that wrapped around me like vines and squeezed all the fight out of me, so that I woke feeling hot and tangled and defeated. When I rolled myself down the stairs, Da whistled through his teeth.

"You look like something's been gnawing on you all night."

"Thanks, Da."

"Didn't you get any sleep?"

"I did."

"You sick?" He toddled over to feel my forehead. "Someone been cooking you? You're about ready to serve."

Sick. Maybe I was sick. That would be a relief.

"I might have caught something."

"Can't have you around the meats, then," said Da. "Go back to bed."

Bed didn't sound inviting. I had left it a sodden, roiling mess, sheets half-off and trailing on the floor, and my pillows soaked through.

"I think I'll go for a walk. Blow the cobwebs."

"All right. But then back to bed, understand? I can't afford for you to have a holiday." He sounded stern, but I knew he was joking. He loved me, did Da. More than I deserved. Mam's death in childbirth haunted me, and I knew he grieved for her, but he didn't hold it against me. I was lucky, I knew it.

"I'll see you in a bit, Da."

The square was back to normal. No crowds goggling. Just the usual mess of peddlers and people, arguing and gossiping and wasting time. I went to the spot where I had fallen down the day before and stared at it.

"You all right, Foss?" someone said. It was Hallie, one of the girls around my age. One of the comeliest, as well, and the sweetest. She was always taking in birds with broken wings, or blind kittens, and nursing them, and she was always eager to be kind to me for much the same reason. If she could, I think she would have folded me up in a box and taken me home to be given milk-soaked rags to suck on.

"I'm fine," I said.

"We were just talking about the sorcerer," she said. She was standing with a gaggle of others, all pretty enough, as most young women are pretty.

"Oh yes," I said, trying to sound uninterested.

"None of us got a wink of sleep," said one of the other young women, at which I perked up.

"Bad dreams?" I asked. "Feeling sick?"

Maybe I wasn't alone.

"No, just thinking about him," another sighed.

"So handsome," added another, and then they all started chirping.

"Well, he has to be handsome. If he's like the ladies."

"Do you think they do it to themselves? Change their faces?"

"D'you think they're even human?"

"I think they're people like us," said Hallie. Of course she did.

"What do you think, Foss?" said someone, carefully including me.

"I think they're trouble," I said. "And I wish they would take their trouble elsewhere, rather than bringing it to us."

I stomped back to the shop and home.

There was no escaping him. All people could talk about for days afterward was the sorcerer, how handsome he was and how grand, how eldritch his eyes had been and how tall he was, whether he would come back, whether he was different from the ladies or just like them.

The menfolk got a taste of what it was like for the women after the sorceresses left, and they went about glowering, with caps pulled low to muffle the chatter of their wives and daughters and sweethearts. *He's long gone. Just shut up about it, won't you?* they told the women. But the women wouldn't, and they didn't.

They drooped about during the days, minds a mile off, and sighed in their beds at night, probably diddling themselves under the covers. Some of the men too, I was sure. I thought about it, thought maybe that would help to fix whatever the ailment was the sorcerer had given me.

Maybe if I could just twiddle my fingers about a bit and have a release and get it all over with . . . But it didn't work. It was like trying to kick a stubborn donkey over a puddle. I rubbed until my fingers were raw, until it started to chafe, but my quaint just lay there sullen and dumb and refused to help me.

What, then?

I went in search of Dav Mallet, because I couldn't think of anything else to do. I had never exchanged more than a few words with him before he was taken, and none at all since he had come back.

There was an unspoken rule that the girls and women of the town shouldn't talk to Dav, for fear of hearing the possibly unsavory things to which he had been subjected, so I sought him out at a time when not many other people would be around to gossip and speculate—when he was leaving the pub at closing.

He sat there every night at his table off to the side, weeping into his ale. Everyone ignored him now, too accustomed to him to even be embarrassed any longer. He had become one of the town oddities, like the man who kept ferrets and walked them on bits of string, and the mad old woman who slept with the pigs on Goodman Marrow's farm.

Da was a hardworking man and had little time or inclina-
tion for drinking, and so he was long abed by the time I slipped
out to wait for Dav. I stood in the shadows until he emerged
from the pub, one of the last to do so. He had an odd, sham-
bling walk that wasn't due to drunkenness, but it was a kind
of disorientation strange to see in a man who had lived in the
same village since his birth.

"Dav," I said, and then, "Mr. Mallet," because that sounded
more respectful.

It took repeating his name a few times for him to stop and
look about for me. His eyes were unfocused and lost.

"What do you want?" he said. "What do you want with me?"
He raised his hand, perhaps to shade his eyes to see me better,
but it looked like he was warding off a blow.

"It's me, Foss Butcher," I said. "From the shop."

"Oh. Foss."

"I wanted to ask you some questions." I took a deep breath.
"About the sorceress."

He moaned a little. "I didn't do nothing," he said. "She
took me."

"Yes, I know she took you, Dav. I wanted to ask you about it."

"I didn't do nothing."

"Right, but . . . when she took you, how did you feel?"

He looked at me properly, then, as if he was really thinking
about it. "It was the happiest I had ever been in my life," he
said.

"And you went with her, right? To the city?"

His eyes went blank again.

"You don't have to tell me everything, Dav. It's just . . ." I hesitated. "I think something happened to me, when the sorcerer
came the other day. I feel . . . well, strange, and I think it's something he did to me. I think I have to go and find him."

"No." Dav shook his head vigorously from side to side, and clasped my forearms with hands that were surprisingly bony and strong. "No, no, no. No, you mustn't."

I writhed in his grip. "I have to do *something*," I said. "I feel like I'm sick. Like he made me sick, and only he can fix it."

"Don't go," said Dav. "There's nothing worse."

He took one of my hands and guided it to his chest. I curled my fingers in, unwilling to touch him. I could smell his fishy sweat—or perhaps he had been around fish for so many years that their oils just seeped from his pores now.

"She took it," he whispered, and put one finger of his other hand to his mouth in a hushing gesture. "I don't know where she keeps it, but I know it is still alive somewhere, because I am. But not for long. Not for long."

I twisted myself out of his grip. "But you're here, Dav. You came home. You got away."

"No, I didn't," he said, and shambled off with blank eyes, as if forgetting I was standing there. I wiped my hand on my dress, feeling my skin crawl where he had touched it.

I went home and collapsed into bed again, feeling as if I could sleep for a year. I fell into another crowded and claustrophobic dream, where everything was black, black, black, and tunneled my way through to morning. I saw Dav again through the window the next day, and he looked up at me when I called, but without recognition.

I went back to the shop, because we couldn't afford for me to take any more time away. Those tangled-up and suffocating dreams still bothered me every night, however, and I still looked like someone had leeched all the color out of me.

Da was worried, and got all kinds of tisanes and herbs from Goodwife Tilly with which to dose me, but nothing helped. I don't remember exactly what was in those dreams, if anything.

There were no images, no stories. Just this feeling of being wrapped tight all around, like a baby in swaddling, and then feeling suffocated.

And I thought about the sorcerer all the time. I hated myself for it. I wasn't even mooning, like the others, and talking about his hair and his eyes and the muscles of his legs. I thought of him with resentment, with anger that he had done this to me— and yet I thought of him.

I still felt that tugging and pulling, fainter now than it had been on the first day, and I imagined him sitting on a great black throne somewhere, hauling on a rope he had wrapped around my innards somehow and made invisible. A shining black rope, made out of the same rock-hard stuff as his carriage.

"You're not thriving, Foss," Da said, weeks after the visit. We hadn't seen any more carriages since then, which was unusual for this year, when one had been showing up almost every week.

The excitement of the sorcerer's visit had faded, and people were concerned again with the meager crops and the unusual sickening of livestock.

Big Cully had lost three newborn lambs, which was almost unheard of, and the incident was much talked about in the pub of an evening. If I hadn't been so preoccupied with the sorcerer, I would have been worrying about whether this had brought the circumstances of my birth to the forefront of their memories again, but right then, I didn't care.

"I know," I said.

"Still feeling poorly?"

"Yes."

"Getting any worse?"

It was. I felt sick but also antsy, reckless, as if I might break into a lopsided run or start kicking at the hanging carcasses in the shop, anything to get that dark, frenetic energy out of my legs.

"I don't know what else to try," Da sighed.

"I'm not dying, Da," I said, although, truthfully, I wasn't quite sure. I didn't know what dying felt like, but if it felt like you were going to fall over at any moment, and if it turned your insides to black custard, I might indeed have been dying.

The restlessness got worse as I thought about it. I felt like shite, but I could have run a thousand miles without stopping, it felt like. So long as it was in *his* direction.

I suppose it was inevitable. Perhaps this was how all the sorceresses and sorcerers got hold of folk now, infecting them and then buggering off and leaving them to follow like ducklings. They didn't even have the decency to truss someone up and throw them in the carriage anymore, like they did with old Dav.

I had thought that exchanging the odd heart for prosperity and peace was a small price to pay, but it felt rather different when it was your *own* heart.

I'd like to say I gave it a lot of thought, turned it about in my head, but I didn't. I just reached a point where staying put became impossible in the same way that standing calmly in a fire becomes impossible, and I had to go.

As I was packing for my journey, I muttered and swore under my breath. The last thing I wanted to be doing was leaving Da in the lurch and going off to a city I'd never seen to look for someone I hated, someone who was gods knew where but was tugging on me nevertheless, like a farmer pulling his great, heavy plough.

Well, he wouldn't get what he had bargained for, that was some comfort. He had probably wanted to snare one of the pretty girls, one of the Hallies, but no—his gaze had settled on me, and here I was, readying myself to journey across the countryside to find him. *Here I am, Your Lordship.*

I imagined the look on his face when he saw what flavor of heart he'd harvested, and it gave me some kind of satisfaction.

I didn't tell anyone I was going. It was embarrassing enough telling myself. I left a note for Da on the counter, saying that I was headed to the city for a few days. I wanted to write more, but I didn't know what to say, or how to explain it.

I left the note as it was, scrawled and inadequate, and hoped that I would fix myself up and be back before long. I opened Da's door, just once, to peer in at the great lump of him in his bed and listen to his whistling breath.

He would do well enough by himself in the shop, for a little while. And if it turned out that having your heart hooked by a sorcerer was fatal, if I was ground down to little bits, or my soul was sucked empty like marrow from a bone, he would find some other girl in the village to do my job.

And perhaps it was a blessing in disguise. Without me to worry about, Da would have a chance at a new life—even marrying again, perhaps. He wasn't too old to father a sprout again, either—one not cursed with the circumstance of my birth, not destined to live in his house forever as an old and increasingly crotchety spinster.

I tried not to think of how it would hurt him.

CHAPTER 5

It took hours, but I managed to make it far enough out of the village that night that I was unlikely to bump into any folk I knew on the road come the morning and have to try to explain what on earth I thought I was doing.

The very first cart I waved at stopped for me, and the driver even helped me up into the hay-stuffed back with his own hands. I spun him some story about an aunt with a sickness, how I had been sent by the family to care for her.

I don't know if he believed me, but he pitied me enough to say he would carry me all the way to her fictional house in the city. I told him I didn't know the exact address, that I had been told to ask about for it when I got there, and at that he did look at me a bit oddly.

I had forgotten how large a place a city must be, and how difficult it must be to find one person in the whole crowded mess of it, not like in our village where you just had to collar one old biddy to find out the affairs of the whole damn place.

He obviously decided not to ask anything further. I realized why when I saw his quick glance down toward my belly. He thought I was "in trouble," in the way of village girls, and was leaving to spare my family shame. People didn't usually travel unless, like him, they were delivering goods, or had some kind of dire need.

"I'm not going straight there," he told me. "I have stops to make further out first—you caught me on my way out to the border villages. You might want to wait and find someone else."

But I couldn't wait. I had to be moving, to ease the roiling in my stomach and brain. "How much longer will it take?" I asked.

He shrugged. "A day at most."

I had never been to the villages along the border. You heard strange things about them. From the stories, it was the outcasts and the oddities who moved there, close to the edges of the kingdom, people who had disgraced themselves irreversibly at home or who had other, private reasons for wanting to leave the comforts of the central villages for the straggling, struggling settlements on the edges.

I didn't know quite why the kingdom's borders attracted strays, nor did anyone else seem to know, but all agreed that you didn't go there except out of direst necessity—and, if you did, you took a stout stick with which to beat off any suspect characters.

Drivers like this one did a roaring trade ferrying goods out to them, though; for some reason, very little grew along the border. The soil was unforgiving, perhaps. The few people I had seen from those places had been small and weedy, too. Apparently, nothing thrived out there.

There were other stories, too, about something sinister that lurked around the kingdom's edges, but I didn't put much truck in that. My need to get to the sorcerer was such, however, that rather than take the risk of not finding someone else who seemed trustworthy enough to drive me to the city, I chose to take the roundabout route with this cart driver.

He was gruff, but well-mannered, and I had no sense of

danger from him. He would provide some protection. Not everyone I encountered on the road would be a safe bet, and I wasn't desperate enough to take unnecessary risks. Not yet.

As we wound our circuitous and bumpy route to the border, the villages grew gradually dirtier and less prosperous. I looked with interest, having never seen any place but my own village before, and noticed the houses turning from brick and mortar to weathered boards, and the roads from cobble to pockmarked dirt.

Crops browned in the fields, and the cattle that grazed alongside the road looked thinner and larger of eye. The children grew skinnier too and chased our cart with their hands out, shouting for coin and candy, but I had none to give.

We passed through those villages without stopping, until we were right on the edge of the kingdom, a full ten hours' ride from home, and the cart driver pulled up outside a rough-looking tavern.

This village had an odd feel about it that I couldn't quite put my finger on. It had a scruffy, scrounging air, true, like the rest of the border settlements, but the oddness was more in the angle and mien of the buildings. They seemed poised either to run or to snarl, like so many flea-bitten stray dogs that had been kicked one too many times.

The driver cleared his throat. He had said so little that this gave me a start.

"I'm not staying here tonight," he told me. "We'll set off after dinner. You can sleep on the cart."

Sleeping in a pile of hay after sitting in a pile of hay all sodding day. Delightful. But it would save me some coin. I nodded. "Are we running behind, then?"

"No." He rubbed his nose. "I don't like to sleep here, is all. Always drive straight through."

"Why don't you like to stay here?" I asked, emboldened by what was our longest conversation since setting off.

"Just don't," he said. "No one does."

He was clearly done with talk, and so I shut up as well. I did help him unload some of his crates of produce, though, as thanks for the lift, and he seemed pleasantly surprised at the strength of my arms.

I asked if I had time to stretch my legs, and he nodded, but told me to be back within the hour, as he planned to finish his transaction as quickly as possible.

I didn't want to wander too far in this unnerving place, so I took a brief walk around the tavern, just enough to shake the cobwebs, and then I huffed out a great breath and sat myself down on a wooden crate.

I made sure I could see the cart driver from where I sat, in case I ran into any trouble. I don't know what sort of trouble I imagined would find me, but the whole village had the stench of danger about it, no less worrisome because it was so undefined.

The light of the setting sun glanced off the windows of the buildings around me in odd, disjointed patterns, like a smile missing some of its teeth. There were few people about, and they walked with their heads down and their eyes determinedly on their shoes. Gave me the shivers, like I said.

Chastising myself for my childish fears, I forced myself to stand up and walk with as much confidence as I could muster. I needed to stretch my legs further before an uncomfortable night in the cramped cart, sandwiched between the hard boards and the itchy hay. And no matter how unsavory this village felt, I would be sorry later if I didn't take the opportunity to work my muscles a bit.

I found myself whistling under my breath, more for the

small measure of company the noise gave me than for any desire for a tune, and wound my way through the buildings, keeping to the main road and the lit path.

Abruptly, I reached the end of the village. Usually, buildings would trail away from a village center, getting smaller and farther apart, until they dissolved into farmland again.

This village, however, just ... ended. Even the road petered out, coming to a halt just beyond the shadow of the last house. Dandelions grew luxuriantly in the gaps between the last few cobblestones. There were no wheel marks or hoof prints in the mud beyond, still a little illuminated by the last gas lamp.

It occurred to me that this village had an extraordinary number of gas lamps for how poor and hardscrabble it seemed, and was better lit than the roads back home. Almost as if they were frightened of the dark.

I peered ahead into the gathering dark. I couldn't see anything more frightening out there than fields and the shapes of cows, but a prickle at the nape of my neck told me to go no further. If I squinted, I could see what looked like a thick, swirling fog on the horizon, pale against the darkness. It was a desolate place, and the blessing of the sorceresses' magic seemed scant out here.

I was not sorry to leave that town behind.

We stopped each night after that to rest the horse and ourselves. At night, I used the little coin I had to purchase a room in the least expensive inn I could find, usually dimly lit and evil-smelling, with portraits of the king of varying degrees of quality glaring down from the walls.

The cart driver stayed somewhere better, I am sure, but I

never knew exactly where. He helped me down at the end of each day, brushed the hay off his hands, and stomped off, leaving me to find my own way.

I woke every morning in a panic, washing up as quickly as I could and running out to the cart, fearful that he would have traveled on without me. But he never did. He was always there to help me back up, grumpy but polite. It could have been a lot worse.

On the evening of the fourth day, the driver called back to let me know we were nearly there. We had reached the very last village before the city. I found it hard to feel too much excitement, however, because waking up in a pile of hay is not an experience I'd wish upon anyone, and one that I'd had more than enough of by then.

My hair was a mad red tangle, and my skin was covered in red pinpricks from the thousands of little needles, as if I'd germinated another thousand freckles overnight.

Still, despite all that, I felt a tingle of what might have been anticipation. After all, it was the city! I'd never expected to see it in my lifetime. I twisted about and raised myself up as best I could to see over the driver's head, but my first impression of the place was still framed by his ears and the wisps of hair either side of his bald pate, which detracted from the grandeur a little.

I saw yellow stone walls, with an expanse of tents and market stalls spread out before them. The walls were so high that if the city itself hadn't been on a hill, I wouldn't have seen a thing.

As it was, though, the whole thing rose up like the crown of a hat with a wide, flat brim, and I could see roofs and chimneys of all colors poking out all the way up to the castle perched on top, upright as a trussed pork chop. If you squinted, you could see the sun winking off the guardsmen's spears.

As usual, the driver left me to my own devices once we had found a spot for the cart and he had unharnessed his horse.

I was down to my last bit of coin, barely enough to pay for a room and board, so I thought the sorcerer had better either rip my heart out as soon as I got there to save me the trouble of sleeping and eating, or put me up for a couple of nights.

One good thing: The pain was much easier the closer I came to the city. It was like gradually getting over a bad head cold—I could think more clearly and breathe more easily. The tug at my gut, which sometimes felt a lot like desperately needing to go to the privy, had eased, but the anticipation of growing closer had set my belly to grumbling and growling as if it were waiting for a good beef dinner.

This last village was the most prosperous of any I'd seen, which made sense, since it was so close to the city. The people were friendly and open faced, and looked well-fed. We found a pub. I bought a gray, greasy bowl of bone soup and a mug of warm ale. I sat apart from the driver, who wanted little to do with me when I wasn't on his cart (not that I could blame him), and I listened.

One of the advantages of looking plain and nondescript is that it allows you a sort of invisibility sometimes, where a pretty woman would draw attention.

"Thin times," one hairy-chinned fellow was saying. I looked down at my soup, which was little more than dirty water with a lick of oil on top; it seemed to add weight to his words. A lone cube of onion bobbed in the center.

"Getting worse," said his friend, bald except for a few strands of hair slicked across his dome.

"It's because they're buying less, up there," said the first one, jerking his head in the vague direction of the city. "I think"—and he leaned in close, but, in the way of drunkards everywhere, his whisper was louder than his speaking voice— "that They've come up with a way to make everything they need themselves, without coming outside the walls."

The way he said "They," you could hear the capital letter. "The magic-workers?"

I stiffened and listened more intently. We called them by a different name, of course, but he had to be talking about the sorceresses. And my sorcerer.

"Who else?" said the bearded man.

"I don't see how," said the other, sucking at his remaining teeth. "Never heard anything about them making food and such. Just potions and hexes and murderous brews. Things for the nobles. They've been buying their foodstuffs from us for a hundred years or more."

"Then how do you explain it? Three carts of my peaches, rotted, because I was told they didn't need the usual order. Told by letter, no less. They didn't even bother to say it to my face. Twelve years I've been supplying them!"

A man at a neighboring table with a shock of pale hair chimed in. "Parsnips! Turnips!"

For a moment I wondered if this was some strange way of swearing in this particular village, but then he went on, "Wurzels! Carrots! All useless. I held them back for the usual city order, and it never came. Now they're tough as feet and smell as bad."

Who would have thought that those hoity-toity sorceresses—and my sorcerer—would have had anything to do with something as everyday as fruits and vegetables? It was hard to imagine them sniffing at peaches like housewives and poking apples to see if they bruised. Why would such powerful beings need to concern themselves with foodstuffs? Surely they had other servants who could do the job just as well?

"I'm telling you," said the first man. "They're making it themselves. They're cooking something up. Those . . . *women*."

There was a collective moment of loathing and longing as everyone thought about *those women*. I took a slurp of my soup.

"Haven't seen one of them for weeks either," continued the bearded man.

"Because they don't need us anymore."

"They'll always need us." The bearded man lowered his voice. "*For hearts.*"

The room seemed to darken, shadows closing in from the corners, and the men scraped their chairs in close to the table and lowered their voices.

"They get those from the outer villages," said the bald man. "They don't trouble us."

"They used not to," said the blond man at the adjoining table. "Because we grew their food. But now"—he took a swig of ale—"they don't need our crops any longer, apparently, or soon won't."

"They wouldn't," said the first man, sounding more sober. "We've had this arrangement for a century. Longer. My great-grandfather told me on his knee. They don't take hearts from us because we grow their food, and they don't take them from the city folk either."

"And how long will that last, d'you think?" said Baldy. "All they need to do is sign another fancy bit of paper, and we're done for."

"Maybe they've found something else to use instead of hearts," said the blond man, without much hope.

I felt a tug under my own heart, as if to remind me of my purpose. I got up and walked over to the men, ignoring their looks of embarrassment, their edgy glances at one another. Lucky for them, propositioning them was the furthest thing from my mind.

"I overheard you," I said, "and I'm not from around here. You were talking about the magic-workers."

"No, we weren't," said the bearded man automatically.

"Yes, you were," I said. "You were saying they usually order their vegetables and such from you . . ."

The bald man gave in to the inevitable, shrugging at the others as if to say, *What does it matter?*

"Usually," he admitted.

The tension released. They relaxed their postures a little, moistened their mouths, ready to talk. "We grow the food," said the bearded man who had first spoken. "The villages close by. They don't make anything in the city but fine clothing and mischief."

"Someone signed some bit of paper a hundred years ago or more," said the bald man. "Said they wouldn't take from us except in dire need, if we supplied the city."

"And a good thing it was too," said the bearded man.

"Did the ladies come themselves? To collect them?" I asked.

He snorted. "Of course not. They sent their servants."

All the men looked at me as if I was a simpleton.

"Where are you from?" asked the bearded man.

I named my village.

"I had an aunt from out that way," he said. "Things are different out there, farther from the center. You're pretty close to the border."

"Not that close," I said, remembering the eerie border village I had visited just a few nights before. "And the sorceresses don't buy from us. Nothing but herbs from the goodwife, that is. They just come to ..."

"*Harvest*," said the bald man. All three exchanged glances.

"They go out to you for one thing and to us for another. They rarely ... *take* ... from here. That's the bargain. They take from the border towns, mostly."

Was that why it had felt so dangerous there? I had heard that living closer to the city was safer, and now I had an idea as to why.

"Shitting on their own doorstep, 'twould be," said the man at the adjoining table.

"Josef! Not in front of the . . ." The bearded man glanced at me doubtfully. "Lady."

"Something's going on, that's for certain," said the bearded man, warming to his subject. The slowly descending level of his ale was probably helping with this, also. "There's something they're not telling us. We've been supplying them with food for as long as anyone can remember, and now they suddenly don't need any? Something has changed."

Something *had* changed. More sorceresses than ever before had come through our village in the past few months. And then, the most surprising change of all.

"Have you ever seen . . ." I hesitated. "A male magic-worker?"

They all three raised their eyebrows and pursed their lips.

"No such thing," said Josef, and the others nodded.

"Never been heard of," said the bald man.

"Well," said the bearded man, "if there were one, then that's just one more of the strangenesses. Something's up, no doubt." He leaned back in his chair so that the wood creaked ominously.

"I've heard rumors," I said. "But you said they're canceling their orders. Does that mean they'll be *harvesting* here too?"

There was a collective shiver.

"My granny said they don't take the actual heart out of your chest," said Josef. "It's a mettyfor, like."

We all stared at him.

"Mighty big word," said the bald man.

"What's that when it's at home?" asked the bearded man.

"Like, something that means something else." Josef looked embarrassed. "Like, they take part of you away, but we call it the heart because we don't know what else to call it."

"Get away with you," the bald man said. "They rip the heart from your chest, all right? Blood and everything. My granny told me."

43

"I heard that they don't need to take you at all," Josef said. "That they can just call you, like. They set eyes on you once, and you'll come running."

The oily soup churned in my belly. "And then what happens?" I asked, keeping my voice even.

"No one knows," said Josef.

Wonderful. This close to the city and still no real answers as to what exactly had been done to me, or what would happen next.

"So," asked Josef, and by now he was drunk enough to try winking even at me. "What brings you here?"

"Just passing through," I said, and turned my back before he got any bright ideas.

A little of my gruel was left, but I couldn't bring myself to stomach it after all that talk. Instead, I wandered outside to gulp a little of the manure-scented night air and settle myself a minute. I had to think about what I'd heard.

I had no idea that arrangements like those of the fruits and vegetables were in place, and now that I knew it, I felt rage bubbling up in my gut along with the soup.

So not everyone had to sacrifice their hearts to the sorceresses? Just my village, and others like it, while places like this grew their turnips and lived without that creeping dread, no less fearful because it was so unformed?

Another thought twisted my gut: We *were* the turnips, sitting out there on the borderlands, no more than vegetables to be harvested or discarded as the city folk saw fit.

CHAPTER 6

The cart driver let me down right inside the city gates. We had been waved through by guards with plumed helmets and muddied boots, the buttons on their coats all shined up like pennies.

At first I thought it was all terribly grand, looking up at the ornate masonry, but as soon as we rumbled out from under the archway, I saw the midden piles and the narrow streets, houses leaning in on each other like gossiping neighbors, and any awe I might have felt disappeared right quick.

The cart driver came round to the back to let down the gate, and I jumped down frog-legged. I kept up the tale of my sick aunt, although I knew by now that he didn't believe me. He stared into my face from under beetled brows but did not question me out loud. Why should he care if I was running away, or had got myself into mischief? "Be careful," was all he said.

I was picking bits of hay out of my clothes for a good hour afterward.

So. The city. It wasn't anywhere near as frightening as I had imagined—not because it wasn't enormous, loud, and stinking, because it was all three of those things, but because its enormousness meant I was near invisible. No one gave me so much as a glance.

I wandered upward, because that was the only way I knew to go, scratching at the hay rash on my arms and legs, and had a good look at the place as I went. I knew the city was meant to be full of cutpurses and murderers, but I had no purse to cut and, honestly, being murdered might at that point have been a relief, so I didn't trouble myself overly.

At first, I was in the outskirts, where the poorer people lived; I could tell. The roads all sloped upward, and if I squinted, I could see greenery and white walls farther uphill. The king was in his castle at the very top of the hill, and everyone else spiraled out neatly in their correct order, nobles and sorceresses and merchants and poor folk, down to the beggars who squatted right against the city's outer walls.

As I climbed, the smell of shite about the lower levels gave way to the scent of fruit from the trees that lined the streets, and of the city's blooming flowers that clambered over every wall, great, fat things with too many petals, like women wearing all their best clothes at once.

The uphill wasn't kind to my tired legs, but the pulling at my ribs drew me forward, like a toddler hanging onto my hand and dragging me on to show me a favorite toy. The pull became more and more enthusiastic as we drew closer. I was panting already from the climb, and this didn't help.

About halfway up, where the houses were neat but small, I came upon a pebbled market square. I didn't look too closely at the items for sale, because I was so preoccupied with my journey to the sorcerer, but there were definitely more frills and furbelows and sparklies than there would be at the market back home. There didn't seem to be any shortage of produce either, and I wondered about what I had overheard in the pub about the magic-workers and their orders.

A man at a stall covered with scrolls and papers and a sign saying "Letters Read and Written" peered at me over his wire-rimmed spectacles. Before I could walk over to him, though, there was a commotion in the middle of the market that immediately threw the whole place into chaos. A crowd clustered all about something in its center, drawing yet more people as they spotted the drama and wanted to join in.

Folks were the same everywhere, it seemed: willing to postpone just about anything to get a bit of gossip. I wanted a rest, and so I propped myself against a dried-up stone fountain and watched the show.

There was a lot of scuffling and grunting from the group. The crowd parted for a moment to show two men fighting in the center, with their arms on each other's shoulders, staring, red-faced and panting, into one another's eyes as each tried to wrestle free. They looked like two sweethearts clenched in a dance.

Some of the spectators were egging them on, others begging them to stop. It was the usual drama you'd see outside a pub any day of the week. Or so I thought.

"Gerroff!" one of the men was saying indistinctly through his puffed-up lips. He must have taken a punch or two.

"Gimme!" said the other.

I watched with interest to see what trifling object they were fighting over. One of the men had his fist tightly clasped at his side, and so probably had the thing, whatever it was. The crowd was milling about so much that it was hard to see.

"It's not yours!" said the first man, sounding like a child whose favorite toy had been taken away. They wrestled again, and the crowd shouted around them, and something came skittering out of the second man's hand across the cobble-stones. It made its way almost to my feet, as if seeking the one spot of calm in all the chaos. I could almost see it shaking its head. *Can you believe all that fuss?* it was saying.

No one seemed to notice that the object of all that bother had made its escape. The crowd still cheered the two on as if they were in a boxing match. I bent down and picked up the Thing.

It was wizened as a peach pit and about the same size, but softer, misshapen. Clearly pickled or dried. Some kind of preserved fruit, maybe? It reminded me of something, but I couldn't put my finger on it. There was a faint squish to it be-tween my fingers, and it gave off a dry puff of powder when squeezed.

I had no idea why it was important, but no one had no-ticed it was missing. And if it was worth a street brawl, maybe it would help me barter, bargain, or bribe. I put the thing in my skirt pocket and glanced at the commotion, which had not halted a bit.

I almost wanted to stay and see their reactions when their precious object was found missing, but the urge to find the sor-cerer tugged me on and upward, through the spiraling streets.

Higher up I went, and higher still. The houses here were whitewashed, with glass windows and wrought iron gates through which I saw gardens or tiled floors. These gave way to even larger buildings, made of stone, with great doors twice the height of a man, and offering no glimpses inside at all, as if the valuables within made the houses close themselves up all tight and unfriendly.

I had expected that the houses would grow grander and larger as I wound my way up to the palace—and they did—but they also became stranger. No longer whitewashed plaster or stone, they were instead of odd, outlandish materials, strangely colored.

One looked to be made all of mirror; another of a smooth, flatly gleaming green stone. One was stained glass, patterned all over with birds and foliage; and another was luminescent and pearly, which yielded gently to my fingers when I dared to touch it, like the faint ripeness of a plum. These were magic materials, clearly, which meant I was getting close.

When I came to the sorcerer's house, I knew it at once. It was made of that same black, shiny stuff as his carriage had been, smooth as glass. When I ran my hand over the wall, it left no grease or fingerprints, despite my hands being dirty and slippery with sweat.

So. I was here at last. I plumped myself down for a moment, my back against the shining wall, to catch my breath. There were few passersby up here, and they walked with urgency, barely glancing left or right and certainly not down at the girl in the gutter, so I felt safe enough taking a breather. I was proud of myself, I have to say, for making it all the way to the city by myself—a journey that so few from my village had ever taken.

When I felt well enough to stand, I made my way along the shining black to what looked like the gate. It was set flush into the wall, with no knob or knocker or anything announcing its presence, except a line as thin as a hair that traced its outline.

I probably wouldn't even have noticed the door if it hadn't been for the spell on me, which was practically jumping up and down by now, so eager was it to get inside. I was all set to rap my knuckles against the door, but it swung open as I approached, making no sound at all, the gap just wide enough for me to squeeze through.

The door was a good three feet thick, it turned out, all in that same featureless black stone. I found myself standing in an open-air space and staring at another door across the way, this one leading into the house itself.

The sorcerer had either a great love of that black stuff or very little imagination, or both, because everything out here was made out of it: the courtyard tiles, the fountains (although the water appeared to be of the usual sort), the house itself with its great front door.

He'd set dark jewels here and there—they never could resist a shiny, these magic-workers—but for the most part, it was that same expressionless, smooth, smothering blackness.

Despite its shine, it didn't seem to have any reflective properties; bending over, I couldn't see my face or even my shadow in the black, mirrorlike tiles. The shine came from inside it, somehow. Just as well, because it would be a right bitch to clean.

It had the smell of magic about it, magic made solid and polished to a fine sheen, and I imagined the sorcerer had invented this stuff to make himself look all the more dark and impressive. Well, it was working on me, for certain.

I found myself almost tiptoeing across the courtyard to the bejeweled front door, all hung about with spangles and sparklies glittering in all directions, like the thousand-faceted eye of a fly. Like I said, they couldn't resist shiny things, these magic people.

The front door opened for me like the street door had, but it was nowhere near as thick. I was expecting guards barring the way, or at the very least, a snooty butler, but there was no one inside that I could see. Just more black, lit with black and glittering chandeliers that were powered by something other than fire.

The tugging directed me down the long corridor, and I followed it. I wondered why it had been so easy to get inside such a grand house. Perhaps it was so that people like me would wander in like mice into a trap. Or perhaps everyone was so frightened of the magic-workers that they would never dare to try to rob them, making guards unnecessary.

Something soft against my knee made me yell, thinking it might be a trap of some kind, but it was only a cat—black, of course—who had heard me coming and decided to investigate.

"Hello," I said quietly, feeling a little foolish as I bent down to offer my hand. I knew better than to reach for him or presume to touch his fur without permission. After a suspicious, slit-eyed moment, he proffered the underside of his chin for a scratch, then whirled around and proceeded to escort me down the corridor.

He was the only living thing I had seen in the house so far, and so I was grateful for his company as he stepped a few feet ahead and led me forward, tail up and twitching, his little cat arsehole winking at me with each step.

He could have been leading me to his master, to the kitchens, to my doom, or just on a wild-goose chase, but I didn't care. I was just glad to be almost at the end of my journey.

As it turned out, he was leading me to his master. The door at the end of the corridor was even grander and blacker than any of the others. The cat sat on his haunches and scratched away at the door, just as if he were any ordinary old moggy begging at any ordinary old door.

I looked behind me at the long corridor and wasn't too surprised to see that it wasn't long at all anymore, just a score or so steps away from the front door. Magic-workers were tricky like that, and it no doubt amused the sorcerer greatly to make his guests traipse about and lose their breath before knocking.

I knocked. The cat squawked and twined itself about my leg.

"What?" came a voice from inside.

Well, I wasn't about to shout the whole story through a door. There wasn't even a keyhole I could peer through. I opened the door a crack, just enough to let the cat slither past with another squawk and a quick burst of purring as if to say, *Thanks very much, and you're on your own from here.*

"What? Who is it? Come in."

The voice was a man's but petulant: the kind of voice that deserved a clout around the ear. I pushed the door open with more courage and then immediately regretted it, because my heart gave such a leap from the power of his presence that I thought I might actually keel over.

"Who the hells are you?" said the sorcerer.

At first, I couldn't see anything but the mess. Plates and plates of food, only half-licked clean by the cat's tongue, and still loaded with enough bones and bits of gristle and crust to feed a herd of pigs.

Fine food, as it turned out, stank worse than plain food when left to rot. All those creams and sauces, maybe. The worst stale bread and old cheese could smell of was stale bread and old cheese, but this room smelled of the overripe armpits of a dozen fancy ladies.

How could he bear it? Wouldn't it just take one wave of his hand, the magic of one purloined heart, to keep his dishes clean forever? Of course, I didn't know anything about how their magic worked, but it wasn't much use if it couldn't even mop a floor.

I looked up from the mess and saw that the sorcerer was sprawled across a throne, a big, dark throne, just as I had pictured it, made of the same diamond-bright blackness as the rest of the house. It was magnificent, no doubt, but didn't he long for a cushion or two? Was even his bed made of the same mad stuff?

His head was on the seat; one arm was dangling down and the other thrown up to hang over the back; and his legs were folded up into a black triangle against the other arm of the throne. He seemed boneless as a scarecrow. As I watched, the white hand draped over the back of the throne twitched its fingers, setting its rings all to sparkling.

"I said, who the hells are you?" he repeated, but he hadn't even bothered to turn his head from where it was fixed, staring at the ceiling. I could see his profile, that aristocratic beak of a nose and the strong chin that I remembered from the village.

Even strewn all about like a cut bundle of rushes, his limbs looked elegant. I could have taken each of them in my mouth and sucked them like sticks of cinnamon. I could have pressed my cheek against the sole of his foot and been perfectly happy, so happy that it just might have killed me.

I came closer, and he finally looked at me properly. I imagined what he must be seeing: a short, solid figure with travel-mussed red braids (probably still with some bits of straw sticking out), an unremarkable face, plump in the cheeks, and a pair of rather small blue eyes.

I also wondered if his elegant, magical nose could smell the bad fortune that clung to me from my cursed birth, or if it had some visible aura he could see. Honestly, at that moment, I didn't much care.

He raised an eyebrow as he looked me up and down, but the pain in my chest had eased so greatly that I felt almost joyful, despite the strangeness of the place and my uncertainty. I could put up with being stared at and no doubt deemed unworthy, for the cessation of that terrible pain.

"Foss," I said. I debated adding a "sir," but decided that he didn't deserve it, what with all the trouble he had caused. I hated how much I was drawn to him. The closer I got, the closer I wanted to get. It felt like the only way to satisfy the straining of my guts toward him would be for him to unbutton his skin like a suit of clothes and let me climb inside.

He swung his legs around and sat up, his hair fanning out in a perfect black swathe before settling itself back into even waves about his jaw and neck. This close, I could see his gray-blue eyes had gold rings about the pupils. I could have stared at them until I starved.

It was strange to feel these things, and yet at the same time to be aware of feeling them, and to know how ridiculous it was to be feeling them.

"Foss? What kind of a name is that?"

Rude little so-and-so, my da would have said. He really did have the kind of face that begged for a good punch—indifferent and arrogant at once, as if he couldn't be bothered with the world. He leaned his elbows on his knees and his chin on his hands, looking for all the world like a gargoyle perched on a window ledge, and stared at me, still waiting for an answer.

"It's a type of flower," I said finally, reluctantly. "Where I come from."

I imagined I could see him thinking he had never seen any-thing less flowerlike. *Fair point*, I thought. My name had always been something of an embarrassment. He rubbed at his nose, violently.

"Have you come for a spell? I haven't the energy today," he said. "Go ask someone else."

The irony of it. I didn't even want the spell I had. "No," I said.

"Then why have you come here?"

Well, you leave the doors unlocked and unguarded, I wanted to say, *and surely people wander in all the time.* I searched those gold-rimmed gray-blue eyes for a hint of recognition, but there was none. I felt affronted. Clearly he had no memory of me at all.

"What do you want? A charm? Something to ensnare a sweetheart?" He spoke with self-mockery more than scorn, but I still felt my whole self bristle.

"You sell those things?"

"I can. I'm no better than a hedge-witch in that respect. Although my charms are more expensive."

"I don't want a charm."

His interest was waning, like a little boy's. He picked at his sleeve, looked about, chewed at the edge of a nail.

"Well, then . . ." he began.

"I've come to be your housekeeper," I said, before I had realized the words were queued up on my tongue and ready to jump out.

"Oh," he said. "Well."

He clicked his fingers. The black cat appeared like smoke.

"The cat will show you where things are."

I blinked. I hadn't expected him to accept it so suddenly and without question.

"Go on. Clear off. I'm thinking."

I bent down to pick up one of the dirty plates.

"Leave it! Leave it. You can get it later. Go on."

The cat raised its tail like a banner and started marching back toward the big doors, glancing back over its shoulder to make sure I was coming. I straightened up and followed, feeling with each step away from the sorcerer that the ache was becoming worse again.

Still, it was a thousand, thousand times better than it had been in the village. And if I had to live with something permanently that was no worse than a mild stomachache, I could manage that.

The doors opened as if, well, as if by magic, and the cat sauntered through. I glanced back, once, and saw that the sorcerer was sprawled out again, staring at the ceiling, but now with one hand clicking its fingers in the air as if to inaudible music. I had not asked his name.

CHAPTER 7

"I've come to be your housekeeper." What an addlepated thing to say. As if I wanted to spend the rest of my born days scrubbing that strange black tile and washing those filthy dishes!

But it had popped into my head as soon as I had realized that he did not recognize me. I had expected . . . well, even if he had not recognized me, I had expected him to at least recognize what he had done to me. Surely there was some sign on me, some invisible magic signature, that showed he had harvested up my heart, even just a portion of it?

I felt oddly insulted and unsure of what to do next. He hadn't swallowed me up or drained me dry upon my arrival, as I had half expected, but he hadn't given his piece of my heart back to me in a paper bag either.

I could tell by the ache in my chest that it had not been restored (as I had half hoped it would be as soon as I turned up, as if it would have flown to my breast like a homing pigeon coming in to roost), and that he probably still had it somewhere on his person, or in his house.

Had he taken so many hearts that he had lost count? Did he

forget their previous owners as soon as he grabbed them? And why, then, was I the only one who had felt compelled to drag myself all the way to his doorstep and had felt I would surely die if I did not?

Of course, I hadn't asked him about it yet, which was the most logical course. I had to work up enough courage for that, and perhaps being his housekeeper would give me the time to do so.

"These blasted corridors," I said to the cat as we traipsed our way through the shining black. I knew he couldn't understand me, but I had no one else to talk to. "Ridiculous. How long does it take him to get to the commode?"

As if it had heard me, which I suppose it had, the corridor made a noise very like a sneeze and folded itself up smaller, as you would fold a bedsheet. From standing in the middle of nowhere, I was suddenly at another door, with the door to the throne room barely five steps behind me. It left me breathless.

"Thank you," I said to the empty air when I had composed myself. I opened the door, not without caution.

"Well, Master Cat. What have we here?"

The kitchen, it turned out, or what passed for one. The cat ambled in, looking back to make sure I was following, and sprung up onto a long table made, of course, of that same polished black. You could barely tell what was table and what was cat, but for the yellow eyes blinking.

How could the sorcerer stand to live in all this dark? It set his pretty eyes and cheekbones off nicely, to be sure, but there was more to life than pretty eyes and cheekbones, and besides, there was no one else here to see them but the cat.

There were more dirty plates in here, of course, so far gone that there would have been flies buzzing about them, if something as prosaic as a fly could have made its way into this place. As it was, the kitchen had a sweet stink and no windows to open.

As far as I could tell, there were no windows in the whole giant house. The darkly glittering chandeliers provided all the light.

"I'll need water," I said to the cat. "There must be water, somewhere, to clean the plates. And soap. And wood for the fireplace, so I can warm it up. I need a wash myself, bugger the plates. How does he arrange his meals usually?"

I turned a slow circle on the spot. I couldn't see anything— no cupboards, no baskets of food. Nothing. Just the table and the plates. Did he make his own meals, then? With magic? The thought of eating magical food made my stomach churn.

The black cat squeaked.

"I wish you could talk," I said.

"All right then," he replied.

I looked over my shoulder, as if the voice could have come from anywhere besides the cat. Eventually I was forced to admit that he was the only possible source and turned unwillingly back to him.

"You can talk, after all?"

"Not usually," he said. "But you wished for it."

The words came out in strange shapes through his cat throat and cat jaws, giving him an odd, foreign-sounding accent. He had trouble with his "b"s and "w"s.

"How is that possible?" I asked.

"That's how things work around here, for the most part," he said.

"Oh." Well, at least I seemed to have one ally in the place. "What do you go by?"

He looked confused.

"What should I call you?" I clarified.

"I've always rather fancied Cornelius."

I raised an eyebrow. "Well, Cornelius. You wish for things,

58

and they appear?" It sounded far too much like a fairy story. The idea that a place could be organized in such a ridiculously fanciful, mealymouthed way made me itch with irritation.

"Not really," explained Cornelius. "It only works if you have a real need of things. You can't just ask for anything. And it decides what you do and don't need, so no asking for velvet gowns or anything like that. Believe me—I've thought about salmon for months, and no luck."

"I'd look a fright in a velvet gown," I said. The cat nodded in agreement, which didn't bother me overmuch. At least the creature was honest, or seemed so.

"You say 'it' decides," I went on. "The House?"

"The House, Him. It's all the same thing, more or less. The place grew up around Him." I could hear the capital "H"s of House and Him, even through the little triangular cat mouth.

"All the same?"

"You'll see, if you stay," he said. "But as to water and a fire"—his voice was becoming more confident, the sound more fluid, as he spoke—"that shouldn't be a problem."

I cleared my throat. "I need water," I said to the House. "And a fire in the fireplace. And . . ." Well, there was nothing, nothing in the whole place. "Soap," I continued, "and rags, and tubs, one for bathing and one for the dishes. And food."

"Steady on," said Cornelius.

"Bread, for certain, and meat, and fresh things. Vegetables. Fruit. And I don't know where you keep the plates and cups and such."

I had that same strange feeling of the place sneezing around me and rearranging itself. It was a disorienting sensation, like missing a step on the stairs—things didn't appear, exactly, but had suddenly always been there, and I had just failed to notice them, somehow.

A fire bloomed like red lilies in the grate. Two tubs of hot water stood simmering before it, towels and linens draped over their sides and two long bars of green soap laid between them.

There were bread baskets and sacks of green vegetables, all full—I hadn't seen such healthy produce in a while, with the terrible harvest we'd had—and an expensive-looking black crystal bowl full of fruit.

A door swung open to show a cold room where meat hung from silver hooks. The table was covered with dishes and cups of all sizes, as well as a kettle, and a teapot wrapped in an embroidered cozy (black). I lifted the cozy and the lid of the teapot. It was full of tea, steaming and fragrant.

"That's a nice touch," said the cat.

"It is at that." I ran my hands over the dishware. Fine china, so thin you could see through it if you held it to the light, with a spindly pattern of black and silver at the edges that reminded me faintly of crows sitting on tree branches. There were saucepans too, great, heavy things.

"No stove, though," I said, and then heard a *clank* and turned to see a stove installed on the wall behind me, made out of the same black stuff as everything else.

"I think the House likes you," said Cornelius. "It's not usually this helpful."

"How does it normally work?"

He did something with his shoulders that would have been a shrug if he had been hinged properly for one.

"I have food and water when I need it," he said. "And the odd mouse."

"Mice? In this place?"

"I think the House makes them for me. They taste peculiar. Have a funny texture, not like the real ones. But it's a change, having something to chase." He stopped to wash a paw. "I think it's worried I'll get bored. Maybe it's worried you will, too."

I looked around at all the new things. "I suppose I could have wished for the dishes to have cleaned themselves."

"I don't think that would have worked," Cornelius said. "More of a want than a need, if you see what I mean."

Well. I rolled up the sleeves of my dress, which, frankly, would have to be made into rags soon enough anyway, and piled up the dirty plates. I scraped the leavings into the fire, where they crackled and shriveled, and then dumped the dirty dishes into one of the tubs of water to scrub them with soap and a linen rag that was made of nicer stuff than any dress I'd ever owned.

It was satisfying, having my arms up to the elbows in hot, soapy water, and made me feel a thousand times better and more at home.

Cornelius watched for a while, then curled up on the hearth rug—had there been a rug there a moment before?—and appeared to fall asleep.

He opened one yellow eye when I had finished, however, and watched me pour the dirty water down the sink that had politely introduced itself to one corner while I wasn't looking.

"You close those eyes," I said. "I'm going to take a bath."

The cat snorted. "You think I care?"

"You may not, but it'll make me more comfortable."

"Fine." He yawned, rolling out a carpet of tongue, and flipped himself over to toast his other side.

The hot water was glorious. It seemed such a long time since I had felt anything good, anything at all, besides the terrible pull of the spell, and I had forgotten what it was like. I lay in that water until my skin was wrinkled and soft as a baby's bum.

I dried myself on the fine cloth that passed for a towel and groped for my old bodice and skirt, but I found them exchanged for something altogether sturdier and handsomer, of better cloth, and with fine silver fastenings.

My boots had been repaired, I saw, and cleaned, and there were new underthings draped on a rack in front of the fire so that they warmed my skin when I pulled them on.

I had never known such luxury. My old clothes were folded in a length of fabric beneath the new ones, I found to my relief. I didn't want to lose them entirely.

When I had dressed, I smoothed my hands over the skirt, and felt it firm and soft beneath my fingers, the nap of the cloth springing back like new grass. I had never been so comfortable. I thought about what Cornelius had said about not wishing for velvet gowns. I suppose something—or someone—thought I really did need them.

I leaned over the edge of the bathtub to see my reflection in the water. The new clothes fit like the best tailor in the city had stitched them directly onto my body. The movement of the water blurred my face a little, and I almost didn't recognize myself. I had a brief moment of vanity before I remembered I wasn't a fancy lady, but a solidly built butcher's daughter who had no business preening in front of her reflection.

"Is he doing this?" I asked, trying to tamp down the unreasonable flush of warmth and affection in my belly at the thought of the sorcerer caring for me.

The cat snorted. "No. At least, not in the way you mean."

"How, then?"

"It's complicated," said Cornelius. "I'm still just a cat, whatever you and the House have done to me, and I don't fully understand it myself."

"Try to explain."

"Well, him and the House are the same thing, but aren't, if you follow me, as far as I can tell. We're pretty good at seeing things that people don't see, we cats, and I can see both all tangled up together. Like the House just grew up around him.

They have the same scent, so to speak. So his magic might be the root of everything the House does, but it doesn't mean the House consults him about all of its doings."

"That is complicated," I agreed.

"Told you."

"Well, do you think I'll be able to untangle it all somehow? Make sense of it?"

"Frankly, no," said the cat.

"And does he have a name, this sorcerer?"

"He does," Cornelius said, "but I can't recall it right now. I don't hear it that often, you see."

"I see. And how does he normally arrange things for himself? Food and such, when there's no one else here?"

"It arranges itself for him, I think. He's in that big room most of the time, and sometimes he isn't here at all, and it all seems to shake down well enough, no matter where he is."

"Does he sleep here? Does he have a bedchamber?" I hated my blush.

"If he does, I haven't seen it. I've never even seen him sleep."

"And where do you sleep?"

"There's usually somewhere. There are a few places I go back to, and they seem to have stayed hollowed out for me in the right shape, but the House doesn't mind me trying somewhere new if I'm in the mood."

"And the commode?" I asked, uncomfortably aware that I was going to need one before long.

Cornelius blinked.

"The loo. The toilet. Where you do your business."

"Oh, I have a spot. It seems to clean itself up. It's always clean when I go back there, at least."

"That's very accommodating. And for humans? Where does he go?"

"I don't know," said the cat. "I've never seen him use one. Maybe he doesn't have to. But I wouldn't worry about it. I'm sure one'll show up when you need it."

There were no needs more pressing than that particular need, certainly, if that was the way the House arranged itself.

I busied myself in the kitchen, trying to ignore the black stuff all around me—it still made me feel unsettled to be surrounded by solid magic, instead of wood or good, ordinary bricks—and settled to the tasks I knew: peeling potatoes, chopping up vegetables, and setting two pork chops in the oven to cook while I boiled water on the stovetop. Cornelius watched me.

"Don't suppose you could throw a third in?" he asked. "I don't get cooked meat, usually."

There seemed no harm, since the magic store would probably replenish itself, and so I found a smallish one with a good amount of gristle and added it to the pan. Cornelius blinked at me slowly, which I knew was a good sign in cat language.

"It's just you and him?" I asked. "No other animals? No servants?"

"He doesn't need servants," said the cat before remembering himself. "Didn't, I mean. Seems to have taken a fancy to having one now."

"Your speech is getting much better," I remarked.

"Thank you. It does seem to be coming easier, now that you mention it."

I sat myself down at the long table, waiting for the water to come to a boil. "Any idea what he gets up to all day? We know about them a little, back home, the sorceresses, but we never saw a male one until he came along."

"He's either here or he isn't," said Cornelius.

"Well, that much is obvious."

"When he's here, he sits in the throne room picking at his nails or playing games—juggling, tossing a ball, things like that. He'll pet me, sometimes, if he's in the mood, and I'll purr for him. He seems to like that."

"What else?"

"He gets visitors. Mostly ladies."

The jealousy that gripped me was all the more terrible for being unnatural, a constructed thing that I knew was the result of the spell and not any real feeling. I let it pass through me like the runs and, like the runs, it left me weak afterward. Cornelius watched me sidelong.

"You all right?"

"Yes."

"They come and talk with him. He won't let me in the room when they do. I don't know why. It's not like I would say anything. Maybe they don't want fur on their nice dresses."

So, Cornelius wasn't likely to have overheard any useful conversations—such as where the hearts were kept. Still, he spent all his days wandering the House and seemed to know his way around at least some of its mysteries. "How would you ever find a secret room in a place like this?"

The cat performed that strange movement of his shoulders again that passed for a cat shrug. "I suppose you would find it if you needed it."

Well, I certainly needed it, didn't I? That was the whole reason I had come here, after all—to get my heart back. Or whatever it was he had taken, if the heart turned out to be a mettyfor, as the man in the village pub had said.

True to Cornelius's promise, the House produced a bedchamber when I required it that night—decorated all in that black stuff, but with sheets and pillows, and a mattress so high and thick that I had to clamber up onto it like a child onto their mother's lap. It had provided a commode, too, to my relief.

I was ready to collapse into sleep then and there, as soon as I saw the bed, but a washbasin announced itself in one corner of the room and stood there pointedly, and I supposed the place wanted me to use it.

So, the House was finicky: that made the filth of its master's throne room all the more odd. I took off my new fancy clothes, folding them as carefully as I was able, and found a clean (black) nightgown in the wardrobe that stood in one corner. Finally, I was able to climb into the bed.

I waited with the covers drawn up to my chin for a little while, wondering (and hoping, if I was being honest) if the sorcerer would come press his attentions on me, but the door did not open. I had delivered his dinner to him that evening, and he hadn't even looked up. Clearly my face and form were of little interest to him.

My brief flutter of pride from earlier, at making it to the city and the sorcerer, turned to a chill of apprehension. What had I let myself in for? Before I could think about it too much, slumber pulled me under, and I slept dreamlessly for the first time in weeks.

I do remember a small, chirruping noise, a thump, and a weight on the bed when Cornelius jumped onto my feet. He kneaded my legs pretty violently, and I grumbled into my pillow.

"Sorry," he said, and retracted his claws. "Better?"

"Yes, thanks."

Cornelius started to purr, a low, soothing rumble. I found that I liked it. I had never seen the point of cats before, really, other than for catching mice, but the warm weight and the peaceful sound were pleasant, and they helped me fall asleep again.

CHAPTER 8

In the morning, I opened my eyes to blackness. I listened for the sound of Da's bed creaking as he swung his legs over the edge, and his slow footsteps down to the kitchen to light the hob for tea, but heard nothing. When I remembered where I was, I felt a shiver of fear, laced with excitement.

There were no windows, but when I stretched and yawned, there was suddenly light, as if the House had been watching and waiting for me to wake, which was an unsettling thought. I couldn't tell where the light was coming from, exactly; it was diffuse and mild, seemingly coming from everywhere all at once, as if the black stuff had decided to glow. I suppose the House had thought that lighting one of the magical chandeliers for me would be too much of a shock at the start of the day, which I appreciated.

I noticed an extra blanket had appeared across my knees, an enormous, thick, black fur, and my feet were toasty warm.

Cornelius was still asleep, or mostly asleep—little fingernails of light showed beneath his eyelids—and when I stirred, he started a half-hearted purr that clicked in and out, like a fire sputtering in the grate.

I swung my feet onto the floor, which was warm and uncomfortably fleshlike—it would take me a while to get used to that—and washed up in the basin. Cornelius snorted and complained a little at the splashing noise, but then roused himself and stretched, lengthening his tail and legs, and even his ears and whiskers, and then letting himself settle comfortably back into shape.

"What does he do for breakfast?" I asked when I was clean.

"Usually leftovers from the night before," said Cornelius.

"Off those dirty plates!"

"Yes. He's not too fussy."

He lived like a pig, it sounded like.

"And who makes those meals in the first place?"

"The House, I suppose? Probably in the same way it makes my mice. They don't taste all that good. I don't even like to lick the plates."

"The meals looked pretty fancy."

"Oh, they *look* fancy, all right," said Cornelius darkly.

I sighed. "I suppose I'd better make His Nibs some breakfast, then," I said. "Since I've apparently volunteered to be the maid-of-all-work about the place."

I dressed in my fine, new clothes, marveling again at the intricacy of the stitches and the richness of the cloth.

They seemed to have sprouted new clusters of embroidery overnight. I also spotted that the neckline seemed noticeably lower than it had the day before—still modest, by most standards, but exposing more skin than I was used to in that area. I gave the House a sideways glance for that one. Was it going to tinker with my garments every day?

"Listen," I said out loud. "These are very nice, thank you,

but they're a bit on the fancy side. I'm a butcher's daughter. I'm sure I look ridiculous. All I need is something serviceable and an apron to tie over the top, and I'll be set."

A small movement at the edge of my vision made me glance sideways to the bedpost, where a black lace apron had apparently hung itself. I couldn't have imagined a more impractical garment, but I rolled my eyes and put it on.

When I judged myself ready, I opened my chamber door and had the impression that the House had gathered itself together in order to look like a respectable, normal dwelling. There was that sense of movement suddenly stilled.

I stepped out carefully and made my way to where I thought the kitchen probably was, based on my memories from the day before. The House undulated a little underfoot, guiding my feet one way or the other when I lost my way. It was being gentle with me, I thought, trying to help but not startle me.

I did find the kitchen, and I am ashamed to say that, on that first morning, I barely thought about the village and my da at all, even as I cooked the little cakes that were Da's favorites and floured the potato wedges for breakfast just as he liked them.

It was just a relief to have the pain dulled at last, and to be near the object of my tortured, involuntary love, and I reveled in it rather than think about it too deeply.

As well as the cakes and potatoes, I made the sorcerer eggs and bacon, fried mushrooms, and tomatoes. Everything appeared at my fingertips when I needed it: butter, milk, anything I might want, and good stuff too, not rubbish. My initial reservations about eating magical food melted away soon enough when I got a whiff of it all, although I wondered what it what it would do to my body if I ate it day in and day out.

The House seemed enthusiastic about breakfast. The fire roared and sputtered, the eggs danced in the pan, and the bacon rashers curled in on themselves like so many bashful girls hiding their faces. There was even coffee, so dark and rich smelling that I felt I could have dyed my hair black with it.

I gave Cornelius a piece or two of bacon, and the way he went at them, you would have sworn they were still alive.

"I'll give you more in a minute," I said. "Let me take this tray up first. Will he be in the throne room this morning? Or in his bedchamber?"

I imagined him in bed and felt my whole body flush. The pain and almost irresistible tugging was much better, being this close, but it seemed to flare up when I pictured things like that. I wasn't proud of it.

"I don't know if he has one, I told you," said Cornelius.

"You don't ever want to sleep on his feet, like you did on mine?"

"No. He's never wanted me to, I suppose. I'm not sure why he brought me here in the first place. Maybe he thought I would amuse him. I was outside the walls, being a perfectly respectable alley cat, and then I was in here. Haven't been out since. Haven't been able to."

"Have you tried?" *Was I trapped here, too?*

"Once or twice. But what's the point, really? It's warm in here, and dry, and I get regular meals."

"Does he play with you?"

"He did a little, at first. He made fireballs for me to chase, but they singed my whiskers when I got too close. He never got the hang of it, really. Eventually, he gave up." Cornelius gave his whiskers a quick wash. "It's not a bad life."

"All right." I piled a tray high with breakfast and silverware. The House produced a bowl of exotic fruit that I did not recognize, as if dropping a hint, and so I popped a couple of pieces on there, along with a paring knife, just in case.

My heart thudded as I walked back down the black corridor.

I was on my way to see the sorcerer again, and I could barely stand the anticipation. Again, the House guided my feet, and I found myself at the throne room door within seconds.

As far as I could tell, the sorcerer hadn't stirred since the day before. He was still slouched across the throne, legs drawn up, staring at the ceiling.

What was left of my heart gave a joyful leap upon seeing him, and I was disgusted with myself. He did at least turn his head when I came in this time, just the slightest bit.

"What?" he said ungraciously.

"Breakfast," I said.

"Oh." He heaved himself up on one elbow and looked about, as if it were perfectly normal for him to have a servant bringing him breakfast in the morning. "Put it anywhere."

As if there was anywhere to put it. The floor was still littered with filthy plates. I wanted to give him a piece of my mind, but instead I picked my way through the mess like a frog jumping lily pad to lily pad, and found a spot of bare, black floor on which to lay the meal, since there was no table.

This was closer than I had been to him yet, and my stupid, cursed heart yearned in my chest. I imagined that I felt his warmth and smelled his scent—a faint spice, unfamiliar and inviting.

Despite myself, I wondered what he thought of the new clothes the House had provided for me and how I looked in them. I hoped desperately that they didn't look like a fancy cozy on a stout little teakettle.

"You can go," he said airily, waving his hand.

I supposed he would eat the meal, eventually, although I was sorry to miss the look on his face when he got a taste of Da's potato wedges.

I reached for one of those dirty plates, then another, and started to stack them on my arm. The sorcerer pinched the skin between his eyebrows, as if the chinking and clinking were giving him a headache, but I didn't care.

It served him right for living in a pigsty and for dragging me all the way here to clean up after him, even if he didn't seem to realize he had done it. I thought with a pang of Da, at home, who never drank so much as a cup of tea without rinsing his mug and putting it away. "My mam brought me up right," he would always say with a wink.

I half thought the sorcerer was going to say something as I collected the dishes—tell me to be quiet, perhaps—but he must have seen the no-nonsense expression on my face. He watched as I gathered up as many plates as I could carry, which was a decent amount. I had pride in the strength of my arms.

"Have you seen the cat today?" he said at last, startling me so that I nearly dropped everything. I turned to face him.

"He's in the kitchen."

"Oh. All right. I hadn't seen him for a while."

"He's there. He showed me around."

"So, you're finding everything all right, then."

Oddly, the sorcerer seemed to be trying to *make conversation*. It was like hearing an eagle try to cluck. He stared at me, and I stared at him right back, feeling what was left of my heart fluttering in my chest, and wondering if he was beginning to remember who I was.

Somehow, it would be even worse if he had snagged a piece of my heart by accident rather than design, like stepping on a toilet rag and dragging it out of the privy with you, stuck to your boot. I waited, but he showed no signs of recognition, just continued to stare.

What was he thinking? I wanted to flush and turn away, feeling every imperfection of my face writ large upon it, but resentment rose in my gullet. Why should I feel ashamed and look at my feet, when he was the one who had dragged me here? If he wanted to stare and judge, so be it.

"More or less," I said. "Most things seem to stay where I put them."

"I built the place when I first came of age," he told me, "but it has rather taken on a life of its own."

"Came of age?"

He looked wary, suddenly, as if he had given too much away. "Yes. We are all given a house when we are ready. What we do with it is up to us."

"You and the sorceresses?" I pressed.

He suddenly became very interesting in cleaning under his thumbnail.

"The cat told me you and the House are one and the same," I said.

"The *cat*?"

I suppose Cornelius's gift of speech was news to him. "He said this great black House grew up around you, from your magic."

"Clearly the cat should have remained voiceless," the sorcerer said, still seeming a little perturbed.

"Is it true?"

"I suppose that's one way of putting it," he responded. "It started out as part of me, of my magic, but it has . . . taken on a life of its own. I let it do what it likes, now, mostly."

"But are you aware of everything it does?"

"Impossible. It has grown so large and sprawling that even I don't know how many rooms it has. In theory, I suppose, it could be an infinite number by now."

"But from the outside . . ."

"Space and time work differently in here, as you may have noticed," he said. "The House is much larger on the inside. I tried to map it once, out of curiosity, but it was quite impossible."

Since he seemed to be in a chatty mood, I ventured another question. "What's your name?" My heart beat faster at my own audacity.

He wrinkled up his forehead and cast his eyes upward. Was he trying to *remember* it?

"I rarely use it," he said. "It begins with an 'S,' I think. Yes, I'm almost certain it is an 'S.' It's on the tip of my tongue."

Another long pause.

"*Sylvester*. That's it."

What kind of a person forgets his own name? I stared at him. And was he a person at all? That was an uncomfortable thought. We stared at each other for a moment.

"You may go," said the sorcerer—*Sylvester*—at last, waving his hand grandly. I fought the urge to roll my eyes and made my way out of the throne room as best I could while balancing the plates. I made it to the kitchen without incident.

Cornelius was waiting for me.

"I didn't eat your breakfast," he said. "I wanted to. Shouldn't have left it out like that."

I sat and poured myself some of the coffee and started on my eggs. I twitched a couple more rashers of bacon off the plate and onto the floor for Cornelius.

"Ta very much," he said.

It was an odd first day, but not a bad one, entirely. I was used to work, having spent my whole life in the butcher's shop—first underfoot, as a sprout, then behind the counter, when I was big enough to see over the top of it—and the work distracted me from the more bizarre parts of my predicament. It wasn't too different from cleaning a non-magical house, except for the occasional appearance of a new item when I needed it. I did find that one or two of the rooms I had explored had either disappeared or moved to a different part of the House when I tried to return to them, but was relieved to find that the kitchen, my bedchamber, and the commode stayed where I had put them.

I scrubbed the kitchen to within an inch of its life, while Cornelius watched. I heard him start to snore, eventually, a tiny, comforting noise, while I rifled through the cupboards to make a plan for lunch and dinner. It was a luxury, having so many different ingredients all at once, and I intended to make the most of it.

While I cleaned, I thought about my heart and how to retrieve it. If the sorcerer truly didn't remember me, he wouldn't expect me to be hunting about for it, and I should be able to explore the House on the pretext of cleaning it.

I was surprised he had so easily allowed a stranger access to his home, however, and that he seemed so uncurious about my origins or motives—but I suppose that, to him, I was no more than another inconsequential stray who had just wandered in, like Cornelius, and the cat and I were diverting enough in his shapeless days that he tolerated our presence.

As soon as I had finished cleaning up after breakfast, I started the search for my heart in the kitchen.

No matter how many drawers or cupboard doors I opened, more appeared, sidling in at the corner of my vision and then solidifying when I turned to look at them.

It was a hopeless task, but I kept at it, opening door after door to see more and more outlandish spices, herbs, and dried foods, and then finally (when the House had run out of ideas, I suppose), empty shelves. I sighed and straightened, smoothing my skirts.

It was unlikely the sorcerer kept his hearts in the kitchen. Unless he was planning to eat them, which—well, it was something I didn't like to imagine. I was pretty sure the magic-workers absorbed the hearts' magic in another way, because the alternative didn't bear thinking about.

"What are you doing?" asked Cornelius from somewhere by my ear, making me jump. He had woken from his nap and was perched on top of one of the open doors. I felt like a burglar.

"Nothing," I said reflexively.

He gave a derisive sniff.

"All right," I relented. "Look, have you seen any . . . hearts about?"

"Hearts?"

"Or pieces of hearts. Or anything that could be such."

"What?" Cornelius cocked his head to one side.

"The hearts. That he uses, in his magicks. That the magic-workers all use. That's what they do. They take bits of hearts and use them to make their sorceries. Sometimes they take the whole thing and sometimes just a little; sometimes it's the real, fleshy thing; and sometimes it's more the essence of it, I suppose. But he's a sorcerer, and he took my heart somehow, or part of it, and it has to be somewhere in this House, and I have to find it."

Cornelius blinked, impassive.

"Don't know about that," he said. "Haven't seen any. Haven't smelled any."

"No hearts at all?"

"No. He doesn't even bother to put them in the mice I eat, far as I can tell."

"Are you sure?"

"If there was a heart about the place, I would smell it," he said. "I get so little fresh blood."

I abandoned my search of the kitchen and started wandering the House, letting a duster dangle from my hand lest the sorcerer question me. (Although, he seemed to care very little what I did.) Those other rooms, then.

They seemed less like rooms and more like the living organs of some strange, incomprehensible giant creature. The hallway gave a shiver under my feet, like a horse whisking a fly off its neck, and I found myself facing in a new direction and looking at a new door. Cornelius appeared at my feet, as he seemed to do whenever anything interesting was going on.

"Was this here before?" I asked.

"I don't pay much attention," he said. "I just find a warm spot, if one opens up. But I don't think so."

The doorknob had placed itself invitingly below my hand, like a dog looking for a pat. I opened it and stepped into the new room, Cornelius at my heels. He made a pleased chirping noise when he saw a long, low sofa, and jumped up and started kneading at it immediately.

"Not bad," he commented.

It was a bedchamber. The sorcerer's bedchamber? I imagined him tangled in black sheets, his skin even whiter against the shining dark, his hair mussed about and slick on a black pillow. I flushed hot and pressed one hand to my ribs to keep the rest of my treacherous heart inside.

But it was not the sorcerer's bedchamber. It clearly belonged to a woman. *That* kept my heart firmly in my chest—the thought of another woman living here, and a beautiful one, judging by the room. Everything in it, although made of the same magical black stuff as the rest of the House, was delicate and feminine and gorgeous.

I inched my way inside, feeling as if a giant, manicured hand was going to appear and flick me away like a speck of lint from an embroidered sleeve. After a second, when no such giant hand appeared, I made my way about the room.

I fingered the flocked wallpaper, velvety black on black, a pattern like crows on bare branches, and opened the closet door to riffle my hands through the row of fine dresses within.

Well. I had thought myself very fancy in my new garments, but these made me aware all over again of how squat and forgettable I was compared to other women.

The clothes were also black, but they were the black of starlings, or ravens, iridescent-like, with a rainbow of colors peeping out from beneath the black like painted ladies smiling from behind veils. A strange and beguiling perfume hung about them, something like honeysuckle at evening and strong, sweet wine. The waist span of these dresses was barely more than the span of my hand, it seemed, and the shoes I found at the bottom of the closet were just as dainty.

I gave in to an unusual girlish impulse and kicked off one of my shoes in order to try one on, but they might as well have been made for mice. I gave one particularly fussy pair a shove with the toe of my boot, just to show them what was what.

"Who lived here?" I asked Cornelius.

"I don't know. Must have been before my time," he said through his purr. The sofa must have been comfortable. "It's only ever been him here, as far as I know."

Jealousy roiled in my stomach like a bad stew. I walked to the dressing table, a frivolous thing on spindly legs that looked like they were about to take off running, and stared into the mirror. The thing was surrounded by a frame like that around an oil painting, which looked very odd encircling my face, I can tell you.

The room made me feel all sorts of painful longings that I thought I had long ago suppressed. I felt a pang of anger at my mother, for dying when she did and leaving me without anyone to talk to about such things—how to care for your hair and skin, how to dress, how to talk to someone you found appealing.

And then I felt a great surge of guilt, because whose fault was it that she had died? Perhaps I was better off alone, rather than subjecting someone else to the curse of my bad fortune. I turned my back on the mirror, walked over to the bed, and touched the coverlet. Black lace.

"You said the House would show me things as I needed them," I said. "Why do you think I need this room?"

"How should I know?" said Cornelius. "I'm just a cat. The House probably has its reasons."

I opened every drawer and cupboard. Mayhap this was where the sorcerer kept my heart, amid his lover's frills and furbelows. In an ornate box perhaps, like a piece of jewelry to be presented to a lover; because this was the kind of room a rich man would give his lover. I couldn't fool myself into thinking he kept it for when his mother visited (if he had one)—there was far too much skimpy lace nonsense in the drawers for that. I rummaged about but didn't find anything but more clothing.

After a while, I gave up and left the room, closing the door softly behind me as if to avoid disturbing an invisible occupant. There was such a strong sense of *presence* in there.

"So will this room stay here, like the kitchen?" I asked Cornelius.

"I keep telling you, I don't know for sure," said Cornelius.

When I tried the doorknob again, however, giving in to a shameful desire to finger those soft fabrics again and imagine the fine lady inside them, the room was gone.

I had missed my opportunity, whatever it was. I hadn't seen what the House wanted to show me. Or maybe I was giving it too much credit or imagining it to be too much on my side. Maybe it had just wanted to taunt me with the specter of the kind of woman I would never be.

The next room of any interest that appeared to me was more prosaic than the boudoir. I was on my way to the kitchen, this time, when another door appeared in front of me, and another doorknob insinuated itself under my hand. I rolled my eyes and opened it.

I don't know what I had expected—another bedchamber? Very little would have surprised me. A room full of nothing but pungent black lilies, for example, or a torture chamber hung with blades and screws, or an enormous corridor lined with oil paintings with eyes that followed you about. Any of those would have seemed quite at home in the sorcerer's black mansion, and plenty stranger things would have fit right in, too.

What I saw, instead, was a plain room, still black, lined with locked cabinets, with a wide plain table in the center. There was a floor that needed sweeping, some cobwebs, and a painting covered by sackcloth. Or perhaps it was a mirror; I couldn't tell.

Before I could step in, the door wrenched itself from my hand and slammed shut, as if from a gust of wind, leaving me gaping.

"What are you doing?" said a voice from behind me, and I almost jumped out of my skin. I whirled around. The sorcerer stood just behind me, so close that it set my senses swirling. He was watching me rather as a well-fed cat watches a bird—with speculation rather than predatory intent.

"You're exploring," he said.

So he knew about my wanderings through the House. I almost apologized, but I managed to stop myself in time. "It's my job to clean, isn't it?" I said. "And I wouldn't call it exploring. My feet get twitched out from under me, and I find my hand on a new doorknob, that's all." As casually as I could, I added, "I found a bedchamber. A woman's, by the look of it."

"My sister's."

His sister? But I was shamefully relieved it hadn't been the chamber of a lover.

"She lives here?"

"She used to." Something flickered across his face that I couldn't identify.

"Oh."

I waited for him to tell me to stop snooping, but he did not. He stared at me for a moment, then turned on his heel and strode away, his hair lifting and settling about his shoulders.

And so things continued for the next several days. The sorcerer and I barely spoke. I came in at every meal, announced myself, announced what was on the plate, and left. After a day or two, however, he started to request certain dishes, or protest petulantly that he didn't like cabbage, or clams.

It was no skin off my nose. The House provided everything I needed, however exotic, and it all seemed real enough. I did wonder, though, if the food we ate was like the mice the House created for Cornelius to chase—convincing, but not quite as nutritious as the real thing.

Whether it was real or not, Cornelius had already grown plumper on my cooking, and the sorcerer's throne room was clean of plates and smelled of soap rather than rotting meat, which could only be an improvement.

It had been a satisfaction to scrub that room properly for the very first time and see the stains disappear. The sorcerer had watched me in silence while I worked, chewing on his nails, and hadn't offered any charms or cantrips to help speed the process.

I learned my way about, for the most part, if the House behaved and kept things in the same places, and I grew used to sleeping in the huge bed with the enveloping black covers.

The House also continued fiddling with my clothing, which grew richer and more intricately detailed by the day; although when the bodice started dipping lower again, I had a few choice words to say. We compromised on a little more skin than I was used to showing, but not enough to make me feel self-conscious.

Those first days took on . . . I wouldn't quite say they took on a shape, exactly, because time seemed to operate differently in that dim place, stretching out like rubber, then snapping back and coiling in on itself, dizzying and disorienting—but a routine emerged.

I couldn't tell you for certain how many days passed, as I never saw real daylight, only the odd, off-color stuff manufactured by the House, and I only knew which way was up by the clockwork regularity of the meals: breakfast, lunch, supper, breakfast, lunch, supper, and cups of tea or coffee in between.

Back at home with Da, there had never been a moment when we weren't either boiling water for a hot drink, drinking one, or rinsing out our mugs ready for the next one, and I saw no reason to alter this pattern just because I was in a fancier house with fancier teacups.

The sorcerer raised his eyebrows when I first brought in his tea, but when I would come back in a couple of hours with the next cup, the previous one was always empty, so he wasn't complaining.

He also wasn't complaining about the tea cakes and sweet breads I made to go with the tea, because those disappeared right quick as well.

He liked the sugary things best, I found, and when I brought him the sugar bowl to go along with his tea or coffee, it was always half-empty when I came to retrieve it. It replenished itself each time, of course.

We talked a little, now and then. He commented on the food, mostly, and I managed to reply without falling to the floor or professing my undying love, so I thought I was doing rather well when it came to keeping myself together in the face of the spell.

I was handling it all magnificently, really, if you didn't count sobbing into my pillow at night when I longed for the sorcerer or remembered Da. At least I wasn't sighing about the place like some wilting flower.

I was impressed with myself, to be quite honest, that I wasn't just mooning after him pathetically and was instead able to make myself useful as best I could—even if all I could do was cook meals and make sure the sorcerer didn't bury himself in a charnel house made of crusted plates.

I did not know where he spent his nights. Not with me, that was for certain. I must admit, I had expected (or feared, or hoped for) something a little more salacious than cooking and cleaning when I turned up on the sorcerer's doorstep, but my bedchamber remained silent and still each night, save for Cornelius's snores.

Even so, I tucked myself in with a mixture of fear and anticipation at the end of each day, half hoping and half dreading that he would come.

I was a little surprised. When the magic-workers took someone, it appeared that they owned them, body and soul, for as long as they wanted to. Surely even a magic-worker had . . . urges? I obviously hadn't expected the sorcerer to throw me on a bed of silk sheets and ravish me as soon as I showed up— although if I had looked different, perhaps I would have expected different. But I was a woman, after all, and I was completely devoted to him because of the enchantment.

Of course, I would have let him have his way. I *wanted* him to have his way. That was the horror of the spell. But he hadn't done anything of the sort, and disappointment was stirred in with my relief.

Maybe he had lovers whom he snuck in, or maybe he had magical ways of sating himself that were more elaborate and satisfying than our sweaty, commonplace human ones.

Of course, I still had my own urges, which I took care of by myself under that thick black coverlet. And if I pictured the sorcerer's face while doing so, well, it was his fault for ensnaring me the way he had, and so I didn't feel too peculiar about it.

I didn't come across anything resembling the sorcerer's bed-chamber, and because the House had not provided it to me, I assumed I did not need to know its whereabouts.

If I'd had to change his sheets, for instance, the House would have practically shoved me through the door. As it was, however, the only sheets I needed to worry about were mine, and I washed them in the big tub before the kitchen fire whenever I needed to.

It was an odd sort of life, and odd how quickly I got used to it, ferrying plates back and forth between the kitchen and the throne room, sudsing them up, putting them back in those blank, black cupboards.

I continued looking for my heart, of course. More rooms appeared to me as I looked, gradually, as if the House was flexing its muscles after a long sleep. I ransacked them, but most were empty, and the rest were filled with black furniture covered with swathes of black cloth.

I could only see the rooms the House chose to show me, and I suspected it was giving me just enough new rooms that I felt the illusion of progress, as you might occupy a small child with a pencil and paper to distract it.

Every so often, I stood with my hands on my hips and confronted the House.

"Go on, then. Where is it? Where is he keeping it?"

The House fanned the flames of the fire a little higher, or produced a whistling kettle for me, trying to ingratiate itself. Or distract me.

"You know where it is. You know where everything is here."

It shouldn't have been possible for a House to look sheepish without a face or a body to look sheepish with, but it did.

I made the sorcerer Da's famous meatloaf one night. I put all my missing of Da into the meal as I worked in the ridiculously well-stocked kitchen, every ingredient I thought of at my fingertips.

Da would make it with all the cuts of meat that were left over, put them through the mincer, and mix that with flour and water and chopped vegetables to make something like a cake that you could slice, crusted with herbs all the way round. He served it with mashed potatoes, and so I did, too.

When I took the dinner to the throne room, I was rumpled and cross from frustration. The fine velvet dress was immaculate, though, not even a speck of dust or a spot of sauce on it from all my day's labors, and somehow that irritated me further.

I entered the room balancing plates of fine meat and roasted vegetables, snappish and ready for an argument, but at the sight of the sorcerer, I melted again into mawkish worship. It was ridiculous.

I knew it was the spell and out of my control, but I turned my irritation inward. Why wasn't I strong enough to resist? Why couldn't I shake him off and get back to my life, rather than waiting on him hand and foot and dreaming about his pretty eyes?

Those same pretty eyes were half-hidden behind a swathe of black hair. As I entered, he puffed out a breath to blow it away and managed to make even that look elegant. He was sprawled across his chair as usual, one hand pillowing his head, while the other bounced something that looked like a yo-yo up and down—although there was no string, and the ball that slid up and down from his finger to the floor looked as though it was made of fire.

Such pretty toys he made, and he seemed to sit there all day playing with them. How many hearts did it take to make them, I wondered? Was mine already all burned up in the makings of some pointless plaything?

He watched me as I set his dinner down on a black table that had politely presented itself to one side, as it always did. He rarely commented favorably on anything I made, and so I was surprised when he tried a forkful and said, "This is good."

I refrained from saying thanks, because I wasn't about to thank him for getting me away from Da in the first place. I had been in tears for most of the time I was cooking it, if I was honest.

"It tastes . . ." He paused, pressing his lips together, as if to squeeze the flavor from them. "I can taste the heart in it."

Well. From anyone else that might have been a nice, if rather maudlin, compliment. From him . . . I felt the urge to clutch at my chest. What else had I inadvertently given him, feeding him my da's recipe?

"You are a good cook," he said now.

"It's not hard to be a good cook with a magic kitchen," I replied. "Anything I ask for is right here, at my hand."

"But this is no illusion," he said. "Whether the ingredients are or not."

I still hadn't learned to look the sorcerer in the eye without flinching—it was too overwhelming, and I was too ashamed of the upsurge of love, and how ridiculous that love must seem to him—but I lifted my gaze now and stared at him. We looked at each other, and I could not read his expression.

"What do you use the hearts for?" I asked suddenly, surprising myself.

He coughed, as if a piece of meatloaf had gone down the wrong way. *Good*, I thought maliciously. "What?" he sputtered.

"The hearts. We all know you take them. What are they

for?" I teetered on the brink of telling him about my own heart but couldn't quite bring myself to do it.

"We . . ." He stopped. Was he really looking *uncomfortable*? He twiddled his fork between his fingers. It seemed to change shape as he did so, becoming a little silver snake with four darting tongues. Another trick. "We protect the kingdom," he said at last.

"So I've heard. But how?"

"Heart magic is the most powerful magic there is," he said. "We take only enough from our people to ensure the safety of all."

It had a rehearsed sound, as if it was something he had been taught by rote.

"The safety of all. Right. Except the people who lose their hearts."

"Rarely a whole one. They barely notice."

I managed to stop myself from actually scoffing out loud. He filled his mouth with another bite of meatloaf, scowling as if he regretted saying that much. I waited, but he chewed for an inordinately long time, as if avoiding further speech.

"I knew someone once," I began carefully, "who had his heart taken."

He swallowed convulsively and did not meet my eye.

"He certainly *noticed*," I continued. "In fact, he hasn't been the same since."

"I suppose it might affect some more than others," he said vaguely, as though he was talking about nothing more consequential than a bad head cold.

"To the point of looking like the walking dead?" I asked. "Barely able to speak?"

He chewed on another mouthful. I got the feeling he was deliberately keeping his mouth full to avoid speech, because while Da's meatloaf was good, it wasn't *that* good.

"What happens to the ones you take from? Afterward?" I pressed.

His strange eyes flickered a little. "I'm not sure," he said after a while.

My own heart pounded with my audacity. "Ever go back?" I asked. "Make sure they're all right? After all, you said you only take what you need, and leave them *barely noticing*. That's what you said, isn't it?"

"Yes," he said. "That's what I said."

There was a long pause. Clearly, he wasn't going to say any more on the subject. Not for now, at least.

"Well," I said, taking up his empty plate. "Good night, then."

"Good night," he echoed.

CHAPTER 9

Eventually, the pace of new rooms appeared to slow down. New doors appeared like cards shuffled and dealt, but when I turned the handles, they opened into an unsettling void, without even the pretense of reality. The House was running out of ideas, I suppose.

I was a little pleased with myself, I have to say, that I was exhausting it so quickly with my sheer determination. If I had sat and thought about my predicament too long, I would have started to fret, and so constant motion was my solution, whether cooking up a storm in the kitchen or stomping about the House and trying to run it ragged with sheer force of will.

"You must know every inch of this place, surely," I said to Cornelius. "There must be some other place I can look."

He gave his ear a quick wash. "I don't know about that," he said. "The House moves about a lot, as you can see. Changes shape. Even I haven't seen all of it. Gets me feeling queasy, sometimes, and then I have to get away for a bit."

"Get away outside?" I asked. "I thought you said you couldn't get out?"

"Not *outside*," he said, as though I were an idiot for suggesting it. "To the Other House."

I stared at him. "You've been watching me ransack this place for days and only now tell me that there's *another* House? Where?"

"It's not any use to you," he told me. "I can go in and out as I please, but I've never seen him do it. It's not magical, you see. It's what used to be here, before he moved in, and this other black place grew up around him and shoved the old place out of the way. It's always the way with these magic people. Cats can go back and forth between such places, but I don't know if humans can."

"I have to at least try. Maybe he's stashing my heart there somehow."

"I've never seen such a thing there. And I told you, it's not magical."

"Please, Cornelius. At least show me how you do it."

He gave his funny cat shrug that I was coming to recognize. "No skin off my nose," he said, and vanished. I jumped back at the shock of it. Then he seemed to wink back into existence, his tail lashing.

"See?" he said, as if it should all be perfectly obvious now.

"How did you do that?" I cried.

"You have to sort of *think sideways*," he said.

I closed my eyes and concentrated, feeling foolish. For a moment, I thought I had it. The world slipped out beneath me as if someone had pulled a rug from under my feet, and I tripped and fell into somewhere dim and dank, with dust swirling about me. Then it was gone, my stomach lurched, and I was back in the black belly of the House.

I tried again, ignoring the rising nausea, and thought for a second it might have worked, but I opened my eyes to find that nothing had changed. I sank to the floor, my magic-made skirts settling around me like the petals of a dark flower, and put my face in my hands. After a moment, I felt a cold, damp nudge on my elbow, and then a shiver of soft fur, as Cornelius tried to comfort me.

"It's all right," he purred. "I told you I didn't think humans could do it."

"I don't know where else to look," I said, knuckling my eyes roughly to discourage any tears from falling. "I could search this place forever, and open a thousand doors, and not find a thing. I might as well be wandering the inside of his *head*, if what you tell me about the House is true. And he'll never give up his secrets."

Cursed at birth, and now cursed to love a sorcerer who saw me as a sort of sentient household appliance.

"Cheer up," said Cornelius. "It's not so bad here."

But he didn't know what I had left behind.

I went to deliver lunch to the sorcerer as usual. Perhaps I could ask him more questions and find out something about my heart that way, without tipping my hand overmuch. Once the door to the throne room creaked open for me, however, I saw that it was empty, save for his throne. Where was he? I backed out, keeping the tray steady, and stood at a loss.

I noticed that the House seemed to be twitching a little underfoot. It wasn't quite forcing me to walk in a certain direction but was definitely encouraging it. If it had been a person, it would have been winking and jerking its head meaningfully.

"Fat chance," I told it. "I'm leaving his lunch here, and if it goes cold, that's his own fault."

The twitching underfoot increased in urgency. I turned to head back to the kitchen and almost walked into a wall that had suddenly appeared in front of me. I glared at it, and it stared right back. I balled my fists under the tray and turned, determined not to let the House bully me, but found myself confronted with another dead end. I sighed.

"Fine," I relented. "Show me where you want me to go."

A corridor unrolled before me, and I followed it. I didn't see that I had much choice. The House led me around a few winding corners before plonking me down in front of a door. I reached for a doorknob that already seemed to be pressing itself up into my hand. What would I find this time? Another bedchamber?

The door opened cleanly and silently, and I saw the same oddly plain, homely room I had found once before. The cabinets were now open, showing its full shelves, and the rectangular frame was still covered with its piece of black sackcloth. The shelves bowed with the weight of jars and canisters, and rough bundles of herbs. Was this the Room of Hearts that I had been searching for after all? My breath caught in my throat.

Several books lay open and dog-eared on the black floor, as well as crumpled notes scrawled in a dark and untidy hand— lots of question marks and exclamation marks, I noticed, as if the author had grown increasingly more agitated and frustrated. The papers littered the floor like fallen blossoms, and thick dust hovered in the air, making it hazy and golden.

I tore my gaze away from the floor and looked up to find the sorcerer sitting behind a black desk that he must have conjured for the occasion, because it hadn't been there the last time I had glimpsed the room.

I hadn't noticed him before because his back was to me, but as I walked around the room towards him I could see the curve of his cheek and the flickering movements of his hands before his face. More papers littered the desk, and pools of black ink shone bright and iridescent on the black surface, turning the scrawled notes to purple mush where the ink had soaked the papers.

He seemed absorbed in an intricate net of sparkling thread

strung between his hands, something like the cat's cradles we made as children back in the village, and hadn't even looked up at my entry. I set down the lunch tray—on the floor before him, amid the mess, since there was no room on the desk—and it made a soft clinking sound.

The sorcerer spun around, his hair lifting and falling about his face. It was constitutionally impossible for any of these magic-workers to do anything gracelessly, it seemed.

"What are you doing in here?" he demanded. "How did you get here?" A sharp frown line carved its way between his brows. I felt like a child caught with her hand in the jam jar, but I rallied.

"Don't ask me," I said. "I was just trying to bring you your lunch, and the House brought me here."

"Oh." He looked at the plate. "What is it?"

"Pork chops," I replied.

"Again." He sighed and made a petulant face. I wanted to turn on my heel right there and march out, but I was too intrigued at the possibility that I had found the Room of Hearts at last.

It certainly felt like *something* significant. The air tasted of metal—it made my tongue feel thick and sluggish in my mouth. My ears buzzed faintly. *Magic.*

I recognized the flavor of it at once, despite never having felt it this strongly before. Perhaps it was an instinct built into me, to recognize its signature, the way a baby mouse knows from birth to fear the shadow of an owl.

The sorcerer continued to fiddle with the sparkling cat's cradle between his hands. He seemed to have sprouted several new fingers to manage the threads, manipulating them with manic intensity. Staring at it and trying to determine exactly how it worked made my head hurt.

I discreetly stirred the discarded papers on the floor with

ANDREA EAMES

my foot, looking about for any sign of a heart. Perhaps it was in one of the jars or bottles on the shelves, ground to a powder or dissolved in liquid. I started making my way slowly toward the cabinets, but he looked up sharply, and I stopped, trying to look like I was just idly wandering.

"What are you doing?" I asked. "What is all this?"

I bent down to unfold one of the hysterically scrawled scraps of paper. The sorcerer immediately threw the cat's cradle down to the floor.

"Don't touch anything!" he cried.

The cat's cradle exploded where he dropped it, making me jump, and turned into a handful of glittering ash that descended onto the pork chops, looking like expensive seasoning.

The explosion sent the papers on the floor swirling like a cloud of moths—and it also blew the sacking cover off the frame on the wall. The sorcerer noticed and grabbed at it as it fell, but he was too late. It escaped his grasp and left its secret uncovered.

It was a painted portrait that hid behind the sacking, and I could see it now in full. I was no expert on paintings and had barely seen any besides the portraits of the king that hung in taverns and public buildings, but it didn't seem like a very accomplished portrait to me.

Rather, it seemed like the work of an excessively average painter, someone who was still learning, and who had scrubbed out and painted certain patches over and over. There was a laborious, many-layered quality to it, and the colors were muddy.

I would have expected a beautiful woman, if I'd had to guess at the sort of secret portrait a man might keep in a locked room in his house, but despite the painter's lack of skill, I could tell this was definitely a picture of a boy. A very young boy, no more than five years old, perhaps, although I wasn't much use at judging the ages of sprouts.

The portraitist clearly had trouble with hands, and had

94

erased and redrawn the eyes a number of times, but there was still something of the spirit of the boy there, despite that.

He had darkish, longish hair, a prominent nose, and an unhandsome face that nevertheless had some character about it. The painter had managed to capture a certain stubborn set to the jaw, even if they hadn't quite succeeded in shaping the lips and had ended up with a kind of muddled, fleshy blob instead.

"Who is that?" I asked.

"No one."

I studied the sorcerer's profile as he looked at the picture. Every line perfect. He looked like he should be the oil painting. Or, rather, the oil painting, with all its errors and smudges, looked more human than he did.

He did not seem inclined to tell me more about it, so instead I asked, "What are you doing in here?"

He blew a stray hair out of his eyes, and I tried to stop myself from staring at his pursed lips. He stared ahead for a moment without speaking, then threw his hands up as if in surrender.

"I'm working on a . . . cure, I suppose. For a . . . disease. And it's a particularly infectious and destructive disease, and a cure is urgently needed. The king has tasked us all with its finding."

"Then the sorceresses are working on it too?"

"With more success, I am sure."

I looked around at the mess again. I picked up one of the books at random off the floor and leafed through its pages. It felt unnaturally dense and heavy for its size, straining out of its physical boundaries as if it were a very large object pretending to be very small.

"You can read?" he asked, with a note of surprise in his voice. I don't know why it irked me. It was a fair assumption to make; most village girls never bothered to learn. Or rather, no one bothered to teach them.

They didn't have a da like mine, who loved stories, and who

sat his aching body in front of the fire every evening to read to me and help me shape my letters, guiding my tiny fingers with his coarse hands that always smelled a little of blood, no matter how much he scrubbed.

Most people assumed I was illiterate. Sylvester being surprised at my abilities, though—that stung.

I had expected the magical books to be in another language, perhaps even another alphabet, but I could read it all quite clearly. It was drily academic, from what I could tell.

"This is a recipe for a charm," I noted. "You said you sold charms. Why? I can't imagine you need the coin. Or"—remembering the hearts—"whatever they use to pay you."

He laughed a little. "No, I have little use for coin. I do not accept payment. But the king likes us to make ourselves useful to the common people. It keeps relations cordial, he says."

I snorted.

"If anyone chooses to come to me for a spell, however, they must be desperate," said Sylvester, resting his chin on his hands again. To my surprise, he sounded a little bitter.

"I imagine everyone who seeks out magic must be desperate," I said.

"Not all. Some are simply greedy. No, I am the last resort when it comes to potions and charms. I told you, I am no better than a hedge-witch in that regard."

"But you're a *sorcerer*."

He crooked one eyebrow. "The others are more powerful than me."

"Is that why you're the only . . ." I wasn't sure how to put it. "The only one like you?" I ventured.

"Yes," he said simply. "Magic manifests itself . . . differently, in me. My spells can be somewhat unpredictable in their outcomes. And so those seeking magic come to me last, if the others have refused them."

"What does that mean, unpredictable?"

He snorted. "Exactly how it sounds. Sometimes my magic works, and sometimes . . ." He made a sweeping gesture at the mess of papers and ink. "It doesn't. Or goes spectacularly awry." His eyes flickered upward, unnaturally bright. "This is what I was made for. It should come as naturally as breathing. If not, I have already outlived my usefulness."

I stared at him, and was about to ask another question when I was startled to hear a knock at the door—partly because it was a surprise, and partly because I was amazed I could hear it this far away. I thought at first I was hearing things.

"Did you hear that?" I asked.

"It's the door," the sorcerer said helpfully.

I felt oddly fearful. I had grown accustomed to the House and my role in it, and I was comfortable in my invisibility there. I was not eager to be seen by the world again. "Who is it?"

"I suppose you should answer it," he said absently, preoccupied again with the papers on his desk. "Take them to the throne room."

I muttered to myself about entitled sorcerers as I stomped to answer the door, and the House obliged (or hurried me to my doom) by making the corridor shorter.

Could it be one of the sorceresses? I didn't know how I felt about seeing one of the magic-workers up that close. I'd only ever seen them at a respectable distance. Might she siphon the rest of my heart out of me on sight? Then again, I thought, how exactly would I be worse off?

Perhaps it would be a blessing to get it over and done with rather than continuing to waste away in the sorcerer's House. I decided to risk it, and I made my way to the door. I hadn't opened the big slab of black since I had arrived.

When I did, it let in a mess of noise and light and colors as the daylight sliced across my eyeballs like one of Da's best filleting knives. I blinked to clear my vision, bracing myself to see one of the sorceresses, but instead saw a weaselly little man clutching a leather purse and looking just as scared as myself. He actually jumped when I looked directly at him.

"Who are you?" I asked.

"Who are *you*?" he demanded, and I couldn't blame him. I was the last person you'd expect to see in such a grand place. He seemed to collect himself and spoke more calmly. "I'm here for a charm," he said.

"Oh yes," said Cornelius, who had appeared from somewhere around the region of my feet. "Haven't seen one of these in a while."

If the man had been jumpy before, he was practically vibrating now that he had heard Cornelius speak. I held the door open a little wider. "I suppose you'd better come in," I said.

Cornelius led the way to the throne room, as he had when I arrived. The House behaved itself, and kept everything in the same places as usual, and didn't play any tricks with the floor. The way the visitor acted, however, you'd have thought trapdoors were popping open all around him. I'd never seen anyone so spooked, certainly not by a gloomy black corridor.

"In there," I told him, pointing to the throne room door. The man looked like he was about to melt into a puddle on the spot.

"Aren't you coming in with me?" he asked in a strangled voice.

I exchanged glances with Cornelius.

"All right, I suppose," I said. I must confess, I was interested. I pushed open the door and found the sorcerer lounging in that great black chair, as usual, juggling fireballs with one hand and propping his chin up with the other.

"What?" he said ungraciously.

"Visitor," I said.

"Where?"

I realized the man was cringing behind me. It was hard to tell how tall he actually was, what with all the shaking and cowering.

"Pull yourself together," I said over my shoulder.

The man poked his head out and licked his dry lips. "Greetings, Your Highness," he said.

I almost snorted.

"What?" said Sylvester again. "I'm busy."

"I need a . . . a potion, Your Highness."

Sylvester sighed. He let the fiery juggling balls fall one by one into his open palm, and then closed his fist in a puff of smoke.

"What sort of potion?"

"Er . . ." The man glanced at me. I rolled my eyes. "I'll wait outside," I huffed, and stomped out, closing the door behind me. Cornelius was just outside in the corridor, sitting up with his tail tucked neatly over his front feet.

It was bound to be an aphrodisiac the fellow was after, I speculated—that, or something to rid himself of an unwanted babe. I had chatted with Goodwife Tilly now and then, back in the village, and she had said that whenever someone came to the herbal shop through the back door, it was always to ask for one of those two things. She insisted she didn't sell them, but I wasn't too sure.

"Does this happen often?" I asked Cornelius.

"No. They're always like that, though, when they do come."

The door swung open behind me, sooner than I had expected, and I had to shuffle out of the way. The man emerged, wide-eyed and clutching a little velvet drawstring bag so tightly that his knuckles were bloodless.

"All done?" I asked.

He nodded, seemingly unable to speak. He stood there staring at me until I realized he meant for me to show him out.

"Oh. This way."

I stomped back down the corridor to the front door but drew the line at opening it for him. His knuckles were still white as pearls around the bag.

I couldn't contain my curiosity. "What did you ask him for?" I wondered.

He jumped at my voice. "Do you live here?" he asked, ignoring my question. "How do you bear it?"

"Bear what?"

"Being so close to one of *Them*." He sounded awed.

I wasn't about to go into my whole history, and so I said, "You get used to it."

"I've seen them, of course, and heard stories . . . But being so close?" He shook his head.

"Yes, well," I said, with a little acid in my voice.

The man held out his purse with a trembling hand. "Payment," he said.

Unthinking, I held out my hand, expecting the *clunk* of gold coin. Instead, a handful of unpleasantly squishy, damp things, something like fermented figs, rolled onto my palm.

I swore and let them fall to the floor in my surprise, and the man shot me a furious look and dropped to his knees to scramble them up again. He batted Cornelius away, who had been sniffing at one.

"What are you doing?" he hissed. "Do you know what I had to do to get these?"

"I don't even know what they *are*," I said. I stooped to get a better look at them.

"Hearts," he said.

"*Human* hearts?"

"They'd better be, for what I paid for them." He seemed surprised by my ignorance, and his surprise had driven away his anger. "Don't you know about them?"

I opened and shut my mouth like a fish. What to say? "I didn't know they were like *that*," I managed. "They're so small! And wrinkly!"

"Well, they've been dried a bit," he explained. "These could probably do with a bit more drying, to be honest, but I had to take what I could get."

I couldn't believe it. Did everyone in the city cart a bag of hearts about with them? Was one half murdering the other half? Well. I didn't know what to make of that. It seemed odd that such powerful sorcery was piddled out on little cantrips and potions for the public, and the hearts sold on the black market sounded like one big swindle to me.

"I would have thought you'd seen a lot of them, living here," he said. "They all use them for their magicks, don't they?"

"But . . . they go out and get them on their own," I said. "They don't *buy* them. How do you have so many?"

He cocked his head, puzzled, as if I was asking questions that were common knowledge.

"I'm not from here," I explained. "I'm from the country. *Far* out in the country."

"Oh," he said, apparently satisfied. "Well yes, of course, they get their own. But there's a market for these others, if you know where to find it. Some people say that you can learn to use them for magicks, even if you're not one of Them, but I don't know about that." He had gathered all the hearts back up into the little purse, and handed it to me. I weighed it in my palm. I couldn't imagine anything magical being left in these sad, squishy little things, but what did I know? Maybe there was something yet to be milked from them.

"And these are what they take as payment?"

"Of course," he said. "Usually. But none of the others are selling magicks just now."

"Why not?"

He frowned. "I don't know. Things have been changing, lately. All the others turned me away."

Clearly Sylvester had been a last resort, as he had said. "Well, good luck to you," I said.

The man nodded goodbye and ducked out the door quick as winking, relieved to be out of there. I inhaled a tantalizing gasp of outdoor air before the door swung smoothly shut. I looked at the repulsive little bag in my hand.

"What's that?" said Cornelius. I held it out for him to get a proper sniff.

"Pig, I think," he said, with the air of a connoisseur. I knew it. I marched back to the throne room and found Sylvester hunched over on the throne with his elbows on his knees, glaring straight ahead.

"I was told to give you these," I said. I held the bag of pig hearts out to show him. He barely gave it a glance.

"Useless. The man was a fool to be fobbed off with such." He sighed. "Which reminds me. Our visitor bought my last potion. We may have to go out."

"Go *out*?" I imagined sitting beside him as he rolled into another village in his grand carriage, watching him snatch up another unsuspecting maiden. Did he really expect me to help him gather up hearts?

"To the market," he said, much to my relief.

"What do you need from the market that you can't magic up at home? The fruit bowl fills itself quick as blinking if I so much as think about an apple."

"Some things can't be magicked," he said. "Or lose their efficacy if you try."

"Like what?"

"Certain herbs, tinctures . . . Even the magical food needs to be supplemented with the real stuff from time to time. Eating nothing but magic tends to make one a bit sickly over time."

"Is that why you lot come out to get those things from the villages?" I had thought it was just a pretense.

"Sometimes."

"But I thought all you needed for your magic was a heart."

To my surprise, he seemed uncomfortable. He conjured one of his little fireballs and started flickering it between his fingers, as practiced as a street magician. "Well, that's not *all* we need," he said, rather sharply.

He straightened up suddenly, his clothes shimmering around him, and quick as blinking, he seemed dressed for travel: the heavy, many-caped cloak he now wore looked to be made of leather, and his boots were sturdier and squarer of toe than the ones he usually sported. (I had noticed that he had a particular vanity about his shoes, which were often the most extravagant part of his dress.) "You will accompany me to the market," he said, still short in tone.

To fetch and carry, I supposed. I looked down at my clothes. Even though the fabric was richer than anything I owned back home, they weren't best suited to a city outing.

As if reading my mind, the sorcerer made a gesture with one hand, and I felt the garments scramble around my body like cats after a mouse. The metallic scent of magic filled my lungs.

In a panic, I yelped and tried to hold the fabric down to cover myself as best I could, but I needn't have worried—as quickly as the old clothes slithered off my body and raced away like shadows, new ones spiraled up my legs like vines and wrapped themselves around me, leaving no room for naked-ness in between.

"You could have warned me!" I snapped. The new garments were heavy, made of something like velvet but with a finer nap, warm and close-fitting. Glancing down, I could see a row of gold buttons and some intricate embroidery on the placket.

I wondered how much of a fright I looked—a butcher's

daughter dressed up like a fine lady. There were no mirrors in the sorcerer's House other than the one in his sister's boudoir, and none had been provided me—perhaps because they were the last things I would wish for.

The sorcerer seemed satisfied with my appearance, however. "Come," he said simply, and swept past me in a gust of cinnamon- and copper-scented air, into the dark corridor.

Giddy from the magic and the nearness of him, I could only follow, tripping over my new fancy skirt as I did so.

Outside was fresh and biting and bracing, with a wind full of city smells and the humming of city noise. I hadn't realized how flat my senses had become inside the magical House, how deadened and dimmed.

Now, more than ever, I realized that nothing it produced was really real, and *here* was the real stuff, the dazzling, stinking mess of it, ready to be swallowed down and spat back up with each breath.

The sorcerer looked back at me curiously. I must have looked like a landed fish, gasping and gulping there on the pavement.

"Come along," he said, and turned on his heel.

I followed at a slight distance, struggling to match his pace. He noticed, I think, because he slowed a little, which made me feel like a dog trotting after his master.

I had enjoyed my anonymity in the city, but there was none of that now as I trailed behind the sorcerer. Eyes stared first at him, lingering on his beautiful face and fine clothes, and then passed to me, and widened.

I felt their gaze hot on my cheeks, and I kept my head down. I dreaded looking up and seeing pity on any face, even just one. I was pitiable, no doubt about that, but I didn't want to be reminded of it.

"Keep up," the sorcerer said over his shoulder. I made a face at his back.

We arrived at the same market I had passed through when I first arrived in the city. It was certainly fancier than the one in our little village square back home.

As well as the usual meat and fish and vegetables and flowers, it had a whole stall devoted to ornamental cages, some of which were filled with feathery creatures of all colors, and one to little jeweled collars for dogs, of all things. One stall even sold an assortment of cheap furnishings featuring the king's familiar face—plates and tea towels and such.

There was nary a beggar to be seen. They probably gave them a kick and sent them rolling downhill if they dared to venture up this far.

I was surprised at the ordinariness of the sorcerer's shopping—herbs and powders, twisted roots, even a bunch of evil-smelling flowers. He ambled between the stalls, seemingly oblivious to the stares and whispers, and I trotted along at his heels.

As he made his purchases, he stowed them away in his cloak pockets, and I came to realize that they were magically capacious, as there was no way they could hold such a bulky assortment of plants, herbs, and spice packets without spoiling the perfect line of the tailoring.

I don't know what use I was, trailing after him, as he didn't give me anything to carry, nor send me to fetch anything he needed. I suppose he just wanted to keep me from cleaning the House into oblivion. Or exploring it further while he was out and unable to keep an eye on me.

I became aware of a susurration in the crowd, and a wave-like movement as people drifted to either side of the market, clearing a path. I craned my neck to see what was coming and saw another one of *them*. The magic-workers.

The sorcerer came to a halt, and I went careening into his back. I clutched at the warm leather of his caped cloak for a moment to steady myself, and the warm spice of his scent rushed up at me and made me giddy.

I let go and stumbled back, stepping one foot into a puddle of mud, right up to the ankle. Lovely. I closed my eyes and tried to breathe, fighting back the wave of adoration that muddled my head.

It was quite the sight. A sorceress with hair as golden and gleaming as a sweet wine, trimmed with expensive cloth and fine jewels, was riding something like a fancy rickshaw. The rickshaw was all decked out with shinies and curlicues as well. Of course. Pulling it was a youngish man, tall and gangly, but with wiry muscles visible on his bare shoulders and arms. He would need them, clearly, pulling that jewel-encrusted monstrosity around.

Why couldn't she use a horse? I suppose it was to show off her power—to intimidate. I would have expected her servant to be straining and panting at the weight, but his face was oddly blank and rigid.

What surprised me most was that the crowd started to cheer as she passed—respectfully, no rowdiness or rude remarks. I heard, "Bless you, my lady!" more than once. Back home, we would have goggled and stared, of course, but silently— certainly no cheering, as we knew what they had come to us for.

Things were clearly different here. Children laughed and pointed with no fear, and the men and women gazed and smiled with not just the expected adoration, but with approval. I was used to seeing the magic-workers worshipped—but *liked*? That was a new one.

Sylvester hadn't even looked up.

"It's one of your lot," I said.

He glanced her way. "So it is," he said without expression.

She had spotted him too. He was hard to miss. She reached for a pair of reins—*reins*? She was really using reins on her servant?—and pulled on them, bringing the rickshaw to a halt. I could hear the tinkle of her bracelets as she lifted her hand, and her dress shivered and sparkled before settling, all those elaborate folds reacting to the movement.

I watched her servant come to a halt. His bare torso gleamed with sweat, but his face remained impassive. The jewel-encrusted reins linked to a collar around his neck, also elaborately decorated, so they seemed more for show—and humiliation?—than practical use. If he felt shame, though, he showed none. I could see nothing living behind his eyes.

As far as I could tell, no one in the crowd seemed surprised or outraged at the sight of him, as we would have been back home. A servant drawing a rickshaw for a fine lady, all right, but wearing a collar and reins? There would definitely have been some mutterings back in the village.

The people around us dispersed respectfully, muttering prayers or blessings as they departed and went about their business. I knew enough about the nature of people, however, to be sure that their attention was still fixed on us, even if they turned their backs and pretended to be absorbed in their shopping.

"Sylvester," the sorceress greeted him. Her eyes flickered over me, widening just a little as they took me in. I was face-to-face with a sorceress, closer to one than I had ever been.

The word "dazzling" didn't even come close. It was like looking into the blue heart of a fire or tasting a spice that set your mouth to burning. The perfection of her face hurt me; the symmetry sliced me open.

It would not matter who was behind that face—the most evil-minded, meanest, and most rotten-cored person could have been inside there, and it would not have mattered. I would have worshipped her all the same. Anyone would have.

"Clarissa," said Sylvester. Of course she would have a name like Clarissa.

"I don't often see you at the market," she said, and a thread of judgment wove through her crystalline voice. "I am glad to see you out and about among the people."

I stole a glance at the sorcerer. I'd never seen anyone less pleased to be out and about. "I needed more herbs," he said shortly.

"You've been selling spells? Even better." She seemed pleased, which made him glower even more.

"Go," he said, turning to me. I blinked. Go where? Then I realized that, of course, they would want to speak alone, and embarrassment stung my cheeks. Dismissed, like the servant I was.

I swallowed down the ache in my heart as best I could and walked away, trying to look like it didn't matter to me one way or the other. The bespelled part of me felt jealousy twist in my gut, even though he hadn't seemed overly pleased to see the sorceress.

Well, it was a chance to look about for someone who seemed likely to have the knowledge I sought about retrieving my heart. I wasn't going to accost just anyone.

I wandered around the market for a while, wondering how to broach the subject and whom to speak to, until I saw again the sign I had seen on arriving in the city: advertising quills and paper, and "Letters Read and Written." Behind it sat a bespectacled man.

I started toward him, with the vague idea that someone who was around ink and paper a great deal would have more knowledge than the average person. And then I realized—I couldn't believe this hadn't occurred to me before—I could write to Da! I could explain where I was and what I was doing, far better than in my hastily scribbled note that I had left on the counter back home.

"Need something read?" asked the scholar when I approached, eyeing me dubiously. I suppose my fine clothes made me look less illiterate than usual.

"You're a scribe?"

"That is my trade," he said, tapping the sign.

"Could you get a letter out of the city? If I wrote one?"

"A letter? Nothing easier. Shall I write it for you?" He was still looking at me oddly, as if he wanted to say more.

"No, my hand is fair enough. But I will need pen and paper," I said.

He passed me both, wordlessly, and I palmed him a coin. I wrote a few lines, telling Da where I could be found, and that I was working as the sorcerer's housekeeper ("and *nothing else*," I added and underlined it, because I knew he would worry). I told him I would be back as soon as I found a way, and then I signed my name and addressed the letter.

I feared it would do little to ease his worry. He would know better than to come to a sorcerer's house looking for me, of that much I was sure, but we all knew what the magic-workers did to a person. Well, we had thought we knew.

"Thank you," I said to the man as he stashed it in a leather bag filled with papers. I waited until he had tucked it away safely and then said in a low tone, "I'm looking for someone who can tell me about the sorceresses."

He jumped, then rearranged his face into a neutral expression. "The what?"

"The sorceresses. The . . . beautiful women. The magic-workers." I gestured vaguely at where Sylvester and the sorceress were still talking.

"The Magic-Workers!" I could hear the capital letters he added, dropping them like a couple of sugar cubes into tea.

"Right. Them," I said.

"What do you want to know about them?" he asked, still guarded.

I hesitated, wondering if anyone was eavesdropping and if it would matter. The man saw me twisting my skirts in my hands like a bashful country girl and took pity on me.

"What's your name?" he asked me.

"Foss Butcher," I replied.

"My name is Basil," he said. He looked at me narrowly and moved a little closer, although the bustle of the market already smothered our voices, and I doubted anyone would have over-heard us.

"You want to know about the *hearts*?" he whispered.

"I know that they take them. But I don't know why, exactly, or what they do with them afterward."

He peered behind me, as if expecting an army of guardsmen to jump out from behind the fruit stalls.

"Why do you ask?" he said. He leaned in even more. "Have you been *snagged*?"

I wondered if it was a dirty question.

"I don't know what that means," I said.

He looked at me closely, peering into my face as if he could read it like one of his scrolls. It was disconcerting, I tell you.

"I think you have," he said. He scribbled something down on a scrap of his paper—an address.

"Come here tonight, at midnight," he said. "It is best if no one sees you."

I raised an eyebrow. A strange man giving me an address and telling me to go there alone, in the middle of the night? He must have read these thoughts in my expression, because he waved his hands.

"No, no, it is nothing sinister, or dangerous. Our gatherings are merely . . . frowned upon."

"By whom?"

"All of them. The king. The Magic-Workers. They prefer to keep their business . . . quiet."

Well, that was reassuring, all right.

"Fine," I said. "I'll think about it."

"Here," he said, folding the little paper and holding it out. I started to open it, but he flapped his hands at me urgently and hissed, "Hide it! Hide it!"

I wondered if he was slightly unhinged. Maybe I'd open the paper back at the House and find nothing but a meaningless scrawl. Still, it was the best chance I had, so I tucked it away in my pocket.

Idly, I cast my eye over his wares and saw a little seal and picked it up, so that I would look like nothing more than a customer should the magic-workers glance my way.

The wood was smooth in my hand, and the design looked like an amateurishly drawn carrion bird—a crow, perhaps, or a raven. It reminded me of the dishes in the sorcerer's House, and of him. It appealed to me. A memento, for when I left, then—if I were ever able to leave.

"I'll take this," I said, and waited as the scribe wrapped it in waxed paper. He tapped the side of his nose, as if to remind me of our shared secret, and I left.

I did feel better, though, having written to Da. Sending that letter to him was almost like reaching out my hand to him and feeling his larger, rougher one take it. I felt warmed and strengthened.

I walked back to the magic-workers, who stopped speaking abruptly when I turned up. The sorceress parted her lips for a moment as if to say more, then seemed to think better of it.

"I will call upon you soon, Sylvester," she said. She twitched the reins again, and her expressionless servant picked up the rickshaw shafts.

"Come," said Sylvester abruptly as she moved away. He

turned on his heel and started back toward the House. Again, I had to trot to keep up with him.

I imagined the letter I had written to Da, nestled in that leather bag and waiting for the mail coach that would take it all the way back to our village. It took a piece of my heart with it as surely as the sorcerer did.

CHAPTER 10

When we returned, I felt despair settle on me like rain as the black House engulfed me once more. After having been outside, I was more aware than ever how alien the place was, how alien *he* was.

The *he* in question spoke not a word to me upon entering, just strode off down the long corridor, muttering to himself and rifling through the herbs in his pockets. Cornelius appeared and wound himself around my ankles, purring. I gave him an absent-minded pat.

"Are you all right?" he asked.

"Yes. I might have a way to find my heart. I'm not sure yet. I have to go and talk to someone tonight about it."

"Be careful," said Cornelius, giving me a gentle nip on my ankle.

I was in the middle of cleaning the kitchen, ready to prepare the evening meal, when I heard it—a sound like a great wind.

Then the floor started to shake beneath my feet. I grasped the stove to keep my balance.

"What's going on?" I shouted to Cornelius above the noise. He had flattened himself beneath a cabinet, and all I could see were two glowing yellow eyes.

"I don't know," he mewed.

I made my way on unsteady feet to the kitchen door and looked out into the passage. The whole House trembled, and a greenish light flickered from one end of it. I raced toward the light and noise, my feet scrambling for purchase on the black floor.

Cornelius had more sense, hiding from the commotion rather than running toward it. But any sense I had fled with the thought that the sorcerer might be in danger. What I planned to do about it, gods only knew, but I ran until I reached the doorway to his room of cabinets and bookshelves, from which the green light and terrible banshee wind emanated.

Sylvester was spread-eagled on the wooden table, gripping the edges as if either holding something down, or keeping himself from blowing away. All his discarded papers spiraled around him in a whirlwind, and some detached part of me observed that I would probably be cleaning up the mess later.

"What's happening? What's wrong?" I shouted above the roaring and screeching.

"Get out!" he yelled. I didn't take it personally, though, because I could see the strain on his face. The greenish light was coming from beneath him, as if he were holding closed the trapdoor to hell. I struggled forward into the room, clutching at my skirt as it swirled around me.

"A spell," he panted. "Gone awry."

I was close enough to see now that he was putting his whole weight on an open book on the table, and the light came from that book. It shuddered and twitched beneath him as if trying to escape.

"There's nothing you can do! Take the cat, and get out of the House!"

So he was about to blow the place up, it seemed. It might have been more sensible to do as he said, and take my chances on the ensnaring spell dying with him and setting me free, but my heart wouldn't let me.

I forced my way through the hurricane of papers to the table. Don't ask me what I was thinking; I hardly knew. I just knew that I had to get to him, somehow; touch him; do something to keep him from coming apart. I reached out to where his hands gripped the table on either side and put my own over his, as if that would do much good.

Amazingly, it did.

As soon as I touched him, every swirling piece of paper in the room froze and hovered in place. The green light blazed once, so brightly that it left an imprint of the room behind my eyelids, and was gone.

And then it was just the two of us, him still flat on the table and me clutching at his hands, and the papers floating peacefully down to the floor like a swarm of moths. We stayed like this for a moment in the sudden, ear-aching silence.

"What did you do?" Sylvester whispered, more expression on his face than I had yet seen. His hands trembled under mine, just a little.

"I don't . . . I didn't . . ." I stared at my own hands. They were the same old hands, chapped and work-roughened, the nails sensibly short.

"You did something," he snapped.

"I didn't! I . . ."

He straightened up, pulling himself away. The book lay on the table, inert now, but steaming a little.

"What *was* that?"

"You did something," he muttered, ignoring my question and leafing through the book. "You must have."

"I . . ."

"Please. You have to let me think."

I stepped back over the threshold, and a gust of magical air slammed the door in my face.

After that, I was more eager than ever to visit Basil and find out whatever esoteric knowledge he had to share with me. I prepared carefully for my escapade that night, knowing I wouldn't have long outside the House and away from Sylvester before the heartsickness set in. I wanted to make the most of my time as a relatively sane person.

I dressed myself in my old clothes—the new ones, though warmer and richer, were too conspicuous. With luck, the sorcerer would never know I had gone. I had taken him his dinner as usual, so he should not be looking for me. I had made the blandest meal I could, as I obviously wasn't feeling very charitable toward him that evening.

"You're coming back?" asked Cornelius as he watched me fasten my cloak. He had been hovering about me anxiously ever since I had returned from the market.

"Yes, I promise," I said. "Honestly, I don't think I'll have much of a choice."

When the time came, I walked down the corridor as casually as I could, headed for the front door, as if I was on my way to nowhere special, but I wasn't fooling anybody. The House didn't want me to leave.

In a wink, walking down the black corridor became as

difficult as trying to climb back up a throat when you'd been swallowed. The floor stretched out endlessly underfoot, doors ranked on either side as far as I could see. I could feel the House's sulk all around me, as thick as if I were wading through water.

I had treated it like a sort of disobedient but basically eager-to-please dog up until that moment, ordering it around and scolding it when it misbehaved. As it showed me its temper, however, I felt a little afraid of it, and the fact that I was afraid of it made me furious and therefore a little less afraid. I stopped dead.

"Listen, House," I said. "I'm leaving, but not for long. Let me go. I'll come back."

The walls rippled. Silence. I felt a creeping along my spine. The House wasn't a person. It didn't have the same thoughts or feelings as a person, if it had either at all. Whatever was listening was not human.

The walls seemed to inch a little closer. The floor felt unpleasantly alive and warm even through my sturdy boots, as though I stood on a giant tongue. If I showed it I was afraid, I thought, I would never have any chance of getting out. I had to stand up to it.

"Let me *go*!" I said, and stamped my foot.

And then, just as suddenly as it had closed around me, the House released me. I staggered forward, legs buckling. The black corridor stretched before and behind me at its usual length, docile and still, as if it had never moved.

I listened for the sorcerer—surely he was aware of all this commotion? I still didn't know if he ever slept—but heard nothing. I took a wary step forward, but the floor was solid beneath my feet, and the door allowed me to open it. I staggered across the black courtyard and flung open the door to the street.

Outside was just as much of a shock as it had been earlier,

but the nighttime smells were different from the day's—at once stronger and more mysterious. I took a cautious breath. Despite bracing against it, I could tell already the heartsickness was setting in.

Not too badly, as yet. I could feel it nagging at me, like a child tugging at my skirts, but it was ignorable, not the all-encompassing, whole-body ailment it had been back in the village, thank the gods. I had a little time before it would set in again in full, it seemed.

I unfolded the paper. *Oyster Lane.* I had no map of the city and no way to find my path other than to ask the strangers who passed me in their hundreds—even at night, the city was bustling—and so I summoned up my courage and did so. I did not tell them the exact house for which I was searching, for fear it would have meaning to them, but I found that the street I sought was down in the lower reaches of the city, by the river, where the beggars sprawled against the outer walls.

Part of me enjoyed this expedition—and liked this new Foss. The sheer variety of faces that filled every street and alleyway made me realize how little feeling like the plainest girl in my tiny village mattered. I was just one more face in a crowd, and though far from the best of them, I was also a long way from being the worst.

It made me wonder whether I was really as bad as I had feared, or whether the whispers about my mother's death had made me feel ugly and wrong out of proportion to the reality of myself.

Here, where no one knew that story, I in no way stood out from anyone else on the street. I found I liked being away from the gossip and the stares of people who had known me since I was a sprout, who knew every detail of my history and my family's history, who thought they could predict all my movements and see my life spooling out ahead of me as clear and inevitable as a fairy story told so often that your mouth finds its shape without thought.

Here, no one cared anything about my life, much less had any visions for it. At home, all I'd had to look forward to was working in the shop and taking care of Da until he finally passed on, then running the place myself until I was too old and gray and had to take on an apprentice—or perhaps marry a widower who had passed the age of being fussy about trim figures and pretty faces, and only wished for someone to make his tea of an evening.

I shuddered to think of it, and then immediately felt guilt twist in my gut. How could I feel this surge of gladness at a life away from Da, who had loved and cherished and protected me since I was born? Aside from a wet nurse right after my mother passed, he had refused to take on any help to care for me and did it all himself—all the nappies and nighttime wakings, all the hair-braiding and bandaging scuffed knees that came later.

And now I was enjoying a life without him, while he worried about me? I should be ashamed of myself.

I did not want to walk for too long, lest my time run out, and so I paid for a pony cart to take me down. The driver set me down as close to my destination as I dared, since I did not want anyone to know exactly where I was going.

I found myself almost by the city walls in a dank row of houses beside a river that smelled as badly as old Dav's fish stand.

The heartsickness was a larger presence now, twisting my guts as though I had eaten something that disagreed with me. I hoped that my relative closeness to the sorcerer would keep it from becoming debilitating before I had a chance to learn what I could.

I was no idiot, whatever else I might have been. Nothing going on in an alley like this could be good. But my feet were killing my lower half, and the exquisite pain in my chest from being away from the sorcerer was starting to niggle at my upper half, and I had to do something if I didn't want to live in his House forever, making his meals and drooling over his pretty cheekbones. So I found the right door and knocked.

The man who answered was the scribe from the market—Basil.

"You came," he said, as if that weren't obvious. He darted a look down the street, first one way and then the other. I tried not to roll my eyes. If this was nothing more than some sort of secret society devoted to rumor and speculation about the magic-workers (I refused to give them capital letters, even in my thoughts), I would be tempted to turn on my heel and march back up the hill. My borrowed time was too precious to waste.

He creaked open the door to reveal a room that had probably been a tavern once, with a long, low counter and wooden stools around a handful of tables, the ubiquitous royal portrait glaring down from above the bar. Some of the stools had been drawn into a circle. On the counter were cups, a small pitcher of wine, and some plates of bread and dried fish.

Secret society, just as I had feared. If I had braved the possibility of another bad bout of heartsickness just for a gossip circle, I'd feel like a fool.

Basil indicated a spare stool, and I sat, happy to take the weight from my feet. The others stared at me. There was a sense of wariness, even of fear.

"This is . . ." said the scribe and flapped a hand at me.

"Foss. Foss Butcher," I said.

"Foss. She came to me in the market this morning. Came directly to my stall, as if she had been *led* to it . . ."

Oh no. One of those. If he started talking about fate or destiny, I was out.

". . . and asked me about the Magic-Workers, and what they do with the . . ."

"*Hearts*," someone else whispered. All the faces were frightened. It was an odd mix of people, old and young. One woman was very richly dressed, richer even than my House-made clothes, while one youth was ragged, and the rest ran the gamut. I counted nine people, in all.

"There are more of our number," said Basil, indicating the group. "Not all could come tonight. There are certain . . . *restrictions* that come from our . . . shared condition."

Questions were popping up in my head like bubbles in broth.

"What do you mean, *shared condition*?" I asked. The older lady with the fancy clothing cupped her face in her hands and started to weep. And I do mean *weep*, not cry. Crying was a low-bred thing to do, but weeping was higher-pitched, and involved a lace handkerchief and small, ladylike sniffs.

"It is a terrible affliction," said Basil, "and yet there are those worse off than us."

"You must be similarly affected," said the rich lady, raising her face to me. I saw her slight wince as she allowed her well-bred eyes to rest on my face. She settled on staring at my left ear as she spoke. "Or you would not have come here."

"Afflicted? Affected?" I looked around. I felt a strange shame about the sorcerer—strange because it had been in no way my own fault that I was connected to him, nor was it my fault that I . . . loved . . . him, but everything in me rebelled against the humiliation of it. I wasn't eager to talk to these strangers about it.

"So, you've all been . . ." I let my voice trail off.

"*Snagged*," said someone.

"Taken," said another.

"Used," said a third.

I leaned forward. "How does it happen?" I asked. "What do they *do*?"

"You have to tell your story first," said a motherly woman. "That's the way it works."

Nodding of heads. Murmured agreement.

"All right," I said, and took a deep breath. I told them what had happened to bring me here from my village—the edited version, without my sweaty, imaginary tanglings in the sheets, although they probably knew all about those anyway. There was a knowingness in their gazes that wasn't entirely comfortable.

"You live in his *house*?" said someone.

"Yes," I said. "I didn't know what else to do."

"You poor thing," said the elderly lady, and everyone shook their heads in sympathy, exchanging significant glances. But was I imagining it, or was there a touch of envy in their gazes also?

"So, you still have it?" asked Basil.

They all looked at me intently.

"Have what?"

"Your *heart*, of course," said the older lady. "How much is missing?"

"I don't know," I admitted. "I don't think any of it is *missing*, exactly. It's more, sort of, caught up. Like a fish on a hook."

They leaned back and sighed. The youth with dirty clothes spoke up unexpectedly.

"I wish I had a piece of mine left! Just a piece! To mop the rest of me up with, like a scrap of bread mops up gravy!"

"There, there, Nat," said the motherly woman, handing him a handkerchief. Not a frilled, lacy affair like the one the rich lady had, but a proper cotton handkerchief big enough for a nose like mine. He blew his, loudly.

"Thank you, Em," he said, and seemed to brace himself to tell his story. "I were buying fruit," he said. "The carriage stopped, and the pretty lady called me over. She looked like sunshine."

Sunshine? I wondered if it had been Clarissa, with her golden mane of hair.

"What happened?" I asked.

"She called me into her carriage," said Nat, "and then reached right in and popped out my heart, like we pop peas from their pods. She wrapped it in a handkerchief and put it away somewhere. Worst thing was, I *wanted* to give it to her. And I told her me mam were waiting for me, and she said she wouldn't be more'n a minute. Said she didn't usually let children into her nice carriage, but that I was a special boy. She put me out after that, but I came after her. Walked all the way to the city. I would have followed her anywhere."

"Were you in love with her?" I asked.

"No," he said, looking at me as if I was mad. "She was pretty, that's all, and smelled good. Me own mam did nothing but scold me and pinch my ear." His mouth twisted as if he were about to cry. "I'd give anything to be back with her now, though."

"There, there," said the motherly lady again—Em. "You sit quiet for a while."

This was news to me. I had always assumed that all the sorceresses' victims fell in love with them, but it was more insidious than that—it seemed there were other ways they could *snag* their victims.

"Tell them about yours, Em," Nat sniffed.

"They only took a piece of mine," said Em. I got the feeling that these were stories they had all told many times. There was a comfortable rhythm to them, despite their gruesome content.

"Just a piece!" said a middle-aged man with a protruding belly. "Lucky!"

"Fenn," said Basil in a reproving voice. "We have all suffered. We do not compare our suffering. Let Em speak."

This, too, sounded like something that had been said often.

"Carved it out of me with a spell as easy as you'd winkle out a clam," said Em. "Two pretty ladies, and they didn't have enough magic left to ride their carriage home as quickly as they would like. They told me a crumb of heart would do, that I wouldn't miss it. Well, I would have given them anything, wouldn't I? So beautiful they were. I didn't think. 'Twere like a maze were on me. I didn't feel a thing, until afterward. And then I had to follow them here." She glared at me suddenly. "And before you ask, yes, I was in love with them, all right?"

Taken aback, I said, "I didn't . . ."

"I spent my life raising babes and caring for a house," she said. "I was a good wife, and a good ma. I did my duty. My children were all grown. And I never so much as looked at another man or woman after I was married, until they came along— and I could have! I had plenty of offers! Well, I lived with one of the ladies for a while, until she tired of me, like Nat. It's always the way. They use us up, then cast us out."

"I'm sorry," I said inadequately.

"I was not seduced by any promises," said the wealthy-looking older lady. "I offered my heart freely."

"You . . ."

"I needed their magic. My daughter was sick." She pressed her lips together and dabbed at her eyes with her lace handkerchief. "There was no other way. And I couldn't bring myself to buy a heart on the black market. I was *not*," she said vehemently, "going to have anything to do with *that sort*."

"Still. Your own heart!" I said.

"She lived, and that was all that mattered," said the old lady. "I have not seen her in a long time. She lives with other family now, and I am here. I do not want her to see me like this . . . and I do not have long."

I was ashamed of myself. I had dismissed her as a snooty old bag. Of course, she *was* a snooty old bag, but that wasn't all she was.

"They took a piece of your actual heart?" I said, turning to Em. "Your real, live heart, out of your chest?"

"As I said."

"And your whole heart?" I said to the boy. "The whole thing?"

"Right," he said.

"But . . . then how are you walking around? Talking? I don't mean to be rude," I added quickly, as Em bridled. "It's just . . . Take the heart out, and you take the life out. I don't mean to be rude," I repeated to the roomful of eyes staring at me.

"It's magic, innit," said Nat.

"Right, but . . . there has to be something in there, to keep the blood going."

"I don't know how it works."

"But you can't live without a heart!" I argued. "It isn't possible!"

Nat glowered at me. I appealed to Basil, spreading my hands. "I'm not doubting you. I'm just wondering what you've got in there instead, that's all."

"Oh, there's something in there, all right," Basil said grimly. "They want to keep you alive, I suppose, in case they can harvest from you again. Wears off after a while, though. Takes longer for some than others."

"I were nineteen," said another man who looked to be only a little younger than me, "when a sorceress came to my village. She looked at me out of everyone there and crooked a finger. At me. Not any of the big lads, nor the handsome ones. I couldn't believe it. She took me into her carriage, and she promised me . . . things."

He blushed. The rest of the room nodded, as if in understanding.

My sorcerer had never promised me *things*.

"She brought me here," he said, "and . . ."

Em patted his shoulder. "It's all right, Jol," she said.

"I don't remember it very well," he said. "I remember it hurt."

"What did she do?" I asked. I realized I was leaning forward on my rickety stool.

"Like I said, I don't remember it well," said Jol. "She kept me for a while, afterward. I don't know how long. I lived in her house. I was happy, I think. She was kind to me. And then she sent me out to the market, and when I came back, the doors were locked. I waited outside for a while. Weeks. I slept on the stair like a beggar. But they never opened for me again."

I felt a shiver of fear as I imagined the House closed against me tonight, Cornelius waiting, unknowing, on the other side of the door, for a friend who never would come home.

"And what about you?" I said, turning to Basil.

He fussed about with his collar for a minute, as conscious of his dignity as a cat. Two spots of high color showed on his thin cheeks. He was embarrassed, I realized, despite his air of officious assurance. We were all embarrassed, to have fallen in love so deeply and ridiculously, romantically or otherwise, and to have discarded our lives and families for the sake of that hopeless, helpless love.

"I met a Lady," he said stiffly, giving the word one of his capital letters. "And the rest is much the same as the others. She did not take the whole thing. Just a part of it. I do not remember the actual taking, as Jol does not."

"You do not feel it?" I asked. "You live, as normal?"

"It is different," said Basil. "I have a portion of my heart left, and so I do not suffer as Jol does. And as others do." He cast his gaze around the room.

"But . . ." I clasped my hands together, struggling to understand. "I work in a butcher's shop. I slice bodies up for a living. I know how they work, the machinery of it. It is not possible for anyone—an animal, a person—to live without a heart pushing your blood about. It just isn't."

"We do not know the manner in which they take it, or what exactly they leave in its place," said Basil. "There are many who lose so little, barely a speck of a heart, that they can live a long life without missing it. But those of us who are called by them and follow—they carve pieces from us."

"I remember jars," Jol piped up unexpectedly. "Rows of jars, like someone was making jelly."

"But you all survived it," I said. "You all still live and work. And you meet here to talk about it. They *released* you. And if you stay close enough, you're not in pain . . . ?"

It's not so bad, a soothing, lying inner voice said to me. *You can stay with him. You can live this way, too. They do. It's not so bad.*

"I wouldn't say we survived it," said the elderly woman sourly.

"We were all taken in the last year or two," said Basil. "That's about how long we last. Afterward."

"What do you mean, how long you last?"

"How long *we* last," said the elderly lady sharply. "You're one of us."

"Whatever replaces our heart seems to wear out after a few years," explained Basil in a village-preacher voice. "That's why time is of the essence. For all of us. More so now than ever, as you'll see. Some seem to live longer than others, which may be due to the varying severity of their harvesting, or to the relative skills of the sorceresses. Some of the Ladies may be more powerful than others, we speculate."

"And then what happens? When it wears out?" I asked.

"We . . . go away," he said.

"Are you saying we die?"

"We don't know," said Basil. "Some of us have died, certainly, at our own hands, or from the inevitable heartsickness, but others just . . . disappear, eventually. This . . . society of the similarly affected has been in place for many years, and we have written records of all who have come here. Aside from those who, as I said, decided to take their own lives, we have never received *any* information about the hundreds who have come here for help and then vanished."

"Hundreds?" I repeated faintly.

"Hundreds. And we have, as I said, been operating for a long time. There may, of course, have been others who were 'harvested'"—he winced a little saying the word, as if it offended his delicate sensibilities—"of whom we don't know, but they, perhaps, did not make it to the city, to their . . . captors. We cannot be sure."

"It's not such a bad life," said Em bravely. "We keep each other company. You know, for as long as we can. I have a job in the fish market. So long as I stay close enough to the sorceresses, it doesn't hurt too badly. And who knows, I might have a good year left in me."

"It *is* a bad life," said Nat violently. "It's no sort of life at all. And it's getting worse."

"Show her," said Basil.

There was a stirring, a feeling of sudden, focused attention. Nat hesitated, then began to unbutton his shirt. I could tell this was for my benefit only—everyone else had seen this before. I watched, unable to imagine what might be there. My mind was numb.

When he had unbuttoned it far enough, he twitched aside the left-hand side of his shirt, revealing his chest. Which was . . . missing. The left-hand side of his rib cage had caved in, exactly like the overripe peaches eaten out by fruit flies in our garden.

What was there instead? A furred cavern of mold. A hole in his chest, obscuring what would have been nipple and muscle. Ashen and rotten, and, I think, spreading. The veins that snaked out in tendrils from this hole were an unhealthy greenish black, and the very edges of the skin surrounding it were pink with sepsis.

"What's that?" I asked after a long pause. "Is that what you all look like?"

"No. Not yet," said Basil. "Not all of us."

He unbuttoned his shirt. I watched as if mesmerized. Was this what had happened to Dav? If so, I owed him a drink when I got back home, if nothing else.

When Basil opened his shirt, there was no gaping hole, like the boy's, but a gray patch like a bruise. The same greenish-black lines spiderwebbed out from it, and the skin between them was tender.

"This started a month ago. Maybe two—I remember the first faint greening of it," he said. "Before that, you could see nothing from the outside. But now . . . well, you see."

"It has happened to all of us," said Em. "We don't know what it means."

"We are afraid," said Basil in his precise, dry voice, "that it might shorten our already decreased time."

"What do you think it is?" I asked. I tried surreptitiously to peer down the front of my dress. I hadn't noticed any mold sprouting there, but perhaps it had been obscured by the eerie light of the House.

"Some new spell, perhaps?" ventured Basil. "Or something going awry with the old one. We can feel it creeping in our veins, alongside the love we still bear our sorceresses. It is sapping what little strength we have."

Everyone in the room nodded.

"We are so glad you are here," he added earnestly, rebuttoning his shirt.

"Why?" I said cautiously.

"You are uniquely positioned," he said. "You are *inside* a Magic-Worker's house. You can find his store of hearts. You are closer than anyone else has been, *after*."

I looked around at all the expectant faces. "I don't know what to tell you," I said. "I have been in every room in that place—or every room that it's possible for me to enter, at least—and I have seen nothing. What do you want?"

"A way to get the hearts back," said someone.

"And once you have them, then what?" I asked. I had wondered this myself. I had a vague hope that, if I found my heart, it would flutter back into my chest like a homing pigeon. But what if it didn't?

"We have found someone who may be able to help us," said Basil. "After much searching and studying. We have a network of Snagged all across the kingdom, and we correspond as best we can, sharing any information about ways in which we might free ourselves. One such Snagged on the border received a message from beyond our kingdom—from someone as powerful as the sorceresses themselves. Someone who can help."

A wave of nods and murmurs around the room.

"This person feels strongly that they will be able to help us to repair ourselves, if we provide hearts that can be used as replacements. Of course, we understand that we were all *taken* by different sorceresses, and so might not be able to retrieve our own exact heart, but apparently that should not matter."

"This . . . person can use any old heart?" I asked. "Then why not just go to a butcher's shop and buy a bagful? We usually give them to the dogs."

Basil closed his eyes briefly against my crassness. "Not just any old heart, obviously," he said. "But any human heart, taken by a Magic-Worker, and stored and preserved in whatever way they store and preserve them. Yes, she can use any of those. If you can find them, or tell us where to find them . . . Well, it has the potential to save us all."

There was someone who could help? Someone who could fix my heart and break the spell? I couldn't help thinking that Basil had been taken in by a clever charlatan, but I couldn't deny him—nor myself—the faint stirring of hope. Even if it did mean someone else's heart would be banging about in my chest in place of my own. It was better than nothing.

"I can try," I said. "I have to try, at least. But I can't promise anything."

"That's all we ask," said Basil. "That you try. Whatever you can find out will be more than we already know."

There was hope in the many pairs of eyes that stared at me, but there was also greed, and that same shimmer of dark envy that I had noticed before. I shivered. On top of that was the unsettling feeling that they weren't quite telling me the whole of it.

"Is there anything else I should know?" I asked. "To be careful of?"

"We have told you all we know," said Basil.

"Hells, I don't even know what they *do* with the hearts, exactly," I said. "Do you?"

"Everything," said the old lady, unhelpfully.

"Like what?" I prodded. "And not just guesswork and horror stories. What do they *actually* do with them?"

"We are not sure," admitted Basil reluctantly. "But whatever it is, the city seems to run on it. The whole kingdom, maybe. The Magic-Workers are very deep in the king's counsel."

I took a deep breath. "All right. I'll find out what I can, while I'm in the House. But . . . none of you were harvested by my sorcerer? *The* sorcerer, I mean," I added, remembering there was only one.

Shaking heads all around the room.

"I'll try, all right? I can't promise anything more than that."

"That is all we ask," said Basil. "Can you come here again? We are here most nights."

"Yes," I said. "I will return as soon as I know anything. Or have anything."

There was a collective sigh and a feeling of relief.

"But right now, I have to go," I said.

"You will come back?" said Jol.

"I promise." I felt the weight of that promise settle on me like an iron collar on a cart horse.

CHAPTER 11

The journey back to the House was excruciating, and I hoped Sylvester hadn't managed to blow it up in my absence. The nagging ache had worsened as my hours away from the sorcerer wore on.

When I finally reached the door, I was so eager to get inside—and so fearful that I might be shut out—that I tripped and fell. I lay prone on the threshold, knowing that I must have looked like a sack of potatoes but unable to move.

The heartsickness passed from me like a fever, soothed by the sorcerer's proximity, and left me weak and shaking and empty.

I don't know how long I lay there, but eventually I gathered enough strength to open the blank, black door and stagger inside. I was surprised, and a little unnerved, by how much it felt like coming home.

In the kitchen, the kettle was already boiling for a cup of tea. The House knew me well.

"Did he notice I was gone?" I asked Cornelius.

"I don't think so."

Of course not. I had been there to bring him his dinner, and I would be there to bring him his breakfast, and that was all he cared about. I set about making my tea while Cornelius watched me.

"Well?" he said.

"Well, what?"

"What happened? Outside, I mean."

"Nothing very helpful." I didn't usually take sugar in my tea, but I felt the need for it after my ordeal. I scooped in several spoonfuls, almost as much as Sylvester. "They want me to bring them a heart. More than one, ideally. I can't even find my own, so I'm not sure where they expect me to find someone else's."

"Why?"

"Some harebrained scheme to replace the missing ones. Apparently, they know some other magic-worker who can fix us all up." I stirred the tea with unnecessary force. "So now I have to find a heart. Either here, or on the black market, I suppose, if they indeed sell some real human hearts and not just the pork bits they fobbed that fellow off with yesterday. If the House lets me leave again, that is."

That was a thought. Would the House release me again? I had proven that I would come back, hadn't I? But then, I didn't know how the mind of a sorcerous building worked, or if it had a mind at all.

Just as I thought this, the floor seemed to turn liquid beneath my feet, sending me lurching and my sugary tea spilling all over. I swore and clutched at the kitchen counter. Was the House punishing me for my midnight excursion?

Cornelius leaped up onto a shelf, his fur bristling and his eyes big as saucers.

"What's going on?" I cried. "Is this more of what happened earlier?"

"No, no," said Cornelius. "It's not that again. I can smell the difference. This happens sometimes." He shrank back as far as he could into the relative safety of the corner. "It'll pass. Just hang on to something."

"It *just happens*?" Another queasy lurch almost sent me sprawling. It felt like being on the deck of a ship during a storm. I righted myself and, clinging to a wall, started feeling my way out of the room, thinking to lie on my bed until it passed, but the House gave a shudder that sent me staggering down another path, as it had when it had shown me the way to the sorcerer's workshop.

There was something it wanted me to see again, clearly, but I didn't know how it expected me to get there if it was planning to toss me about like a piglet in a sack. I'd had more than enough of that for one day already.

Still, I knew there was no point in resisting it, so I let myself be bullied down a long corridor until I reached another of the seemingly infinite black doors and opened it as soon as the House was calm enough for me to turn the handle.

So, this was the sorcerer's bedchamber, and apparently, he did sleep—or something like it. Like the throne room, it was near empty and bleak.

The only furniture was a large bed, rather like the one the House had provided for me, with black blankets and furs that had been kicked and tossed into a snarled heap along one side and were trailing onto the shining floor.

There was a haphazard tower of books on the other side of the bed, with a few open volumes scattered around it as if tossed aside in fury or frustration. There was the portrait I had seen hung on the wall of his workshop, leaning against one of the walls, with the sacking that had covered it half-torn off.

And there was the sorcerer, naked but for a pair of black drawers with lacings down the sides that were probably supposed to tie at his knees but had been rucked up by his flailing to sit more at mid-thigh, exposing a cool, hard stretch of muscle in each leg. His chest was bare.

As I watched, trying not to blush, he kicked out his legs and sent yet more blanket sprawling onto the floor, and the House heaved again.

His eyes were tightly closed. He was asleep, then, and perhaps having a nightmare? I took a step back, intending to leave him to it rather than risk him waking to find me gawking at him, but then I saw him lash his head back and forth on the pillow, so violently that it looked like he might break his neck.

The House juddered and shuddered as if it were about to break apart, and I was relieved that it wasn't made of bricks and mortar.

Was he having some sort of fit? I hesitated. If so, I couldn't just leave him, loath as I was to go any closer and intensify the spell with my nearness to him . . . and nearness to his half-naked body, and his bed, and everything that implied.

Was this why the House had practically pushed me through the door? To entangle me with the sorcerer and his spell even further? Or was it concerned for him?

They were connected, after all.

I blew out an exasperated sigh and stamped over to the bed as best I could through the House's rocking, trying to keep myself feeling as practical and unromantic as possible. The fact that I was tired and grumpy helped, and I focused on that, trying to pretend I felt nothing but irritation, and not a fluttering of excitement and pleasure.

I was fearful that I would lose all control as I approached the bed and throw myself on his flailing body or something equally as mortifying, but the state of him soon shook me sober.

He had thrashed his head with such force that he had bitten clean through his bottom lip, and the blood welled from it in generous red bubbles, mixed with saliva. I could see the white of the fat through all the red, and it made my stomach turn.

He was in a bad way, every muscle of his body rigid and trembling, the cords standing out in his neck. His black hair was drenched with sweat, clinging to his skin in coils thick as rope. He grimaced as I leaned over him, his lips pulling back from his teeth in what seemed like an involuntary snarl. What with the blood from his cut lip, it was a grisly sight.

If I didn't wake him, he could do more damage to himself. I took him by the shoulder as emotionlessly as I could, trying to ignore the spell, and shook him hard.

His response was immediate. His eyes snapped open, darker than I had ever seen them, with the pupils huge and staring. He flung out an arm at me, and although I was quick to dodge, my foot twisted under me, and I fell, sprawling onto the black tile. He leapt from the bed with animal speed and landed over me on all fours, his hands on either side of my head.

I froze. He stared at me with those great black eyes, panting open-mouthed like a dog, the blood from his almost-severed bottom lip dripping on me, stinging hot. I had forgotten how inhuman they could look, the magic-workers. He looked like something out of a children's story, a monster made up to terrify the wee ones into good behavior.

He didn't seem to recognize me. I wondered if he was going to rip out the rest of my heart at last or ravish me. Both options seemed utterly terrifying and, because of the spell, darkly enticing.

"Sylvester?" I said tentatively. It was the first time I had actually spoken his name to him, I realized. It sat oddly in my mouth. He blinked, and his dilated pupils shrank to a normal size. He brushed his hand along his jaw and stared at it when it came away, taking in the blood.

"Foss . . ." he said, his voice trailing off. He looked more human now as he stared down at me. I could feel the heat coming off him. He looked about him, at the tangle of bedclothes. "Ah," he said—an entirely inadequate syllable, in my opinion.

"You were having a nightmare," I said. I would have been mortified to be discovered in his bedchamber if I weren't so shaken by the state of him—and annoyed that he had knocked me on my arse, intentionally or no. "The House . . ." *Sent me?* It seemed ridiculous to say.

He seemed to realize that he had me pinned, and he heaved himself off me and stood. I scrabbled on the floor, trying to right myself. There was a swishing sound, and I looked up to see the sorcerer extending a hand—he was clothed now, by magic means, and I suppose the noise I'd heard was the fabric slithering into existence and onto his body.

I gripped his hand and allowed him to lift me, surprised a little at his strength. The spell was still dizzying me, of course, but I fought to keep my face expressionless.

"Thanks," I said grudgingly, once I was upright. I saw that the bed had tidied itself, too. I reached out to touch the pillow that had been such a bloody mess. It was dry, and the blood was gone, as if it had never existed—either magically evaporated or dissolved into the black fabric, I suppose. When I turned back, the sorcerer was looking at me, his mouth slightly open and his breath still a little ragged.

"Thank you for waking me," he said after a long moment.

You're welcome seemed an altogether ridiculous thing to say. "Do you have those often?" I ventured. "The nightmares, I mean."

"Yes."

"And is it always . . . like that?"

"They are not always as bad," he said. "I cannot observe

myself while I am sleeping, of course, so I don't know what you saw."

His lip had knitted itself back together, and there was nary a trace of where his teeth had severed it. I glanced down at myself, and the blood had vanished from my clothes as well.

"And do you remember them?" I pressed. I knew I was being nosy, but who would blame me? After what I had seen, a bit of nosiness was natural, surely.

He sat down on the edge of the bed and rubbed his temple with a weariness I hadn't yet seen in him. "I do."

Even I wasn't ill-mannered enough to ask any more. I did let the silence stretch out between us for a moment, though, just in case.

"It helps to think of other things, afterward," he said. "Perhaps you could talk to me."

"*Talk* to you?"

"What is it like, where you come from?" he asked, surprising me again. He seemed to be demanding a bedtime story. He even had his head propped up on one hand, ready to listen.

I sat gingerly on the bed beside him, leaving as much space between us as I could, and smoothed my skirt down before folding my hands in my lap like a well-behaved schoolgirl, lest they reach out to him involuntarily.

What sort of story do you tell the sorcerer who holds your heart in his hand? I decided to keep it as prosaic as possible, for my own sanity. As he lay down again, I told him about the butcher's shop in the square, about Da with his gentle hand that could yet wield a cleaver like no other, and about the blood and the mess that a butcher's shop makes.

I told him about plucking chickens and turkeys, and skinning larger game. I told him about the poachers who snuck their prizes in for butchering by the back door, and to whom

Da turned a blind eye. It was both a bloody and a rather tedious tale, at least to me, but he seemed fascinated.

It was odd, seeing him fascinated by me, but I knew he was fascinated by my commonness, my ordinariness, and not by me myself. Despite my brain's good sense, however, my body responded, and sent a flush to my cheeks, a brightness to my eyes, and made me gesture more than I would normally.

He asked to hear more about Da, and I told him. My grandfather had been a butcher, and my great-grandfather, and all before him, as far back as anyone could remember. My da had been a dreamy boy, from what he told me, prone to making contraptions out of wood and metal, and sometimes even the cleaned-off bones from the butchered carcasses.

When you're born with a name like Butcher, though, and a shop with its doors open and inviting, and an apron with your name embroidered on the pocket, there's not much else to do but pick up the cleaver and resign yourself.

"And your mother?" asked the sorcerer.

The word "mother," so cozy and rounded, sounded odd coming from his perfectly formed mouth. It was too ordinary. Still, it was the same mouth that had been wrapped around my very ordinary meatloaf, so perhaps it was the very ordinariness that fascinated him.

"I didn't know my mother," I told him. "Da told me she was very . . ." I hesitated. "Beautiful."

The sorcerer didn't react.

"Beautiful," I repeated, the word sitting oddly on my tongue. "All the lads were after her, Da said, but she liked him, because he folded the paper we wrap the meat in into little shapes for her. Animals and such. She liked his blue eyes and his dreaminess."

"You have blue eyes," said the sorcerer.

I thought I was getting used to him, living in his house, and used to my ailing heart. I had started to treat it something like a fungus on my toe; it bothered me occasionally but was largely out of my control.

Now, however, I realized that my detached assessment of it was a pile of shite, because I could have died on the spot right then and there when I realized he had noticed the color of my eyes. And then, a split second later, I was furious at my own heart for its gullibility. I sprang to my feet, ready to race out of the room before I did something to embarrass myself.

"You're probably wondering how I turned out so ugly," I said, chewing on the word as if it were a bit of gristle. I didn't wait for his reply, nor look at his face. "I don't take after Da's side of the family, and I certainly don't take after my mother's."

I rarely talked like this. Perhaps that was what made me hate the sorcerer most, despite my love—that he had woken in me again the desire to be pretty. To hold hands with a sweet-heart. To wear the stupid white dress and carry the fresh ears of corn, as tradition dictated, and marry in front of a holy man. All that rubbish.

The sorcerer stared at me. "Ugly?" he said.

Like he'd never heard the word before. I waited, but he did not look as though he wanted to say more.

"My mother died when I was born," I said at last.

"I'm sorry."

"Thank you, but . . ." I was doing my best not to look at him. "Part of the sorceresses' protection—your protection too, I sup-pose—is that everyone is born healthy. Almost everyone. It's rare for anyone to lose a pregnancy or have a stillbirth. And it's rare for a mother to die in childbirth."

"So I have heard," he said.

"But my mother died. Having me. So there must have been something very wrong with me, for her to die, something stronger even than your magic could fix. Or she wouldn't . . ." I stopped and cleared my throat. "Anyway."

"It wasn't your fault," he said.

"Well . . ."

"And your father doesn't blame you."

"No." I felt the prickling of tears. "No, Da loves me."

"I'm afraid I have been rather a disappointment to my own father." Sylvester sighed.

"You have a father?" It was hard to imagine.

"Oh yes. You've seen him, in fact. Or at least a picture of him."

I stared blankly.

"The king," he said, moving his hand in a lazy impression of a royal wave.

"The *king*? The king is your father?"

"Of a sort. We are all his children, my sisters and I."

"I . . . I didn't know."

"It's not something he advertises."

The king had fathered all the magic-workers?

"I don't know what, exactly, is wrong with my magic abilities. Sometimes they work, and sometimes they don't. When they do, they are apparently more powerful than the others'. When they don't . . . Well, the results can be messy, as you saw. He was elated to have succeeded in creating me, at the time, but despite all his best efforts, I haven't the same control as my sisters, the other magic-workers. Clarissa tried to teach me how to be more like them. She did her best."

"She was kind to you?"

He thought about this. "It is hard for me to know what is kindness and what is not," he said. "But I think my father would have discarded me like the other boys if it weren't for her. I tried to do what she taught me, but my spells either wouldn't work, or would work far too well."

"What do you mean, 'too well'?"

"They were too powerful. Not that that was of any use to

me. Flooding a spell with too much magic is almost as useless as giving it too little. It's like pouring an ocean into a wineskin. It will overflow, go in directions you did not intend. It is a delicate balance, gauging how much power to give to any particular spell, and I don't seem to have the . . ." He waved his hands vaguely. "Finesse."

"So, she tried to teach you how to control it."

"At first," he said. "With little success. And then she came up with a way for me to . . . siphon some of that power away, so I could control it better."

I couldn't imagine any of Clarissa's ideas being without their sinister side. "What was it?"

"The House," he said simply. "The others built their magical houses on top of real structures, as I did, but theirs aren't so . . . chaotic. If I gave too much power to a spell or felt a surge of it coming upon me with no immediate purpose, I could send the excess into the House. Give it more magic. Each time, it expanded to accommodate it. It got a little unmanageable, but it was better than letting the magic run wild."

"So that's why the House is . . . how it is."

"Yes."

He let out his breath in a sigh. His hair fanned out behind him in annoyingly perfect curls.

"I do wonder though," he said, "what is to become of me if I am unable to fulfill my single purpose."

"Maybe magic doesn't have to be your purpose," I said. "Couldn't it be something else?"

"No. I was made for one thing and one alone."

"Well, that's what your father wanted, but why can't you do something else?"

"I was not given the skill for anything else."

"Right," I continued, exasperated. "But that doesn't mean you're doomed to be this one thing forever. You don't have to do what the king tells you to do every hour of every blessed day. Fine, you don't have any other skills. So learn some."

I had spoken more sharply than I intended. There was another long silence. He rubbed at his eyes.

"Well," I said. "I suppose I should let you . . ."

"Wait." He reached out to hold me by the wrist. I stopped.

"It is hard for me to sleep again, after," he said. "We need little sleep, thankfully, but even a magic-worker must rest now and then. Stay."

"What?" I said stupidly.

"Stay until I am asleep," he said. "I would not be alone tonight."

I couldn't concentrate on his words for the touch of his hand on my wrist, heavy and encircling and precious as a bracelet. He seemed to realize this and withdrew it.

"Where?" I wondered. I looked around at the room. "I mean . . ."

An overstuffed black chair sidled in at the edge of my vision. Another one of those large, shaggy black throws lay temptingly over the arm.

"You need not," he said, and it was the thread of uncertainty in his voice that decided me.

"All right," I said, and made a show of settling myself in the plush chair and drawing the blanket over my knees, taking time to tuck it in under me and arrange it perfectly so I didn't have to look directly at him.

I could feel him watching me until I stopped moving, and when I dared to look up, he had settled himself down and turned his head from me.

"Good night," he said, and the light in the room extinguished as if a giant, black hand had descended to snuff it out.

CHAPTER 12

I woke with a crick in my neck and a sour taste in my mouth. As soon as I remembered where I was, I snapped my eyes open.

The events of the previous night crowded my mind: my walk to Oyster Lane, the Snagged, the sorcerer's nightmare. I felt like I had lived a thousand years in the space of sundown to sunup. And now I was in the sorcerer's bedchamber, of all places. His *bedchamber*. And to make it even worse, Sylvester was still in the bed.

As I watched, he stirred, and the dark blankets fell away a little, exposing part of his chest. I sat frozen, barely daring to breathe. The bespelled part of me wanted to climb into bed beside him, but the rest of me wanted to get out of there as quickly as possible before either he woke up, or I spontaneously combusted.

I got to my feet, letting the blanket slither to the floor, and tried to creep away quietly, but I knocked into the portrait, and of course it fell over as spectacularly as possible, clattering on the black floor. I swore and grabbed at my shin where I had bruised it, and only then did I turn around and see Sylvester sitting up in bed.

His unbuttoned nightshirt had fallen open, and his chest was now fully exposed in all its pale, chiseled glory. The blood rushed to my head. And elsewhere.

"Sorry," I said weakly, then rallied. Grouchiness was an excellent cover for the confusing feelings a half-naked Sylvester awoke in me. "Well, it was a stupid place to put it. Right in the way."

He blinked. "Noted," he said.

"Why did you bring it in here, anyway?" I grumbled, massaging the sore spot on my leg.

"It should be on the wall."

He leaned forward, further disarranging the covers and seeming wholly unselfconscious. "Oh . . ." He passed his hand over his mouth. "Sometimes I like to examine it, before I sleep."

"Why? Who is it?" I asked.

"It could be the right boy," the sorcerer said softly. "In the portrait. It's from around the right time, as far as I can tell. And he's about the right age and has dark hair—although that doesn't mean much, as my hair could have been changed along with everything else."

I stared at him. The outlines of something horrifying were starting to form in my mind.

"Changed from what? From whom?"

"Of course, I could only guess at the age. I could be off by as much as ten years, in which case, this has no chance of being the boy."

"What *boy*?" I said, exasperated.

He pressed his lips together, as if wondering whether to speak. Then he seemed to come to a decision. "The boy from whom I was made."

I wanted to thump right down onto the floor in shock. "Made? Who *made* you?"

"My father made all of us," he said. "He could not birth his own children, I suppose. Or perhaps he could, and the making of magic-workers requires a different way of birthing. I do not know. I have never asked him."

"So when you said the king was your father . . . ?"

"I meant that he made us, raised us. Trained us to do his bidding."

All I could think was that Basil would be bursting in his fancy waistcoat with excitement if he could hear all this.

"So, you were a little boy?" I prodded. "A little boy named Sylvester?"

"Years ago, yes. But I doubt I was named Sylvester. I'm not sure who gave me the name. Probably my father. It doesn't sound like the sort of name given to an urchin, and I was probably an urchin. I almost certainly had no family, no entanglements of any sort. It is simpler that way, you see."

So the stories of children vanishing in the city were true, it seemed, and even more horrifying than we had imagined when we were sprouts. I blinked. "You were kidnapped and turned into . . . this?"

"No." He sounded impatient with me, as if I was failing to understand something very simple. Perhaps I was. "Not kidnapped. Bought, in all likelihood, as you buy wood to whittle it, or flour to make bread. Shaped for a purpose, by my father, over the course of many years, as I grew to adulthood. I am no more that boy now than a handful of flour is a loaf."

I wondered what that was like—being a loaf of bread, as he had put it, baked to perfection, rather than the raw dough the rest of us presumably were. Did that sort of thing trouble him at all, or was he so removed from folk like us that such musings were unimaginable to him? But I couldn't hide my horror. "Who would sell a child?"

He shot me a glance. "You would be surprised," he said. "Such happenings might not occur in your little hamlet, but things are different in the city."

"And your father *bought* them? Bought children to make them into . . . you? And your sisters?"

"Yes."

I sat, taking it in. "Why are you telling me this?" I asked.

He looked at me. "You told me about your mother," he said.

"So . . . this is a portrait of who you *were?*" I said slowly.

"Perhaps," replied Sylvester. "I found it in a marketplace. The artist had made several such studies of the local street children, years ago, and was selling off some of his old canvases. This one had enough of a resemblance that I thought it might be possible."

I looked at the portrait again. I could see no likeness, but then, Sylvester's perfect face barely looked human. It certainly resembled no other face I knew, as the men in our village tended to look more and more like sprouting potatoes as they aged.

Questions bubbled up inside me, but I didn't want to ask too many of them at once for fear of him clamming up altogether.

"You said your father made you," I said. "*How?*"

"It is a complicated process," he said. "He made all of us. Me. Clarissa. My other sisters. Thirteen, in all. The transformation process gave us the magical ability, and then he had years to train us in its use, until we came of age and he deemed us ready to work on our own."

Thirteen children, at least, stolen or bought, and transmuted by some magical *process*—the seemingly innocuous word made my stomach turn—into powerful magic-workers.

"And you were the only boy?"

"Not the only one, but the only one who . . . succeeded," said Sylvester. "My father had tried with male children before, but apparently, I was the only one that ever 'took,' as he put it. I don't think he expected me to come along when I did. Twelve is a nice, even number. Thirteen . . . well."

"'Took'?"

"Apparently, his other attempts failed rather spectacularly."

"What happened to the children he used? The ones who failed?"

"I don't know. He never told me."

I hated to think what that could mean. I shuddered. Who could look at a child and think of something to be bought and sold—worse, something to be taken apart and reassembled? I doubted he let the "failed" children skip merrily back out onto the street to live lives full of puppies and apple carts.

I stared at the portrait again. I had no idea whether or not this was the boy the sorcerer had once been, but I could see why he had been attracted to it.

There was spirit to the thing. You got the feeling the subject was sitting for the portrait under duress, and wanted to spring up and go chase frogs by the pond, or something similar. He looked like someone who didn't want to sit about in fussy clothes in musty rooms, tinkering with fancy toys.

It was hard to imagine the sorcerer as a boy, but even harder to imagine his sisters as little girls. Presumably they, too, had been regular children once, before spending unimaginable years being transformed and trained into the beautiful, terrifying *things* they had become as adults.

"I . . . am sorry," I said. I couldn't imagine being that boy, taken and twisted into something unrecognizable, with no father but the man who had ruined him. I thought again of Da and how lucky I was. Had been.

Sylvester was still staring at the portrait.

"I had better go," I said. "Breakfast."

And with that dazzling piece of repartee, I crept out of there and to my own chamber, as if I really were sneaking back after a night of debauchery.

I wouldn't have minded a bit of debauchery.

When I got back to my own chamber, I washed my face and changed my clothes to another elaborate black number that the House provided for me. Cornelius had slept on my bed, and when he heard the water splashing, he yawned and stretched.

"Where have you been?" he asked.

He was completely unbothered, but I still felt a flush of shame.

"In the sorcerer's bedchamber," I said gruffly. "He was having a nightmare."

"So that's what it was! It stopped a lot sooner than it usually does."

"I woke him up," I said.

"Well, good," he said. "I could get some sleep."

I suppose I could have gone back to sleep. There was really no reason for me to keep so rigidly to my self-appointed duties, except for my slavish devotion to the sorcerer.

But that almost religious routine was the only thing stopping me from going completely mad, and getting dressed and making breakfast was better than lying in bed and feeling my mind melt like butter in a pan.

So, I had learned that the magic-workers had been made rather than born, and weren't fully human—made from street children, no less, by Sylvester's "father," and then trained by him into adulthood. And what kind of power must someone have to take one person and shape them into something else entirely, into a being with the ability to steal hearts and make magicks?

Oddly, I felt sorry for Sylvester. I told myself that was the spell talking, the spell that bound and enslaved me, making me feel a connection that simply wasn't real . . . But it had *become* more real, though, I thought, by sheer virtue of being in his presence day after day, and talking to him.

The love, the dogged devotion, might still have been an ensorcelled illusion, but something else had grown up around it, like a vine curling around a tree. It had to. You could not live with someone, day in and day out, and feel nothing genuine for them at all, good or bad. At least, I didn't think *I* could.

I was spellbound to the sorcerer, but I felt a growing sympathy, or even affinity, for the man behind the sorcerer—or the little boy who had been the flour to make his bread, as he had put it.

I made breakfast in thoughtful silence, dropping scraps for Cornelius as I rattled the pans and sipped on my tea. My hands shook a little as I prepared it, and I spilled some hot butter onto the fancy new dress. As always, it left nary a mark.

When I had finished, I piled up the tray as usual with potatoes and bread and eggs and bacon, poured the sorcerer a cup of tea, and poured another one for myself for good measure, and took the breakfast through to the throne room.

My heart thudded with anticipation as I stepped in. Would he be different now? Would he confide in me further?

The answer was, of course, no. He was slumped in the throne, flickering a little fireball between his fingers, and didn't even look up when I came in, although I lingered and fussed about with the crockery more than usual. I even ostentatiously cleared my throat, but he didn't budge. When I finally realized he wasn't going to speak, I left.

I suppose I was relieved. I was still pitifully in love with him, of course, and would have aimed my own meat cleaver into my head if he had asked me, but he seemed reassuringly unaware of that fact. I doubt he had any idea of my feelings at all. I was around, like Cornelius, and I was company, and I was useful, and that was enough.

I hated myself for it, but it was enough for me, too, no matter how often I lay awake in my black bed wishing so hard for his kisses and his hands that my skin stung as badly as if I had fallen into an ants' nest.

Over the following nights, I listened out for more cries in the dark, signs of his nightmares, but I heard none.

The one change was that he asked me for more tales about the village at the end of each day when I came to collect his dinner plates. I was happy enough to oblige. I had twenty years' or so worth of them, after all, and the duller, the better, as far as he was concerned.

I resisted any impulse to embroider the stories, because their ordinariness seemed to be what he enjoyed. There certainly wasn't much that was ordinary about the House, or him.

He found the story of Goodman Whelk making a fool of himself over the baker's pretty young daughter, for example, more entertaining than my tale of the birth of a two-headed calf. The deformed calf had entertained the whole village for months, but he barely raised an eyebrow at it before asking me to tell the saga of a pub brawl over again.

He listened like a child being told a bedtime story and, like a child, wanted each story repeated in the same way, with the same details. He even corrected me when I left something out.

I have to admit I enjoyed his attention for the short time he gave it to me. Most of the time, while I talked, he was sprawled across his chair doing something pointless, like throwing and catching a ball, or making a cat's cradle with a tangle of glowing string, but I could tell he was listening intently.

Maybe there was some eldritch meaning to his little baubles, but I suspected not. He reminded me of an indulged little boy, allowed to sit inside and be idle, rather than being pushed outside to go play with his friends and get out from under his mother's feet.

I suppose I would be the mother, in that scenario.

I talked and talked about my life until I was fairly sick of it, but he said little more about his. Perhaps he regretted telling me so much when he had woken from his nightmare. I did not press him—although, if I didn't find my heart soon, I was going to have to. I dreaded the thought.

And I was supposed to find hearts for the Snagged, too; any heart, so that even if I never found mine, I would at least be able to replace what I had lost—or so they believed. I didn't know if I shared their belief in this mysterious person and process that claimed to hold the key to their cure, but I understood their desperation.

One morning, perhaps four or five days after my visit to the Snagged, there was a crash that sounded at first like the whole place was caving in.

"Aren't you going to get that?" said Cornelius, appearing seemingly from nowhere.

"Get what?"

"The door."

"That's the *door*?" Who could hit the door with that amount of force? Another supplicant looking for a hex or a charm?

Surely they wouldn't break the door down before asking for a favor.

I stomped over there and hauled it open, ready to present my most cantankerous self to whoever stood there, but as soon as my eyes focused on the visitor, I was lost.

I had grown used to being almost invisible in the sorcerer's house. There were no mirrors in my chamber, which suited me just fine, and Cornelius couldn't give a bald bollock what I looked like as long as bacon kept showing up on his plate every morning. As far as the sorcerer himself went, I might as well have been a piece of his black furniture.

On the doorstep now, however, I felt my plainness again in full force, because I was met with the most beautiful face imaginable, every exquisite line of it a poem. It was the sorceress we had seen at the market, Clarissa.

But seeing her so much closer, breathing her in face-to-face, was dizzying. I must have staggered a little, because I felt myself clutch at the doorframe.

She said nothing to me. She brushed past me with a rustling of silks, and the House opened for her as if it recognized her.

I smelled the scent of her as she passed—strange night-blooming flowers and the drifting mystery of her skin. It smelled familiar, and I remembered the sweet-scented dresses in the mysterious bedchamber.

She walked down the corridor as if she knew where she was going, leaving me gasping in her wake. Her servant followed close behind her, but I could barely take him in, so blinded was I by her presence. He didn't so much as glance at me, either, but kept his eyes on his sorceress.

"Oh yes, it's one of them again," said Cornelius from somewhere around my feet. "Told you."

I was still breathless from the beauty of her and couldn't say anything.

"It'll pass in a second," said Cornelius, understanding. He dropped to the black floor and started to wash his tail, keeping it carefully in place with one paw. "I'll wait."

He was right enough. Whatever influence the sorceress had over me started to fade when I could no longer see or smell her, leaving me with my usual heart-tugging from the sorcerer's magicks and just the faintest trace of her perfume.

"Don't you feel it?" I asked when I was able to speak again.

"No. Not even a little," said Cornelius. "But I can see it on them. Like a cloud. Like pollen. And I can smell it. It works on all the humans."

Something dreadful occurred to me. "Did she take any more of it?" I clutched at the fabric on my chest, ridiculously, pulling it away from my body as if I had an apronful of blackberries and was afraid to spill them.

"Any more of what?"

"My heart!"

Cornelius gave me a withering stare.

"That's what they do," I reminded him.

"You look fine to me," said Cornelius.

"Well, it doesn't matter if I *look* fine." I patted myself down. "I don't feel any different, though."

"Then you're probably all right."

"Thanks. Very helpful."

I started back to the kitchen.

"I'm going to make them tea," I said.

"No need," said Cornelius. "They'll just talk for a while, and then she'll go."

"It's not really about the tea," I said. "I want to hear what they're saying, and I can't get in there unless I have a good reason."

In the kitchen, the kettle boiled most reluctantly on the stove, huffing out its displeasure. I shook it about a bit, to show it who was boss.

The cups and saucers hid from me in the cupboards, but I hunted them out and forced them onto the tray, and then stood with my hands on my hips and stared down the stove again until it baked me a tray of seedcakes. It singed the edges a bit, just to show its disapproval, but they were good enough.

I had to laugh at myself for a moment, fussing about with tea and cake like some housewife preparing to entertain the preacher back home.

"You'd better not try any tricks," I said to the House. "All right?"

There was a pause and then a general, bad-tempered sense of agreement. I stamped my way to the throne room. As if in protest, the House made the corridor long again, unspooling the floor out in front of me like a dropped ball of yarn in front of a kitten. I was of two minds as to whether the House would let me into the throne room or not, and it probably was, too, but when I got there, the door opened seemingly as usual.

I could smell the sorceress's perfume again as soon as I walked in. It made me light-headed, but just for a moment this time. I wondered if it was possible to build up an immunity to them—or if, perhaps, already being bound to one kept me safer from the other.

It gave me a malicious twinge of satisfaction that the sorcerer did not sit up straight for his visitor, either. She had manufactured herself an ornate seat out of something that looked like crystal, sitting regally straight with her hands folded in her lap, and still he lay flopped across his black throne, hair in his eyes, like a puppet with its strings cut.

He was staring at the ceiling, as usual, and she was glaring at him with those gorgeous, unnatural eyes, shaped and colored as smoothly as fresh-grown leaves. Her servant stood behind her, hands clasped in front of him and head lowered, as full of animation and personality as a mushroom.

I hovered with the tray. There was nowhere to put it except on the floor. Seeing my plight, the sorceress flicked her eyes in my direction and created a column of that same crystal, something like a fancy upturned wine goblet, growing like a flower out of the black floor.

I wondered if this was her equivalent of the sorcerer's black substance—if they all worked with their own particular material. Mayhap she had a castle made of that sparkling stuff somewhere else in the city, like the sorcerer's House.

I put the tray down with a clatter, deliberately, to make them look around. The sorcerer blinked at me briefly, setting my heart to thudding, and then looked away as if he had always had a personal maid bringing tea and seedcakes to his meetings, and it was nothing worth a second glance. The sorceress glared at me like an owl glares at a weasel.

"What is this?" she asked, gesturing in my direction. "It answered the door."

"Really? The cat usually does that."

"Well, this isn't a cat."

I bit my tongue to stop myself from retorting. I wanted to see what he would say.

"This is Foss." He waved a hand at me. "She's doing the housekeeping."

"You don't need a housekeeper."

"Apparently I do, or the House wouldn't have provided one."

"The House didn't come up with . . . this," she said, taking me in with one sweeping green glance from head to toe.

"It must have brought her here, Clarissa. I didn't."

"Sylvester. This is clearly from Outside."

He looked at me directly then, the beauty of his eyes startling me all over again. I held his gaze for a second, then dropped it, ashamed of what might be showing on my face. I was sure the lady had seen it, however; when I raised my eyes again, she was looking at me with the same sort of amused, pitying knowledge that I had seen on the faces of the girls back in the village, when I was pining after Aron.

The village! That jolted my memory. Clarissa was the one who had taken Dav, I'd swear to it. As I've said, the ladies all looked mighty similar in their perfection, but I remembered the tale of the gleaming golden hair like wool all combed out for the spinning, and the yellow-green eyes so full of color that the irises almost crowded out the whites. She was the one who had pointed her finger at Dav that day and led him to his doom.

She must have seen something in my stare besides the naked adoration she was used to, because her eyes narrowed.

"What is it looking at?" she said, but she reached for a seed-cake as she did so.

"Careful," I said maliciously. "They're hot."

I had half expected the House to be on her side, but it showed gratifying loyalty when it made the seedcake steam, just a little, and burn her hand. She dropped it in her lap and sucked at her fingers. Her servant gave a twitch, as if responding to his mistress's pain.

"You may go," she said to me irritably.

I cocked an eyebrow, but the sorcerer waved a hand vaguely in what seemed like agreement, and so I heaved myself back out the door. I let it close behind me, but the House obliged me in its own way by opening an ornate little keyhole in the door that hadn't been there before. I felt like it was trying to get on my good side again after its sulk earlier.

"I really don't see why it's necessary to keep that creature around," the sorceress was saying when I pressed my ear to the keyhole.

"She just showed up," said the sorcerer.

"Well, it's cleaner in here, at least," she said, brushing some speck of imaginary dust off her perfect skirts. "Careful, though.

It's not a good idea to keep *them* around for too long. They get . . .
clingy. Remember what happened with Father? When he tried to
keep them? It never worked."

"You have one," the sorcerer pointed out.

"Yes, but I replace them regularly, darling," she said. "I've
only had him for a month, and he's already half-used up."

Used up?

I could almost hear the sorcerer shrug. "I didn't bring her
here. Can we stop talking about it? It's boring."

"You must have snagged her without realizing," said his
sister. "I'm just telling you to be careful. She might be a novelty
for now, but unless you plan to harvest her, there's really no
point keeping her around."

He sighed. "Why are you here, anyway?"

"We're concerned about you."

"Who's *we*?"

"Your sisters."

"Any particular ones, or the whole lot of them?"

"All twelve of us, Sylvester."

"I do have a ridiculous number of sisters," he said, examining the dirt under his fingernails.

"You're not producing much," she said, steepling her fingers and tapping her perfect nails together. He huffed a sigh.
"Nothing at all, in fact. We're all expected to meet a certain
quota. You know that. Now more than ever."

A quota? I thought sharply.

"I've only just started," I heard the sorcerer say sleepily.

"Well, you only came of age a few months ago, of course.
But the king has high expectations of you, as the only brother."

"I don't *like* going out to villages. They're boring. And they
smell like manure."

She huffed an impatient breath. "More boring than sitting
in your chair all day?"

"I like my chair," he said.

"Well, you brought that ugly housekeeper girl back from somewhere, so you must have visited at least one. But one heart isn't enough. Father has given you a lot of leeway with your training, but he expects you to produce nearly as much as the rest of us by now."

"I told you, I didn't *bring* her here. She just showed up."

"You mean you haven't taken anything from her *at all*?" The sorceress sat up, and her voice became shrill. "Sylvester, she's living in your *house*. You don't even have to leave your beloved *chair*. At least have *one* heart to show Father at the next meeting. It might be enough to keep him happy. For now."

"*Foss's* heart?" he said, as if startled at the thought. I bit my lip hard as he said my name.

"Well, she's right here," said the sorceress. "It would be convenient. And a start."

He sighed and tapped his fingers on the arm of the throne.

"You don't have to take it all at once, if you don't want to," she said. "Sometimes it's useful to have one around in case of need. Like Colin, here. But you can't leave it intact for too long. Just take a little at a time, like sips from a glass. She'll barely notice."

I couldn't see Colin from my angle—just his shadow—but as far as I could tell, he hadn't moved.

"Of course, it could be shriveled already," said the sorceress. "It goes one of two ways, with the ugly girls. It's either ripe and ready, because no one else has picked it, or it's dried up and bitter. Either way, it's a lot better than nothing."

"Look, just leave me alone, all right? I'll go to one of the villages tomorrow. Or the next day."

"Not good enough, Sylvester." She stood with a rustle of skirts. "We're in a crisis. We need more from everyone, you included. And start with the girl, for goodness' sake. You need something to show the king."

As you can imagine, I wasn't rightly excited to be seen by either the sorceress or the sorcerer after hearing all that, nor would I put it past her to poke her sharp nails through my skin and pull out my heart like the stone of an apricot as soon as she emerged.

I scuttled away as quickly as I could back to the kitchen, where the kettle whistled at me reproachfully, as if to say, "I told you so."

I stood by the stove and sipped my own tea as I thought about what I had overheard. Well, that had been enlightening. The sorcerer clearly had no idea he had captured me in any way, a thought that was both a relief and a torment. I was just a burr that had caught on his cloak; an accident, like the babes the unmarried women went to the hedge-witch to flush out back home.

One thing had me addled. He had told his sister that he didn't have my heart, and he had seemed sincere, but I had definitely been hooked, or I wouldn't have come here at all. So, did that mean that whatever portion of it had clung to him was knocking about here someplace, unbeknownst to him? Or was my heart whole, and I was simply under another spell of some kind? Or was he lying? I had no reason to trust him, after all.

To my surprise, a few minutes after I had closeted myself in the kitchen, the sorceress's mushroomlike servant wandered in. He looked around the room with a glazed, slack-jawed look, and then his gaze landed on me. He didn't speak.

"What?" I snapped after a moment.

He moved his tongue in his mouth for a moment before speaking, as if he had to remind himself how it worked.

"My lady requires an herbal tea," he managed.

The kitchen table gave me a nudge, and I turned to see that a black cabinet had installed itself on one wall. I sighed and tromped over to it, hauling open the door to see rows of herbs neatly bundled with twine and hanging on little hooks inside. Of course.

I gathered them and filled the kettle to boil water, flicking my eyes to the servant now and again. When he wasn't moving or speaking, he was oddly lifeless, like a toy that needed the key in its back wound up.

"So, you live with the sorceress," I said, pretending to have trouble with the string binding the herbs in order to delay him. He didn't answer. "What's your name?"

"Colin," he said, after a long pause.

"I'm Foss. Where are you from?"

Another long pause. "I don't remember."

I could have made a cup of tea several times over by then, but I was affecting clumsiness. "How did you come to work for the sorceress, then?" I said, putting on the chatty manner of all the twittery housewives I had served in the butcher's shop.

He blinked. His blink was slow, like a reptile's. He barely seemed awake. My skin crawled. Is this what would happen to me, if most of my heart was taken away?

I poured the tea into a black china cup as fine as a beetle's wing case and moved close to him to place it in his hands. As I stood right before him, close enough to see the freckles across his nose, I whispered, "Do you need help?"

His eyes flickered, more rapidly than I had yet seen them move. He mumbled something indistinct and grabbed at the cup with hands as dexterous as if he were wearing oven gloves, almost dropping it.

Before I could say anything else, he turned and fled back to the throne room. I hastened after him, determined to get *something* out of him, but stopped short when the sorceress emerged.

She clicked her fingers at her servant, and he hurried to her, almost tripping over his own feet. Then she looked past him, to me.

The shock of her green gaze was like a splash of cold water to the face, and I stood numb as she strode to me and lifted my chin with her hand.

I felt a surge of adoration and awe, despite myself, gazing at her, and shame, too—because her relentless, gorgeous eyes magnified every inch of me and shone it back so that I was more aware of myself than ever before, even more so than when Aron had drawn me as a toad on his wine bottles.

"Be careful, girl," she warned.

She dropped her hand suddenly, leaving me gaping, and turned to leave in a swirl of silks. The manservant followed her out, his eyes fixed on her, still carrying the teacup.

He didn't even flicker his glance in my direction. He was clearly infatuated with her in the same way I was with the sorcerer—desperately, helplessly. I hoped I didn't look as much of a fool as he did, though, as he stumbled in her wake like a baby lamb staggering after its mother.

I hid in the kitchen until dinner, chopping vegetables and slicing the gristle off meat as if it were any ordinary day. When I had prepared the meal, I put a plate of meat and gravy down on the floor for Cornelius and took the silver tray through to the throne room, with some trepidation.

If the sorcerer had taken his sister's words to heart, it might very well be my last march through the dark corridors.

Pushing open the door to the throne room, I could see at once that something was different. For one, the sorcerer was not lounging in his chair, but standing. I was surprised all over again by how tall he was.

The more striking difference, however, was that he was surrounded by a hundred tiny bonfires that lit the room as bright as day and brought sweat pearling on my forehead. He stopped when he saw me, looking like a little boy with his hand caught in the cookie jar.

"What are you doing?" I asked.

"Nothing," he said, and I almost laughed, I swear it.

"Half the place is on fire," I pointed out.

"I was bored."

"I'm not cleaning this up."

He clicked his fingers, and the fires went out, and the throne room returned to its usual dim self. I plonked the tray down and turned to leave.

"Wait!" he said.

I stopped and turned back.

"Just, wait a minute," he said, pinching the bridge of his nose.

I waited for a minute.

"Can I go?" I said at last.

"Why did you come here?" he asked.

"To bring you your dinner."

"No, *here*. To the House."

"To be your housekeeper."

"No. Why did you come?"

I found myself strangely shy. "You came to my village," I admitted.

He started to massage his temples. "I remember going to a village. I do not remember you."

I desperately wanted something to do with my hands. I wished I had not put the tray down. I took the fabric of my apron between my fingers instead, and twisted it as if I was wringing the neck of a pullet. "You bought some plants from the herbalist—I don't know what—and then you stepped back into your carriage. Before you did, you looked out at all of us, at the crowd. And you looked at me."

"I do not remember," he said again, looking directly at me this time. *How could I possibly have looked at something this hideous and forgotten?* I imagined him thinking.

"Well, you . . . *snagged* me," I said, remembering the sorceress's words.

"Oh." He pinked, which surprised me. He looked about as embarrassed as I felt. "I did not mean to."

So, it had been like walking out of the privy with a rag stuck to your foot, as I had suspected. Flattering.

"Why didn't you tell me who you were, when you arrived?" he said. "Why did you come here?" There was more agitation in his voice than I had ever heard previously, and I wondered why. After all, he had been *made* to take hearts, as he said. Why did he seem so horrified?

"I do not want to be here," I burst out. "I *had* to come. You did something to me. I was in terrible pain until I got here."

In the dim light, his cheekbones stood sharp as folded paper, and his eyes were shadowed so that they were black rather than gray blue. I found it difficult not to watch his mouth while he talked and hated myself for it. "You were . . . caught?"

"You should know," I said sharply.

"Why didn't you tell me?" he repeated.

"I needed time . . . to figure things out. To try to find my heart."

"You've been looking for it all this time?"

"Yes! What do you think? Of course I have!"

"Even when . . ." He caught himself, pinching the bridge of his nose again and breathing deeply. "So since you've come here, you have been trying to find your heart. You thought I had it."

"Yes!"

"So all the times we have talked . . . you were trying to find out where it was? That is why you asked me all those questions?"

Did he look *hurt*? It was so hard to read his face. "You don't know what it's like," I said. "It's torment. Of course I wanted to be free."

"To be free," he repeated. He was silent for a moment, and then, "I did not mean to take you," he said, more gently. "I promise I did not. It must have happened without my knowing about it. I haven't been doing this for long."

As if he were one of Da's apprentice butchers who had waved his cleaver too wildly and chopped off the tip of a thumb. Just that easy, to accidentally take a piece of a person and barely notice.

"Where is it?" I demanded. "Where is my heart, then, that you took without meaning to? Where are you keeping it?"

"No! I took nothing from you. If you are . . . attached to me, then it is a spell that went awry."

"What *spell*?"

"The spell for heart-taking is a strong one," he explained. "Even though I chose not to cast it in the end, I had been preparing to cast it. Spells don't like that. It's like throwing a stick for a dog to chase, and then telling it not to run. I suppose some of that . . . preparation caused the spell to reach out and attach to you somehow, without my intending it."

"Why did you choose not to cast it?" I asked.

He looked uncomfortable. I could tell he was desperate for another magic toy to fidget with. "I just did," he said.

"So, you don't have my actual heart? Like, in a box or some such?" All my searching had been worthless. All my time spent here—worthless. I had nothing to take to the Snagged. No way of freeing myself.

"No. You are bonded to me by a powerful spell, that is all. I have no piece of you."

"But you meant to take a heart. You came to my village to get one."

He rubbed at his temples violently. "I went to your village to harvest, it's true," he said. "But then I got there and . . . I didn't. I left without taking anything. Or so I thought. I would never have chosen you."

I would never have chosen you. Of course. No one would pick me out of a crowd of Hallies and other lithe, young love-lies—girls who knew how to dress and how to smile, how to look up through their eyelashes and laugh at the right moments. Girls who hadn't spent their whole lives behind a shop counter trussed in an apron. Girls who hadn't been cursed from birth.

I looked up sharply, expecting to see disgust or even mockery, but all I could see were his brows drawn together a little in concern. Somehow that made it worse. Thank goodness for that apron to twist. I stared down at my hands as they wrung the fabric: strong and red, the proper hands for a butcher girl to have.

"Can you break the spell?" I wondered, the words coming out more plaintive than I had intended. "Can you let me go? Without using me? Without damaging me?"

There was a pause. He pursed his lips. "I do not think so."

"Can you try?"

He came toward me. I forced myself not to back away.

"May I?" he asked.

"May you what?" I managed to say through the surge of desire that rose in my throat.

He gestured at my chest. What on earth . . . ? But then I chastised myself for being a lovesick fool. He was hardly going to rip my bodice open now if he hadn't done so previously. He wanted my heart.

"Will it hurt?" I whispered.

"What?" He seemed startled. "No. I want to look at the spell. There are ways to . . . Please. Just trust me."

I shut my eyes. There was a rustle of rich fabric as he raised his arm, and then I felt his palm against my rib cage. I almost groaned but managed to swallow the sound.

"It's strange," he said, so close that I could feel his breath touch my cheek. "It's . . . tangled. Many threads all tangled together. I can't see a way to pull them loose."

He stepped back, and I opened my eyes.

"So, I am to be your housekeeper forever," I said. "Or I die. I am doomed, is that it?"

His jaw worked, but he did not reply.

"I will come back to clear your plate," I said, and I turned with as much dignity as I could muster.

"Wait," he said, and I paused. "I am not going to harvest you. My sister . . ."

"Your sister will know that I still have my heart, when she comes again, and she will harvest me herself," I said. "I am damned if I stay and damned if I leave."

"I promise that I will take none of your heart, nor will I let her take it." He sat again on his dark throne, clenching his fists on its arms. "If I knew how to release you, I would."

"*Why* can't you?" I asked. "There must be a way."

"We have never learned it. We have never needed to." He rose and started toward me again, as if to stop me from going.

"That doesn't mean it's impossible!" I insisted. "You could try! If it can be done, it can be undone!" Couldn't it? I was crazed with fear, with the possibility that I might never be free.

He just stood there.

"In the old stories, a kiss would undo the spell," I said,

unthinking, and then went beet red as I realized what I had said. Now he would think that I wanted him to kiss me, which of course I did, but I didn't want *him* knowing that. But it was too late.

He stared at me for a moment, then crossed the distance between us again. I froze.

"You don't . . ." I began, but before I could continue, he leaned toward me with complete seriousness and brushed my burning lips with his cool, dry ones. It was my first kiss, and I had nothing to compare it to, but I imagine that kissing a sorcerer would have trumped all other kisses anyhow.

If I had been red before, now I must have been a rich purple shade. My heart throbbed in my lips, and they felt unnaturally sensitive, as if chapped by a cold wind.

Our lips parted. The sorcerer held my gaze, seemingly completely unembarrassed. "It doesn't seem to work," he said.

"Well, I . . ." I began, and then realized I had absolutely no idea how to finish that sentence, and that I should just leave before I made an even bigger fool of myself. "Well, I'm going to bed," I said eventually. "If you feel like setting fire to anything else, feel free to snap your fingers and clean it up before morning."

He said nothing, and I could not read his expression. I left him there, and I was so angry that I could have spit.

CHAPTER 13

I cried myself to sleep that night. Of course I did. It was my first kiss, and it had been given without love or even the mildest affection, as an experiment. To him it was nothing, and to me it was everything.

I cried for my cursed heart, and for the misfortune of my birth, and for my da, and for the knowledge that I was trapped here with no chance of freeing myself, at the whim of a magic-worker who didn't even want me.

I was an accident, as usual. I should never have been snagged, never should have come here, just as I had always believed I was never meant to be alive at all. I gave in to self-pity entirely and soaked my black pillow with tears that were absorbed by the House's magic, leaving the cloth dry and cool as ever.

This made me feel even more as if my tears didn't matter—didn't have any impact on the dreadful blank blackness of the House and of the sorcerer's heart. Cornelius curled himself around my head, letting his tail fall across my neck like a scarf, and tried to purr the sobs out of me as best he could.

I spent a restless night, as you can imagine, thoughts

scurrying about like ants. I thought about making a run for it, trying to go home to Da, but I couldn't see how I'd be much better off once the heartsickness kicked in, in force again. I'd probably end up staggering back within an hour, begging to be allowed to serve the sorcerer all over again.

The only chance I had was to stay here and hope that he would stir himself and put some effort into learning how to undo the spell or mend me somehow (fat chance of that).

Or, I suppose, hope that he would just finish the spell and take my heart and put me out of my misery before his sister could. Or perhaps the Snagged were right and their method really would work. They were fast becoming my only hope.

I thought about the sorceress's manservant, too. Colin. He had shown a flicker of remaining humanity, right at the end. Would he be able to help me? Or, if I found some solution, would *I* be able to help *him*? I had to try at least, didn't I?

I woke up without any sort of solid plan, but with a raging headache that made me grump about the room as I got dressed and glower at Cornelius when he mewed. The House stayed out of my way as I stomped through to the kitchen, making the floors especially smooth and obstacle-free for me, and the kettle boiled in record time on the stove. I made a cup of tea so strong that it could have dissolved a spoon and swallowed it all down while I stared at the fire.

"Why are you in such a bad mood?" Cornelius asked me.

"That shiny bint in the fancy dress told her brother to harvest me, and he's going to do it. If not today, then someday soon. Or she will."

"He wouldn't *really*," said Cornelius. "He likes you."

"He's amused by me," I corrected, "and only sometimes, at that. And it sounds as if he might not have much of a choice, if she's making him. Or if the king is making him."

"So, you're leaving." Cornelius stared at me with wide eyes.

I could almost see the word "bacon" imprinted on his little forehead.

"I don't know," I said. "I'm thinking about it. I don't know if it's even possible for me to leave, but I might have to try. I'm sure the House will give you more bacon if I go, now that you've got a taste for it."

"It's not that." Cornelius washed his chest quickly, as he did when he was embarrassed. "Could you take me with you?"

"You want to come with me?" I was startled.

"I don't want to stay here," he said.

"But you said it wasn't a bad life."

"It's not. But it's not a particularly good one, either."

"It's a long road. And we're not fancy back home, like him."

"I don't mind. I'm a good mouser. I think." Cornelius paused. "Actually, I don't know how I would do with real mice now. I'm a bit out of practice."

"We have a butcher's shop," I said.

His eyes brightened. "Well, that's perfect, then," he said. "Plenty of meat."

"Right," I said, still a bit startled. "Well, if I do leave, I'll bring you with. Like I said, though, I don't know if I can." Something occurred to me. "Will you still be able to talk, away from the House?"

"I wouldn't think so," said Cornelius. "Which is a pity, because I'm getting quite good at it. I think it's something the House gives me, and outside of the House, I don't see how I'd be able to keep it." He looked at me a little uncertainly. "Would I still be good company, if I just mewed like any other cat?"

I felt an ache in my heart. "Oh, yes," I said. "You would always be good company, Cornelius."

"Oh. Good," he said, and looked away as if he was thinking of something else. There was a pleased tremble to his whiskers, though.

I suppose the House had been listening and wanted to distract me, creaking open one of the drawers in the kitchen. I was used to the House's ways of communication by now.

Sighing, I rummaged about, looking for whatever it wanted to show me, and my hand closed on something small and slightly furred to the touch. Tough, but with a little give to it. I lifted it out. It was the thing that had rolled to my feet in the courtyard.

I had almost forgotten about this odd, peach-pitlike thing. I probably wouldn't have thought about it again, what with everything else going on in my head.

"What is it?" asked Cornelius.

"Well, I found it on the street. Two idiots had been fighting over it. I hung onto it out of curiosity, but I didn't know what it was . . ." I held it out to him. It felt oddly alive in my palm. "Have a whiff. What do you think?"

He made a face, but sniffed it, and coughed a delicate cat cough. "Dusty," he said. Then he stuck out the very end of his rough little cat tongue and just barely touched the surface of the wrinkled thing. He made a face.

"It's meat," he said. "Or it *was* meat."

"It's a heart," I said with certainty, putting it in my skirt pocket. I remembered the little bag of pig hearts with which the sorcerer's visitor had tried to pay him. "Is it rotted? Molded?"

"No, I'd smell that a mile off. It's just . . . dry."

"Can you tell what kind of meat it is? Was?"

Cornelius thought for a moment, giving one ear a quick wash. "If I didn't know better," he said, "I'd say it was human."

A heart. A *human* heart. No wonder they had been fighting over it so furiously. I could only imagine the price a human heart would command on the black market, no matter how wizened.

I didn't dare think about how it had been procured, but now

173

that it was in my hands, I thought I might as well use it. I could take it to Basil and the Snagged. I could give them what they had asked for—their price for the cure. I could leave the sorcerer and his House and his cursed kiss behind.

I should have been elated. I should have run out the door there and then. But I didn't. I stood very still, pressing my hand against my pocket, thinking. I then made breakfast in a daze, preparing all the foods and making more tea without really being aware of what I was doing.

I almost forgot to be angry and embarrassed about the kiss until I entered the throne room, and then it came back over me in a rush.

To my surprise, Sylvester was standing on the black tile just inside the door, adjusting his cuffs. The fact that he was standing at all was a shock, frankly, as I almost always found him lounging in his throne as if half-asleep.

He was dressed differently, too. His hair was brushed back neatly, showing the fine planes of his cheekbones and jaw, and he wore a voluminous, black travel coat over his usual shirt and breeches. The fabric of the coat looked like thickly embroidered velvet, with a pattern that moved under my gaze and refused to let it get a grasp on it, and with dozens of buttons the size and sheen of a raven's eye.

"You look nice," I said, despite myself.

He looked at me blankly, as if "looking nice" was a completely incomprehensible notion. He didn't seem embarrassed about the previous night at all.

He did brighten when he saw the breakfast plate, though, and threw himself back into his chair to eat the bacon with his fingers and lick off the grease. He was worse than Cornelius when it came to bacon.

There was an odd tangle of awkwardness and intimacy between us. I wanted to ask him more questions about the spell and what to do now, but I hesitated, hovering beside the door and watching him eat. It didn't seem to make him self-conscious, but I felt like a fool.

"I'm going out today," he announced when he had finished. He seemed . . . nervous, suddenly? His long, white hands twitched, as if he longed to be playing with one of his toys.

"Where are you going?"

"Just out," he said.

"You never go out." My curiosity was getting the better of me.

"Well, I'm going out now. I'll be a day, maybe two." He brushed imaginary dust off his sleeve.

"All right," I said, although my heart had started beating fast. What would happen to me if he went away? Would I fall prey to the strongest bout of heartsickness again? My stomach roiled at the thought.

And how was I supposed to go to the address Basil had given me, if I were barely able to move or speak for the pain of separation?

"Can I come with you?" I heard myself say and flushed with shame.

"No," he said, avoiding my eye. He stood and started to fuss about with his collar and cuffs, his face turned away from me.

I started to clear the breakfast plates, anxiety building in me at the thought of the pain I would feel at his leaving.

If the heartsickness returned in full when he left, there was no way I would be able to take the heart to the Snagged. If it was anything like when I was in the village, I would be barely able to walk.

Then my love-clouded brain cleared a little, and the anxiety was replaced by sudden knowledge, and my anger rose up like bile in my throat. I dropped the plates, and they smashed at my feet. The sorcerer whirled around, startled.

"What did you do that for?" he asked, staring at the shattered pieces.

"Are you going to one of the villages?" I demanded, hardly recognizing my own voice. "Is that where you're going? Are you going to *harvest*?"

For a second, his beautiful face was unguarded, and he looked like a little boy who had broken a window with his ball. Then it was inscrutable and eerily perfect once again.

"You can't!" I cried. I imagined what had happened to me happening to someone else, but worse, because it wouldn't be just another *snag*. He would take the whole of them, their whole heart.

I also had to fight down an irrational stab of jealousy. Whosever heart he took, it would be the heart of someone he chose. Not an embarrassing accident, like me.

"You can't," I said again. "It's not right."

He said nothing.

"Why did you not tell me yesterday you were planning this?" I asked, realizing how ridiculous I sounded. As if he had to keep me informed of his plans. Still, I felt a sense of betrayal.

He sighed. "That's not all I've been doing. I spent the night examining the spell that binds us and trying everything I could to break it, but there is nothing. It is so tangled up in what I am, and what you are."

I didn't know what to say.

"I'm sorry," he said, in what for him was an oddly gentle tone. "All I can do is alleviate the pain a little, or so I hope."

If he wanted me to say *thank you*, he was going to have to resign himself to disappointment.

"So, you're going out to the villages now?" I asked.

"What do you suggest I do? Are you offering yourself to be harvested, then, in their stead? My sister will return, and she will expect me to produce a heart. If I do not, she will take yours. Are you sacrificing yourself, then?"

I stood, glaring at him, unable to think of something to say in response. I wished I could have shouted "Yes!" and meant it, but, shamefully, I was still concerned with preserving my own hide. He was right. I was not about to offer myself up to save someone else, although perhaps I should have. He saw my answer in my face and gave a small, bitter smile.

"You could stand up to her!" I said, knowing I was being ridiculous. Why on earth would he defend his housekeeper against his sister? "I don't care how *kind* your sister was to you," I continued. "Or how *helpful*. She's a horrendous, evil harpy, and you're about to be just as bad."

We stared at each other over the little heap of shattered plates that I had dropped.

"Don't worry about clearing those up," said Sylvester, an edge to his voice, and the chips of china rose buzzing into the air like a swarm of bees, reassembling themselves with sinister neatness and efficiency.

I shrank back, as if they were going to aim themselves at me and pierce my body with their thousand broken points. I felt sick. It was the first time I had perceived the sorcerer's magic for the unnatural, world-bending thing that it was.

The House's antics happened just out of sight, as things sidled into place at the edge of my vision, and it seemed less like true magic than a sort of sleight-of-hand. The toys the sorcerer played with every day were just toys, even if he tossed a ball of fire from palm to palm. I hadn't seen *magic* magic, not like this, so blatant, impossible, and inexplicable.

Seeing these inanimate things rise up, as if suddenly come to life, felt wrong in a sick, visceral way; warped and off-kilter, like a dream where everyone you know looks just a little unfamiliar.

I knew all at once, with a great and strange certainty, that the sorcerer's kind of magic was something wrong and damaging that should not be here in the world, and might even be doing harm by being here.

I watched the plates, now good as new, stack themselves neatly, obediently, ready for my shaking hands to carry them back to the kitchen.

He was making a point, I knew. The House would have provided more, but no, he had to show me what he could do. To scare me with his power? To show me how insignificant I was by comparison?

"You will wait here until I return," said the sorcerer in what was probably meant to be a lordly tone but came off as sulky instead.

We glared at each other. I found it was possible to be helplessly in love and completely disgusted with someone at the same time. I picked up the now-mended plates, holding his gaze.

"I'd smash them a second time," I said, "if I didn't think you would use heart magic to repair them all over again. And it's not worth that. Nothing is."

He fastened the buttons of his coat, all the way up to his chin. "You may go," he said grandly. I rolled my eyes and stomped off, hoping he'd choke on his own high collar.

I fumed in the kitchen, fiddling with a pigeon pie crust and pointedly avoiding the sorcerer until he left, hearts dancing across my brain. I nursed my anger like a beloved babe at the breast, making sure it grew and strengthened, fueling me in preparation for the pain I would have to endure that day.

I had fashioned a heart shape on the roof of the pie without realizing it—a child's heart, simple and symmetrical. Innocent. Nothing like the real thing, which was lumpen and lopsided, valves popping out like tentacles. I had seen more than enough of them in the butcher's shop.

I could not hear any sounds of the horses or the carriage, but as soon as the sorcerer left the House, I felt it. His carriage was swift, and the pain increased just as swiftly. It was like the journey from my village had been, but in reverse, as the pain worsened with every mile between us—the magical horses ran faster than the real thing.

And as that invisible rope that tied me to him stretched and frayed, I doubled over, startling Cornelius, who jumped back with a bottlebrush tail. I ruined my heart-shaped crust as my hand flailed out and caught its edge.

"Are you all right?" mewed Cornelius.

"No." I groped for the black wall, realizing, now that the sorcerer had gone, how fleshlike it felt to the touch despite its hardness. It turned my stomach, suddenly, the warm black mass of it.

The House felt alien and strange without the sorcerer, its familiarity and homeliness gone, as if it had never been. And the pain was a torment. Worse than before, or at least I thought it was—waves upon waves, each growing in power, washing me toward a dreadful shore.

Perhaps I had just forgotten the agony of it, as they say women forget the pain of childbirth and long for another babe after a few short years.

I plopped down into a chair, my head in my hands, and imagined the sorcerer on his journey. I pictured the carriage rolling into a village, as it had on the day I had been snagged, all dark curlicues and jewel-studded spokes.

I pictured the door opening, as it had then, and Sylvester

stepping out with that fine, high shine on his boots and the light glancing off the blade of his equally fine cheekbones. I pictured him brushing his black curls aside, scanning the crowd with his gray-blue eyes, and fixing his gaze on one of the prettier girls, someone like Hallie, maybe, or one of her friends.

She would make her way through the hushed crowd toward him, staggering a little as if mazed, and he would stretch out one white hand to draw her in to the carriage, close the door, and twitch shut the velvet curtains.

Once inside, what? He would fill her ear with sweet words, perhaps, as he dazzled her eyes with his beauty. Perhaps he would dampen her wondering, open mouth with kisses, as well. Perhaps more. Perhaps the long, white hands would open her bodice, or part her legs.

That was what we all believed they did—or hoped they did, in our shameful and fevered imaginings. It is what I imagined him doing to me, although I allowed myself only a minute or two of such dreaming, alone in my chamber at night.

I put up with the pain for an hour, maybe more, sitting doubled over on the kitchen chair, with Cornelius at my side, before crumpling and feeling my way down the long corridors to my bedchamber.

The House sat inert, refusing to make my staggering journey any shorter or easier. Cornelius trotted along by my feet, clearly concerned. As concerned as a cat could get, at least, which was merely one or two notches above complete indifference.

"If I lie down for a while . . ." I said, but couldn't finish the sentence.

I collapsed onto the dark bed like a toad plopping into its pond and fell into a parody of slumber. The dreams of vines and long, twisting passageways were back. The passageways were familiar now, having spent so many days wandering the fickle corridors of the House. But the vines were just as strange and unkind as they ever had been, fat as snakes, and I pushed my way through them with ever-failing strength.

I slept a damp, overheated sleep that left me feeling more exhausted than if I had never slept at all. Cornelius stood guard beside the bed, tail lashing.

In my troubled dreams, he grew sometimes as big as a house, a panther made of black flame, and then shrank down to a flake of ash that could have fit beneath my fingernail. Once, he stood on his hind legs and grew as tall as a man, and wore a shifting, many-caped coat, like the sorcerer's traveling garb.

"Foss," I heard him say once or twice. Or perhaps he was just hissing. With a cat, it was hard to tell.

I had even less perception of the passing of time than usual. The pain was a dark, emaciated figure that picked me up between its teeth and worried me like a terrier does a rat, then dropped me for a moment of relief before dancing back, laughing, to snatch me up again.

"Why is it so much worse?" I panted to Cornelius, but of course he could not answer, because I had not really spoken, but merely dreamed that I had spoken.

The fever-dream Cornelius spread great bat wings and flew to the ceiling, where he hung staring at me with enormous upside-down eyes.

In my few moments of clarity, I thought that perhaps the sorcerer's magic was as chaotic and disorganized as he said, and tinkering with the spell had only made it worse. Typical. He should have left well alone, rather than tangling me in another spell gone wrong.

To my surprise, however, the pain seemed to break eventually, like a fever. I lay on the sodden sheets, gasping, aware that the respite would not last forever, but grateful for it all the same.

I stayed very still, as I had when I was a sprout and had imagined monsters under my bed waiting until they heard movement to pounce. The pain did not come back, though, and I ventured to sit up and look around. Cornelius was at the foot of the bed, curled up and sleeping, but stirred when I shifted position.

"You all right?" he said.

"I think so," I said. I stretched out my arms experimentally. They looked white and frail, but the movement didn't cause any pain. I swung my legs out of bed and staggered to the wash-basin to splash my face.

"Is he back?" I asked. That would surely be the only reason for the sickness easing.

"No," said Cornelius. "Still gone."

It didn't make sense. Perhaps he had changed his mind, had turned, and was on his way back? I stared at my wet face, dimly reflected in the shine of the black walls, and then stumbled back to the bed.

Perhaps the pain was over for good, miraculously, but I couldn't think of any good reason for why that should be the case—however much I wished it were so. Unless he had died or been killed somehow, on the road, and the spell had died with him?

I shuddered at the thought, despite my fury with him. I couldn't imagine a world without him, even if that meant free-dom for me.

After a while, however, the heartsickness started up again, just as badly as before, so I supposed he must still be alive. I did not remember the pain coming in waves like this before I came to the city. Perhaps it was the effect of having been so long in the sorcerer's presence that altered the experience of it?

Whatever the cause, it seemed to be waxing and waning rather than keeping a steady presence. I did not know how long it took, but eventually it eased again, and I was once again grateful for the relief. I knew it would not be for long. I seemed to sense the next wave of it already, gathering itself ominously behind my eyes and readying for attack. Cornelius jumped up onto my chest and kneaded it with his paws.

"Cornelius," I said into the darkness.

"Hmm?"

"If this is what happens when I'm away from him," I said, "I will never be able to go back home. If he discards me, I will die."

"He will be back tomorrow," said Cornelius reassuringly. "Probably," he added, less reassuringly.

"But I have to leave tonight," I said. "I have to go to the Snagged. To take them that heart."

The idea of leaving the House *now* gave me the shivers. Perhaps the House was providing some comfort, some shelter from the full force of the spell, and walking out its door would make everything worse. After all, as Cornelius had said, the sorcerer and the House were one and the same, somehow. It was an extension of his magic.

Maybe being close to the House was a little like being close to the sorcerer himself and thus protecting me a little from the pain, making it wax and wane as it was doing. Once I was outside the walls, I would really be apart from him, without even his strange black substance to surround and succor me.

I would only know for sure once I left. But I had to try. What else was I going to do, lie here sweating and fever-dreaming until he got back, and then gratefully pop on my apron and resume business as usual? No. I struggled upright.

"I need a clock," I said to the House in what I hoped was a commanding tone.

"What's that?" asked Cornelius.

"It's a device that tells you what time of day it is." I realized that I had never seen a clock in all my days in the sorcerer's House.

"What's the point of that?" said Cornelius with animal logic.

"I want to know how long I have. The pain seems to come in waves. If I leave when it ebbs a little, I might have time to get to the address and back."

The House provided with its usual secretive generosity. I turned my head and saw a small, ornate pocket watch on the bed beside me, a gentleman's toy tricked out in black metal and diamonds, dense and complicated. It had a cunning clasp that opened with a *snick*, and inside were the familiar numbers, old friends arranged in the usual comforting circle, as if sitting around a table together in polite conversation.

They seemed as alien here as I was, here where time was ill-mannered and unruly, and refused to be fettered by numbers and flattened behind glass.

I gritted my teeth and stared at the diamond hands as they swung around, and when the pain tightened its grip on me again, I closed my eyes. After a long while, when the pain lessened, I opened them again.

It had been almost an hour of a dull ache that was unpleasant, but bearable. Now I had to wait and see whether the respite was consistent—whether I could trust it enough to risk leaving the House. I lay back and let the pain take me again.

I could feel the walls grumbling around me. The House, although it had reluctantly provided me with the pocket watch, didn't like its presence. It forced the House to belong to the real world (a little), and follow real-world rules (a little), and the self-governing sorcerer magic resented it.

I found it comforting, however. It had a light, sure tick that sounded like the clip of hobnailed boots on tile and made me think of Da coming home after the day's work. It soothed me as the heartsickness worried and snapped at me, when it took me in its jaws and sank in its black teeth.

Without the watch, I could not have guessed how much

time had passed. When the next respite came, I saw it had been about an hour again. I lay still for another almost-hour, listening to the *tick, tick* of my new friend, and then the heartsickness took me once more.

I knew now, however, that there would be an end to it, and so when the black pain snatched me up again for its mad dance, I allowed myself to be tossed and twirled without resistance, waiting for my chance to leave the House.

I lay awake that night, staring at the pocket watch and waiting for it to get near enough to midnight, holding the piece of paper with the address on it crumpled in one hand.

The watch's ferocious, regimental ticking fought against the viscous soup of the House time—or rather, the odd timelike substance, because what filled the House's days like wine in a cup wasn't really true time at all, just something like it, just as the mice Cornelius chased weren't really mice, but just mouselike enough to pass muster with a bored cat.

Although the ticking was faint, it was valiant, and I trusted that it could hold its own.

When the time came near, and the pain stopped again, I heaved myself out of bed, feeling as if I was a hundred years old, and started looking about for my boots.

I buttoned them up, pulled a new dress over my head, and fastened a new cloak at my collarbone. I stuffed the watch into a pocket. I would need to keep close guard of the time. I tucked kitchen knives into my boots and the pockets of my cloak. I was a butcher's daughter, and a butcher myself, really, even if I'd never been given the official title. I knew how to use a knife. Last, I felt for the little wizened heart in my skirt pocket.

"You will come back, won't you, Foss?" said Cornelius, who was hovering at my heels.

I snorted. "I don't have much of a choice."

"All right," he said, looking small.

"Stop fretting," I said. "I told you I wouldn't leave you here for good."

I didn't think it through any more than that, for fear that the House might sense me thinking and throw up obstacles in my way, or that the heartsickness would somehow grip me again before my hour of respite was up.

Once I had myself looking as respectable as I could, I groped my way out of the bedchamber and headed for the front door. The House, perhaps taken by surprise, didn't do more than shiver itself a little, and I found myself with my hand on the knob, then stumbling across the courtyard, then opening the great door that led to the Outside.

"I'm coming back," I said to the empty air, as if I were reassuring the House as well as Cornelius. The whole place seemed to sigh as I stepped out the heavy black door. I felt a suck of air, as if something inside was trying to inhale me back in, and then nothing.

I hurried as fast as I could and reached the tavern without incident. Every so often, I thrust my hand into my pocket to touch the little heart, reassuring myself that it was still there. I was all ready to show it to Basil when he answered my knock, but as soon as he opened the door, he grabbed me by the arm and pulled me inside, shutting and locking the door behind me.

I noticed then that all the other Snagged who were present were standing in a tight circle around something on the floor and had not turned at my arrival. Just my luck—they were probably performing some eldritch ritual in which I'd be expected to take part.

Then I felt a stab of fear—there was a body on the floor. I backed away, walking into the door that Basil had just closed and bolted behind me.

"Open the door," I said. "Let me go. I want no part of this, whatever it is."

"No, wait." Basil tried to lay a hand on my arm, but I shook him off. "It's Jol," he said. "The mold has spread."

Which one was Jol? All the Snagged had blurred together in my mind. Basil went back to the circle, and I followed him.

The Snagged were clustered around a young man—ah yes, I remembered him now—who was curled up on the floor, panting and twitching. A woman had his head cradled in her lap and was washing his face with a soaked rag that she dipped and refreshed in a tub of water at her side every few seconds.

He was shirtless, his torso almost concave, eaten away by the same rot that had corroded Nat's. It was a sickly, queasy green-gray, deepening to a bright sap green under his left ribs, where his heart should have been.

There was a smell, too, like fresh-turned compost—not wholly unpleasant, but strange in that stone room where nothing grew or should be decaying.

I did not want to keep looking at him, but I couldn't seem to tear my eyes away. As I watched, he started to writhe again.

"Shhh, love," said the woman who cradled his head, as if he were a sprout having a nightmare. She even smoothed his hair back from his forehead, and her hand came away wet with his sweat.

A lump clogged my throat for a second, seeing her motherliness. Da had done his best, but there was something about a mam feeling her babe's forehead for a fever that always made me wish for a mother of my own.

"We should call a doctor," I said.

"There is nothing a doctor can do for us," said Basil.

No one else met my eye. We stood, or sat, or crouched, and kept watch while Jol shook and spasmed. The green mold had spread up his throat and was reaching fingers into his mouth. He coughed, and something splattered on the flagstones. Everyone took a step back, except the woman who was holding him. The sputum was bright green.

"Not long now," said Basil.

"How can you just stand there and watch him?" I shouted. "At least *try* something!" I was practically vibrating where I stood, so tensed was I with the desire to jump in.

"We have tried," said Basil. "With others. Nothing helps when it gets this far." He absentmindedly rubbed at his own breast, through his embroidered waistcoat, and coughed. I felt my own chest instinctively, wondering if I was short of breath because I was anxious, or because there was some creeping corruption beneath my own ribs.

"There is nothing to do but wait," added Basil.

No one moved as Jol struggled to his death—no one except the woman who soaked her rag, wrung it out, and dabbed at his clammy forehead, over and over. The water was probably warm by now, and certainly filthy with his sick sweat, but she kept going.

I wished I had been given such a task, something to keep my hands and my head busy, but instead I had to stand and watch as the green decay bubbled in his chest with every labored breath, slowing and slowing, until I could not be certain if the faint movement of his lungs was more breath or just the mold itself shifting and settling.

I looked from one face to another, and saw them all determinedly still and fixed, never turning away, hardly blinking, as if bearing witness to Jol's death was the only way in which they could do him honor.

After a long while—I could not have guessed how long—his

chest stilled. It was my first time seeing death close at hand, human death, and I could tell at once when the life left him.

There was no way of seeing it, exactly, but the body on the flagstones transformed from a *he* to an *it* in an indefinable but unmistakable way. Jol was dead.

Basil knelt and felt his pulse at arm's length, keeping a fastidious distance. "He's gone," he confirmed with a quick nod. The woman who had been dampening Jol's forehead held the wet cloth still, without putting it back in the bucket, and there was a steady *drip, drip, drip* of dirty water onto the floor.

"Best get cleaned up," said Basil, and the watching Snagged came to life as if they had performed this dance many times before.

"What will you do with him?" I asked, staring down at Jol's body. The mold was still bubbling a little.

"Burn him," said Basil, matter-of-factly.

I must have looked shocked, because he added, "We can't be sure that the corruption won't spread. I doubt it, because so far it seems to be confined to those who were harvested. But we cannot take the chance."

"And if someone else saw this," added another man, who was helping to wrap Jol's body in a piece of sacking, "they would ask questions. Talk to a doctor, maybe."

"But wouldn't that be a good thing?" I said, exasperated. "You *should* talk to a doctor. Hells, they might be able to help you. You don't know unless you ask!"

"She doesn't know," Basil told the other man.

"I don't know *what*?" I snapped.

"Doctors might be able to help," said the other man. "Unlikely, but there's an outside chance. Mayhap they have some potion or some such."

"Exactly. That's exactly what I'm saying," I said.

"Or mayhap not. Then maybe they go to one of the magic-workers, ask for a magical remedy for some strange ailment that rots you like an apple. Then the magic-workers come looking for us."

"They already know you're here, though," I said. "Don't they?"

The man avoided my gaze. He wrapped Jol's body with care, paying particular attention to the head and feet, tucking the dead man's arms into the sacking as if tucking a child into bed. Soon the body was an innocuous bundle, like a parcel you might take home from market.

I appealed to Basil. "What difference would it make? At least there would be a chance of finding a cure. Or at least stopping us from dying like *this*."

"We stay outside of the Magic-Workers' notice," said Basil.

"But they know you're here! You followed them here, you said. Jol said he slept on one of the sorceresses' front doorsteps for weeks!"

"They do not know where we are now, nor that we gather together to talk and share information," said Basil. "Why do you think we meet here secretly?"

"You mean you're *hiding* from them?"

"Yes, in a way," replied Basil. "For our own protection. Oh, they let us stay for a bit, sometimes, while it amuses them, or serves them, I suppose, or if we slip their minds for a time. But eventually, if we do not hide from them, they come back for us. To use up what's left. We think it's easier for them to use up a heart they've already snagged. Takes less effort. And when they come back for one of us . . . we are powerless to resist. Because it's what we want, deep down."

He looked at Jol's wrapped body as it was carried out of the door. "The corruption is spreading faster and faster now. It was slow, at first, developing over weeks and months, but now it is more like days. We need to find out everything we can, as quickly as possible. Before this happens to more of us. Poor Jol. If he could have hung on, just until we found the hearts, and took them to our contact for repair . . . He had so much hope."

"You still think you'll be able to heal yourselves? The rest of you?"

"If we all find hearts with which to replace our own, I have every faith," he said. He wiped his hands briskly on his waistcoat.

"What is the name of the person who will repair—or re-place—the hearts?" I asked.

"I'm keeping that quiet for now," said Basil, tapping the side of his nose. I wanted to hit him. I decided to keep the little heart to myself for the time being. I didn't want to stay there any longer, with the stink of corruption in the air.

I had cut it fine. The heartsickness hadn't quite descended yet, but I could still feel it waiting, subtle but dense, like a nagging headache that never quite surfaces, lurking behind your eye-balls and burdening your thoughts.

Outside the tavern, I hailed another cart and perched tensely on the seat, jiggling and fidgeting and willing the driver to go faster, checking my pocket watch obsessively.

I wondered about Dav, back home. According to Basil and the rest, his days were numbered. How much of his heart was left? Was he, too, covered in that creeping mold? I wish I had talked to him more, back in the village. I wish I had found out all I could, while I could.

I felt much more sympathy for the poor fool now than I ever had before. If I ever made it back to my village, I thought, I would sit down for a long conversation with Dav Mallet.

When I reached the higher levels of the city, all I could

think about was sinking into my soft, black bed, resting my aching body, and letting my mind slow its unrelenting race for long enough to sleep a little before breakfast. I don't think I had ever lived through a longer day.

According to my reckonings earlier, I should have started to feel the full strength of the heartsickness again, but I was still fairly hale and hearty when I stepped into the courtyard.

When I opened the door to the main part of the House, however, Cornelius was there to greet me, his tail like a great bottlebrush standing up behind, and his eyes even bigger and yellower than normal.

"Where were you?" he said.

"I told you I would be back."

"He's going mad," said Cornelius. "Smashing everything. Setting fire to things."

"What? Who?" I asked stupidly, before realizing. "He's back already?"

He was back, much sooner than expected, and he knew that I had been out. I didn't know what to make of that. It did mean that I wouldn't be getting heartsick again, though, so that was something.

"Who do you think? He singed my whiskers," said Cornelius. "He didn't mean to, but he did. Now I'm lopsided."

"They'll grow back," I hazarded.

"Maybe," he said gloomily. "Either way, you'd better go in."

He turned and then added, "He's in a right state."

I started toward the throne room. But Cornelius said, "He's in the kitchen."

"The *kitchen*? He's never in the kitchen."

"Well, he's there now."

The House practically hurled us through the door, like a mother handing her child over to the father when he gets home and saying, "I can't do a thing with him, you try."

The place was a mess. Sylvester was standing beside the kitchen shelves and on top of a stack of broken china. Less of a stack, really, and more of a small hill.

There was far more broken china than there should have been, judging from the number of dishes the House had conjured into being for me. It must have made more of them just for him to smash—or perhaps the sorcerer had made them himself.

His arms were upraised, his hair was wild and floating about his face, and his whole bearing had more energy than I'd ever seen in him before. His lean form was a black flame, wavering at the edges a little as he moved, as if his agitation was shaking the air around him.

The House trembled. When he noticed that Cornelius and I had burst into the room, the sorcerer paused mid-smash, staring at us wide-eyed. The final plate hovered with an apologetic air, as if denying its involvement.

"What are you doing?" I asked, because that seemed like the thing to say. I rested my palms very slowly and carefully on the kitchen table.

"Oh," he said. "You're back."

"Yes, I just . . . went out," I said.

He let the hovering plate drop. It only broke in half, rather than smashing into smithereens like the others. The pile of splintered china gave a cheerful, welcoming tinkle as the halves joined their ranks.

"How long have you been at this?" I asked, staring at the pile. "That's quite a stack."

"I don't know."

"Well, stop it."

He paused, seemingly at a loss. His hair, which had been crackling about his head with manic, magic energy, floated down to its normal place about his shoulders.

As he calmed down, a broom appeared in the corner, with

an expectant sort of look on its . . . Well, it didn't have a face, but it managed to look expectant anyway. I grabbed it. Seemed like the sorcerer could have cleaned his mess up himself, but the House didn't seem to be presenting that as an option.

"I thought you had gone," he said.

"And so, your first thought is to come down here and smash up my kitchen?" I asked, starting to sweep and ignoring the little leap my heart gave. *He was worried?* "I needed some fresh air, is all. I've been cooped up in here with no one to talk to but you and the cat . . ." I swept furiously, keeping my eyes on the floor.

"Oi," interrupted Cornelius. "*The cat* is right here."

". . . and I just needed an outing. I didn't think you'd be back until tomorrow." It was a feeble explanation. Why would anyone go for a casual stroll at midnight?

The sorcerer was so removed from the usual rules of time and human habit, though, that he didn't seem to question it.

"Oh," he said. Everything about him was slowly settling, and I realized that his feet had been drifting a tiny way above the pile of smashed dishes. As I watched, they lowered until his high-shining boots rested on top of the stack.

"Can you get off that? I'm trying to clean," I said.

His face looked odd, off-kilter. It was still perfect, of course, every line of it a brushstroke painted by a master in the art, but something about it was different. His eyes roamed around the room, taking in the stove, the fire, Cornelius, the plates, and finally me.

"I thought you had gone," he said again.

I let the broom dangle from my hand.

"I wouldn't just leave," I heard myself say. We stared at each other.

"Where were you?" he asked.

"I didn't realize I was a prisoner."

"You are not." His face was flushed. "You know I do not keep you here deliberately. You are here of your own will."

"Hardly *my own will*," I said, hands on hips, "when I am ensorcelled and bound to you, whether you wish it or not. And what do you care if I go out? You didn't bind me to you on purpose, as you said."

He bit his lip. "I thought you had left. Because I had gone to harvest."

"You'd hardly miss me," I said. "You don't need a housekeeper at all. Your House takes care of itself, and the rare times it doesn't . . . Well, you can just snap your fingers."

"It can't make meatloaf," he said.

I stared at him for a second, then resumed sweeping. "Yes, it can. It can make anything."

"It's not the same," he insisted.

We stared at each other for another moment. I hated the perfection of his face. If I were wearing some sort of silk-and-lace contraption like the ones in the mysterious bedchamber, it might have been romantic.

As it was, I stood stolid as a stump and waited for him to speak further. He did not, but leaned toward me ever so slightly. My heart thumped about like it was trying to throw itself into his hand.

"I . . ." he began, and stopped.

"What?" I whispered. My voice came out dry and thready.

"Nothing," he said, and turned to go, leaving me trembling on my feet and yearning after him. I did manage to overcome my heartsickness enough to ask, "Did you take one?"

He stopped, without turning around. "One what?" he said.

"A heart."

He stayed still for a minute, then kept walking as if I hadn't spoken. Cornelius trotted after him, leaving me with the mess of broken china and the hum of spent magic, and the knowledge that some poor soul's heart had been harvested and bottled like autumn preserves, from a village like mine, somewhere out beyond the city's walls.

Once I was alone in my room, with not even Cornelius as witness, I peeled off my dress and underclothes and examined my own chest. I palpated the skin around my breast and ribs with my fingers and peered as closely at it as I could, but saw nothing—no rot, no decay, not even a greenish cast to my paleness. It seemed I had been lucky so far, but how long before I succumbed to the same corruption that was consuming the rest of the Snagged? I would have to keep an eye on it—and redouble my efforts to find out how to extricate myself from the sorcerer, before I ended up like Jol.

CHAPTER 14

The day of Clarissa's return dawned with an appropriate feeling of dread. I chewed on the ends of my hair. I needed a wash—the fever and exertion of the day before had left its mark. I heated up water in the big tub before the kitchen fire and had as quick a bath as I could manage.

When I felt sufficiently restored, I made a hurried breakfast from the ingredients the House provided for me and went through to the throne room to find the sorcerer. I steeled myself against the inevitable leap of joy my heart would give at the sight of him and determined to stay as angry as possible, to guard against it.

He was clad in a billowing black shirt, a black waistcoat embroidered in silver thread, breeches, and his impossibly shining tall boots—dressed up for this important meeting with his sister. He had something small and fiery in his hand and was playing a sleight-of-hand trick with it, flickering it over and under each of his fingers in turn so that it shimmered like a bright-finned fish.

"Porridge," I said, plonking the plate down. "Need anything else?"

"No," he said, without looking up. I hovered, though, wanting to say something but not knowing what.

"What happened to being more than you were made for?" The words burst out of me. "To thinking for yourself?"

The little fireball winked and shone between his fingers.

"I suppose I'm next, am I?" I pressed.

"I told you that you would not be." He spoke quietly, not looking at me.

"Very reassuring. Did you bottle the heart like a jar of pickles, or is it magicked away somehow?"

He looked up at me, his strange eyes cold and pale. "My sister will be here again soon," he said.

"Right, then. Want me to bake a cake for her?" I tried to keep the sarcasm out of my voice; I was not sure he would even notice it.

"That won't be necessary," he said.

"You'll be able to give her a nice surprise," I said, the venom spilling out of me without my meaning it to. Every time I thought about him harvesting a heart, horror, disgust, anger, and jealousy rose up in my throat and threatened to choke me. The surge of emotion was almost enough to overpower my love, but not quite.

"Yes," he agreed. "I suppose I will."

Hands still shaking, I set his cutlery down and then turned to leave. He surprised me by speaking, and I stopped.

"I knew it would hurt you when I left yesterday," he said. "I did what I could to mitigate it, but it seems like I have little control over the spell, as I suspected. The work I did the other night gave you some relief, though, I think."

"Thank you," I said, after a pause, taken aback.

"I will keep trying," he said, surprising me again. "I will not be able to completely remove the pain, however, and if you travel too far from me, this new spell will not hold. I have to be fairly close to you in order to sustain it. The . . . bond between us allows me to use it as a channel for such magicks. At first, I did not think it would be possible, but it has grown easier for me throughout the day, I find, and I can hold it more loosely now."

I pictured the spell like a fine, shimmering net cast over me, and the sorcerer holding the slender threads between his fingers. I wondered what his magic felt like to him, if it was something tangible he could hold and manipulate, like his endless parade of sorcerous toys. Like Da's butcher's knife, and the slabs of meat. "Anyway. It means that it is easier for me to work magic on you now that we already have a . . ." He waved his hands vaguely. "Connection."

I wasn't sure if that was good news or bad. He seemed uncomfortable. We stared at each other.

"And what does this connection mean for you?" I asked.

He seemed startled. "I . . . don't know," he said slowly. "But I am trying to find out."

My mind was in a muddle. He had harvested a heart, but not mine. He had refused to harvest mine, in fact. He had left me but cast a spell to protect me while he was gone, as best he could. And when he found I had left the House, he had created a thousand plates to smash.

I knew he did not love me, despite what my embarrassingly ensorcelled heart tried to tell me in the dark watches of the night, but could he possibly *like* me? Or at least like having me around? I felt a stab of guilt, that I was thinking about how to leave him, and then an even sharper stab of anger at that guilt.

Of course I wanted to leave! Of course I wanted to go home! I had been *stolen* from my home, whether he had meant to take me or not. And of course he would rather have me cooking and cleaning for him and, yes, providing some companionship and conversation, than have no one at all. I was Cornelius, but more useful. Protecting me as best as he could from the worst of the injury *he* had caused was the very least he could do.

And so I argued with myself, staring into his face and saying nothing, while he stared back and waited for me to speak.

"What are you doing, Sylvester?" I said at last.

"I don't know," he replied. He held my gaze, but the light in his eyes flickered a little.

"You said yourself it's what you were made for," I whispered. "Taking hearts. You are doing your duty, right? Finally? So why are you helping me?"

He sat very straight, so different from his usual slouch. His hair fell in such perfect waves around the fine edges of his cheekbones that I wanted to weep.

Would I ever be free of this terrible pull toward him? I took a step forward, almost involuntarily.

What if I just gave in? Threw myself at his feet and told him that I would endure anything, *anything*, if he would only permit me to be near him always?

His jaw tensed, but he stayed still, watching me. So still. I couldn't even see the rise and fall of his chest.

Another thunderous knock on the door. Even though I had been expecting it this time, I jumped. Thankfully. I had almost let the spell take me over.

"I'd better answer that, then," I said, and waited for him to speak. He said nothing. I turned tail and stomped to the front door, flinging it open with more force than necessary. Across the doorway, Clarissa stared at me with open hostility. *Still here?* I could almost hear her thinking.

I made my face as stupid and simple as possible. It wasn't hard, because faced with the inexplicable pull and attraction of her beauty, my face quite naturally fell into a stupid and simple expression on its own.

Without greeting me, she floated off to the throne room again, Colin following close behind and looking grayer and more mushroomlike than ever, and, again, I went to the kitchen to prepare tea and cakes for them both. My hands shook as I poured the boiling water over the leaves. Cornelius wound himself around my shins.

"You all right?" he said.

"Yes."

Of course I wasn't all right. I had half expected her to reach into my chest and pick my heart like an apple as soon as I opened the door. Well, maybe she would be satisfied with whatever he had been able to harvest.

I carried the tea tray through the throne room and to the crystal plinth the sorceress had created and did my best not to look at either of the magic-workers. An angry silence hung in the air when I walked in, as solid and tangible as a bat hanging from the ceiling. I would be glad to get out from under it and back out into the black corridor. Clarissa watched me closely as I walked back out and waved her hand at her servant.

"Colin. Guard the door."

Well, that put a wrench in the works. Colin followed me out silently and took up station to the right of the door. It closed with a deliberate, final *thunk*, leaving me outside with no way to listen in this time, lest the servant bear tales to his mistress. I stared at his blank, bland face, and he stared back—or perhaps just stared into space, because there was no focus in his pale eyes at all.

I wondered if I could persuade him to let me look through the keyhole, which was still there from the last time. After all, it would be in his best interests as well as mine, if I was able to help the Snagged. He was the most thoroughly Snagged of all of us, as far as I could tell. Was there enough humanity left in there for me to argue—or negotiate—with? I sidled up to him.

"Colin," I whispered urgently. His eyes flickered, just a little, which I took as an encouraging sign. Either that, or my breath on his face had made him blink. I chose to believe the former. He was in there, somewhere. I had to believe that. I didn't want to think that I would end up like that, scooped out like a melon, nothing of me left. I didn't want to think that Dav would end up like that, back home, or all the other Snagged I had met.

"I can help you," I said. "I know people who might be able to fix you—put you back the way you were, before Clarissa got her claws in you."

No reaction. I reached out and poked his shoulder. He swayed a little at the pressure, but it was like poking at an odd-shaped fungus you found in the woods. There was a slight give and squish, but the thing certainly didn't push back.

"In order for me to do that, though," I continued, "you have to let me listen to what they're saying. All right? They'll never know. I'll just look through the keyhole."

He made a small, convulsive movement, as if to stand in front of it.

"Please. I know you're in there, somewhere. Please. I'll try to help you if I can." I hoped the words were reaching him, somehow.

To my complete astonishment, he shuffled a little to one side and turned his eyes away from me, leaving the keyhole unguarded.

"Thank you," I managed to say through my surprise and knelt at the little opening, prepared to listen again.

At first, there was nothing to listen to. I could not see Sylvester clearly, because Clarissa obscured my view of him, but I imagined that he was either glaring back or lounging in his chair, staring at the ceiling.

"Sylvester," Clarissa said at last. She drew something from the soft leather bag that hung at her waist. I squinted. It was a jar, I thought, but she was moving it around too much for me to get a good look. Some kind of liquid sloshed about inside. My eyes couldn't get a good look at it.

"Why are you here?" Sylvester asked.

"You know why I'm here. We have to report to the king in two days' time, and we're concerned about you."

I couldn't see him, but I heard him snort. "Why?"

She did not deign to answer. She shifted her weight, and I heard a faint splash from the jar she held as it moved more clearly into my view. I could see only an ordinary glass jar, the kind that Da kept our pickles in at home, filled with liquid and nothing else that I could see.

"I told you," she said. "He has expectations. If you haven't done anything about them, I'm afraid I'm going to have to take your . . . housekeeper . . . myself. It's for your own good, little brother."

A strained pause. And then:

"I did it," he said. "All right? Are you happy? Here it is."

What? I clutched at my chest, which felt no different, in a momentary panic.

I clawed open my bodice as far as I could and stared at the unblemished skin. There was no bruise, no rot, no spiderweb of inching veins. My breathing slowed as I realized he was talking about the heart he had harvested, and not mine. *Idiot*, I thought to myself.

I heard the chink of glass. He must have reached out to pass something to her, because I saw her lean forward in her seat and stretch out her hand. It was another jar, not as large as hers. The sorceress unscrewed her own, and tilted Sylvester's down to pour from one to the other. The solid thing floating inside Sylvester's jar hit the liquid in hers with a stomach-turning *plop*, and she screwed the lid back on.

"I'm glad you realized it was madness to keep her here intact," she said.

203

"It's not *hers*," Sylvester corrected her.

"Then whose is it?" she asked sharply.

"Someone I . . . met."

"You harvested!" she exclaimed. "I'm proud of you, brother."

I could see the jar again now. It winked in and out of my sight as she moved it in her hand, glowing faintly. There was something floating about in it, something solid but disintegrating, trailing threads of itself as it moved.

It was in some sort of oil, I thought, some golden and viscous substance. The sorceress's mood seemed to have improved somewhat, however, and she smiled a little as she turned the jar over in her hands and peered through the glass.

"It's not very big, is it?" she said.

"It's big enough," said Sylvester.

"Of course, it's not big enough. You know the situation," she said. "We need more, more, more. Much more, if we are to keep the peace in the kingdom, and restore the crops, and keep everyone plump and prosperous. I do not mean to nag you, brother"—and she winked, playfully, which was one of the most disturbing things I had ever seen—"but you understand that it is terribly important."

"You've had enough of them without me for years," said Sylvester sulkily. "You'll live. And there are shelves full of them in the palace."

Shelves full of them in the palace. Now that was something to report to the society. Getting into the palace had to be nigh impossible, but perhaps they knew of some more shady characters who could help, like their mysterious magical benefactor.

"There are not," said the sorceress shortly. "Not any longer. The mold, fungus, whatever it is, has been spreading."

A fungus? Like the one infecting the Snagged, perhaps.

"Whatever it is," she continued, "it has killed more than half of them. We have a deficit to make up. We have had to renege on our agreements with the closer villages."

"Renege?"

"This was in your *lessons*, Sylvester. We agreed to leave them alone in exchange for the produce and meat that we needed."

"Why can't we just grow our own? I know, I know," as she tried to interrupt, "I know that what we do is toxic. I know that the earth of the city is dead, and things do not grow here except by magic. That we"—and I heard the edge of self-contempt in his voice—"*infect* this place. But if we stopped harvesting . . ."

"We need hearts"—as always, the word jolted something in my chest—"to keep us safe. To feed us. To keep Darius on the throne. It affects everyone. It is very sweet of you to want to keep your housekeeper—"

"Foss."

"—Foss, alive. But surely she would want her family to remain protected? Her village? They have not fared so badly, in recent years. For a long time, we have just picked the odd one here and there, plucked portions of hearts, only taken full ones when it was absolutely necessary. It is regrettable, of course, but now with this . . . disease, we must harvest with a scythe if we are to build our stores back up. We will lose a few villages on the outskirts, but that is *what they are for*. In time, they will recover and rebuild, and they will be grateful that we kept them from a worse, more painful fate."

"*Grateful.*"

"Don't be sarcastic."

Lose a few villages on the outskirts? I felt a rush of rage at how carelessly she spoke.

"Foss's father lives in one of those villages," said Sylvester, echoing my thoughts. "He is a butcher. Like mine," he added with a huff of a laugh.

"Don't be so melodramatic. We are not *butchers*."

"Really? What are we, then?"

"If anything, we are comparable to farmers," she said. "We nurture, and then we harvest. And the harvest is for all. Without our magic, would our kingdom be as safe or prosperous? As peaceful? It is a small price to pay."

Only if you're not the ones paying it, I thought. I watched as Clarissa raised the jar to her face and examined it with the eye of a connoisseur. She shook it up, and swirls of oil and little threads and specks of flesh detached themselves from the heart and circled lazily in the slow liquid, like fish in a warm pond.

"Not bad, really," she said. "A bit shriveled, but not bad."

"Now will you leave me alone?" said Sylvester. "I will find you others, if that's what you want."

"What I want? Darling, it's what you're *for*," she said, an echo of her earlier words about the villages. She tapped a long nail against the glass. "It's enough, for now. For today. I will take it to Father. But you still have that girl . . ."

"What about her?" he said, rather sharply. I could see just one of his hands through the keyhole. It had been drumming impatiently on the arm of the throne, but now it stilled.

"She's still here. Untouched."

"What of it?"

"You need to get *rid* of her, Sylvester. Harvest her and get rid of her. You know we can't live with *people*."

I could almost hear his raised eyebrow. "Are we not people ourselves?"

"You know what I mean," she said, sounding a little flustered. "With *ordinary* people."

"You keep servants. You all do."

"Yes, but *empty* ones, darling."

Empty?

"Not whole humans wandering about, getting their sticky

fingers into every corner and poking their noses into what doesn't concern them. You can't keep an intact human in here."

Intact had never sounded like a dirty word to me before, but it did now.

"She doesn't poke her nose into things," said Sylvester, which was patently untrue.

"That's beside the point. You can't keep her here. You can't know what she's doing *all* the time. It can't all be housecleaning and cookery—the place is lousy with magic! You don't need her."

"Food made without magic tastes better," he said. "And we can't eat magical food all the time and stay in best health. Why not have someone to prepare it?"

"I don't understand you," said his sister with a sigh.

"I know."

"Look," she said. "I told Father about her."

"Why?" His voice changed, grew more resonant, as if he had suddenly sat up straighter.

"Because you can't do this, Sylvester. You're new. You don't understand the rules yet."

"I understand them just fine." It sounded as if he were standing and moving about. I still could not see him, but I could see the nauseating little jar of drifting flesh in his sister's hands. The . . . *thing* inside—my mind shied away from it— turned a little, like a babe in a transparent belly. "Why did you have to say anything?"

"It isn't safe to keep her. You know it isn't safe."

"What is he going to do?" There was a thread of panic in his voice, odd to hear.

"I don't know, but I would advise you to get rid of her, one way or another, before he does anything." A silence. The jar in her lap tilted a little, and the *thing* pressed up close and gruesome against the glass.

"Chase out that cat too, while you're at it. It's not natural to have those things around. They're always *watching*." A short pause. "You know I only want the best for you, Sylvester," she said, her voice silken. "I am your sister, after all."

"Sister in name only," he said. "And one of a dozen." But his protest was weak.

"Sister in more than name," she retorted. "We were made by the same hand. Whatever we were before has been erased, and now we are creatures of magic, bonded by magic, closer than any blood siblings could be. No one else can understand what it is to be *us*. Certainly not your housekeeper."

There was a long, unpleasant pause.

"Well, I suppose you'd better be on your way," said Sylvester. "According to you, you're very busy."

There was a susurration of rich fabrics as Clarissa started to get to her feet, and then it subsided. I twisted a little, pressing my eye closer to the keyhole so that I could see her better. She was standing very still, looking closely at the jar.

"What?" said Sylvester.

I heard the sloshing of liquid as she turned the jar over in her hand again. I saw her lift it to her face, frown, narrow her eyes. Then she threw it. I heard the bright, almost joyful sound of shattering glass, and a discomfiting *squelch* that had to be the heart flopping onto the floor.

"Do you think I'm a half-wit?" she shouted. "Or are *you* a half-wit? Has your housekeeper pickled your brains in her sauces?"

Sylvester sounded bored. "Get to the point, Clarissa."

"You were going to let me carry this to the king like a fool," she said. "You would have had me telling him you were fulfilling your duties—defending you—all while you were palming off some wizened little piece of offal you bought from a two-bit hustler in the marketplace!"

"Hardly wizened. I plumped it up," said Sylvester. "I thought it looked pretty convincing, myself. In fact, I'm a little surprised you didn't notice sooner. I thought you fancied yourself a connoisseur."

My own heart, however, was jumping up and down in my ears, and muffling all sound. So he hadn't harvested a heart at all?

"What is *wrong* with you?" Clarissa was screeching.

"It's still a heart," I heard him say.

"A used-up, dried-up little husk of one," she screamed. "I could barely conjure up a toothpick with something like this. And do you think that, if these pathetic baubles did any good, Father would allow the black market to continue operating? It amuses him, is all, seeing the little people squabble over his leavings. He could gather all the black market hearts in a second, with one word, but he doesn't. Because they are useless."

She pointed a finger at him. "And you thought to fool him with one? By reddening it and swelling it out a little? I don't understand what goes on in your head, Sylvester. And then *I* look like a numbskull for bringing it to Father like a good little go-between and pleading your case. He will be *furious*, Sylvester. And I can't protect you any longer. You need to start pulling your weight, and fast."

"I will," he said.

"When?"

"Now. I will go today."

She snorted. "And what, try to find another black market heart, but plump it up a little better this time? No. You are going to harvest, and I am going to watch you."

"Fine," he said, with a bite in his voice. "I will call for the carriage, and you can *watch* me as I take some poor villager's heart. Happy?"

"No," she seethed. "You will call for your housekeeper, *now*, and I will watch as you take hers."

209

"Clarissa . . ."

"I gave you a chance. *More* than a chance. It's too late, Sylvester. It has to be done. Either you do this, or Father will."

From the way she said it, I got the impression I really didn't want "Father" anywhere near me.

"Really, brother," she continued. "If it means that much to you, you can keep her once she has been harvested. She'll still be able to cook and clean for you, and she won't be troublesome. She should last a while longer once she's been harvested. Long enough for you to get tired of her."

"It's not the same," he protested.

"I assure you, it is exactly the same," she said. "You just haven't been around enough intact humans to realize how deadly boring they really are." She raised her voice. "Colin, come in here."

I shuffled backward as fast as I could, nearly falling over. The House provided a little alcove just in time for me to scramble into it as Colin came back to life and walked inside the throne room.

When the door closed behind him, I crawled back to the keyhole, my heartbeat thundering in my ears. I saw Clarissa standing before her servant, smiling into his blank face.

"It's easy, Sylvester," she was saying. "No need to be squeamish. It doesn't *hurt* them."

To my horror, she shook back her sleeve so that her hand and arm were exposed almost to the elbow, her fingers curled like the petals of a flower, and thrust her hand into her servant's chest.

"Of course, most of his heart has been taken already," she said conversationally as she twisted her wrist in his chest, and he writhed around her hand. "I'm careful to do a little bit at a time, if it's a really good one. It's surprising how long you can make them last, if you're frugal."

Colin's face contorted, but he made no sound. His eyes were closed. He looked almost drugged. Perhaps he was—or perhaps she had bespelled him.

I watched in horror as his mouth made the shape of a scream, but no noise came out. I still couldn't see Sylvester's face. Was he bored? Yawning while he lounged in his chair? Watching avidly? I had no idea.

His sister withdrew her hand with an awful, incongruous *pop*, as if she had pulled a plum from a pie. Her servant's heart was in her hand, a pocked and shrunken thing, clearly not whole.

She pulled an empty jar from the pouch at her waist and shook it. The shaking must have been part of a spell, because the jar filled with a golden liquid like runny honey. She dropped the heart into it and screwed on the lid in a business-like manner.

"A pity to use him up all at once," she said. "I was planning to hold onto him for a while. It's better if the heart is freshly plucked. Still, I hope the demonstration will prove worth it."

Colin swayed and staggered but did not fall. I could not see his chest. I wondered if it was a sunken cavity, like the boy's I had seen at the secret society meeting. I knew Colin couldn't have long to live.

But did Sylvester know that? Did he imagine I would survive the harvesting just fine, and keep on living in his House and cooking his meals as if nothing were wrong?

Well, I wasn't sticking around, waiting to be mutilated. I turned from the door so quickly that I slipped on the slick floor and fell on my backside, the hard black substance sending a jolt up my spine. It made quite a thump, and I hoped they hadn't heard me. I scrambled away, pushing myself along the floor with my feet, before getting up and running as best I could along the corridor.

I was trying to get to the heavy front door and out into the courtyard, to run out into the city, but the House undulated under my feet and would not let me. I almost sobbed in frustration, but could not keep my already unsteady footing, and so I obeyed it and turned around, cursing. I had to pass the throne room door again, but thankfully, it was still shut.

"Hide me, hide me," I said under my breath as if chanting a spell. I couldn't go to the kitchen, or my bedchamber. There was nowhere to go. Perhaps the House had decided to betray me after all—another of its whims, and a dangerous one this time.

Cornelius appeared at my feet.

"What's going on?"

"She's coming out to harvest me," I said. "I need to hide."

I scooped him up.

"Oi!" he protested.

"I'm sorry. But I have a bad feeling about you, too. I think it's better if we're both out of her sight."

He wriggled in my arms. "Put me down."

"I told you, it's better that we both hide."

"No, put me down, I can help."

"How?" I looked around wildly at the black walls. "Why can't you open one of your doors for us now, damn you?" I pleaded to the House.

"There are other ways," said Cornelius.

"What other ways?" I put him down.

"I'm a cat," he said, as if this explained everything. "There are always other ways."

"Yes, well, I'm not a cat, and I can't fit in your little spaces."

"You won't need to. You just have to sort of think sideways, like I said. Remember? To get to the Other House."

"*Think sideways*," I repeated. It made as little sense to me now as it had the first time.

"Like this," he said, and vanished, as if that demonstration was going to help me. Shite on a pile of shite, I thought. The House has swallowed him up, and it will finally swallow me, too. And then he reappeared.

"I don't know how to explain it any better," he said. "I've only been able to talk for a few weeks. You have to . . ."

"Think sideways, I got it."

Right. This was going to be a challenge. I cursed myself for not trying this more when Cornelius had first brought it up, and when I had had leisure to try and fail and try again. But if I didn't figure out Cornelius's secret paths to the Other House, fat chance of either of us getting out, and odds were, I'd be chewed up and spat out by the sorceress without ever seeing Da again.

So, I took a step back inside my head to take a look at how I was thinking, which was confusing enough without asking the question, *if I'm watching the Foss who's thinking, who is "I"?* Which is not the sort of question I was in the habit of asking myself, nor was it in any way helpful. So, I pushed that aside. I remembered the time I had first tried, back when Cornelius told me about the Other House and I had caught just a glimpse of it. I cleared my mind as best I could, and tried to make a sort of sideways *leap* in my head, like a fish twitching on a line.

Admittedly, I hadn't expected anything to happen, so it came as a shock when the corridor seemed to make a leap of its own and change shape for a moment. A trick of the light?

"That's it," said Cornelius. "Only this time, do it better."

"Thanks. That's really, really helpful advice."

The door to the throne room opened. I almost screamed, but then I saw Colin stagger out, and the door slammed shut again behind him. He seemed to be trying to take his position by the door again, to guard it, but he was having trouble staying upright.

"I can't leave him," I said to Cornelius.

213

"What? He can barely walk. We can't take him with us."

"I have to try. That's how I could end up, if I'm not careful."

If Cornelius could have rolled his eyes, he would have. I went up to Colin and grasped him by the shoulder, shaking him a little. "You have to hold onto me, all right?" I told him. "I'm going to get us out of here, but you have to hold onto me. Don't let go."

It was too good to be true, though. I don't know if it was pure coincidence that Clarissa left the room just then, or if she had some eldritch way of knowing what we were doing, but the throne room door blew open on a blast of hot air and noise—something like how I would have imagined a dragon's cough to feel and sound—and Clarissa burst out of it.

I staggered backward and fell, feeling my face to see if my eyebrows had been singed off, but they seemed to still be there. Cornelius clung close to my side, bristling, as Clarissa blazed in the doorway like a phoenix, lit up, and practically steaming with rage.

I thought at first that her rage was directed at us, that she had emerged from the throne room to ambush us and rip out my heart. But then I saw that she was looking back at Sylvester, who had become a dark, wavering shape, like smoke, behind her fiery fury. Her face was almost too bright to see.

She was shouting something at him, but I couldn't make out the words, and I couldn't see his face. Her hair lifted off her scalp, just as Sylvester's had when he was smashing the plates, limning her head like a saint in a painting.

Even her skirts were floating, as were her long bell sleeves, although the embroidered and bejeweled fabrics had formerly seemed too heavy to walk in, let alone to blow about like washing on a line. The House shrank from her and warped around her, making me feel seasick as well as nervous and overheated.

She spotted me, of course, and lunged toward me with her

mouth open and snarling, as if she was going to bite my head clean off. Her teeth were very white and sharp. I kept hold of her servant's shoulder, more out of terrified instinct than fellowship. Cornelius launched himself toward her face, and she put up her hands and screamed.

I didn't stick around to see what happened next. Trusting that Cornelius would be able to take care of himself, I scrambled down the corridor as quickly as I could, dragging Colin behind me. I could feel the heat of the sorceress's anger singeing the hairs on the back of my neck. Cornelius yowled, and I heard his claws skittering on the floor as he ran after me.

"Foss! Wait!" I heard Sylvester shout.

Like I would fall for that old trick. I didn't care if I dropped dead of heartsickness at the first corner; I wasn't letting that magic harpy take my heart. As I was almost to the front door, however, I skidded on the smooth blackness—the House had given a twitch—and went sprawling, bringing Colin down with me.

Clarissa was upon me at once, glowing like a bonfire. As I quivered like spilled jelly on the floor, unable to stand, she reached out with one long-fingered hand and lifted me by the shoulder as if I weighed nothing at all.

She shook back the lace of her sleeve on the other hand, flexing her fingers into a claw. Three ripe, red scratches from Cornelius's claws rent her perfect face. They were already healing as I watched, tiny invisible hands stitching them up until you'd never know anything had ever marred her flawless complexion. I shuddered. She flexed her hand, a twist of triumph at the corner of her mouth—and then hesitated. I had the sense that she expected something to happen, and was surprised when it did not.

"What are you?" she hissed at me. "What is protecting you?"

Sylvester appeared as a dark blur over the fire of Clarissa's shoulder. I saw his mouth open and shut, and dimly heard him say my name.

"Foss!"

No, it wasn't him after all—it was Cornelius, appearing and then disappearing, winking in and out of my sight, showing me what I should do. But Clarissa still had a grasp of my shoulder like an owl's talons on a ferret, and I couldn't twist free. She was examining me with cold curiosity, staring into my face as if trying to read something there.

Taking advantage of her distraction, I turned my head and bit her wrist as hard as I could, tasting her oddly metallic skin and then the warm flooding of blood that told me I had bitten deep. She cursed and released me, just for a second, but a second was enough.

My mouth full of her bitter blood, I *thought sideways* as best I could, and felt myself shiver out of one existence and into another. Just before I was entirely gone, I reached out and grabbed Colin by the ankle, hauling him with me.

It seemed to work, and for a moment, I was looking at the bare boards and cobwebs of the Other House. But a pain in my shoulder made me gasp and set my vision to shimmering, so that I was seeing first the sorcerer's black House, then the Other House, back and forth, flash-flash-flash, until I thought my eyes would melt.

Then the pain stopped, and I sank to the floor in the silent, dusty hallway, and Cornelius was wrapping himself about my ankles as if trying to tie a knot around me with his own furry body.

CHAPTER 15

I spat onto the dusty floor, a repellent glob of saliva and spicy, sorcerous blood that left my mouth as numb as if I'd been sucking on cloves. When I put my hand to my shoulder, it came away wet with my own blood. Clarissa's nails had been sharp.

I tried to slow my breathing and clear my thoughts. I was kneeling, I discovered, but on dirty floorboards now. I looked to the side and saw that Colin was sprawled beside me. Only the faint up-and-down movement of his spine showed that he was alive and breathing. One of my hands still gripped his ankle like a manacle, so tightly that I could see his skin reddening around it. Cornelius was at my other side, quite composed.

"You did it," he purred. "I wasn't sure if you'd be able to."

"I almost couldn't," I said. I patted myself down, less to check for injury than for the reassurance that I still existed, that I hadn't left a leg or an arm somewhere between the two Houses. I felt watery and weak, fuzzy about the edges, as if the journey had stripped me of something essential.

As I calmed myself and steadied my breathing, however, I

started to feel solid again. I was still here—me, Foss, the one unchanging, unchangeable thing in all this magic mess.

"She was going to harvest me," I said. "Something stopped her."

"You bit her."

"No, before that. She tried, and couldn't."

"Well, whatever it was," mewed Cornelius practically, "we made it."

There was none of that black stuff to be seen. We stood in a drafty hallway (which was a relief, honestly, after the stifling warmth of the House), laced with very impressive cobwebs and smelling of a fair amount of damp—and thick vines everywhere, twisting and dark.

I let my eyes travel slowly from one unfamiliar corner to another. It was lavishly coated with dust, like an old woman puffing on her face powder with a too-heavy hand. Every surface was furred and blurred with layers of it. Clearly, no one had come here for a long time—the dust was undisturbed except for a few of Cornelius's paw prints.

"This is what the House really looks like?" I asked.

"No," said Cornelius.

"But you said . . ."

"It really looks like this, and it really looks like the other thing," said Cornelius, twitching his tail. "They're both real, at the same time."

"And one is on top of the other?"

"No," he said, exasperated. "I *told* you. They're both in the same place, at the same time."

I suppose I had to accept that both places could exist at once in exactly the same space, but I did wonder what I had been sleeping on for the past month in this Other House. A nest of hay and field mice, perhaps? It made my head hurt to think about it.

"Don't think about it too hard," warned Cornelius. "It might be listening."

"Can the magic-workers follow us?" I asked. "They have magic. If I can get here, surely they can get here too."

"I don't think so," said Cornelius. "Probably because there's no magic in it at all. It's the *absence* of their magic, if you see what I mean. There's nothing they can draw on in here to do their castings, so it's beneath their notice, so to speak."

So, there was one place safe from their spiderweb of spells. I found I could breathe easier, stand straight. That constant, nagging presence of the heartsickness was not quite entirely gone, but it was certainly lessened. I took in a deep breath of air, then immediately regretted it when the dust set me to coughing and spluttering.

When my vision cleared, I could still see the dust swirling about me. I thought of hiding in here indefinitely, escaping the spell that way, but from what I could see, there was no way to survive.

Nothing lived besides the twisting vines, and there was no water source that I could see. Unless Cornelius could somehow be persuaded to bring me supplies every day for the rest of my natural-born life, which wouldn't be much fun for either of us.

I pressed my fingers to Colin's wrist. His pulse was still there—faint, thready, but even. "We have to get out of here. We have to leave. Clarissa is going to kill us both."

"We're leaving for good, then?" asked Cornelius.

"We have to." I ignored the pain that leaped up as soon as I thought about leaving Sylvester. *You're not real,* I told it sternly.

"Where will we go?"

"We won't be able to get back to my village. Not straight away," I said. "The sorcerer cast a spell that makes the heartsickness come in waves, but it won't work if I go that far. I'll get sick again. We'll go to the secret society people I talked to. They're the best chance we've got."

"All right," said Cornelius, "if they have food."

"I think they had sardines last time," I said.

He brightened. "Let's go."

I looked at Cornelius doubtfully.

"Once we get outside, I suppose I'll have to carry you in my arms," I said. "Unless you have any better ideas. It would look pretty odd to have a cat trotting alongside me."

"Put me in a pocket, then," he suggested. "The ones in your cloak are big enough."

"Really? That doesn't sound too comfortable." Or dignified. I knew how Cornelius valued his dignity.

"Just until dark," he said. "Then I can come out, and no one will be any the wiser. I'm good at being invisible."

"Remember, you won't be able to talk to me once we're out of here," I said. There was a pocket in my voluminous skirt plenty big enough for a smallish cat, and lined with velvet, which was a nice touch. I held it open so Cornelius could take a look.

"Looks comfortable enough," he said, "for a little while."

"Then we'll both be comfortable for a little while." I tried to speak lightly, but I felt a weight settle on me. I would not survive too long away from the sorcerer, I knew, no matter what I told myself about the secret society and their supposed magical friend who could heal hearts. Still, dying in a ditch was infinitely better than letting Clarissa reach between my ribs with her pointed nails and harvest me herself.

"Let's go," said Cornelius.

"Wait," I said. I nudged at Colin with my toe.

"I think you should leave him," said Cornelius. "He'll be safe enough."

"I can't *leave* him." I grabbed him under the armpits. He

was startlingly light, like a child. *Hollowed out,* I thought. He groaned. I heaved him up and supported him on one shoulder.

"He's coming with us," I insisted. "We'll get out of here, and go to the secret society, and get the name of that person who repairs hearts. And she'll fix us up, me and Colin."

I spoke with more certainty than I felt.

"You only have one heart in your pocket," Cornelius pointed out. "Don't you need one for each of you?"

"I'll figure something out," I said through gritted teeth.

"Fine, if you want to lug him about. Let's get moving, then."

"How do we get *out*, though?" I asked, looking around. The place looked like it was about to cave in at any minute. "Is there a way to get to the street from here?"

"I don't know," said Cornelius. "But I'll follow my nose, and we'll find out."

Walking through the Other House was an unsettling experience. The ceiling seemed to bulge downward with the damp. Spiders scuttled overhead. Colin was a deadweight against my side.

I thrust my hand into one of my pockets and found the little raven seal I had bought from Basil's stall. My one souvenir, if you didn't count Cornelius. I also had a knife, out of habit.

I had always carried one at home and in the shop, and I had nabbed one from the House's kitchen to ferry about with me in the House in the same manner. It was black, of course, with an ornate handle, barely larger than a paring knife, and its sharp edge was a comfort to me.

Cornelius followed his nose, and I followed Cornelius. There seemed to be no logic to the arrangement of this place. We might as well have been in a labyrinth. I voiced this to Cornelius, and he gave his odd cat shrug. "It's not so bad. I come here sometimes just for a change of scenery. Look for mice, eat a few spiders. Sleep in the rafters."

The walls shimmered oddly when our shadows fell on them, as if they were deciding whether or not to be solid. "Is that normal?" I said, pointing at them with my free hand.

"Just ignore them," said Cornelius. "If you pay too much attention, you'll go back."

"That's reassuring," I panted. Even though Colin wasn't that heavy, he was limp and uncooperative, and it was becoming a strain to support him.

The place made a sort of groan, like the creaking of an old tree in a bad storm. The spiderwebs quivered. And what happened to the spiders, when the sorcerer's House was taking up this space, I wondered?

"Stop *thinking*," said Cornelius sharply, as if he could hear me.

"It's a human thing," I protested. "It's hard to stop."

Cornelius gave a disgusted sniff that summed up all his opinions regarding humans.

"Why is it *shaking*, though?" I asked. "Is this usual?"

"Not as far as I know. The sorceress may be looking for us, I suppose."

"That's not very comforting. What if she brings the place down around our ears?"

"Not much we could do about it," he said.

I did my best to ignore my thoughts and just concentrate on following Cornelius's tail down this new corridor.

"How do you know where you're going?" I asked. My breath was coming shallowly.

"I just do," said Cornelius, and looked back over his shoulder. "It's a cat thing," he added ironically. "It's hard to stop."

The Other House was not the same shape as the sorcerer's House, exactly, but there did seem to be points where the two were a little closer together, like two streams of water flowing into one.

In these places, the walls shimmered more decidedly, as

if the wood and plaster had become a curtain between one place and the next that you could draw aside with your hand. I avoided looking at the shimmer for too long lest, as Cornelius had said, I sent us back to the House before we were ready.

The magical House seemed to be wrapped around this one like a vine choking a tree, stifling what it used to be, but there was a hint of life left. Standing in one of the abandoned rooms, I felt a twinge that told me *this* was the kitchen, in the same way you might see the memory of old beauty in a wrinkled face.

We pushed open a door that seemed to have been long shut—or tried to. Something pushed back. I put my head down and shoved it as best as I could while still supporting Colin, and with a great sound of crackling and snapping, whatever was behind it gave way, and I practically fell through into a cloud of dust and plant matter.

The corridor behind the door was choked with dead and dying vines, crowding every inch of space, and smelling of rot and must. Cornelius sneezed. "I haven't seen this bit before," he said.

"It looks familiar," I said. I had dreamed something like this, before coming to the city and then again during my heartsickness fevers. Those long, black corridors, so like the House, and those tunnels of vines. I felt a shiver.

"Well, my nose tells me this is the way out," said Cornelius. "So we'll have to push through."

We picked our way through the vines, most of which were dead and dry, but some of which still had a little bend and juice to them.

Colin had woken a little, enough to move his limbs sluggishly, but he kept getting tangled up in the vines and coming to a standstill, his eyelids flickering and his mouth hanging open as if he were still half-asleep.

The vines were covered with little thorns that reached out

with malicious hands to snag clothing and skin. I had to use my little knife to cut him free several times, and the thorns left my hands crisscrossed with red lines and bright beads of blood. I cussed and muttered as I tried to maneuver Colin through each new obstacle.

"Just leave him," Cornelius kept saying. "He's barely alive as it is. I can smell it."

"I can't just leave him," I grunted, lifting each of his legs in turn to guide him over a particularly nasty muddle of vines, tangled all together like a nest of snakes. "Barely alive is still alive. We might still be able to help him."

Humans, I could hear Cornelius thinking, but he said no more and even helped to free a trapped piece of clothing with his little teeth.

"We're nearly at the door," he said. "I can feel it."

I didn't know if we would be able to get to the Outside from this House, or whether we would have to pass back into the sorcerer's House to do so. All these layers of reality, one on top of the other like folded pastry! I couldn't keep them straight in my head. What if there was another House beneath this one, and another beneath that, and . . .

The walls shivered. The vines rattled their thorns.

"You're thinking too much again," hissed Cornelius.

"Sorry," I said. I hefted Colin past a last mess of thorns. We both looked like we'd lost a fight with a pack of rabid weasels. Our clothing was tattered and blood-smeared, and our skin was cut to ribbons.

There was a door in front of us, small and narrow, like the door to a cupboard. It certainly didn't look important or large enough to be the door to the Outside, but Cornelius trusted his nose, and I was coming to trust it too, so I supposed it might be the key to our escape.

I put out my hand for the handle, and the Other House

roared around me, a roar that wasn't exactly sound but managed to be deafening nonetheless. I clapped my hands to my ears, letting go of Colin, who staggered but miraculously managed to stay upright.

It sounded like all the boards and dust and spiders and vines had swirled themselves up into a maelstrom. The door spun in front of me like clay on a potter's wheel, the handle a black blur at one edge.

"Why is it like this?" I panted, struggling to stay upright. "Why won't it let us *out*?"

"It doesn't like the House being in its space, I think," said Cornelius, his voice also straining. "I suppose it thinks we're part of it."

"It *thinks*?"

"It's kind of . . . shoved under the House," said Cornelius. "By the sorcerer's magic. And it doesn't like it."

"Wonderful," I said through my teeth. "Let's get out before it figures out how to crush us."

Fighting the wall of soundless sound, I reached out again and grasped for the door handle. Astonishingly, I found the smooth curve of the handle in my palm, the chaos stopped, and I was able to open the door.

"Let's go before it changes its mind," huffed Cornelius, a little out of breath.

He jumped through, seemingly with no difficulty. I pushed Colin through first, then followed. The door pulsed around me, unpleasantly warm and tight, but then I was free and standing in the sorcerer's courtyard. It was night. It was not possible for it to be night—not enough time had passed.

"I forgot to mention," said Cornelius. "Time does seem to pass differently in there."

"How differently?" I asked. "Is it tonight? Tomorrow night? A hundred years later?"

He snorted. "Don't be dramatic," he said. "We've probably only lost a few hours. But we need to go."

I nodded, but looked back, just once, as all the fairy tales tell you not to do. I had to go, I knew that much, before I ended up with a rotten peach pit in my chest and my heart in a jar.

I had thought to myself previously—staring at the ceiling in the early hours of the morning, contemplating the fix I was in—that perhaps I could carve out some sort of hollow life, as Dav had, and live out my shortened days with no husband or sweetheart, sobbing in pubs until the rot took me.

Hells, that's probably what would have happened to me anyway, even if I'd never encountered the sorcerer at all. It would just happen a little faster now, that was all, with whatever this spreading mold was, if indeed I had become infected like the others.

But the thought of leaving Sylvester was almost unbearable. I hated myself for it. I knew the love I felt for the sorcerer was artificial, not a real attachment.

I would be Sylvester's footstool, his nursemaid, I would scrub out his privies, just so I could stay near him and feel that nonsensical and unearned happiness that his presence gave me, false or no. To be leaving—really leaving—felt impossible. I told myself not to think about it, to just keep walking.

We ran across the courtyard to the outer wall, hurrying, lest the magic-workers feel our presence, and wrenched at the handle of the final door.

Colin had roused himself enough to move on his own and keep up with us, but he still seemed little more than a hollow puppet, trailing along after us as if attached by strings.

We stepped out into the same old night as always, and the black door closed with a hollow *clonk* behind us, shutting me away from the sorcerer and the sorcerer away from me. For good. I imagined I could actually feel the severing, like something snapping in my chest, but of course, it was my imagination.

I wondered if he and his sister were still inside the House, or whether she had dragged him off somewhere to force him to harvest his "quota," however many hearts that was supposed to be. I would probably never know now.

I held the pocket at my waist open for Cornelius to jump in, and once I felt his weight settle into it, I walked as fast as I could away from the House without actually running, fearful that I would change my mind, let my heart overpower my good sense, and turn back.

Either that, or I'd hear the *clip-clop* of the sorceress's heels coming after me. I wasn't sure which would be worse.

Once I felt we had gained enough distance, I held Colin's arm within mine, hoping that we could pass for two sweethearts out walking. Even if one of the sweethearts looked like he could keel over at any minute.

The streets were only dimly lit by lanterns here, and as we got farther down toward the walls, there would be no light at all, so hopefully people wouldn't be able to look at us too closely.

"Are you all right?" asked Cornelius from inside the pocket. "You look a little green."

"I'm fine," I said, and then realized something. "You can still talk!"

I looked around, but there were few people on the street; it was so late. No one turned their head to see where the voice at my waist level was coming from.

"Yes," he said. "I'm not sure how long it will last, so we should make the most of it in case it goes away."

"All right." So, the spells were holding so far—both mine and Cornelius's. He could still talk, and I did not yet feel the full pain of separation from the sorcerer.

It had all happened so quickly and perhaps that was for the best. I didn't have time to grieve for Sylvester and maunder over him. This was the easiest way, I told myself—a clean break, with no time to hem and haw about it.

As we set off for Oyster Lane, we attracted few curious glances. We were just two more cold, preoccupied pedestrians among many others. It didn't seem long before I was down in the reeking lower roads of the city, picking my way through the damp, unpleasantly squishy refuse to get to the old tavern.

Cornelius kept silent, protesting only a little when I stumbled over an uneven cobblestone or turned a corner too abruptly.

The heartsickness had only just started to kick in when we turned onto Oyster Lane itself, thank goodness, and again seemed less than before. I suppose this meant the sorcerer still held the spell, like one of his cats' cradles, rather than letting it fall and fail once I had disappeared to the Other House.

I wasn't sure what this signified. Had he simply forgotten that he was protecting me and hadn't thought to undo his working? Whatever his reasons, I was grateful for it and hoped that it would hold at least while I was in the city, before I traveled too far from him to sustain it.

"There it is," I said, spotting the old tavern. Cornelius poked his head out to look.

"Smells like fish here," he said with approval.

"Smells worse inside," I said. I gave Colin a little shake, to see if he had perked up any. His eyes flickered, and he let out what could have been a groan or just a sigh.

"We're here, Colin," I said in the falsely bright, cheery voice you use for little children. "They'll fix you right up."

I hoped that some of the Snagged would be there. Basil had said they were there most evenings, and so my odds were good. When I knocked, however, the swift opening of the door startled me, and I almost fell inside. Cornelius let out a tiny mew.

Basil was standing just inside the door, clutching its handle, his normally pin-neat hair disheveled and his spectacles askew. He looked surprised to see me and my companion at first, and then his expression hardened.

"Come in, quickly," he said.

I thought he was being unnecessarily dramatic, but I hurried through the door all the same and brushed some dew droplets from my cloak as best I could.

"I didn't know you were coming again," he said.

"You said any night," I reminded him. "And I need to talk to you."

"Tonight is not just any night." He blinked at Colin. "Who is this?"

"Another Snagged," I said. "More than snagged. I don't know how much of him is left, to be honest. His name is Colin. He has been Clarissa's servant for a while—one of the sorceresses. I don't know how long. I do know that she has been slowly using up his heart, and I saw her take all of what was left of it today, with my own eyes. He's pretty far gone, but I thought . . ." I gestured helplessly. "Even if you can't help him, he will be among others like him. At the end."

Basil stepped briskly up to Colin and unbuttoned his shirt. He pushed his spectacles up his nose and peered at the skin revealed beneath the cloth. Cornelius tried to peer out of my pocket, and I had to push him down.

I was surprised to see that Colin's chest was nowhere near as badly diseased as Jol's, despite his heart missing. There was a bruise and a few threads of green spiraling out from it, but nothing more.

"Yes," confirmed Basil, correctly reading my expression, "he's not too bad as yet—when it comes to the mold, at least. That means she didn't take him too long ago, and she has been using him up pretty quickly. Some of the Magic-Workers like to keep a source close by, almost like a pet, in case they need heart magic in a hurry."

He let his spectacles drop back to the end of his nose. "I'm not sure if we can do anything for him," he said. "He might not be too badly infected as yet, but there's very little of him left, I'm afraid. We can't take him with us." He pulled a piece of folded paper from the pouch at his waist. "I have our contact's name and location here. Getting out of the kingdom will be quite the undertaking, and the journey beyond . . . he would never survive."

"The journey?" I said quickly. "To where?"

Basil tucked the paper back into his pouch.

"I'm sure you understand that I have to be very careful with that information," he said. "It could get us into a lot of trouble if it fell into the wrong hands, and our salvation depends on it."

"Of course," I said, cursing inwardly. He really wasn't going to give it to me, the sod, was he? He had it stuffed away in his stupid little pouch of papers, it seemed, and I couldn't get my hands on it without wrestling him for it. I briefly considered actually doing that, but there were so many other Snagged about that I would probably be overpowered.

"I am glad you brought him to us, just the same," said Basil. "You said his name was Colin? At least he can be among friends for his final days. I assume his Magic-Worker discarded him?"

No, I stole him from her while she was trying to rip out my heart, too, I thought, but I got the feeling Basil wouldn't be too pleased that a riled-up sorceress might come storming in looking for her lost property, so I said, "Yes."

"Well, thank you. We will take care of him," he said. He took his spectacles off to clean them with a handkerchief he pulled from the little bag of papers. I felt my gaze drawn to it again. There *had* to be a way to get the name and address of whoever was repairing hearts out of there. "When are you going?" I asked.

"As I said—tonight is not just any night. We have sourced some good-quality hearts on the black market, and confirmed their authenticity," he said. "A select few of us are leaving in the morning. We will be the first. Once we are healed, we will return for the others. They'll be looking for more genuine hearts in the meantime."

"I need to come with you," I said.

"I'm afraid that's impossible," said Basil. "We chose by drawing lots."

"I have a heart," I said. I held the little thing out, and when he reached for it with greedy fingers, I closed my fist about it.

"Look," I said, "I've run away, and the magic-workers might be looking for me. I need to come with you."

"*Looking* for you?" he hissed. "And you came here?"

I blinked. "Well, of course. Where else would I go?"

"You risk bringing them down upon us," he scolded me. "This is our last night of preparation before we leave. Are they looking for this other one, too?"

"I suppose so," I replied truthfully this time, taken aback.

"We can't risk anything interfering with our plan," he said. "You have to leave."

"But . . ." I began, but he was already walking away.

There was enough commotion with all the cleaning and clattering about the rest of the Snagged were doing that I felt able to talk to Cornelius without being overheard. I turned so that no one could see my mouth moving, and whispered to Cornelius. "He has the paper in the pouch at his waist. I have to see it."

"I can get it," hissed Cornelius.

"What? How?" I mouthed.

"Just let me out somewhere where he can't see me."

I sidled behind one of the old pub tables. Cornelius poured himself out of the pocket, slick and quick as ink, and disappeared into the cobwebby shadows.

I stood watching the others, trying not to look too awkward or expectant, my heart thudding in my chest. I saw Basil ordering a couple of them about as they packed bags, and then I saw a darting shadow under his feet. Basil cursed and tripped, and would have gone sprawling if it weren't for the bar stool behind him that he was able to grab.

The other Snagged scrambled to get Basil to his feet and brush him off, and in the commotion, no one noticed a small cat neatly grabbing Basil's leather pouch with its teeth and negotiating the forest of legs to carry it to me.

I snatched the fistful of papers from the pouch Cornelius dropped at my feet, turned my back, and shuffled through them as quickly as I could.

Basil seemed like the sort of fussy little man who would immediately notice anything amiss with his person, so I couldn't risk taking too long.

Most were notes in Basil's tiny, spidery hand, with footnotes and reference numbers, but one looked different—a map, drawn in green ink on thin parchment paper, like the kind used for wrapping meats, and a name: *Weftwitch*.

Underneath it were several copies of the same map, made in blue ink, and marked with Basil's handwriting, so I didn't feel too guilty about taking the original.

"Oh, these fell out of your pocket," I turned around and said, stooping as if I were just then picking them up off the floor, and hoping that the crinkling of paper in my skirts didn't give me away.

"Thank you," Basil said, distracted, wiping his face with his handkerchief. He tucked the bundle away without looking at it. I felt a weight as Cornelius poured himself back into my pocket, quick and silent as a whisper.

Just then, the door disintegrated—not as if blown away by wind or fire, but as if the wood were rotting at a thousand times the usual speed, turning dark and damp as leaf mulch, and puddling on the threshold. It happened silently, as silently as decay, and a musty, forgotten smell like a long-closed room filled the tavern.

Perhaps that is why no one turned until the first sorceress entered, radiant as a second moon, and the room seemed to fill with light and fragrance. Following her came others—all the others.

It happened so quickly that all the Snagged seemed frozen for a moment—or perhaps they really were frozen, captivated despite themselves by the beauty of the women who strode in, bracelets jangling, and skirts and capes sweeping like great wings about their bodies. I was dazzled, truth be told, at that first glance.

It could have been a painting, "Avenging Angels," or some such. They looked that regal and that fierce. And then movement returned, as the Snagged gathered themselves and started to run, pathetic as a scatter of cockroaches fleeing from a struck match.

Clarissa was the last to enter. She smiled upon us as if imparting a blessing and then raised her arms.

Em was the first to fall, gasping like a landed fish and clasping her withered, heavily ringed hands to her bosom.

Everyone was scrambling to get out of the dank little room that was now filling with the miasma of mold and decay, the stench of fear sweat, and the odd metallic tinge of magic, and no one stopped to help Em. It would have been useless, anyway.

The sorceress curled her fingers as if ready to pluck an apple from a tree, and what was left of the old heart streamed out, gay as ribbons from a maypole, toward those reaching fingers, red and black and sickly green altogether. It was almost pretty, if you didn't know what it signified, and if that terrible, deathly stench hadn't been filling the room.

One by one, the Snagged fell. The elderly lady crumpled without a sound. When Basil was struck, his glasses fell off, and his face looked naked without them. Nat made it a good distance, but not far enough.

He was young, so young. I remembered how he had spoken of a mother who had beaten and scolded him, and how the sorceress had seemed so perfect and loving by comparison. When he fell, he curled in on himself like a babe who had just fallen asleep.

The sorceresses snatched the paltry remains of the hearts from the Snagged who still had them: the last, rotting, vanishing morsels to which they had clung for so long in hopes of a cure. Shredded hearts flew every which way, like lengths of yarn spun on a wheel. It was the stuff of nightmares.

Cornelius leaped out of my pocket, no longer worried about concealment, and nipped at my leg, startling me into running. I grasped Colin by the hand, and the three of us darted up a back stair. Well, Cornelius and I darted, but Colin stumbled.

He would slow us down tremendously, but I felt a fierce protectiveness toward him, as a sort of symbol of what I could turn into if I wasn't careful, and I was loath to leave him behind.

Clarissa saw me. I felt her sharp green gaze like a blade in my back. I turned my head to look at her, unwillingly, drawn by her stare and the pull of her beauty, and saw her raising one hand and pointing one painted, beringed finger directly at me, a finger that seemed all at once unnaturally long and over-jointed.

I expected my own heart to stream from my chest in a bright ribbon, and clearly so did she, and so we stared at each other for a moment of almost comic surprise when nothing happened. Then she screamed, doubling over and clutching at her stomach as if she had a sudden bout of terrible cramping.

I had no idea what could have caused it, but her moment of

complete bafflement and then pain gave us a small sliver of time, and I pushed Colin ahead of me up the stairs before following.

Of course, running up the stairs then presented us with the problem of where to go next. This was no magic-worker's dwelling, and "think sideways" wouldn't be of any use here.

We could hide, or we could jump out a window and run. As far as I could tell, those were our only two options, and neither would be any use. They would find us if we hid, and even the slowest sorceress could easily outrun us. I hovered by the open window, deciding. When Colin grasped my arm, I jumped a foot in the air, thinking Clarissa had got hold of me.

"Leave me," he said in a rasping voice. This was the first time I had heard him speak all day. I reached for him, but he drew back, taking his hand from my arm. It felt cold where he had gripped me.

"Don't be an idiot!" I whisper-shouted. "She'll kill you!"

"He is already dead," said Cornelius from beside my feet. "He's right. We have to go."

We were already dead too, as far as I could tell. I had no idea why we weren't already.

"I can't leave him," I said.

But I could hear and even *feel* Clarissa coming for us up the stairs, like the slow warming of a rising sun. I gave Colin one last, useless, despairing glance, and then left him there and jumped out the window, gracelessly, landing like a sack of potatoes and miraculously avoiding a twisted ankle. Cornelius, of course, landed as lightly as a flake of ash.

We ran out into the incongruously ordinary streets, damp and stinking from a light rain that had started falling while we were inside, and Cornelius and I sprinted away as fast as we could—or as fast as I could, because he slowed his pace to stay with me.

Something odd seemed to be happening, though. I was

moving as fast as I could, but I seemed to be trotting more and more slowly, as if trying to run through thick soup, or honey. I swung my legs and arms as violently forward as I could, trying to push through whatever was restraining them, but I just seemed to be getting more tangled up.

"Why are you slowing down?" hissed Cornelius.

"I'm not!" I cried. "At least, I'm not trying to."

The mist seemed danker and thicker than usual, and it covered my mouth and nose as if someone was holding a damp cloth over them. I was unpleasantly reminded of the cloth that the woman had soaked and wrung, soaked and wrung again over Jol's clammy forehead. It had a similar stink to it.

"This is no natural mist," I said to Cornelius. "Something is amiss."

He flattened his ears tight against his skull. We stared together into the thickening air, which had grown so dense that we could no longer see the shapes of buildings through it. Sound was muffled. Those few passersby we had seen seemed to have vanished—whether spooked by the mist, or spirited away by it, I did not know.

Cornelius and I could have been alone in the vast city. It had become harder and harder to move through the mist, or whatever it was, and finally, I could no longer force my legs to move at all. I stopped dead. Cornelius's eyes shone wide and unblinking.

Shapes formed in the mist. Long, tall shapes that I thought at first were thin figures, but then looked more like blades, gray against the darkness. Like pairs of blades. Like scissors, opening and shutting, cold and sharp.

"Cornelius," I said under my breath, "any idea what these might be? Ghosts? Phantasms?"

"I don't know," he said.

There were dozens of them. Hundreds. I could see clearly now that they were in pairs, but even when I looked up and up,

I could not see where the pairs joined. They snapped open and shut, clicking toward us, slicing up the mist. Were they machinery, or living creatures?

They were just close enough to human form to be unnerving, shifting in and out of shape so that one minute they appeared to be headless, the next limbless. They reminded me of the chains of paper dolls I used to cut out when I was a sprout, flimsy and wavering and misshapen.

"They look and smell pretty real to me," said Cornelius.

"Smell?"

"If they were phantasms, they would have no scent. I've seen my share of ghosts. These are real, whatever they are."

"And what do they smell of?" I knew I would not like the answer.

"Sulfur," he said. "And bone."

"Lovely." I was getting a whiff of the sulfurous smell myself now. They surrounded us, impossibly tall, impossibly sharp, slicing the mist itself into vertical ribbons that floated around us like ghostly prison bars.

"Run!" mewed Cornelius.

"I can't," I said, moving my mouth with difficulty, so that the words came out sounding slurred and drunk. I blinked, and my eyelids slid down as slowly as a sunset over my already dry eyeballs. I was preserved in amber, swirling in a sticky oil like a heart in a jar. The world around me had become thick and viscous. "Cornelius . . ."

I was going to tell him to run, if he still could. But before I could say anything, the terrible, life-sucking slowing down reached my belly and my chest. Breathing felt like inhaling molasses, my heart strained to beat, and when my eyelids finally closed, it was a relief.

CHAPTER 16

I awoke blank and frightened. Not blank as you wake from a dream—dazed and groggy—but as if my mind had been scraped bare, skinned by an expert knife. I was aware of a chunk of time gouged from my life, a gap where something should have been. I couldn't help trying to explore it, prodding and poking at it with my mind like you'd investigate a missing tooth with your tongue, but there was nothing to find.

My eyes flashed light-dark, light-dark, before focusing, and my heart gave a jagged, sideways leap in my chest as it seemed to start beating again after that terrible *nothing*. My breath came in pieces, too, juddering and shuddering until I feared it would never settle back into rhythm.

I had never before realized how crowded and rich sleep really was, even when it seemed dreamless. I had thought, before this terrible morning, that I closed my eyes at night and fell into oblivion. Now that I really had fallen into oblivion for a period, I knew that time spent asleep was still time spent alive.

Sleep had depth and texture and purpose. The dreadful empty place where I had been had none of those things. I even missed those old familiar nightmares in which I had wandered the long, black corridors and had pushed the twisting vines from my face.

Now awake, or what passed for it, I scrambled for even the simplest memories—who I was, my name—and found nothing. My consciousness came back in little pieces, as if the monsters, or whatever they were, had scissored it into strips. There was one advantage to the nothingness, though: for just a few moments, I had forgotten all the events of the past months, and it was a blessed relief.

My heart felt ordinary, just for a moment, as I wondered what orders Da and I had to fill on the morrow. I hoped it wasn't hunting season, with deer and quail to dress, because their wild, dark eyes made me a little sad.

Of course, that relief lasted about a minute before the wrenching pain in my chest made me remember that, oh, yes, a sorcerer had bespelled me to fall in love with him; I had left Da and my whole life to trail after him and act as a servant in his enchanted House; and my heart was probably about to be cut out and pickled in a jar, leaving me as some kind of inhuman *thing* that would leak green slime and die in a stinking puddle.

I could have been safe in my own little trundle bed at home right now, rather than slumped in the corner of a dark room like an old sack of bulbs.

But where was I, exactly? The magic-workers had clearly found me—Clarissa, or one of her sisters—and so I was probably imprisoned either in one of their houses, or in the king's palace itself. My guess was the palace. I roused myself enough to look around.

The dark seemed impenetrable at first, but I could tell from the feel that I was chained up. My wrists and ankles were in shackles. I almost laughed. Me, in chains! As if I were some sort of dangerous criminal who needed to be restrained. Locking me in a room would have been more than enough. Hell, in the state I was in, you could have left the door unlocked; I wasn't going anywhere.

Cornelius was nowhere to be seen, and I hoped he was all right. He probably was, I told myself. Cats were notoriously difficult to capture, slippery as ink. I didn't have time or the leisure to contemplate his fate, however, because I had to concern myself with my own.

Someone had stripped me down to my underdress (I filed that particular shame away for another, less urgent time), and my knife, the heart, and the precious paper—with the map! I could have cried—were gone.

Weftwitch, Weftwitch, Weftwitch—I repeated the name I had read to myself, making sure I remembered that, at least. I still had the little raven seal; I suppose they hadn't seen any use for it.

I took a cautious inventory of my body, searching for injuries. I found an uncomfortably dry mouth, and aches and pains all over, but nothing all that serious as far as I could tell. The heartsickness was still there—mild enough that I knew Sylvester's spell to alleviate it was still in effect.

This surprised me. Didn't he know yet that I had run away for good? As soon as he found that out, he would surely whisk the spell out from under me and send me sprawling back into the agony of separation.

I tried pulling on one shackle, then the other, because I would feel silly if I didn't at least try to wrest myself free. Of course, they stayed put. There was nothing to do but wait and hope that they would let me use the privy eventually, because my bladder was knocking urgently on my stomach to let me know it was ready to relieve itself, thank you very much.

As I sat there in the dark, I started to feel very sorry for myself, and very homesick.

Oh, Da. How I missed him, in his great, filthy apron and

240

clogs, beaming ear to ear and telling me always how beautiful I was, and how lucky was he to have such a blessing of a daughter to help him in the shop and keep him company at home.

How could I have left so blithely, leaving my dreadful scribble of a note, and not think about my da lonesome at home, getting his own tea of an evening and drinking it by himself, while the room darkened, and the fire died? Did Basil ever send my letter to Da?

Well, I knew the answer. I had been more concerned with ridding myself of the pain of the sorcerer's enchantment than I had been with doing the right thing by my da. That bloody sorcerer and his bloody spell, intentional or not.

A teaspoonful of early-morning light had started to trickle in through a grate high in the wall, just enough to show me that I was in a stone room—probably the palace dungeon, as I had thought.

I had imagined dungeons as dank and noisome places, but this room didn't even smell damp. It was dry and stale, the air unmoving. Sawdust coated the floor, but it seemed fresh and swept, for the most part.

To my horror, something shuffled about in the sawdust on the other side of the room. A rat? I shivered. I'd seen my share of rats in the shop, of course, but I hated the things. The thought of little pink feet scampering over me while I was chained up—well, it made the urge to urinate even more pressing, I can tell you.

I peered into the darkness, however, and could just make out another figure—not shackled, as I was, but sitting in the dust with their knees drawn up to their chest, which is what had made them difficult to discern at first.

It was the feet I had heard rustling in the sawdust. I could see them squirming about, toes white with cold. A fellow prisoner, I guessed, and I wondered how they had stayed so still all that time. Someone who was used to remaining quiet and unnoticed, I supposed.

"Who are you?" I asked, loudly enough that the sound of my own voice startled me.

The shuffling stopped. The feet drew in closer to the body again. I wondered why the other prisoner was not chained, as I was.

My senses had been deadened by my time spent asleep—if you could call it that—but they stirred enough now for me to smell the sweet stink of body odor coming off my roommate. It mingled with my own nervous sweat and the mustiness of the sawdust to create a cocktail of scents that, if I had to bottle and label it, I would have called "Fear."

"Don't be frightened," I said helplessly, having no idea whether the figure was frightened or not, as I couldn't see their face. *I* was frightened, however, and I suppose I was trying to comfort myself.

The other prisoner shuffled themselves forward a little on their bottom, just enough for the dim light from the tiny window to illuminate them.

It was a girl, as far as I could tell. I'm not much good at judging the ages of sprouts, as I think I've said before, but if I had to take a guess, I would say she was perhaps seven or eight years old, judging from the level of wary intelligence in her eyes, but undernourished enough that she could have passed for five. She had a small, heart-shaped face surrounding big eyes, with petals of darkness underneath them, and skinny ankles protruded from her grubby, oversized dress.

The girl looked over at me without much interest, seemingly so resigned to her fate that she didn't even look frightened. I was just one more potential threat in a lifetime of potential threats, and her flat stare told me I was by no means the worst of them.

"Why are you here?" I asked. I couldn't imagine that such

242

a waif could have committed much of a crime. Stealing food from a market stall, maybe, or picking pockets—that would be the extent of it. Certainly nothing bad enough to warrant being locked up in the palace dungeon.

She kept her mouth pressed shut and did not answer me, but her filthy toes twitched a little. The nails on them were ragged. Their uneven edges caught the light, what little of it there was.

"I'm Foss," I said. "What's your name?"

"Millie," she said, so quietly that I almost didn't catch it.

"And what are you doing here, Millie?"

"*They* told me to wait," she said, placing a sinister emphasis on *they*.

"Who are *they*?" I asked.

She did not answer.

"Do your parents know where you are?" I tried.

"I don't have any," she said.

She was a street urchin, it was clear. That haunted little face and the ragged clothes; that elderly way of shrugging off fear and resigning yourself to your fate.

A terrible thought occurred to me. I remembered the portrait hanging in the sorcerer's room and the face of a little boy who had that same air of old-soul resignation about him.

"When did you come here, Millie?" I asked.

Another shrug. "I'm not sure. They bring me food sometimes."

I tried to tell myself I was jumping to conclusions, that she could be here for any number of reasons, but it made terrible sense, after what the sorcerer had told me. Easy enough for the king to buy another child off the streets, or lure one in with the promise of food and a place to sleep, as he might have bought the boy in Sylvester's portrait.

I didn't know what dark alchemy turned these gaunt, hollow-eyed children into gorgeous magic-workers, but it seemed like

243

none of the child itself survived the process. Quiet, world-weary Millie would die, essentially, and a beautiful sorceress would be born from her ashes.

Perhaps the new sorceress would wonder a little about the child who had given her life, as Sylvester did, but mere nostalgia seemed a poor exchange for a real life fully lived, even if it was a meager, short, and lonely one.

"Do they treat you well?" I prodded. Surely, they wouldn't abuse the child if she was going to become one of their own.

"I get food," she said again. She seemed to be entirely focused on food to the exclusion of everything else, but I suppose that was natural for a sprout who'd been foraging on the streets for most of her tender years.

Being indoors with a regular supply of victuals and water was probably enough, after her experiences, to put up with all manner of oddities and strange folks.

"How long have I been here?" I asked next.

"Not long," she answered. "I don't know. I've been asleep. I woke up and you were here."

The light coming through the slit of the window grate now had a cold, daylight quality, and I supposed it must be the next day. I had been unconscious for several hours, then.

I wondered again where Cornelius was, and hoped that he was safe and had found shelter. It was likely. He was a cat, after all, in a city that was teeming with food and potential hiding places. Still, I missed him.

I was not surprised when the heavy door opened on a waft of honeysuckle-scented air to admit one of the sorceresses, but I was relieved to see it wasn't Clarissa.

The room seemed to glow as soon as the magic-worker stepped in, and even Millie's sharp little face took on a sort of beauty in the reflected light. As usual, when confronted with one of the magic-workers, I felt a queasy blend of inferiority and mindless adoration.

This one had black hair as rich and iridescent as oil, and eyes like copper coins. Although she and Clarissa looked nothing alike, there was an affinity between their two faces that I could not explain: not just the unnatural gorgeousness, but an exquisite ferocity, an unidentifiable sense of threat that set the heart to beating faster.

And yet I was drawn to her—wanted to draw near to her as you would creep toward the warmth and light of a fire.

The sorceress looked at me with disgust. The ugly expression sat oddly on her beauty, like a skin forming on custard, and let me better shake off her spell and force my face from gaping with awe into something more like a glare.

Millie shuffled herself back against the wall and turned her shoulder to me, seeing that I was in disgrace with the pretty sorceress, and distancing herself from her disapproval. Millie was under their spell, for certain.

"*You*," the sorceress said to me, with loathing.

"Me," I said, agreeably, striving to keep myself from smiling at her. There was still that terrible instinct to please, to worship. I was a mouse mesmerized by a cat, a ferret paralyzed by the sweep of an owl's wings above. She stood there and stared at me, flexing her long fingers with their pointed nails.

"Does Sylvester know I'm here?" I asked her.

"*Sylvester*," she spat, "knows nothing. That is why we are in this ridiculous situation in the first place."

Ridiculous, indeed, because even though I knew I was chained to the wall and probably about to be butterflied like a piece of meat, I still felt a surge of *specialness* and, yes, joy, to be in her presence and to be the object of her undivided attention. I could have slapped her just for that.

Would they ever just leave me alone, these magic-workers? Was my heart to be pushed and pulled and worried about by them until the end of my days (which was probably rapidly approaching)?

"Why am I here?" I demanded. "Why not just let me leave? I was trying to go home. I would have been out of your pretty hair for good."

She gave me another flat stare.

"If it were up to us, you'd be dead already."

"Charming."

"The king wants you here and alive," she said, giving me a look that indicated I should consider it an honor that he bothered with me at all. For a moment, I almost believed it was an honor myself—that's how powerful her presence was. I could look at her and know she was a monster, but still want to throw myself on her bosom and have her stroke my hair.

"What am I here for, then?" I asked. "If he's not going to kill me."

"I didn't say he wasn't," she said. "He just wouldn't let *us* do it."

Oh.

"And he will likely do it soon," she added, "because we will all be riding out before long. Enjoy your last few hours."

The sorceress turned on her heel and left the room. It was sudden and left me disappointed, as I was ready for a good fight. I had hoped she would stand there and explain, even out of spite, exactly what was happening, but I supposed I would have to wait.

My bladder, sadly, didn't have that patience. Frightened, and not knowing when it would be able to relieve itself somewhere respectable, it loosened and spilled itself all over the floor under me, until I sat in a pungent, yellow puddle with islands of mushy sawdust floating about in it. Just one more shame to add to the mounting list.

Millie drew her ragged skirts away from the spread of it, but surreptitiously, as if she didn't want me to know she had noticed. That small kindness wrenched at me, from someone in such dire straits themselves, and a child at that.

From the looks of the stone and straw in one corner, now that I could see better with the daylight, she too had been reduced to relieving herself almost where she sat. That bastard the king wasn't content with snatching sprouts and slicing them up to make sorceresses, or however he did it—he treated them like animals in the process it seemed.

"Wasn't she *pretty*," gushed Millie, startling me. Her little face was glowing. She gave a great, gusty sigh, as if yearning after the sorceress.

"Handsome is as handsome does," I heard myself say. One of Da's sayings.

"They're so *shiny*," said Millie.

"They're not to be trusted," I said, more sharply than I had intended. "Do you hear me? Don't trust them."

Millie recoiled, folding into herself, her face going still again.

"I'm sorry," I said. I had been too harsh. If a grown adult fell under their spell as easy as winking, how much more deeply would a little girl fall in love with the beautiful ladies? Especially a little girl who had seen few shiny, beautiful things in her short life, and probably saw in these women the sort of sweet and pretty mother she had dreamed of having since she was little. I know I had had the same dream, once upon a time, although I had never mentioned my missing of my mother to Da for fear of hurting his feelings.

I don't know how long I sat there in my own filth—it was hard to gauge time down there, especially with the last groggy dregs of magic oozing out of my mind—but after some time had passed, a fellow in a fancy uniform came and unshackled me. Millie watched expressionlessly as he turned a key in the metal at my wrists and ankles.

"Wait," I told him when he hauled me to my feet. I held out my hand to Millie.

"Come with me," I said, more from desperation than any hope I would actually be able to help her. "I'll take you away from here."

"Girl stays," said the guard.

Millie shrank back from me, tucking her bare feet under her skirts, flicking an apprehensive glance at the guard. I didn't know what exactly I planned to do if she came with me, but I felt a desperate need to keep my eyes on her and, therefore, somehow, stop whatever horrific thing the king had planned.

"I am a friend, I promise," I said to her, wondering how frightening a sight I was to the small child in my current state—filthy and half-dressed, and stinking of my own urine. I wouldn't trust me, either.

"Please," I said, trying not to let my desperation creep into my voice. "I'll make sure you're safe." *Somehow.* "You're not safe here. I'm sorry I was short with you before."

"Girl stays," repeated the guard, grasping me by the arm and pulling me after him. Millie kept staring at me with her big eyes.

"I will come back for you," I told her as I was pulled away, but the words rang hollow.

The guard very determinedly avoided looking me in the eye as he led me out of the dungeon and up several flights of stone steps, and I was very conscious of the stench of urine that wafted up to him from my soiled skirts. Still, he probably de-served it.

Just as Sylvester's House had been unmistakably a part of its master, I could sense the character of the king all around me. The palace was made of the usual human materials, as far as I could tell, but there was a sharp, cold quality to it all.

The stones were laid in thin, vertical lines, and the width of the steps up which the guard was pulling me felt pinched and ungenerous, with cunning little pits and bumps placed perfectly for tripping. I stumbled up thousands of them, it felt like, the guard gripping my upper arm so hard that I could almost feel his fingerprints impressing themselves onto my skin.

We walked on, and the absence of any other human began to nag at me—just at the back of my mind, at first, and then becoming more and more prominent as we passed through dozens of rooms and passageways without seeing another living soul.

I had imagined that courts would be full of people: the king himself, of course, but also all sorts of courtiers, ladies-in-waiting, seneschals, guards . . . Where were all the servants, even? The guard who had brought me out of the dungeon was the only such person I had seen.

I knew that servants, especially those of very high nobility, were meant to stay out of sight as much as possible, but I would have expected to run across at least one under-housemaid or a scurrying pageboy. I neither saw nor heard so much as a whisker of anyone. It became eerie.

The guard was silent, and all I could hear was the slap of our footsteps on bare stone, turning to a soft shushing when we crossed carpet. We spiraled up and up through the palace, until I wondered whether he was trying to walk me in circles so that I wouldn't be able to find my way back.

Finally, we reached the end of the last hallway—not black and stark, like Sylvester's, but paneled in rich wood and hung with tapestries—and faced an ornate door. He pushed me through it.

Another long, unfriendly corridor, and another door, and

then I was in a surprisingly luxurious room: a reception room of some kind, with a large, long table surrounded by perhaps a score of chairs, uncomfortable-looking sofas against the walls, and a puce carpet that prickled at my bootless feet.

Unusually for a room like this (I thought, at least, although who knew what royalty got up to behind closed doors), there were more shackles set into the walls, and the guard fastened me into them again.

I had recovered myself enough by now to feel thirsty, my whole body shriveled up with the want of water, and when he offered me a skin of cheap wine, I drank it gratefully—if clumsily, without the use of my hands—feeling it spill over my face as he tipped it into my mouth.

His face twisted in disgust as he poured out the skin, but I did not care. I was so grateful to have the liquid; I felt myself coming to life again, like a plant greening in the rain. After that, he left me alone and seemed relieved to do so.

This room was more comfortable than the dungeon, at least, and although there were no windows, the guard had left a lamp burning, so I could look around at the unwelcoming furniture at my leisure. After an hour or so, I had memorized every ugly but intricate pattern of the various upholsteries.

I could have been there for hours. I slept for a while again, I know, because I encountered those old dreams about the vines and the long, black corridor. The patterns of the vines got tangled up with the ugly botanical embroidery on the fancy couches and sent me wandering through tunnels of misshapen maroon flowers and bulging velvet fruits. Even so, it was a relief to dream again after that stretch of nothingness the night before.

When I woke, there was still no sign of Cornelius, which I hoped was still a good thing. I found I had wet myself again, which wasn't a good thing at all, but seemed unavoidable. The thirst was back, along with the ever-present heartsickness, and now hunger had joined it—a gnawing, painful hunger that made it feel like my belly was sticking to my backbone. My mouth became very dry again, so that I could feel every contour and detail of my tongue, palate, and teeth without the softening of saliva, which was a lot more unpleasant than it sounds, I can tell you.

Eventually, the black-haired sorceress returned—but she was not alone this time. She sashayed in with ten others, differing in the color of their skin, hair, and eyes, but essentially just the same, with that same power to entice and enchant.

They filed into the room in a line, bringing sunshine with them, as I sat helplessly and stared. There were as many different colors among them as a bed of wildflowers, from slippers to shining headdresses, and the effect was dazzling.

All of them together were overwhelming. I adored them, haplessly, helplessly. I was bathed in a love that was motherly, sisterly, and loverlike, all at once, rocked by the gentle waves of an ocean composed of eyes in shades of gray, green, blue, brown, and hazel, and strands of hair that were golden, chestnut, brilliant red, and equally brilliant iridescent black. All sisters.

How could we not have noticed this before, back in the village? It seemed so obvious, now, seeing them together. I could not distinguish the sorceress I had met earlier from the other black-haired ones. That was how similar they were.

I searched for Clarissa among their ranks, but she was absent. And where was Sylvester? Why was he not among them?

"This is the girl?" said one.

"Yes," said another.

I felt the burn of eleven pairs of perfect eyes assessing me for specialness and coming up with nothing. They could have harvested me in a second, all of them.

251

"Father is coming," said one of them.

"He'll deal with her."

I felt dizzy, drugged, drunk. Their perfume and their presence filled me up like wine in a glass, so that there was no room for anything else. I felt myself smiling a wide, foolish smile. False well-being warmed all my limbs and fluttered in my stomach. It reminded me of those old tales of mortals who wander into a faerie glade, eat the enchanted fruit, and find themselves dancing until their feet become bloody stumps. The sorceresses gazed at me with loathing, and I gazed back with servile adoration.

Through my haze of enchantment, I noticed two more people enter the room: a final sorceress, this one with hair as yellow as a sweet lemon—Clarissa!—and a man.

Of course, I knew it was the king at once. Every public establishment in the kingdom has a painting of him on a wall somewhere, copied from the one perfect oil painting that I assumed resided in his palace.

Some were good copies, but others made him look like a goat in a robe—and those, I was discovering now, were possibly more accurate than the perfected versions.

He wore a gown that could have been an elaborate cake, it was so curlicued and decorated, set all about with bright jewels and woven with glinting, heavy thread. His headdress must have been a foot tall, wobbling about up there like a dab of cream on a jelly. And I had thought the sorceresses' gowns were elaborate! I had no idea how they all moved about in those contraptions.

My head cleared a little as I looked at him, because he was certainly no unearthly beauty. Quite ordinary-looking, in fact, aside from the magnificent garb—and his shadow, thrown on the wall behind him by the lamplight, behaved strangely, seeming larger and more complicated than it should have been, and moving a little more than it should.

Clarissa flickered her green glance over me. I saw triumph there, and spite. Despite my bedazzlement, I roused myself enough to say, "Where is your brother?"

She smiled and said nothing. The king waved her over to the table and then walked to where I knelt chained to the stone wall.

His eyes were colorless and clouded, as if by cataracts, and his head moved with snappish speed as he looked this way and that. He could have been an automaton, for all the human warmth he exuded. Even his skin was colorless, shadowed almost blue under his jaw and in the gaunt hollows of his cheeks.

He was an unassuming, almost comical figure, if you took him at face value—skinny, pale, balding, with a pronounced belly and birdlike legs not concealed by his rich fabrics and jewels—and yet there was something about him that stopped my breath.

I suppose that was what real power felt like—not seductive, sinuous power like Clarissa's magicks, or playful, erratic power like Sylvester's, but the harsh, inhuman strength of the truest power that had spawned them both.

He smiled, showing his yellowed teeth. "You poor thing," he said, looking at my soiled underdress and general state of disarray (to put it mildly). He didn't have to speak or make a gesture; quick as thought, my underdress was as clean and fresh as the day it was made. I didn't see this as any kind of charity; he just wanted to stop me from stinking up his fancy palace.

"Why am I here?" I asked. "Why bother with me? I just wanted to go back home."

I still couldn't quite believe I was talking to the king. The actual *king*, whose (inaccurate) picture hung in every tavern and shop, glowering over me since birth. No one I knew had ever even seen him in person; he rarely went on procession and seemed to stay within the confines of the city.

Yet here he was in front of me, talking almost like a normal human being and smelling faintly of perfume that even I could tell must be expensive, with a base note of perfectly ordinary human sweat.

There was something exceptionally odd about his face, though. Not its ugliness, because I was used to ugliness, and even found it a little comforting now, after the malicious beauty of the magic-workers—but a flickering in its expressions.

It was as if two beings occupied the exact same space, rather like the House and the Other House. Flick: a goatlike old man with a discolored beard. Flick: a grinning death's head. Flick: an avuncular smile. Flick: teeth like knives in a cavernous mouth. It made me dizzy to look at him directly.

He turned away from me, which was a relief, and spoke to Clarissa. "We must begin the council meeting," he said. The sorceresses moved as one, graceful and united as blades of grass bowing to the same wind, and filed out. The king followed, and then Clarissa, who cast one last, triumphant glance at me.

Despite myself, I felt the melancholy of their absence. Their color and brightness had filled the room, heady and golden as wine in a glass, and I was left alone and depleted.

A shadow flickered. I stiffened, but it was Cornelius this time, popping out of the thin air, it seemed, and trotting over to me.

"Cornelius!"

He gave a brief nudge of his head against my calf, but then was all business.

"You have to get out of here," he said.

"Well, I know *that*."

"They're going to cut you open. I heard them talking about it."

My heart, I supposed, although if that were the case, I didn't know why they hadn't done it already. "Any ideas?" I asked, a bit snappishly.

"Think sideways," suggested Cornelius. He twitched his tail and vanished, then reappeared. "See?"

"That would work here?" I felt a swelling of hope, which I quickly tamped down. There was no room for hope, only surety.

"Of course," he said. "I just did it. This is a sorcerer's house, like any other. And because it's the *absence* of magic, none of them can see it."

"Not even the king?"

"Not even him."

I took a deep breath, trying to clear away any remnants of the fog and confusion from the night before, and tried to push away my fear, exhaustion, and hunger. I didn't succeed.

It took several deep breaths, and Cornelius sitting in my lap and purring vigorously, before I was able to clear my mind enough to do the requisite twists and turns to enter that Other place.

Thinking sideways here felt entirely different. Stepping into the Other House had felt like stepping into an abandoned, but still living, place. Whatever was left under the king's palace was dead. There was a building there of some kind—I felt a floor under my feet—but the air felt stale and poisonous at once.

It reminded me of the time Da and I had helped lay out Goodwife Tilly's husband when he died, helping her wash the body, wrap it, and position it on the kitchen table. He had been a drunkard and a violent man in life, although Tilly would never admit it, and to hear her now, you would think she had married a saint on earth (although she was notably plumper and happier since he had gone).

As I had helped Da sponge his yellowing skin and thumbed his eyelids closed, I had still felt a sense of malice about him. Even in death, the husk of his body seemed imbued with a poison, a stench of who he had been in life. The Other Palace felt like that—a husk, a dead thing, but one with a lingering and wicked animus. I felt like I was feeling sick, just sitting there.

I clutched at a wall to steady myself, and it was so cold, it burned. In doing so, however, I realized that my shackles didn't hold me here, and I was free. I took some satisfaction in imagining the sorceresses coming back to see the shackles emptied, as if by magic.

"Now let's go," urged Cornelius, appearing beside me. His fur rose along his spine, and his tail turned into a bottlebrush. Clearly this place was as comfortable for him as it was for me.

"Not yet," I said.

"Are you mad?"

"I have to find a heart," I said, "to take to the Weftwitch, the person Basil said could mend my heart."

"They'll be back soon. They'll see that you've gone," mewed Cornelius, his tail puffing out even more.

"If I don't find a heart, I'll be just as badly off when I get out of here. I have to break the spell somehow, or I'll turn around and come right back."

Cornelius huffed out an irritated breath. "Fine," he relented.

"Can you help me find one?" I asked.

"I can help you find hundreds. They're stinking up the whole place."

"What?"

"There's a room full of them. I can smell it, rotting away down there."

"Can you find it? Can you take me there?"

He snorted, as if that should be obvious, and started walking, tail up. "Come on," he said, without turning.

Walking through the king's Other Palace was no picnic. I felt blind—even though shadows of the walls, floor, and ceiling remained—because it was so difficult to think, let alone see, through the sickly miasma. I might as well have been wandering through one of the city sewers.

I concentrated on Cornelius's upright tail, like a soldier focuses on his flag bearer in the midst of battle chaos, until I grew somewhat used to it, and the sickness eased enough for me to look about a bit.

It was still recognizably the palace, and so I suppose there had been a fairly solid castle here onto which the king had simply superimposed his magic, rather than a chaotic and overgrown mess like Sylvester's House that had strangled the structure beneath. All the rooms seemed to still be there, just a little shadowed, with an odd halo around the edges of all they contained.

I discovered quickly where all the servants had been lurking. Evidently, the king didn't like to see the commoners wandering about his palace, for there were doors hidden behind tapestries that led to a rabbit warren of narrow, evil-smelling corridors and rickety back stairs, the ceilings almost black with lamp smoke.

There were no windows that I could see, and so I imagined the servants breathed the sooty air in all day, every day, scurrying about in the dark and stink like a panicked litter of mole pups.

Plenty of them passed by us, and through us, because here in the Other Palace, they were as insubstantial as the choking smoke that was probably blackening their lungs every working day.

I felt a chill when they passed through me, and they seemed to shiver a little as well. I wondered if they thought we were ghosts.

Like Colin, they seemed mazed and absent to varying degrees, some with a little more life in them than others, but all were clearly missing part or all of their hearts. I seemed to have developed a sense for it: sniffing out those who had been snagged, or worse.

"How much further?" I asked.

"It's right down underneath everything," said Cornelius. For a moment, he became a shadow cat as he passed back through to the king's palace to snap up a slice of ham one of the kitchen maids had dropped, and then he reappeared in the Other Palace with it lolling from his mouth like an oversized tongue. A manservant that had been about to trip over Cornelius righted himself and looked about for a moment, puzzled, before continuing.

There were definite advantages to being a cat. No one batted an eye at a cat wandering about the palace—I'm sure they had dozens, official and unofficial, for the inevitable army of rats that lived in any such large household. And no one batted an eye at a cat suddenly disappearing, either. It was just what they did.

I was starting to feel dizzy again from the noxious air. I made my way down another few flights of steps. The scurrying of shadowed servants increased the farther down we went, and I felt their rush and urgency even from the Other Palace, shivering the air around us like a heat haze. Something was clearly going on down there.

"Are you sure we're going the right way?" I asked Cornelius, whispering even though no one could hear us. He shot me a look of utter contempt over one shoulder.

At the base of the last staircase was a door, humble, as befitted a servants' entrance. Everyone who entered and left through it closed it very carefully behind them.

"That's it," said Cornelius.

I had imagined the Room of Hearts as some dank and secret cellar, not a thoroughfare. I pushed against the door of the Other Palace, and it opened sure enough, but into nothing.

The shadow servants passed through us with trays full of food and glasses, setting the air to shimmering, but the ones who went into the nothingness just disappeared. There must be a banquet taking place in the room.

"It must not exist here, whatever it is," said Cornelius. "I can still smell it, though. It's that strong."

I supposed that made sense. Somewhere that stored that many hearts, if Cornelius was right, was bound to be warded with powerful magicks and perhaps entirely made of the stuff. So, I would have to pass back to the king's palace in order to find it.

Cornelius could probably pass unnoticed as one of the palace cats, and the worst that could happen to him was being shooed away. I, on the other hand, could hardly stumble in wearing my shift, appearing out of thin air.

I stood in the doorway and thought, shivering now and then as the servants passed through me. Dozens of them. Scores, even. They had probably called in extra help for the occasion, because this seemed like an excessively large staff, even for the palace. That gave me an idea.

"Can you take me to the kitchen?" I asked Cornelius. Silly question—he could sniff out bacon anywhere.

We wended our way through the labyrinth of back stairs until we reached the kitchens—a vast and bustling space, fogged with steam, that probably felt warm and muggy and smelled wonderful on the other side of whatever barrier we had crossed.

Cornelius and I found the busiest, steamiest spot where we would least likely be noticed. I took a deep breath and managed to sidle my way into the king's palace again, bumping into a thick-armed cook who was elbowing her way to the sink.

"Watch it!" she said sharply, but otherwise gave me nary a second glance. I fit in down here, among the plainly dressed, harried, and sweating kitchen maids—as I had hoped—and everyone was far too busy with what seemed to be a grand banquet to be concerned with me.

I spotted a mobcap and apron drying over the range and snatched them up quick as winking; with the apron tied over my underdress, it could pass for a servant's outer garment if no one looked too closely.

My bare feet I could do nothing about, but the dress brushed the floor and hid them well enough. Cornelius kept close to my heels.

I saw the finished plates for the banquet lined up and waiting on a long table, resplendent with elaborate garnishes and fiddly bits of decoration. I grabbed the nearest one and did my best to blend into the hustle and bustle, as if I was just another servant taking a dish to the banquet.

When I entered the Room of Hearts this time, I took a deep breath and pulled the mobcap a little lower on my head. Because of that, I couldn't get a good look around at first. I followed the line of servants to the great, shining tables that lined the walls, groaning with food waiting to be served.

Most were dropping off their trays and immediately scurrying back to the door behind the tapestry to fetch another, but some were doing complicated-looking finishing touches on the plates, so I hovered by the table and tried to look busy and purposeful.

Under the cap, I was sweating profusely. When I had calmed a little, I dared to look up. And saw absolutely no hearts. All I saw was a large banquet hall, dark and ornate. An ordinary room—for a palace.

I looked about at ankle level for Cornelius but couldn't see him. He might not have followed me in. His nose couldn't have been wrong, surely—this had to be where the hearts were kept. Why else would this room have been inaccessible from the Other Palace if it contained nothing more eldritch than a ridiculously long table? I would have to wait, and watch, and hope that I could find some way to find them.

The king and his daughters were already seated, most looking bored or impatient, some *rat-tat-tat*ting their long nails on the polished wood. I quickly turned my face down again, lest the sorceresses' beauty enchant me . . . or lest they recognize me.

Was this the meeting Clarissa had talked about, to which all the magic-workers were to bring their harvest? It was certainly a bit grander than I had imagined from her description.

And was this where they planned to bring me, their little prisoner that they still imagined safely shackled to the wall? Was I to be some kind of grand finale to the sharing of the harvest, like a primitive sacrifice? Was Clarissa going to finally rip out my heart in front of all her sisters? It seemed a tad excessive to throw a party for it when she could have done the job just as efficiently behind closed doors. And why wasn't Sylvester here?

When the king and his daughters had been served with goblets of clear, honey-yellow wine and plates of cut fruit, more servants began to pour in, all with the absent looks of those under the sorceresses' spell—a good thing for me, because I could lose myself among them.

They came bearing great wooden chests with brass handles, which they stacked against one of the walls until it was almost completely covered. I could not count them all, but I would guess there were at least a couple dozen of them.

The last servant to enter bearing a chest was Colin. I was glad to see him alive, I suppose, but he might have been better off if he had died with the rest of the Snagged.

More thralls followed him and lined up against the walls in their dozens.

I looked about. The kitchen servants had slipped away, their job apparently done for now, and only the thralls were left to serve the banquet and perform whatever doubtless sinister duties the magic-workers commanded. I mimicked their distant stares as best I could.

When all the chests were in place, Clarissa stood and walked with a sense of ceremony to the one Colin had brought in. She lifted the lid. I craned to see as best I could while still keeping my face in shadow, although I already suspected what would be inside.

I saw jars, stacked neatly, as many as if someone had been busy turning their strawberry harvest into jam. Instead of preserves or pickles, though, each one that I could see contained that same yellowish oil, and a heart.

Some were whole, and looked like the hearts I saw in the butcher's shop back home. Some looked like the little, wizened one I had found in the square. Some were partial, cut in half or smaller. Some were little more than nuggets of flesh. All were floating in that golden, viscous liquid, something like dirty honey.

More chests, and more, and more, each filled with a clinking, sloshing mass of jars. Hundreds. Thousands, maybe.

"It's more than we have ever harvested before," announced Clarissa, taking out one of the jars and turning it in her hand. The heart inside revolved slowly, looking like a hairless baby bird. "As you can see, Father, we have all worked hard."

The king stood and walked along the line of chests, opening one here and there to glance inside, then continuing to stroll with his hands clasped behind his back. The sorceresses watched him. When he came to the end of the line, he turned.

"It is not enough," he said.

Clarissa seemed startled. "It is all we could take," she said. "If we had harvested any more, the people would revolt. We cannot take too much from each person, from each village. They would notice. They would rebel. This is already more than we would bring to you in a year or more."

"And yet it is not enough," said the king. He tapped a long, yellow fingernail against the glass of one of the jars. It gave off a hollow *clonk clonk*, its resonance dulled by the oil inside.

He then did something I couldn't quite see, something that made his heavy coat lift and settle as if caught by a gust, and then the whole back wall of the room seemed to rush away into the distance, as if a hand had whisked it away like a cloth, revealing an immense chamber beyond. I braced myself for a room of nightmares—blood, needles, even a butcher's block where humans would be chopped up like so much meat.

It was nothing like that. It was a wide, utilitarian room— more like a barn than the sort of room you would find in a palace, if a barn were the size of a cathedral.

Several bright lamps placed on a long, plain table near the front of the room gave some light, but the room stretched out so far to either side that the light of the lamps faded into darkness long before it hit the far walls, wherever they were.

There were scores of rows of shelves, and dozens of long tables between each, and all of them were crowded with jars of varying sizes, thousands upon thousands of them. They were filled with hearts. Of course they were. Each column of shelves went all the way up to the high ceilings and stretched the length of the room, groaning under the mass of the jars.

I couldn't even begin to guess how many were there— thousands upon thousands upon thousands, as I said—and each of them had once been a person, or part of a person, with wants and wishes, and a warm body, and the right to grow old and die naturally rather than being gutted like pigs for a holiday feast. I forgot to hide my face as I stared, but none of the thralls around me reacted at all.

The sorceresses gasped and murmured among themselves. There was something wrong with nearly all the hearts that we could see. Some looked like the fresh jars brought in by the servants, but most of them did not. The thick, golden liquid that kept them floating was only halfway up the jar, or less, rather than filling it to the lid, and the space above was furred with a powdery green mold, the texture of a moth's wing.

All about me, overwhelming even the sorceresses' sweet perfume, was the stink of decay, a scent like vinegar, like fruit fallen to the ground, and like spoiled meat, all at once. No wonder Cornelius had been able to sniff this place out through who-knew-how-many thick stone walls.

"I knew it was bad, but I had no idea it was as bad as this," said Clarissa.

"And it is spreading, no matter what I do," said the king unemotionally. "The hearts you have brought today will replace some of the store, but as you can see, they rot as rapidly as I can replace them. And the kingdom rots with them."

"What if they were stored somewhere else?" asked another sorceress. "If the tainted jars are separated from the new?"

"It makes no difference," said the king. "The corruption is not spreading from one to the other as they touch. Somehow, it is in the hearts themselves, even those that have been here for a hundred years."

"Then how?" cried Clarissa. "How is that possible? The jars are sealed with magic, protected by magic wards! Nothing should be able to touch them!"

"It is a magic-made sickness, but I know not by whom," said the king. He clasped his hands behind his back and rocked a little on his feet, surveying the vast storeroom of corrupted hearts. "I have used all my skills to try to find out what exactly is causing this, and how to stop it. But even with my centuries of knowledge, I have found nothing. How any magic but my own could possibly have entered the kingdom, I do not know."

The sorceresses murmured among themselves, sweet as

a morning chorus, if you didn't know what they were talking about.

"Luckily," he said, "Clarissa has discovered that Sylvester's little pet has some kind of resistance to magic. She is harder to bespell, and appeared to lose none of her heart at all when Sylvester accidentally caught her in his enchantment, leaving her untouched by the mold. If we can't stop the corruption from spreading, we can at least inoculate new hearts against it, using whatever we can find out from hers."

Resistance? That was something to chew on later, when I had time to think. Certainly, Sylvester hadn't actually taken any of my heart with his wayward spell: just hooked it like a fish on a line. If I had been more susceptible to enchantment, would his magic have torn out a piece? Would I be like Nat or Jol right now?

"For now, we will keep these new hearts separate from the others, and hope that we will be able to treat them with that inoculation. Even if we are able to replicate whatever it is that gives this girl her resistance, however, we have lost far too many hearts for this harvest to be enough. We are losing a century's worth of them, or more."

The sorceresses were silent.

Only Clarissa spoke up. "It is impossible to replace that many," she said. "And without them, we will never be able to keep the kingdom protected."

"Protected? My dear, we won't even be able to keep it *alive*. And it is not impossible," said the king. "Just costly."

"You have always told us to keep the balance," said another one of the sorceresses. "We can't take too many."

"We shall start at the outskirts of the kingdom," said the king. "We need fresh meat and produce to supplement our magic, and the closest farms and villages can bring it to us much quicker. We need as many workers there as possible. Farther out, we don't require such a . . . dense population."

"We could survive without the food," said Clarissa.

"*We* could, for a time, but the city folk wouldn't last as long on our enchanted produce before their bodies needed the real thing. And what is a king with no subjects?"

A moment of silence—and then Clarissa said, "Then we must take the girl's heart as soon as possible, before we leave, or all our efforts will be in vain."

"I quite agree, my dear," said the king.

He turned, and his eyes fixed directly on my face. And he smiled.

CHAPTER 17

Stupid. I should have run when I had the chance, dealt with the heartsickness. Then, even though I would never have been healed, I would at least have been able to see Da one more time before I succumbed. And it had been such a faint hope, taking a heart to the Weftwitch—even fainter now that I had seen the state of them.

I made a convulsive movement, thinking to at least attempt to run, but there was a spell upon me that had me frozen to the spot. I felt even more of a fool standing there in my mobcap and apron, and the underdress beneath, in front of the richly dressed magic-workers. I wondered again where Cornelius had gotten to.

I had a feeling the king had known I had been here all along and had let me see what I had seen deliberately. To what end, I had no idea.

"And here she is," he said.

The sorceresses glared at me collectively, like one creature with many limbs and eyes—a malevolent spider. The thralls moved nary a muscle. I tried desperately to will myself into the

Other Palace again—but of course, it didn't exist here in the Room of Hearts, and there was nowhere to go.

"Clever of you, my dear, to find a way out of your bonds," the king said to me, "but I am aware of all that goes on in my palace. All the layers of it. It will not work again. I'm afraid I need you. You are going to prove crucial to the kingdom's survival, if that is of any comfort."

I glared at him. Glaring was about all I could do, as it didn't require movement.

"Of course, first your heart has to be extracted. Clarissa has volunteered. In fact, she seemed eager for the task." The king smiled at her, exposing those terrible teeth again.

Where was Sylvester? I wondered again. Was he slumped in his throne room, playing with some frivolous magic? Did he know what was happening, or even care? Clarissa smiled at me, more a baring of teeth than a true smile.

"I will return when you have finished, my dear," said the king, letting one hand rest on the smooth slope of her shoulder. She shuddered a little under his touch, but did not drop her gaze from mine.

They all rose from the table. When the king and his personal servants had filed out, followed by the sorceresses and their thralls, the room felt even more vast than before. Only Colin remained, and he stood expressionless as Clarissa walked over to me.

After a moment, she reached out with those long fingers and I flinched, but she was merely releasing me from the spell. I couldn't help flopping over when I was freed. My bones felt like they were made of ice that had suddenly melted.

She let me sprawl there and nodded to Colin, who came over to me and heaved me up from under the armpits, in an odd reversal of our position from the day before. I muttered, "That's gratitude for you," but I wasn't sure he even heard me.

Clarissa sashayed over to the storeroom. Colin walked me over to a large, slanted board fixed to the floor with metal struts. There was some kind of mechanism beneath it, perhaps to adjust its angle, and metal cuffs placed where hands and feet would be. It didn't take much imagination or intellect to figure out where I was about to end up. Colin lifted me onto the board and clicked shut the cuffs. Nearby, an assortment of unpleasantly sharp and pointy instruments were laid out on one of the long tables, and Clarissa busied herself with them.

"What are those for?" I bit out. "I thought you'd just pluck my heart out with your fingers."

"Nothing would give me more pleasure," said Clarissa without looking at me. "Your heart requires more precision, however, now that we know its worth."

"So, what's going to happen to me?" I asked. "I'm going to have the heart carved out of me and stuck in one of those smelly jars?"

"Not quite that crudely," Clarissa answered. "But, essentially, yes. Eventually."

My stomach lurched.

"It isn't that bad," she said. "You won't miss it."

Part of me wondered if this was true. After all, my heart hadn't been much use to me since Sylvester came along. Perhaps having the whole thing removed would take away whatever pain was left and stop me yearning after him. It might be worth ending up like Dav, who had about as much life now as one of his own dead fish, in exchange for being rid of that tugging, shameful pain. Clarissa saw me considering it.

"It is not so dreadful, what we do," she said. "It keeps all of you safe, for a price. You have no idea of the horrors beyond our borders. The invaders we beat back. The armies we keep from your doorstep."

"So, our hearts are taxes, then?" I argued, trying to keep the quiver from my voice. "Why not cut off our fingers and toes while you're at it? Why not dice up our livers, or pop the noses right off our faces?"

"So dramatic," she murmured. She reached out to stroke one of the jars. "With these many hearts, you can summon armies of which no other kingdom could dream. Or at least you could when they were whole and well." She licked her lips, as if unconsciously savoring the flavor of such a heart. I recoiled.

"They are so powerful, in fact, that we have to store them as you see—in these jars, and then in this room with thick stone walls, and powerful wards placed upon it. Even then, despite our best efforts, some of the power still radiates out." She looked around her.

"An unfortunate side effect of our work is that the presence of so many human hearts stored for magical purposes here in the city stunts the growth of our plants and animals. So, we grow our food elsewhere, and bring it in. That has been becoming more difficult, lately, as the blight has been spreading to outlying villages as the hearts decay, contaminating the food. We have had to use more magically created to compensate, but the human body needs more than we are able to create, long-term. Obviously, this is not a state of affairs that can be allowed to continue." She sighed, and rolled her shoulders a little, as if to relax them. "You'll understand, then, why the king finds you so interesting."

"Not really," I said.

"No? Finding out what exactly causes your resistance to our magic would be invaluable to us in protecting other hearts in our store. Perhaps in healing some of those already affected, as well. That should please you."

"Where is Sylvester?" I asked Clarissa, as I had asked her father. Maybe someone would finally give me a straight answer.

She snorted. "Not here," she said. "And he probably never will be again."

My stomach roiled. "What do you mean?"

She rolled back her sleeves in a businesslike manner, and picked up a strangely shaped knife from the table. I strained against the bonds, but they held fast. I could not even try to escape to the Other Palace—this room existed in an entirely magical place that I hadn't been able to reach from there, and there was no comfortingly mundane human dwelling concealed beneath it.

"What do you mean?" I asked her, louder.

"Sylvester has disappointed Father," she answered. "Grievously." She shrugged. "It was clear he was a lost cause. Luckily, we have already found a replacement."

Millie. I thought of all the king's experiments—each one a human child, to be dissected and stitched back together into an abomination. I didn't know how exactly he went about creating a sorceress out of a street child, but all the ideas with which my imagination supplied me were horrifying.

"What's going to happen to him?" I said sharply.

"He will be disposed of, like all the other experiments that fail," she said lightly. "Poor boy. I tried my best."

I allowed a little venom to spill into my voice. "It didn't sound like you and Sylvester parted on the best of terms."

"My brother is stubborn," she said, "and tender-hearted. He gets . . . attached to things. It is my job to remind him that we cannot afford attachments—not in our position."

"The position where you rip my heart out? No, I suppose not."

She smiled a gentle, sympathetic smile, wide and sweet. It took all my effort to resist her magic and remind myself that she was a monster, not a mother.

"I think he was a little sentimental about you," mused Clarissa. "Well, he is very young, after all, and still a little squeamish about our work."

She was moving toward me, slowly, speaking softly, as you approach a horse you don't want to startle. Her wide skirts swayed like the sound bow of a bell, rustling and releasing a faint, teasing perfume.

I couldn't get any further away from her without melting into the planks. All the skin on my front felt like it was trying to crawl round to the back, as far away as possible. It was an interesting sensation that I didn't care to have repeated.

"Come," she said. "I will make it quick and painless. It will be better than living here and longing for him, day after day." Her gaze flickered from my head to my toes. "He would never have touched you, you know."

"I know that," I said, too quickly.

"We do use our thralls that way, sometimes. Colin is one such. We keep them, for a little while, before discarding them, in almost the same manner that we keep our servants . . . although with other, sweeter duties. I'm sure my brother would have availed himself of that little perk with one of his thralls, some time or another. But it would not have been with you, poor thing."

Her voice was warm, sympathetic. Loving. The voice I would have wanted my mother to have. The voice I had imagined my mother having. I had felt guilty thinking about her, a little, because my da had tried so hard to be mam and da both for me, but a girl can't help wondering what her mam would have been like.

For a moment, the sorceress seemed like everything I had wanted: a kind and beautiful woman who loved me and wanted the best for me, giving me the best advice she could, even though she knew it might hurt me to hear it . . .

No. I shook my head a little, involuntarily, to clear it. She was not kind. She did not love me, nor want the best for me. She was a sorceress who wanted me harvested, gone, *dead*, and she was coming closer, and I had stood frozen by the glamor in her voice for too long.

She was barely an arm's length from me now. Almost close enough to reach out and touch my chest with one of her long, painted nails.

"Get away from me," I said, although my voice shook. She halted and seemed a little surprised, and then smiled.

"I cannot charm you as easily as I would another, it appears," she said. "Perhaps it is your much-lauded resistance to magic— or because you have already been taken up by my brother. Interesting. Still, we have other ways."

I could smell her perfume. She had a wide, warm smile on her perfect face. I could have bitten into that smile like a cool slice of melon. I would have done anything to make that smile appear again and again. Even now, I found my own lips twitching, desperate to return the smile, to please her. Such was their power.

I felt anger boiling up beneath my awe and worship. I managed to draw enough saliva into my mouth to spit as forcefully as I could. It hit her cheek and trickled down.

"You stupid child!" she shouted. "You don't understand anything. None of you do. You sit there in your little huts and think that the world turns for your benefit."

"And you believe it turns for yours?" I retorted.

"Of course it does," she said. She came closer to me and smiled directly into my face. Despite myself, I smiled back. Then she thrust her hand into my chest, the one holding the knife.

It was a thousand, thousand times worse than the heartsickness, worse than anything I had ever felt. Not only did it hurt, but there was a terrible sense of violation, of wrongness, as if she had opened up the top of my head and rummaged about in my thoughts, then spread the worst and most shameful ones out on the ground for all the world to laugh at. Her knife-wielding hand had passed through me like a ghost, leaving the skin of my chest unblemished, but I could feel it moving about beneath my ribs.

My whole body cringed and shrank. I could not have spoken even if I had the words—my tongue had grown fat and sluggish in my mouth, and it was as much as I could do to force air into my lungs.

Clarissa pulled out the knife, which was somehow as unbloodied as before, and tossed it onto the table. Then she reached into my chest again, stirring up all that sickness and shame once more, and when she removed her hand once more I saw what looked like a perfect half of my heart in her grasp. I gagged. She turned the piece of heart over in her hands, each touch a torment.

"Please," I managed to say.

She put my heart down into a little dish on the table. I collapsed, almost sobbing. It was a relief, to no longer feel myself held by her poisonous hands, but now I felt cold and exposed.

Whatever that oil was in which the hearts floated, it obviously guarded the original owners from feeling the full pain of the missing heart, and it preserved and protected the hearts themselves, or the Snagged would have been in constant torment. I didn't know how much longer I could bear it.

"It's very interesting," she said conversationally, leaning in to examine it.

"What are you going to do with it?" I whispered.

"Merely look at it, for now," she said. "This process will take a while. I'll need to examine the other half too, of course, once we have a better understanding and can risk taking it out. And then the king will do the same."

"And you expect me to just lie here like a lump while you do so?" I gasped, still barely able to speak.

Her lips turned up in a maternal smile. "There's very little you can do about it, my dear, as you see."

She took out a little jar on a chain, full of oil, from one of her voluminous sleeves and shook it gently, then dropped the piece of my heart inside it. The agony eased immediately, but I felt my throat close with longing and revulsion.

With each pendulum swing of the jar on its little chain, the rest of my heart in my chest gave a violent lurch to one side or the other, whether from suggestion or from a real connection to my half heart, I did not know.

I kept my eyes fixed to the winking glass, terrified that she would drop it. If the jar smashed, would the piece of my heart flop about on the floor like a dying fish? Was it still alive?

"The curious thing," she said, watching it pass back and forth in front of her face, "is that there is no corruption on this at all. Not a speck. Not one spore. By now, living with Sylvester for this long, you should have been . . ."

". . . In a green puddle on the floor?" I supplied.

"You put it more colorfully than I would, but essentially, yes. Longer exposure to the magic-worker seems to hasten the process." She stopped swinging the jar and clasped it in her long fingers. "Interesting. You display a remarkable resistance, even now."

She shook it a little. I twitched involuntarily.

"You want it back?" she said. "It won't do you much good. Once it's out, it's out."

"There's no way of mending it?" I asked. I didn't really expect an honest answer, but I felt I should ask anyway, just in case.

"I'm afraid not," she replied. "And we need it more than you do, frankly."

I doubted that. But she seemed transfixed by the sway of the jar on its silver chain, peering at the bisected heart within.

I didn't realize Colin was beside me until I felt the cuffs at my wrists click open, followed by the ones around my ankles. Startled, I slid off the slanted board and to the ground, landing with an undignified "*oof*"—but I was free.

Clarissa's head snapped up, but Colin had moved toward her with astonishing speed, and grabbed her by the forearms in what I suppose was a last burst of his personhood before he succumbed to the magic forever, wresting her away from the table.

He would have been no match for her usually, but she was taken by surprise, and they struggled, moving farther away from me. I had time to back up against the instrument table and let my hand starfish out behind my back, hoping for something, anything, to fall into my fingers.

Something cold and sharp insinuated itself into my palm. I moved my fingers a little, and felt the familiar, comforting heft of a meat cleaver. I closed my hand about the handle and moved around the table to stand between it and one of the tall shelves, bracing myself for a fight.

Clarissa finally managed to wrest her arms free from her servant and then thrust them both into his chest up to her elbows, as easily as if she were plunging them into water. He bent backward in an unnaturally perfect arch, like the shape a salmon makes while leaping, and then dropped to the ground.

I could tell immediately that he was dead. His chest looked like ground meat, a mess of blood and offal. Clarissa's arms were bloody to the elbow, as if she were wearing red evening gloves.

She turned from her fallen servant and advanced on me. I leaned back involuntarily against the shelf, setting the jars rocking.

"Don't be foolish," Clarissa hissed. But the jostled jars had given me an idea. I might not be able to run or stop her from doing what she was about to do, but I could make it more un-pleasant for her at the very least. Thanking the powers that be for my butcher's muscles, I swiped my free hand along the length of the shelf, toppling all the jars that stood on it.

I can't begin to describe the noise. There was the shattering of glass, yes, but also a stomach-turning, wet, plopping, slosh-ing sound as the hearts slid free from their jars and flapped onto the floor like netted fish hauled into a boat.

Clarissa cried out, as much for the gooey mess on her fine dress as for the lost hearts, I imagined, and in that small moment, while she was distracted, I turned and ran for the door, skidding on the slimy golden liquid and trying not to look down as I heard the squish and splat of hearts underfoot.

The poor hearts had done no harm themselves, but their soft and flabby forms, partly dissolved and bleached pale by the liquid, furred with the green-gray mold, made vomit rise in my throat again.

"Stupid girl!" yelled the sorceress. "How far do you think you'll get?"

Power started to swirl around her. Hearts in nearby jars dis-integrated into dust. I could taste the metal tang of magic in the air, like a coming storm, and I turned to look behind me.

She had stretched out one arm, gorgeously sleeved and bejeweled, the bones of her wrist delicate and perfect in con-struction, an intricate little piece of machinery, her hand and many-ringed fingers the culmination of some genius creator's art. That gorgeous hand: the nails red and hard-lacquered, fin-gers spread and ready to reach.

She released the full force of her enchantment on me again, and helpless, hapless, I felt it take me, and I froze. She moved toward me with long, graceful strides. Everything became golden and sweet as honey. She would take the rest of my heart as a fine lady reaches into her canary's cage and lets it perch on her finger, listens to its song. It would be painless, almost beautiful. It was what I wanted.

No.

I shook off her glamor again and remembered that I held a cleaver, and that she was close enough now for me to use it. I closed my fingers tight around the handle, and just as her hand touched my breast, I struck.

I struck at her, and at the same time, I struck at every pretty girl who had ever laughed at, sneered at, or pitied me, and I struck even at the pretty girls who had done nothing to me at all except exist in their prettiness.

It was a mean, petty hatred that added its strength to the thrust of the cleaver, added its strength to the plain old terror and rage, and gave it just that little extra heft and distance, enough to pierce the sorceress's own heart, or whatever it was that they kept inside those dainty chests.

My long-nursed resentment, that I had been born the way I was and not like the other village girls, had directed my hand to the perfect spot. Well, almost the perfect spot. A cleaver is not for precision work, no matter how skilled the hand wielding it, and I hadn't done a precise job on the sorceress's heart, but it did the trick.

It was very different, cutting into a human (or a humanlike creature, because I still wasn't sure about the magic-workers being human), from cutting into a slab of meat on the butcher's counter. I knew it would be, of course, because a steak can't move or answer back, but I wasn't really prepared for how *very* different it would be.

Even slaughtering is different. Not pleasant, but different. There is a purpose and an honor to it, killing for food. There was no honor to this. There was a lot of blood, viscous and syrupy and dark, spreading from the knife across her jeweled bodice and down the handle of the cleaver onto my hands.

That beautiful bodice! I felt a twinge of dismay at ruining the expensive fabric, slicing up that masterful bosom-swelling structure of whalebone and stiff cloth, because it was easier to feel dismay at that than it was to look into the beautiful, startled, dying face.

I don't think she had expected me to fight back at all, despite what she had said about being unable to charm me. She had trusted in the power of her beauty and charisma to keep me frozen as she reached for my heart, and she looked surprised as she died, surprised and irritated, as if I had performed some indignity as mild as tripping and spilling something on her gown.

She stayed upright for a moment, staring at me, at the cleaver sunk into her up to the handle, then sagged to her knees, the complicated upholstery of her golden gown collapsing around her. Her skirts were so wide and billowing that it looked like her torso was reaching up out of a yellow sea as she drowned in it, hoping for someone to pull her out.

"*Sylvester*," she . . . Well, it is hard to describe exactly how she said it, through all the blood. Bubbled, or gurgled. Sounds that you would never imagine could come from that elegant, pale throat.

The words came out in gasps, and pink froth formed around her perfect lips. Her eyes looked almost human. She reached up one hand, impossibly, and grasped at my leg with improbable strength. "You must find him. The king will kill . . ."

But she never finished, because I gave the cleaver a final tug, and freed it from the twin prisons of her rib cage and the stiff corset. With it came a gush of blood. I staggered backward and retched, still clutching the cleaver as tightly as I could.

I wasn't sure if I could unbend my fingers from its handle, at that point. I thought I might have to spend the rest of my life brandishing a bloody cleaver at everyone I met.

Still holding it, I threw up a puddle of mostly bile on the black floor, then stood bent in half and panting until my head stopped feeling like it was about to detach and float away.

I leaned against a table to support my suddenly quivering legs, and, one by one, released my fingers from the cleaver until it fell to the black floor, ringing against it with an incongruously bright, appealing sound.

The blood. So much blood. On her, on me, and all over the floor. It had even landed on places that seemed impossible for it to reach, lumpy and viscous and bright as paint, thicker and stickier than anything that had come across Da's butcher's block.

My eyes stung with it. I wiped my arm across my face, and it came away red. It *stank*, too, even though it was fresh. Meaty. Metallic. It began to seem deliberate, as if the sorceress's malice had liquefied and conspired to stain and surround me, creeping into every crevice.

I felt filthy, besmirched. The blood was so thick on me that it cracked as it dried and began to fall off my skin like scabs. Lovely. And my clothes were beyond salvaging; I would have to burn them.

I thought about these things to avoid thinking beyond them.

Clarissa's face was so beautiful, even in death. I had half expected her to turn into a hideous old woman when she died, or to crumble into dust, like a witch in a fairy tale, but she looked the same as ever.

Well, not quite the same. Without light in those leaf green eyes, she no longer seemed frightening or full of menace. She looked very young, in fact. Like someone's daughter. Like Sylvester's beloved sister. Like the child she might have been before, all those years ago, when the king had taken a little girl and made her into something else, then spent however many years since then filling her with his poison as she reached adulthood and became one of *them*.

I passed my palm over her eyelids, closing them gently. Her eyes were already drying out, and the skin rasped over them unpleasantly, making me shiver. I swung away from the sorceress's body—and saw the king.

I do not know how long he had been standing there. I wished I hadn't let the cleaver fall. I wished I wasn't clothed in bloodstained rags, panting and panicky and barefoot in the spreading, sticky puddle of red on the floor. He was smiling, just a little, as if he enjoyed the sight.

"I felt it," he said. "Did you not think I would feel it when one of my children dies?"

"They are not your *children*," I spat at him. "They are your puppets."

He shrugged. "I fail to see much difference."

"You *love* children," I snapped. "They are not just tools for your benefit. You had no right to take children and make them into your playthings."

"You have no idea what you're talking about," he said, still smiling. He walked past me, so close that I could smell his stale skin below the rich perfume, and bent beside his daughter's body. He stood again, holding my heart in its little jar, letting it dangle from the silver chain. *My heart.* In my panic, I had forgotten to take it from her. I clutched at my chest.

"She performed her duty to the last," he said. "My very best daughter."

He straightened, and I took a step back. Here in this room, in the light of the faintly glowing jars, I saw him clearly.

He wasn't human, not really, and not in the way that Sylvester wasn't quite human. He was rotting from the inside, somehow, the soul of him, and it wasn't from the creeping mold destroying the hearts in those thousands upon thousands of jars. He stank of corruption, seeping up from somewhere deep and secret inside.

"You saw the little girl, of course?" he said, with something like relish.

"Millie," I said. "Her name is Millie."

"Most inconvenient, of course, to have to make another right now, but twelve does seem to be the magic number when it comes to casting the most powerful spells."

"Twelve?" I croaked through a dry throat. "With Sylvester, there are thirteen."

He kept moving toward me, smoothly, unhurriedly, and I kept moving backward.

"Ah, Sylvester," the king said. "Sylvester's magic is ... chaotic. It's a shame. I had high hopes for him. I tried over and over again to create a male magic-worker, but I'm afraid all my experiments had to be discarded."

All his experiments. Each one a human child.

"Sylvester was the first one that worked," he said. "Or seemed to work. He is certainly powerful but lacks the discernment and focus of his sisters. He seems squeamish about performing his duties, and his spells often go awry. Snagging you, for instance. Still, without him, I wouldn't have you, so his clumsiness is good for something after all. We'll have to see if he is worth sustaining after I have finished here, or whether it would be better for him to ... retire."

The way he said "retire" made me think he didn't mean to a nice little cottage in the woods.

"What are you going to do with him?" I asked sharply.

The king did not answer me, but stood turning the little jar in his hands, smiling a little. "We will need to use both halves of your heart, eventually. Clarissa did a neat job of bisecting it, and the cross section is of course very useful, but not enough." He enfolded the jar within one of his elaborate sleeves, and it disappeared.

"Give that back!" I shouted, but my voice rang hollow, and

he knew it. I could do nothing. I felt the terrible miasma of his magic creeping around me—a sickening, head-muddling blend of fog and sharp-pointed malice slowing everything down, my heartbeat, my breath, my thoughts. It was worse than Clarissa's magic—there was no dark beauty, no false hope in it.

I knew it was useless to run, but I ran anyway, as you run in nightmares, your legs heavy. With each stride, I slowed further. I heard the king chuckle a little as I passed him, and I felt his gaze on my bloodied back—a cat allowing the mouse to scurry a little, for sport.

I was almost to the door when it flew open. I flinched back, expecting guards, or another of the sorceresses, but it was Sylvester, with Cornelius perched on his shoulder, tail lashing.

Sylvester was wearing his many-caped black traveling coat, and it flew out about him in a wind I couldn't feel, a wind that lifted the hair from his scalp and blew the hem of my underdress about my ankles.

"Sylvester," said the king in a surprisingly calm voice. "Do not be a fool."

I saw that Sylvester had a handful of jars of his own, hanging from his belt. *He's come to finish me off,* I thought madly. *He wants to be the one to do it.*

"Let her go," he said to his father. Then he looked past the king to the still form of Clarissa on the floor, and a flash of emotion I couldn't quite identify passed over his face.

The king took advantage of that moment to raise his hands and send a pulse of sickness toward his son, a nauseating heave of air like the heave you give before you vomit. The air smelled of poison. I was now completely frozen, suspended in the fog, like one of the hearts in the golden oil, my limbs stiffening and losing their life even as I expended all my energy trying to force them to move.

"You will throw your life away for this peasant girl, then?"

said the king. He swept a glance over me. "Strange tastes you have."

"I have no life to throw away," retorted Sylvester. "You took it from me long ago and left me with this poor semblance instead."

The king huffed a laugh. "A poor semblance? You live in luxury of which none other of my subjects could even dream. You and your sisters command more power than anyone but me. If only you would just learn to use it properly, rather than wasting your time on silly toys."

"I tried," said Sylvester. By now I was completely frozen, my eyes fixed open and unblinking, and I could only stare at him through their clouding surface. "I tried to learn. I tried to please you. And gods know Clarissa tried to teach me, for all the good it did her." Another unreadable, flickering glance at her body.

"Don't be foolish," said the king coldly. "Stop this nonsense. We have work to do."

Don't listen to him, I screamed silently through my paralyzed throat. Even my saliva had congealed in my mouth. *He'll kill you anyway, if you serve him or not. Clarissa knew it.*

Sylvester pushed back one billowing sleeve, as Clarissa had just before plunging her hand into Colin's chest. He thrust his arm out, calling the jars of hearts from his waist to his hands and holding them, hovering about his open palm.

The hearts flared in their oil and then seemed to turn to dust. A ripple of hot, metallic air passed through the room, leaving it shimmering, and then Sylvester let the jars clank to the floor and roll away.

The king dropped to the floor. His spell released me so suddenly that I collapsed, my body tingling with pins and needles all over.

"Did you kill him?" I panted, clutching my head as my blood jumped to life again and set it pounding.

"Come," said Sylvester, stretching out a hand. And then more forcefully, "Come!" when I did not move. "I am not powerful enough to kill him. He is sleeping. Eventually he will wake. We have to go."

"The room is full of hearts!" I cried. "Use them! Kill him!"

"It is not that simple!" said Sylvester. "Come."

"He still has my heart," I said.

We stared at each other for a moment, something unreadable flaring in the sorcerer's eyes. Then I turned and ran as quickly as I could to the king's side.

I flipped back the long tails of his sleeves and fished about in their velvety depths, wrinkling my nose against his too-sweet perfume, looking for the pocket where he must have hidden my jar, growing more frantic as I found nothing.

His skin slithered against mine as I searched, sickening me. Finally, I found a deep pouch, and pulled out a handful of jars, one containing my half heart. I recognized it immediately, as if it were calling out to the rest of itself. The king stirred a little and groaned, and I jumped.

"Quickly," urged Sylvester, who had been examining a row of jars on one of the shelves and pocketing those that seemed least affected by the mold.

"I'm coming," I said. "Give me a pouch. A bag. Anything." He threw me a cloak, much like my old one, that he had apparently conjured out of thin air. It was warm and clean, with several capacious pockets, into one of which I stuffed the jar.

"You have your heart. Now let us go," said Sylvester's voice from above me. He grasped my hand, and I nearly fainted as the spell did its work again and overwhelmed me with false feeling. I was alight with love. I wanted to drop to my knees and kiss his boots. It was horrifying and wondrous all at once.

I could not give in to it, though. I forced myself to stay upright and to move my cramped legs, one-two, one-two, until I was capable of breaking into a run alongside him. Cornelius stared at me from the sorcerer's shoulder, eyes sharp and bright as tacks.

"Cornelius!" I wanted to hug him, but there wasn't time. "I'm so glad you're all right."

"You too," he said. "I found him for you."

"I see that."

"Come," said Sylvester, picking up the pace. "We have to hurry."

I wasn't about to ask Sylvester any questions right then, although hells knew I had no idea where he had been, how he had gotten away, or why he had chosen to rescue me. I was just grateful to have half my heart left.

I did, however, want to know that we weren't just going to run into the king's guard and end up where we started. I stopped, chest heaving, and held myself up with one hand against the wood paneling.

"Oi," I panted. "Aren't they going to stop us?"

"No," he said. Annoyingly, he did not seem out of breath. "I used all the good hearts I could get hold of for that sleeping spell. The entire palace will be asleep for a while. My sisters, too."

"How long is *a while*?"

"Long enough for us to get away, I hope," he said with a ghost of a smile. "My carriage is outside."

"That great, shiny, black thing? The whole world and his wife will know where we are if we parade about in that!"

"We won't be around long enough for the world and his wife to see us," said Sylvester. "We can be out of the city within the hour and gone."

A thought occurred to me. "Millie!"

"What? Who's Millie?"

"A little girl. Your father took her. To make into a magic-worker. Like he did with you and the little boys."

"Where is she?" he asked.

"She was being kept where I was. I don't think I could find it again."

"What did the room look like?"

"It was a dungeon, I think."

I described it as best I could. He nodded and started striding down the corridor, his coat spreading out behind him, dark and iridescent as oil against the crimson carpet.

"Where are you going?" I asked, struggling to keep up.

"To find her."

I was surprised. I hadn't expected him to care, much less delay us to find her. I trotted after him, unable to match his long stride, and tried to remember the turns we took, but I quickly became confused. The place was almost worse than the House for twisting and turning.

"What will he do to her?" I puffed out. "What did he do to *you*?"

"I don't remember," said Sylvester briefly, which I felt wasn't entirely the truth. I wanted to know more, but this was hardly the time to press him, even if I had been able to catch my breath for long enough to do so.

He seemed to know where he was going, however, and after many twists and turns and flights of stairs, we reached the room in which I had been held. There were scuffs of dirt and ash where Millie had been sitting, but no Millie.

"It's too late," said Sylvester. "She has been taken."

"Maybe she escaped in all the confusion," I said. "When you put everyone to sleep. They didn't have her tied up."

I willed it to be so. I pictured her slipping out of the palace, barefoot, creeping back to her life on the street. It would be filled with horrors, of course, but they would be familiar, understandable horrors, the mundane kind that filled every city street—not the arcane and unimaginable fate that awaited her at the king's hand.

Perhaps she could even be found and taken in by a kind family—why not, since I was already imagining an unlikely future? Sylvester, however, looked unconvinced. "No. They work quickly, as I said. She is probably already undergoing the . . . process."

"Your father talked about a *process* as well," I said. "What is it?"

"We might still be able to find her," he said instead, and strode away again. Cornelius looked at me over his shoulder and gave his little cat shrug.

I don't know how long we had been wandering about the palace at this point, but probably longer than we should have been. Sylvester didn't seem concerned that his spell would wear off yet, and so I kept my mouth shut and followed in his wake as best I could.

I took about seven steps for every one of his. It was like a beetle racing a daddy longlegs. Cornelius was lucky to be able to perch on the sorcerer's shoulder—I wished I could have.

I didn't tell him that my legs were starting to ache. Honestly, I was so happy to be back in his presence that I could almost ignore the pain. It was exasperating to find myself right back under his spell when I had hoped to be halfway home by now, but I couldn't resist its pull.

We came to a door that looked exactly like all the others, but Sylvester paused his long stride when we reached it.

"Do you know this room?" I asked, panting again.

"Yes," Sylvester responded, briefly and unhelpfully. He pressed his flat palm against the wood of the door. Cornelius jumped down from his shoulder and wound himself around my shins as he smelled the distinctive scent of magic.

Sylvester had his eyes closed, a frown knitting his dark eyebrows together, and I could see how taut he was holding his body, how the expectation of failure white-knuckled his splayed hand.

Without thinking too much about it, I reached out and placed my hand over his. I felt his slight start as my skin touched his, and his eyes flicked to mine, sending a shock through me like the first time he had looked at me, back in the village. I forced myself not to look away.

"You can do it," I insisted, willing him to believe.

He took a sharp breath and turned his gaze back to the door. The wood curled away from his long fingers, turning from planks to coiling branches that twisted themselves into an opening as neat as a picture frame.

It was oddly beautiful to watch, and even though I knew we had to move swiftly, I found myself mesmerized. I had never seen the sorcerer do anything with his magic other than destroy or burn things, or create pointless toys, and I was surprised by how moved I was by the elegance of it.

I was so absorbed in watching the door that I did not realize my hand was still on Sylvester's, our fingers now entwined on what had become a branch. I snatched my hand back. Sylvester looked at me, his expression unreadable.

"You just have to remind the wood what it once was," he murmured.

"When you've quite finished," interrupted Cornelius.

Sylvester stepped through the new doorway he had created, and after a moment, I followed. The dimly swirling air in this new room had that same metallic taste of magic, stronger than I had ever experienced it. I might as well have been sucking on a coin.

"There she is," said Sylvester.

The only light in the room came from a tall glass cylinder that looked like one of the heart jars, just on a much larger scale—eight feet tall, at least, and a good two arms' breadth around. A thick, honeylike substance filled it and glowed golden, giving an eerie cast to the room.

I could see little else: a long table, bare; a tiled floor that sloped to a drain; and an assortment of gleaming metal instruments hooked onto the far wall, too dimly lit to see in detail. The yellow light had a queasy, unsettling quality that made everything in the room seem like a bad dream.

"That's Millie," I confirmed. I took a few steps toward the shining cylinder and stopped just shy of it, my feet refusing to take me any closer.

The little girl floated in the honeylike liquid, naked, her toes pointed like a dancer's, her arms outspread and drifting. The liquid's slow movement transformed her floating hair into mermaid curls, coiling up from her scalp like the flame of a candle and forming graceful, mesmeric shapes.

I was so engrossed in the eerie beauty of her that it took me a moment to notice the pins—wide as my forearm—piercing her hands, her feet, and, impossibly, passing right through her neck. There was no blood or bruising, no sign of injury. If anything, the curve of her lips was slightly upturned, as if she were having a pleasant dream.

From each end of the pins, which were almost invisible for their fineness, delicate threads like silver hairs rose up to the top of the cylinder, as if Millie had become a madman's marionette. Her heart, removed from her chest by some alchemy, floated a little way in front of her body, attached by another silver thread.

It was visibly beating, a solid, steady pulse, and looked almost indecently healthy for something that was not safely housed in her body, save for a blackening around the edges that was slowly creeping across the red.

It didn't look like a disease or any kind of corruption,

though—the heart was just as healthy and alive in the black portions. If anything, it seemed to pulse most strongly in those places.

I was struck by how small she looked, how young. A child, sleeping, with pursed lips and unblemished, almost translucent skin. She should have been tucked into a trundle bed with a ragdoll, not taken apart like a broken toy and displayed thus, indecent and pierced through.

"It's too late," said Sylvester from just behind me.

I couldn't take my eyes from Millie. "It can't be. We could break the glass..."

"It would kill her," said Sylvester flatly. "She is already transforming. There is nothing anyone can do now."

"What is he doing to her?" I whispered. "What did he do to *you*?"

The little girl's eyes weren't quite closed. There was a sliver of pale light showing under the shadow of long lashes. Her cheeks, despite her half-starved frame, still had some baby fullness.

"We can't leave her here," I said.

"We have no choice. Come."

I did not move. Sylvester took hold of my shoulder, but gently. "Come," he repeated. "We cannot help her."

"Is that what he did to you? To the little boy, I mean?"

"Yes," said Sylvester flatly. "And now we really do have to go."

CHAPTER 18

We climbed back through a doorway he had created and started back on our way out of the palace. Cornelius hopped back onto the sorcerer's shoulder, but I was still struggling to keep up. The floor shuddered and strained.

"My father is trying to break free," said Sylvester.

"How much further?"

"We are almost to the door."

"I don't know if I can run much more," I gasped. My legs were aching, and my feet felt like they were about to fall off. I leaned against the wall, trying to catch my breath. My hair was plastered to my forehead and neck with sweat, and I'm sure my face was bright red.

"You have to," he said.

"I've been chained up for the better part of a day and all night, not to mention that half my heart has been extracted from my chest. I'm doing well to still be standing," I snapped.

The sorcerer gave me a searching look and then sighed.

"All right." He pulled out one of the heart jars. I drew back. I saw him touch his finger to the jar, making the heart inside glow gently. A little of its outer skin crumbled into dust, and then with a queasy lurch, we were outside, on a rain-streaked street somewhere in the city, standing beside the sorcerer's ridiculously ornate carriage and his unnaturally large horses, their immaculate black coats steaming in the rain.

A passerby bumped into me and swore, then stumbled past me into the night. I felt off-balance after being jerked out of the palace, as if I had missed a step on the stairs. I wondered why I wasn't freezing, and then realized I was fully dressed again in rich, black clothing and sturdy boots, any trace of the blood and sweat magicked away.

"We need to be careful with our store of hearts," said Sylvester, tucking the jar away. "We don't have many, and they will deteriorate rapidly as the rot spreads."

The inside of the carriage overwhelmed me. There were so many black cushions and furs and rugs that it was like being inside a giant furry animal, if that animal had also swallowed a bellyful of spangles and sparklies.

I had to push several glittering swathes of fabric aside before I could sit myself down. Cornelius found himself a cozy spot and sat neat as a loaf of bread with his front paws tucked under him. Sylvester climbed in after us and closed the door behind him, enclosing us in a suddenly intimate, breathlessly warm space.

I felt my color rising as I smelled his familiar, spicy scent, and remembered all the things I had imagined the magic-workers did inside their carriages with the people they snagged. To distract myself and conceal my embarrassment, I cleared my throat and crossed my arms across my chest forbiddingly.

Sylvester gave a nonchalant flick of the wrist, and the horses outside snorted and started to move with magical swiftness.

"And how many hearts did that take?" I asked drily.

"No more today," he said. "Once created, something like this will run forever."

"But you used one to make it in the first place."

"It is how our magic works, Foss. I can't change that. If it helps, I didn't harvest it myself."

Maddeningly, I flushed, as I did whenever he said my name. It was exhausting, trying to separate my true feelings and opinions from the ones my heartsickness was giving me. I glanced out the window to distract myself, but the speed of the world slipping by in ribbons of color made me feel sick, and I shut my eyes.

"How did you find me?" I asked instead, to distract myself.

"I found *him*," Cornelius interjected.

Sylvester gave him a startled look. I had forgotten that Cornelius's speech was still relatively new to him. "Yes," he said. "The cat had a long story to tell me. Which reminds me, why did you never speak to me before, cat, in all the years you lived in my House?"

"You never asked me to. And the name's Cornelius, thank you," said Cornelius.

Sylvester raised an eyebrow at me.

"Don't look at me," I said. "I didn't name him."

"Well," continued Sylvester, "hearing the cat's—Cornelius's—story, I knew I had to get you away from my father. They had me locked in a room away from the others while they decided what to do with me. I suppose they thought I would patiently wait for their decision."

"Looks like they'd already made their decision," I said, remembering Millie. "Clarissa interceded for you, though, for what it's worth," I added grudgingly.

"I suppose that is good to know," he said, staring out the window. He seemed untroubled by our madcap speed. I didn't know how we avoided barreling into anything, but then, they were magical horses; they probably passed through obstacles as if they were no more substantial than smoke.

"I'm not sorry I killed her," I said.

"I'm not sure that I am sorry, either," he replied.

I burrowed deeper into the furs and shivered. The events of the past two days were finally catching up to me, it seemed, and I felt like I had to hold myself very carefully to keep from falling apart, as you would when carrying an overfull cup of water. Cornelius kneaded the furs on my lap violently, then twisted himself into a knot and fell asleep.

Despite my head being full of horrors, I found myself starting to nod off, too, by virtue of being warm and rocked gently as the carriage moved, but I roused myself to ask, "Why did you come for me? It would solve all your problems, wouldn't it, if the king boiled my heart down to a soup and made a potion to cure all the hearts. You wouldn't have to be in such a rush to harvest."

What I really wanted to ask was, why bother with me? Why not just let your father have me and be rid of the nuisance I had surely become? Did I matter to you, after all?

Sylvester stared out the window and did not look at me. "You were right," he said. "We should not be . . . doing what we are doing. Harvesting hearts. It is wrong. We shouldn't even exist. We are unnatural things, made by an unnatural master. We shouldn't be in the world."

"Oh." The wind was taken out of my sails somewhat. "Well. No, you shouldn't. But even if you give it all up, your sisters won't. It's getting worse. The king said that all the sorceresses will be riding out to the far villages to replace the hearts that have been damaged. I don't know how many they are planning to take, but it has to be hundreds. Every single heart I saw in your father's storeroom had some mold on it."

"I know," he said. "It has never been done before—all of us

harvesting at once, in such large numbers. But my father is desperate. The heart magic sustains every part of the kingdom. It protects our borders and keeps us safe without the need for an army."

"From *what*?" I asked. "Who are these mysterious enemies clustering on our borders waiting to invade?"

"I don't . . ."

"I think your father is using his magic to keep himself in power and to keep the rest of us under his thumb, and I think he treats his people like apples to be picked whenever he chooses," I said. "And I think we don't need an army because he has *you* and your sisters. I certainly don't think it's to protect us. I don't think he cares what happens to us at all."

"Can you keep it down?" interrupted Cornelius. "I'm trying to sleep."

I sighed. "There's a secret society," I admitted. "Of people like me. People who were snagged. Sometimes they're able to live almost normally afterward—at least for a while. Whatever you and your sisters do to them wears off after a bit, and then they drop dead. The mold made their deaths come quicker. One of them said he knew somebody who could fix the hearts. I don't know much about it, because . . ." *They were all slaughtered in front of me*, I wanted to say, but my mind shied away from the thought. I wasn't ready to remember that yet.

"That's impossible," said the sorcerer immediately.

"Well, maybe it's impossible with your magicks," I said. "But your magicks might not be the only kind in the whole wide world. Your father made you for a particular purpose, like you said. Mayhap there is more than one purpose for magic, and more than one sort of magic-worker out there. This person who can supposedly repair the hearts is outside the kingdom. She's called the Weftwitch, whatever that means. And what if it's true? If you really want to mend what your father and sisters—and you—have done, isn't that a good place to start?"

"It's impossible," he repeated flatly.

"Fine, then," I said. "Let's just give up. Take me back to the palace, give yourself up, and let your father do his experiments on me. How about that? Where else were you planning to hide from him, if not outside the kingdom?"

Sylvester sighed and settled back in his seat. A tiny fireball flared between his index finger and thumb, and he started running it over and under his knuckles. "I have never left my father's kingdom," he admitted.

"Neither have I." I thought about it for a moment. "Nor has anyone else I know."

It struck me as odd, now, although I had never given it a moment's thought previously. You'd think that at least one person from the village would have left the kingdom at some point, whether for trade or family or simply for a visit.

I'd never so much as heard a story about life outside our kingdom. We knew that others existed, out there, at the ends of the roads that snaked out of our villages and away from the city, but I couldn't remember anyone ever having been curious about them.

"Do you think we can reach it before your father finds us?"

"The sleeping spell still holds. I will know when he wakes."

"Right. Well, all we can do is try. But there's something I have to do first," I said. "I have to tell my da that they are coming."

The idea had been forming in my head since I heard the king talk about his upcoming harvest, and now I was resolute.

"We can't afford the time," said Sylvester. "If we are to find this Weftwitch before my father wakes, we must leave the kingdom now."

297

"I'm not leaving without seeing him," I insisted. "And if your own father weren't an evil, murderous tyrant, you would understand."

We glared at each other for a moment.

"Fine," said Sylvester at last. "We will stop there on our way. But only briefly."

"Briefly is enough," I accepted.

I must have fallen asleep shortly after that, because I remember no more talk. I do remember waking once or twice to find Cornelius purring in my lap, but no sooner had I surfaced than I dipped down into sleep again. I had that same old dream, with the long, dark passages and the vines, but it did not scare me anymore. Instead, it made me sad.

We arrived at my village somewhere near midnight, by my reckoning. We all woke as the carriage came to a lurching stop. Cornelius yawned and stretched, his teeth glittering in the moonlight. Sylvester's eyes opened, silver as coins.

We left the carriage and the horses in the woods outside the village. I worried about the horses needing water and food, or even a rubdown, but Sylvester reminded me that they didn't need any of those things, and that, no matter how realistic they looked, they were *made* objects, like the windup dolls visiting toymakers peddled to the village sprouts.

As I touched my hand to the velvety nose of one of the great horses and felt the heat of its breath, it reminded me how subtle and insidious magic could be. Even I, despite knowing the truth, was fooled.

We left them in the thickest part of the wood in which they would fit, and we laid branches against the carriage as well, to further hide it from view, just in case some poacher was prowling in the deep wood before dawn.

Then the three of us walked down the dirt road to the village. Cornelius got tired of keeping up with us after a while and hopped onto my shoulder, wrapping his tail around my neck like a scarf.

Rain began to fall. It was one of those rains that, while not heavy, seems wetter than usual. It trickled down the back of my neck and inside my ears, and my mood dampened as rapidly as my clothes did.

Cornelius maneuvered himself down under my arm and into the pocket that hung at my waist with his magical cat gymnastics. Sylvester, of course, stayed dry. Typical. The raindrops seemed to hover around him in a glittering halo without actually touching him.

The village was asleep. It was late enough that even the pub lock-in had ended, and the last stragglers had staggered home. The sky was still black, but a slender rim of gray showed around the bowl of the horizon.

I looked carefully for any curtain-twitchers but saw none. That didn't mean no one was watching us, of course. There was bound to be one old biddy who couldn't sleep, glued to her window in case one of her neighbors did something scandalous. There was little enough light that she probably wouldn't be able to identify the sorcerer, but she would probably recognize my distinctive shape, and be flabbergasted that old Foss was walking anywhere with a man.

"There's the shop," I said, my heart giving a leap as I spotted its dear old sign and the light glinting off the mullioned window in front. "We live behind it. There's a door to the side."

Really, our house spread both behind and above the shop, wrapping around it like waxed paper around a chop. You could get to our living quarters by going up the staircase behind the counter, but if you picked your way through the alley at the side, there was a door that led into our kitchen and yard. It also had the advantage of being away from any windows and prying neighbors.

Despite everything, I felt a surge of joy walking up the old path to the front door. I held Cornelius in one arm, and I knocked.

The Da who opened the door seemed both shorter and older than the Da in my memories, but it was him, roused from his rest and wearing his old striped nightgown and cap.

"Foss!" His face lit up.

He even smelled like himself, a mixture of soap and the stale blood smell that we could never quite get out, no matter how much we scrubbed. It was the smell that brought tears to my eyes as I fell into his arms, still cradling Cornelius in one of mine.

I felt a sharp pang in my heart for leaving him so cavalierly and for so long. I hadn't allowed myself to realize how much I missed him until now, when my whole self seemed to reach out to him with arms wide open.

"Come in!" he said. "Come in from the rain! You're soaking."

I hovered. "Just a minute, Da."

"You'll catch your death."

I glanced over at where Sylvester was standing. Reading my meaning, he stepped into the spill of light from the open door, and Da saw him. He blinked. He looked at me.

"Foss?" he said.

"Can we come inside? Both of us, I mean," I said.

"Are you safe?" Da asked, narrowing his eyes. I suppose he thought the sorcerer might be coercing me somehow.

"I promise I am, Da. It's pouring down out here. Can we come in?"

He searched my face, then stepped back and held the door open. I had barely stepped over the threshold when he gathered me in a bear hug. I let myself relax for the first time in what felt like forever, feeling the familiar scratch of his stubble against my chin. I almost felt safe. Almost.

I pulled back. "Da, this is Sylvester," I said.

Da looked the sorcerer up and down. He didn't seem enthralled or impressed by him at all, that I could tell, which I put down to the strength of his fatherly concern overriding any magical influence.

"So, you're the one that led my Foss on a wild-goose chase," he said.

Sylvester flushed a little. "I did not intend to. Sir," he added quickly.

"Da, we have to talk," I said.

"Well, then, come into the kitchen," he said. "I can heat up what I made for dinner if you're hungry. Pot roast."

Cornelius shot me a pleased look.

I busied myself in the kitchen, more amazed and comforted by its ordinariness than I had ever been. Nothing appeared magically beneath my fingertips but staying as far away from magic as possible—except for that contained within Sylvester, I suppose—had become my new aim in life, and so I loved every spoon and mug for which I had to hunt.

It felt so good to be back at home again: having good, solid flagstones underfoot instead of black magic, and smelling real food cooking on our trusty old potbellied stove. Cornelius, of course, was right at home at once, leaving my arms to explore the kitchen.

I had told him to hold off on speaking until I gave the word, because I thought my da had more than enough to take in without adding a talking cat into the mix. Da liked cats, though, and bent down to pet him on the head as Cornelius sauntered around.

"Nice kitty," Da said. Cornelius shot me a long-suffering

look but purred enough like a regular cat to pass muster, and then settled himself down on the hearthrug for a good wash, knowing that pot roast was in the offing.

I excused myself to have a good wash, too, at the basin in my old room. All the plain, serviceable dresses hanging in my tiny wardrobe felt like old friends. I selected the most comfortable—a faded green, because I would be perfectly happy if I never saw black again—and laced up a pair of my old boots before going back downstairs.

Seeing Sylvester inside our little house felt completely wrong, as if a panther had wandered in and sat down at the dinner table with a bib around its neck. He had to stoop to get through the doorways, and he looked all kinds of odd sitting in one of our dining chairs. He couldn't lounge in it as he did on the throne—but he clearly wanted to—and he seemed all elbows and knees.

I could see him desperately wanting to conjure one of his magical toys in order to have something to do with his hands, and resisting. His fingers twitched a little.

Da set a bowl down in front of him—pot roast, with a beef rump, potatoes, and carrots that bobbed up and down in a brown gravy, with a hunk of good workman's bread at the side for dipping. He had been the one to teach me how to cook, after all.

Sylvester needed no urging to start slurping it up. Da raised his eyebrows at me as he plonked mugs of tea on the table, surprised at the sorcerer's appetite. I suppose he had imagined that they all lived on gossamer sandwiches and dewdrops or some such. Da picked out some of the choicest bits of meat and gravy and set a plate down for Cornelius, as well.

Da was a man who respected food and enjoyed eating, and so there was a period of silence while we all bent over our bowls. When we paused to take a breath, Da leaned his elbows on the table. "Well, then. Tell me everything."

Well, of course, I wasn't going to tell him *everything*. Da didn't need to know how often I'd come close to being filleted like a side of beef, nor did he need to know I'd murdered one of the sorceresses with my own hand. Not yet anyway.

"Here goes," I began, and tried to explain everything that had happened as simply as possible, leaving out all the most embarrassing bits.

"Wait," said Da, afterward. "The sorceresses are made from what, again?"

"From street urchins, I think," I said. "Orphans. Lost children. Sold children. He trains them up for years in all his magicks until they are of age, like Sylvester. Sylvester only just started being a sorcerer."

Da blew out a long breath and shook his head in disgust. He would never put up with anyone mistreating a child, would Da. He turned to Sylvester.

"So, you were some little bit of a boy when he scooped you up? Disgraceful."

Sylvester looked surprised to be addressed. He had been silent, concentrating on his dinner.

"Yes," he said. "I don't remember it, though. It was many years ago now, of course, and our memories of the children we were before seem to disappear as part of the . . . process."

"That's beside the point," said Da. "You just don't treat people that way."

"I am not precisely a person," said Sylvester with a certain awkwardness.

"Like hells you aren't," said Da. "Of course you are." He reached out and prodded the sorcerer with one of his meaty fingers, startling him again. "That little boy is still in there, somewhere, and he deserved better."

I felt a ridiculous pricking of tears at the back of my eyes. Oh, Da.

"He took another girl, while I was there," I said. "Millie, her name was."

"Oh, the poor little thing," said Da.

I thought about telling him how we had seen Millie floating in the tank, her heart out and floating like a kite on a string, but I didn't want Da to have to imagine such things. Bad enough that we had to bring him such terrible news.

"Da, they need more hearts," I said. "The ones they have are all sick with something, a mold or a disease that's eating them up. They're running out. Until they find a way to fix them, if they ever do, they're going to need to replace them. And there's a whole palace full that they have to replace."

"So, what does that mean?" asked Da, looking at me sharply.

"They're going to ride out, all eleven of them . . . Or twelve, I suppose, if they've changed Millie into one of them already. I don't know how long it takes."

Sylvester shook his head. "It will be many years before she is a full sorceress. She will have the . . . necessary parts for one when he removes her from the chamber, but we are trained until adulthood."

"Right, so eleven. They usually only take hearts from the outlying villages, but this time they're going to almost all of them."

"They will probably start here," said Sylvester. "Partly because they like to take the bulk of the harvest from the farthest places, as Foss said, and . . ." He hesitated.

"And what?" I asked.

"And because this is *your* village, Foss. The king will know it, and he will take pleasure in harvesting from it first and deepest, for your sake and for mine."

"They're coming here?" said Da. "When?"

"I cast a sleep spell that I would hazard still holds," said Sylvester. "I used an inordinate amount of power for it."

"An inordinate number of hearts," I said under my breath.

"They will awaken soon and come here as soon as they have gathered themselves. You have a day, perhaps. Maybe two."

"That's not terribly long," commented Da.

"You need to get out, Da," I said. "All of you. You need to get out and hide."

Da turned his mug of tea between his hands. "Where can we hide, from the king himself, and a small army of sorceresses? Where could we go that they could not follow?"

"I can help a little," said Sylvester. "Perhaps it will be enough."

"If you go deep enough into the woods, you may at least delay them a little," I pleaded.

"And what about all the other villages that aren't lucky enough to have you to warn them?" said Da. "They'll be sitting ducks."

"I know, Da," I said. "But we don't have much time. I had to make sure that you were all right."

"We might be able to get word to them, if we're quick enough," said Da. "Unless you have some magical way of doing it?" he added, turning to Sylvester.

"I am sorry," he said. "I know no such spell that will work without many hearts to power it. Although I might be able to speed the horses, if you can persuade messengers to ride out."

Da looked at him narrowly. "I can't help wondering why you're helping my Foss," he said. "Seeing as how you're one of the magic-workers yourself and should be out hunting hearts with the rest of them."

"I have come to realize," said Sylvester laboriously, "that our presence in the world—mine and my sisters'—makes it worse, not better. Foss has shown me how dangerous we are to people like you."

"I'm surprised you care," commented Da. "I would have thought you were above such things." He shot me a quick look.

"I had questioned it for a while," admitted Sylvester. "But I knew nothing except what my father and sisters taught me. Having Foss in my House was . . . enlightening."

"Yes, she's not afraid of speaking her mind. I know," agreed Da, still looking at me. "Well, seems like the best thing to do would be to gather everyone in the square and go from there. We'll have to ring the fire bell to get them all out."

"You'll have to do it after we've gone," I said. "We have something else to do, and we have to do it before the king awakens and can find us."

"And are you going to tell me what it is?" said Da shrewdly.

I hesitated. "I don't want you to worry overmuch."

"Nonsense," said Da. "I've been worrying about you since the moment you were born, and I'll worry until I leave this earth. Probably after that, too, if I'm able."

"We've heard that there's someone who can help us," I told him. "Some kind of magic-worker or healer, who can fix the hearts and perhaps even give them back to those who are missing theirs. The ones who are still alive, that is. If we can find this person and bring them back, it might stop the king from harvesting all the villages." I shook my head.

"Da, if he has his way, he might kill half the people in the kingdom. More. He doesn't care. He knows more children will be born to replace them, eventually, and I don't think he cares how long it takes."

"Hold on a minute," said Da. "What king would be willing to kill that many of his own people? I've never heard of such a thing."

"Because he doesn't let us hear about it, Da. I don't know why we've never questioned the right of the magic-workers to come out and steal our lives away, but we never have. I never have. It was just the way things were, and we were grateful for their protection, and the health of our crops and livestock, and we just let them do it. Until now."

We stared at each other for a moment, and I saw the same realization dawn on Da's face, as it had on mine.

All this time, we had lived under King Darius's rule without questioning his right to take pieces of our hearts as he saw fit, and we had counted it little more than an inconvenience in exchange for our safety. It seemed so stupid, now, as if we were little more than the unintelligent sheep the magic-workers believed us to be.

"And where is this person you need to find?"

"Outside of the kingdom," I said. "We will leave tonight and hope to be back before too long. If we can offer the king a way to repair the hearts he has, we might be able to stop him from taking the hundreds he needs. And we can save those who have been taken already and still survive."

"Like you?" asked Da. It was the first time he had asked me directly about my heart. "Foss"—he took my hands—"tell me straight. How are you? What has happened to you? Are you going to be all right?"

"I'm fine, Da." I swallowed. "I was just snagged, is all. Sylvester didn't mean to take me. He had his spell ready for harvesting, and I got caught up on the tail of it by accident."

Sylvester looked embarrassed, as he probably should.

"Then you can let her go?" said Da, turning to the sorcerer.

"He hasn't quite figured out how yet," I said. "But he will. Or perhaps the person we're looking for will know a way."

Da sighed and rubbed his hand across his face, looking very tired. "And you say he didn't mean to take you?"

"He says he didn't, and I'm inclined to believe him," I said, meeting Sylvester's eyes for a moment. Was I imagining it, or did he look surprised? I didn't tell Da about the piece of my heart that Clarissa had taken, which was still sloshing about in its jar in my pocket as we spoke.

"Let me at least have a little time with you, before you leave," said Da. Sylvester took the hint and unfolded his long legs.

"I will check on the horses," he said, which of course didn't need checking on at all, but I suppose he was trying to be polite. He hadn't had much practice. He toddled off outside, and with Cornelius asleep on the hearthrug, Da and I settled ourselves in our same old shabby, comfortable armchairs before the fire.

"Foss . . . I never told you the old stories," he said. "You had enough to worry about. But there are tales—true or not—about these harvests, from many years ago. Whole towns full of Davs, with the hearts sucked out of them."

I leaned forward to grasp his hands, desperate to reassure him and take that old, old look from his face. "Da, it's all right. I was just being dramatic. Even if I did lose my whole heart, it wouldn't be that bad. You don't die. Like Dav, like you said."

"Yes, you do die," said Da. "Not at once, but you do. Dav killed himself, Foss. While you were away."

I blinked.

"They all do," said Da. "At least, that's what the stories say. They wander for a while, and weep, and then they wind down like a clock and put themselves out of their misery. Whole villages of ghosts. That's what the stories say."

I felt fear clog my throat like a dose of medicine. "How?" I asked.

Da's eyes shifted. "That's not . . ."

"It is important, Da. How?"

Reluctantly, Da met my eyes. "He cut his throat," he said. "That's how they always did it. In the stories. Either that, or they drowned themselves or hanged themselves. Stabbing themselves in the heart doesn't work, you see. Something about the magic."

My head swam.

"Is that going to happen to you, my girl?" he asked. Da was a fine figure of a man, in rude health, with a ruddy face that matched his meats, but in that moment, he looked drawn and pale.

"No, Da," I said with a confidence that I did not feel. "We're going to find this person who can repair hearts, whoever it is, and they'll fix me right up. I promise."

He knew that I couldn't possibly know that, of course, but I think it comforted him anyway. He drew me in for a hug, and I felt his tears wet against my ear and cheek.

"I couldn't bear to lose you," he said.

"You won't, Da," I managed. "And I'm not alone. Sylvester and Cornelius will be with me."

"I like him," he said in my ear. "Your young man."

I pulled back. "He's not *my young man*," I insisted, flushing.

"Could have fooled me," teased Da, but, like I've said, he thought the sun shone out of my arse, and that I was as beautiful to everyone else in the world as I was to him.

"For being a sorcerer, he's not a bad chap," said Da.

"I'm under his spell, Da. He might not have meant it, but I am. That means that I'm in love with him, all right? And I can't help it. Like Dav and his sorceress."

"Foss . . ."

"I'm just like Dav." I was working myself up now. "Just another fool tagging along after a beautiful face, to be thrown away like yesterday's dinner, not even fit for the cat."

"I don't think he sees you that way," argued Da. "And besides, it's not true. You've done a lot for him, it sounds like. Just . . . put yourself first, all right? As best you can. Even if he's a decent fellow, as he seems, he can't hold a candle to my Foss. And I need you to come home safe."

"I will, Da," I promised. But I know neither of us believed me.

I wished we could stay there just for the night—that I could collapse into my comfortable old trundle bed, with the indentation in the mattress just the right size and shape for me. I wished that Cornelius could curl up on the old blanket my mother had crocheted before I was born, that stayed always folded at the foot of the bed. I determinedly refused to imagine where Sylvester would sleep.

There was no time, however.

Da promised to gather the village together in the morning and tell them about the coming harvest, and to send riders to the neighboring villages to start to spread the word. We hoped each settlement would send out riders of its own, and thus word would spread swiftly, giving many enough time to hide.

It wouldn't keep them safe from the sorceresses and the king for long, but it might keep them safe long enough for us to return with a way to repair the hearts. If such a cure actually existed, of course, which was still by no means certain.

Da pressed a final cup of tea upon us both, as if fortifying us for the journey, and by the time the very first graying of dawn had lightened the night sky, we were back in the carriage and on our way to the border.

Saying goodbye to Da—well, there's no way to describe it. We were both putting on a brave face, but I could barely speak past the lump in my throat, and I could see the tears glistening in Da's eyes.

Sylvester wandered away to give us the chance to bid a proper farewell, and we clung to each other for a long time. Neither of us voiced the fact that this might be the last time we saw each other, but we both knew it.

When Da finally released me, his face was wet. He attempted a smile. "I love you, my girl," he said.

"I love you too, Da." I willed myself not to cry. The least I could do for him is keep it together until I was out of sight, let him see me smile.

"You take care of yourself, all right?" he said.

"You too, Da."

"And don't let that sorcerer get any ideas."

"Da!" I blushed furiously. "It's not like that. He barely looks at me, and not that way."

Da smiled a little. "Whatever you say, Foss."

CHAPTER 19

When I opened my eyes again, the light had taken on the flat, iron gray of a cold morning, and I had a crick in my neck that made it feel like my head was on sideways. I sat there without moving for a while, feeling the rumble of the still-moving carriage and letting my eyes drift, not fixing themselves on any particular spot.

Well, almost. They did have a tendency to float over to Sylvester's sleeping face when I let them, drawn by both the spell and his beauty. Sleep deepened the petals of shadow under his eyes, and even his eyelids themselves took on a violet tinge, making him look almost deathly. Still beautiful, but deathly. They twitched a little as I watched. I wondered what sorcerers dreamed of.

I pulled back the black curtain and looked out the window. The rot infecting the kingdom was even more evident now than when I had ridden out to the border town the first time. Everything looked yellow and sick.

Cornelius awoke with a start on my lap and bristled. He growled, a noise I hadn't heard him make before, which made the skin on my forearms get goose pimples. I roused myself fully and sat up straight. Cornelius stood up as well, back arching.

"What's going on?" I asked the cat.

"I don't know, but it feels . . . wrong."

"What does?" I looked out of the window again and knew that I needed to wake the sorcerer. Outside, a mist had closed in on the horizon—or, at least, mist was the closest word I could use to describe it. It looked like the edges of the world had been erased into a greasy yellow-white miasma. I would have doubted my eyes, except for Cornelius's clear discomfort.

"I think we're at the edge of the kingdom," I said. I nudged Sylvester's knee with mine, trying to ignore the jolt of desire that ran through me. He woke without any of the spluttering or bleary eyes that we normal mortals would have, instead becoming immediately alert and wary.

"What happened?" he asked.

I gestured to the window, and he peered out. The fact that even Sylvester looked concerned when he saw it worried me.

"What is it?" I asked.

"Hmmm," was all he responded.

"Very helpful. Is it magic? Has your father sent it to stop us?"

"I don't know," he said.

I imagined getting lost in that terrifying, ravenous *nothing*. It reminded me a little of the spreading mold that had killed Jol, in a way, with its sense of sickness and corruption, except that the mold had been alive somewhat, while this mist seemed both impersonal and inert. Somehow, that made it more frightening.

I would rather have had a monster with claws and teeth blocking the road. I imagined that I could feel the mist nudging against the glass of the carriage windows, a numb ache pressing with terrible force. It wouldn't eat you up or drain you of blood; it would muffle you into woolly nothingness.

"I will go and see what I can find out about it," Sylvester said, stopping the carriage. "You stay here."

"Fine." I sat back in my seat and drew Cornelius into my arms. He would usually have protested, but he seemed disturbed enough that he succumbed to my petting, which was very concerning. The usual Cornelius would have given me a look of disgust at this indignity and retreated to the other side of the carriage.

Sylvester opened the carriage door, letting in a blast of cold air before slamming it shut again. I watched him through the black crystal window, and saw him pull up his high collar and bury his hands in his coat pockets as he strode toward the mist.

The cold had leeched the landscape of all color, and in the early morning light, everything was gray and white except for his stark, black figure.

"Wait," I said suddenly, sitting up. "What's that?"

I had heard something rumbling on the road behind us. The king's men was my first thought, and I felt my body tense in readiness to run—not that I would get very far.

Then, as I peered out of the window, I realized it was simply another carriage, on the same road and presumably headed in the same direction. So, people did leave the kingdom from time to time, it seemed.

Sylvester continued on his path without turning, and so it was left to Cornelius and me to deal with this new arrival.

The carriage slowed as it neared us and drew abreast. There was no one else on the road, whether because of the earliness of the hour or some other, more sinister reason, and so there was no danger of it blocking the thoroughfare.

I opened the window, and the driver leaned to peer in the window at Cornelius and me, clearly nonplussed at seeing a very ordinary peasant girl and a fairly ordinary cat inside what was clearly a magic-worker's carriage. I suppose he hadn't

314

spotted Sylvester, who was pacing back and forth a few hundred yards away.

"You all right?" the man asked, his brow furrowed. "Trouble with the carriage?"

One of the magical horses snorted through its dinner-plate-sized nostrils, and the man started. He seemed jumpy.

"No, thanks," I said. "Just stopping a while."

"Right you are." He squinted toward the horizon. "Weather looks a bit grim up ahead."

That was an understatement. "Yes, it does," I said. I couldn't help but be curious, and so I went ahead and asked, "Where are you headed?"

"Me? Well, I'm off to . . ." He started confidently and then trailed off.

"Off to . . . ?" I prompted.

He frowned and scratched at his beard. "Right, as I said, I'm off to . . . because . . ."

I waited for a few beats. He reminded me of the few travelers I had met in the village, who always seemed so lost and uncertain about their destinations. This was starting to make a terrible sort of sense.

"You all right, then?" he said again. "Don't need any help?"

Cornelius and I exchanged glances. "No, thanks," I repeated. "We're just stopping a while."

"Right you are," he said. "Well, I'm off home."

He twitched the reins to turn the horse's heads.

"Wait." I stopped him. "You're off home? Back that way?" I pointed behind us.

He looked mazed, like a man who has worked too long in the hot sun and can't quite see straight. "Yes, off home," he said. "I just came out this way to . . ." He laughed a little. "Sorry, it's on the tip of my tongue."

"Don't worry about it," I said. "Thanks for stopping."

"You take care now," he said. He blinked at the ornate carriage, as if trying to focus on it, and then abruptly rattled his reins and steered his carriage round to face the other way. The whole conversation had reminded me of talking to a drunk outside the village tavern.

"He's really leaving," said Cornelius, putting his paws up on the windowsill.

"It's like something made him forget where he was planning to go," I said.

"It's the magic," said Cornelius. "I can smell it."

Sylvester returned, letting in another breath of cold air as he settled himself back in the carriage. His coat smelled of ice and pine trees.

"I don't think this mist has been sent for us," said Sylvester, "although my father may yet send something to pursue us when he wakes up."

That was the opposite of reassuring. "So, what is it, then?"

"Ghosts, of a sort," he said, almost casually, as if he came across such things every day. Maybe he did. "They are very ancient. Almost fossilized. There are ways to tell the age of spells. You have heard how a tree's age can be determined by cutting it open and counting the rings inside? It is something like that. One can take a slice of the spell, as it were—"

"Yes, yes, all right," I interrupted. "You don't need to tell me the whole mess of it."

He pinked a little. I could see he had been a tad impressed with his own cleverness in analyzing the spell and was miffed to be hurried along. "I would be surprised if anyone but a magic-worker could sense them," he continued. "There are so many, and they are so close together, that they create a barrier. But it spreads to either side, as far as I can measure. There is no way around it."

"It's like a moat, then?" I clarified. "Around the kingdom?"

"Something like that, but it has a sort of intelligence. There are souls trapped in there, of some sort. And it is of my father's creation, as we suspected," he said.

"And I can't imagine it's the sort of thing you can just wander through without something nasty happening," I said.

"No."

"Could you tell what particular nature of nasty thing would happen?"

"Not precisely," he said. "There is a spell of forgetfulness bound in it, and one of hunger, and some other strands that I do not recognize. Knowing my father, whatever happens when you pass through the mist is bound to be exceedingly painful, if not altogether fatal."

I told him about the man in the carriage who had seemed to become confused and disoriented. Sylvester listened, his lips pressed together.

"If my father wanted to keep his people within the kingdom, a spell of forgetfulness and confusion would serve to hold them from the mist without causing unnecessary fear or concern," he mused. "And then, if they somehow managed to break free of the confusion, the mist itself would stop them from leaving."

"So, no one can leave," I said, half to myself.

Sylvester suddenly gasped and doubled over as if someone had punched him in the gut.

"What? What is it?" I cried.

"My father is awake," he gasped, still bent in half, his dark hair hanging down and shrouding his face so I could not see his expression.

"How long will it take him to find us?" I said, urgently.

Sylvester looked up, shaking back his hair. Even as my mind worked frantically, trying to think of a way out, I couldn't help admiring how his hair settled back into perfect waves around his face without him even having to smooth it down.

"Not long enough," he said. "We have to leave. Now."

He crumpled again. Instinctively, I reached out to help him, then curled my fingers into fists instead.

"What is he doing to you?"

"He is not at full strength yet," panted Sylvester, breath ragged. "But he is trying to reach out to me."

"And can he?"

"Easily, once he is back to himself. He might even be able to kill me at this distance, if he was willing to use up enough of the good hearts he has left. And he may just be angry enough to do that."

I turned to look at the terrible, churning mist.

"All right, so we have to get through now. But how are we going to get through that? Use a heart?"

My desperation was such that even I, who was so opposed to using them at all, was becoming accustomed to the idea of burning the hearts up in order to get where, and do what, we needed to. I could see how someone like Sylvester could swiftly stop thinking of them as parts of a person at all and instead see them merely as fuel. Kindling for the fire.

He shook his head. "I cannot see a way."

I stared at him. "What do you mean, you can't see a way?"

"Just what I said. I don't know how to pass through the barrier without harm, even with heart magic." He spread his fingers wide in a show of helplessness. "There is no spell of mine that could bring us safely through."

"*No* spell?"

"My father's magic is too powerful."

"How many hearts do we have left? Use all of them!"

"Not enough," he said.

"What are we supposed to do, then?" I almost shouted. "We can't go back!"

"I don't know."

"So that's it, then? We're trapped here until your father finds us?"

It was infuriating. On the other side of that barrier sat a whole other world, a world that apparently contained the magic to heal my heart and save my da, and we could not access it.

The mist might look insubstantial, but it might as well have been a wall a hundred miles high. If we didn't manage to find a way through it, I thought, we were lost. All the hearts were lost, not just mine. And I would become another one of the king's experiments.

Wait. *The king's experiments.* I remembered how he had toyed with the jar holding my heart. How Clarissa had told me that I had a special resistance to magic.

"Use my heart," I said.

"What?"

Even Cornelius was looking at me as if I was crazy.

"Use my heart to cast your spells." I brought out the jar from my pocket and tried not to look at the piece of myself that was sloshing around inside.

"Even if I were to . . . use it," said Sylvester, "it would not be enough. I don't know how many hearts could bring down a spell as strong and old and weighty as this one, but it's probably more than we could gather in a year."

"It will work," I insisted. I felt certain, oddly certain, that this was the right thing to do.

"Foss," argued Sylvester gently. "Even if it did work, we are traveling to find someone who can make your heart whole again. You need both parts."

"That's not the only reason we're doing this," I said. "I am not the only one who is broken and needs mending. There are many. And if your father and sisters do not stop harvesting, there will be many more. I don't know what we will learn outside of the kingdom, but there must be some knowledge out there that we don't have, that will help us. That we can bring back."

"You don't know for sure that we will find out anything of use, or if this heart-mender even exists." He seemed to be pleading with me, oddly.

"We have to try," I urged him. "It will work. I know it."

Sylvester stared at me and then at the jar.

"I know it," I repeated. "And besides," I tried to sound cheerful, "I've survived without it this long."

"You will never again be whole," he said.

"We don't know that. Maybe this Weftwitch will be able to help in some way, once we get there."

He sighed. "Fine. But I do this under protest."

"So long as you do it."

I held out the jar, and he took it. There was not the same sense of violation, of wrongness, as when the king had held it. It actually felt almost comforting, seeing my heart beat in his hands. Perhaps that was all part of the spell. He left the carriage and walked toward the mist again, holding my heart this time.

"I hope you know what you're doing," said Cornelius.

"I think so," I said.

Cornelius curled up on my lap when I arranged the furs about me again, as if to give me some measure of comfort.

I did not understand the exact mechanics of what Sylvester did when casting a spell. I wondered if he would even be able to explain them in a way I could understand, if I asked, or if it would be like trying to explain air to a fish.

From the outside, it had never looked like much. I had

seen him perform minor magicks now and then with little ceremony, to create his toys and little fires. And even the larger tricks I had witnessed—opening the palace door—had been accomplished with little more than a gesture.

If his father's boundary spell was as wide and strong and deep as he had described, however, it would require something of the strength needed to uproot an ancient tree whose roots had become as complex as a city full of streets and alleyways.

Cornelius and I both pressed our noses to the crystal window and watched Sylvester's tall, black figure stride to the very edge of the mist and stand there, arms upraised as if he meant to embrace it.

By a trick of the shifting fog and gray morning light, he looked like a raven gliding over snow. The shapes in the mist seemed to bend and sway in response to the sorcerer's movements.

Sylvester held the jar containing my heart in one hand. I could see the little silver chain dangling from it like a strand of cobweb. His face was turned from us, so we could not see if he spoke, or even changed expression, but the mist flashed white for a moment and seemed to shiver.

"He's doing something," said Cornelius. "Do you feel it?"

"No. I don't feel anything."

I spoke too soon, however. A great pain gripped my chest, and I gasped and fell back. Cornelius jumped out of the way. It was just like the old pain of being apart from the sorcerer, and it only grew in intensity. I wondered if I had made a terrible mistake—if, by urging Sylvester to use my heart, I had signed my own death warrant.

"The mist is fading," said Cornelius from the window. He had both paws pressed against the crystal. "Are you all right?"

I couldn't even answer him. Sweat pearled on my forehead. I managed to heave myself to the window and press my face against it, gasping circles of warm breath onto the crystal. I saw Sylvester lowering his arms, and I saw that the jar that had once contained my half heart now contained golden oil and nothing more.

"It's done," I managed to say. My breath was slowly coming back.

"Look," said Cornelius. The mist was dissipating—not all of it, but enough of it to leave a tunnel wide enough for our carriage to pass through. Sylvester was hurrying back to us, the jar swinging from his hand. He wrenched open the door.

"Foss? Are you all right?" he demanded.

"Yes," I said. The pain was fading. "It . . . stung for a moment. That's all."

"You were right," he said. "It worked. But we have to hurry. I don't know how long it will hold."

The magical horses snorted to life again and went from a standstill to a gallop with a flick of Sylvester's wrist. I felt warmth returning to my hands and face, and only then realized how freezing cold I had been while he was performing the spell.

Sylvester watched me from the opposite seat, his eyes intent. He still held the jar between his hands. My heart was gone, and in its place were swirling dark specks that looked like drifting ash.

The horses sped through the pathway we had created, and the mist arched over us and at either side, swirling malevolently at its edges, as if it would surge in and dissolve us if it could. Cornelius had hunkered down again, his front paws tucked underneath him, and had started an anxious purr.

"How thick do you think it is?" I asked.

"I don't know," said Sylvester helpfully.

The mist boiled and hissed at its edges. I shut my eyes, but I still felt it, an awful presence hemming us in from every side.

"What does it feel like?" Sylvester asked. "The heartsickness."

"What?"

"You experienced some of it just now, didn't you? When I used your heart?"

I opened my eyes. His skin looked even paler than usual against the dark fur trim of his coat. He had drawn it up tight against his long throat, against the cold. If I had let myself, I would have reached forward to stroke the spoonful of white skin that showed. It took all my strength to restrain myself, and even then, my hands wavered in my lap as if ready to obey. I felt the hot dousing of shame once more.

"It is hell," I said, more forcefully than I had intended to. One of his perfectly shaped eyebrows rose a little. "It is like being thirsty, all the time, and never allowed to drink. It is like bleeding inside and dying a little at a time. It is like a fever that never breaks."

His eyes were very steady, but their blue had darkened. I glared at his stupid, unfeeling, perfect, beloved face and wanted to slap it.

"Worst of all, it is *embarrassing*," I said.

"The worst part is the embarrassment. Not the unbearable pain?"

"Yes," I said. "Because yes, I'm a good cook, a competent butcher, and a more than competent accountant, and I did manage to leave my village and follow you to the city, which is more than almost anyone I know has ever done . . ."

". . . And you murdered a sorceress," Cornelius added.

"Yes, thank you—but despite all of that, to look the way I do and to love someone who looks the way you do, that is a humiliation that is worse than any pain. I would gladly take the suffering and leave the love, if I could. I would be in pain every day rather than love you."

"To look the way you do?" He stared at me in puzzlement.

I flushed. I had given too much away.

"But I was just admiring you," he said. "You have . . ."

"I can see the sunlight!" exclaimed Cornelius, who was observant but had no sense of timing. He was right—we passed through the last of the mist, and the world opened up again, bright and full of possibilities.

CHAPTER 20

I had half expected the new kingdom to look drastically different from our own and so was a little disappointed. We had burst in so dramatically that I had hoped for an equally dramatic arrival, but all we saw was the same grass, the same trees, the same road stretching ahead and behind.

I felt a prickle of excitement all the same, because we were really *elsewhere*, somewhere entirely new, where King Darius could not reach us. And it wasn't exactly the same, if you stopped and really thought about it.

It had the brightness and clarity of a world without stolen hearts and beautiful, sinister women. Sylvester opened the carriage window so we could breathe the new air.

"It feels different," commented Cornelius.

"Different how?" I asked.

"I'm not sure. It smells different," he said. "I can't say it in human."

"I know what he means," said Sylvester. "The air has a different texture."

I took a deep breath. I couldn't detect any of what Sylvester and Cornelius were feeling with their heightened senses, but I did feel free. I could stand straighter, knowing that we were safe from the king and the sorceresses. I just hoped Da and the villagers were safe as well.

"I suppose we should try to find a town and ask about this Weftwitch," I said. "Unless you have some magic way of finding her."

"Perhaps, but I think my magic might work differently here," said Sylvester. He created a little fireball and let it play over his knuckles. It danced for a moment, then fizzled. He frowned down at it. "I don't want to risk it. Nor use a heart. We do not know what kind of attention that could draw here."

"Well, until you figure that out," I said, "I think we should keep going along this road. It's bound to lead somewhere, somewhere with people, and then we can ask about to find out where we have to go next."

We followed the road, and, as I had suspected, we reached a village before too long. We stepped out of the carriage, its shining steps unfolding themselves under our feet, and looked around.

The village didn't look all that different from mine, at first glance. I could see a cobbled road lined with shops, a smithy with a horseshoe hung over the doorjamb, and well-tended hedgerows lining lanes that led to houses and farms.

There was even a square like ours back home, where we held the markets and such, or gathered to gawp at the sorceresses. I felt that if I followed the rickety road, I would reach a pub with a sticky floor and a fat black-and-white cat sunning itself on the doorstep, just like back home.

But the village was empty.

I wondered if the entire populace was hiding behind bushes and trees and such, ready to jump out at us. The place had that sort of feel—like something might leap out at you at any second. I looked back at the carriage. Even the magical horses seemed wary, chuffing a little through their dinner-plate-sized nostrils and shifting their weight uneasily from one massive foot to another.

"Is anyone here?" I called out to the empty air.

"I can't smell anyone," noted Cornelius from beside my ankle.

"Nor can I sense anyone," added Sylvester. "My senses are duller here, though. Something like wearing gloves over your fingers. I can still feel things, but the impressions are blunted. Blurred. I could not say for sure that no one else is here."

We kept walking, cautiously, peering in any windows and doorways we passed. The place did seem a little neglected, on closer inspection. Weeds and bright flowers poked through the cobblestones.

"It's foss," I said suddenly, stopping.

Sylvester looked at me as if I had gone mad.

"The flower." I stooped and picked it. It was delicate, greenish white, lacelike, with a distinctive curled petal that made the head look like a chalice. "The flower I'm named after."

I felt foolish for pointing it out, but it was so comforting to come across something familiar in this strange, lonely place.

"May I see?" said the sorcerer.

Feeling even more foolish, I stuck out my hand, holding the flower between my thumb and index finger. The contrast between that intricately detailed and appealing little plant and my strong, red hand seemed laughable to me, but he plucked the flower gravely from between my fingers and examined it. I looked away, embarrassed.

"It is beautiful," he said.

"You don't have to say it," I muttered. "I know it is a ridiculous name."

"I think it suits you very well," he said, holding my gaze with an intensity that made me flush.

"That looks like it was a bakery once," I said, trying to change the subject and pointing at one of the buildings. "I see the chimneys for the big ovens."

"Good place to look for mice, a bakery," said Cornelius. "Lots of crumbs. Mind if I pop in for minute?"

He trotted off. My stomach growled. Like Cornelius, I was suddenly very focused on food.

"I'm going in, too," I said. "There might be something left."

Sylvester made a vague gesture and went back to studying the flower.

There was no one inside the bakery, either. The bread was stale, as I had expected, but only a few days stale. Someone had made it three, maybe four days ago at the most, and set it out for sale on what was probably a very ordinary morning. There was still a dusting of flour on the counter. A fly buzzed around my ear, the only noise in the place.

Cornelius emerged from an open larder door.

"Find any mice?" I asked.

"Not one," he said. "I can see that there *were* mice here, not long ago, but I can't find any."

"This place was full of life not long ago," I said, turning slowly to see the room. The fly followed. "Something happened."

Cornelius hopped up gracefully onto the counter and chewed on a morsel of bread, making a face.

"We're not going to get anywhere if we can't find people to talk to," I said. "And we're clearly not going to find any here. We need to keep moving."

The magic-made horses never required food, water, or rest, and so we were able to continue our journey without interruption. The white horror of the mist diminished behind us, and

I was even able to enjoy our progress a little. The morning was cold but sunny, and the air tasted sweet as an autumn apple.

I think we all felt optimistic, even Sylvester, who still did not believe that hearts could be repaired. That made it even more of a shock when the horses came to a halt, and we found ourselves at a roadblock, surrounded by men and women holding weapons.

"Stay here," said Sylvester. "I will talk to them."

"Not a chance," I said. "We don't know how people here are going to react to a magic-worker. They might start poking at you with their sharp sticks without listening to a word you say. Let me talk to them. I don't look like a threat. And as for you"—I turned to Cornelius—"don't let on that you can talk. Just pretend to be an ordinary cat. All right?"

Cornelius mewed.

"Yes, like that." I took a deep breath and pushed open the carriage door. The people outside stared to see such a homely, everyday person emerge from such an elaborate carriage. It must have been like seeing a sparrow hatch from a swan's egg.

"Good morning," I said to the nearest person, who was holding a spear, for want of any better ideas.

He looked me up and down. "Good morning, ma'am," he said politely. "No one has traveled this road for a long time. We have been charged with the duty of stopping anyone—or anything—who comes this way."

"Why?"

"Am I right in assuming you have traveled here from the Invisible Kingdom?" he asked.

"I have never heard that name," I replied. "We have come here from another kingdom, it is true."

"The kingdom beyond the mist?"

"Oh. Yes," I said. "We traveled through the mist."

A murmur went through the crowd. Concern, at the very least, and maybe even fear.

"You are the first in many years," said the spearman. "We have to take you to our headwoman."

"All right," I said cautiously. "And what will she do with us?"

"It has been so long that I do not know what she will do," said the man. "Truthfully, we never expected to see anyone traveling this road again."

Sylvester opened the carriage door, clearly thinking that I didn't have things under control. I waved at him to go back in, but they had spotted him.

"A magic-worker!" cried the spearman, who seemed to be in charge. A susurration ran through the crowd, and not a pleasant one. "I am sorry, but he will have to travel under guard and in bonds."

Sylvester opened his mouth to reply, but before he could say anything, I said, "Fine. Whatever you say."

Sylvester, I knew, could probably have magicked himself right out of any bonds if he chose, but he submitted to them, allowing his wrists to be tied behind his back.

The person binding him was clearly a little intimidated by the sorcerer's height, beauty, and rich clothing, and he handled him gently, making sure not to chafe Sylvester's perfect skin when he tightened the ropes.

I don't think they knew what to make of him. They had probably never seen a magic-worker before. I did notice that, although they were fascinated by him, they were not in thrall. He did not seem to have the same effect on them as he had on me, or as he had had on those back home who weren't even Snagged. If people in our village had gotten this close to him, they would have been fawning and worshipful; these people were polite, perhaps a little awed, but not enslaved.

"You may leave your carriage here," the leader told me. "We can bring your horses, if they need food and water."

"Uh, no, they will be fine," I said awkwardly. He did not seem too surprised. I suspected that he recognized magical constructions when he saw them. "I do need to bring my cat, though."

He shrugged. Cornelius, who had been waiting in the carriage's doorway for a signal, leaped in one fluid movement and landed on my shoulder, digging in a little with his claws to keep purchase.

The people led Sylvester, Cornelius, and me to what turned out not to be a town at all but a tent city of wooden poles and stretched cloth—large but clearly temporary.

There were animals grazing in makeshift pens, chickens pecking about the dirt paths, and even a gang of children playing some mysterious game involving a broken wagon wheel and a length of rope.

They stopped to watch Sylvester pass, grubby faces wide-eyed and wondering. With his gleaming hair and luxurious, bejeweled clothing, he looked like a butterfly floating through a bevy of moths. Even with his hands tied, he intimidated.

As we walked, we passed a child absorbed in play. He was an ordinary-looking sprog, round in the face and snub of nose. He held his little fingers apart, and a web of light appeared between them, like the cat's cradles with which I had seen Sylvester tinker.

Sylvester watched him, fascinated. The boy twiddled with it a bit, then lost interest, and threw it to the ground, where it popped and wiggled like a firecracker before disappearing.

"So, you do have magic-workers here," I said to the man who was leading us.

"Of a sort," he said. "Not *his* kind," indicating Sylvester, "and no heart magic, either."

"So, spells then? Books? Herbs?"

"I hear of some who meddle with those," he said, "but for most, it is not needed. We use magic for little more here than chasing a kettle to the boil, or persuading bread to rise more easily. Or for pretty toys, as you see."

I couldn't fathom it. So magic was an everyday, throwaway thing here, so simple that even the sprouts could play with it? I had always known it as something red and predatory—something to be dreaded.

Perhaps the people here didn't have the kind of power the king and the magic-workers wielded, but that seemed like a fair trade to me in exchange for a life without fear. It looked to be a good life.

The people, though wary, seemed kind, and were neatly dressed and healthy. The settlement, though humble, was orderly and comfortable.

We reached a tent that was perhaps a little larger than the others, and a woman emerged. She had a kind, plain face, and a brown headscarf covered her hair. She greeted us pleasantly enough, even Sylvester.

"We shall talk," she said. "But first, your magic-worker needs to go in there."

She indicated a rudimentary cage made of wooden planks—the kind of thing in which you would transport pigs to market. Sylvester and I exchanged glances.

"He could break out of that cage before you could spit," I pointed out.

"As a sign of good faith," she said, and made a polite but insistent gesture.

I rolled my eyes, but Sylvester acquiesced easily enough, folding himself small to pass through the door. He sat cross-legged on the bare boards as they closed and padlocked the door behind him. The sight was rather comical.

"We haven't had visitors from the Invisible Kingdom in many years," said the headwoman, "and certainly not magic-workers. But there are certain rules we must follow when we do. Confining the magic-workers is one of them."

"All right," I conceded. "Am I allowed to ask questions?"

The woman looked at me for a long moment. "Are you hungry?" she surprised me by asking.

My stomach had been so tight with worry since we left the empty village that I hadn't had time to even think about food. But as soon as she said this, it growled.

"Yes," I said.

"Let's get you something to eat, then. And don't worry, I'll give some to your man over there, too. And we can talk."

She led me to the bonfire in the center of the encampment, which was surrounded by rudimentary benches made from logs and stumps. People sat and ate, talking quietly. It was an ordinary scene, and one that made my heart ache for the villagers back home.

How were they faring? Were they hidden? Were they safe? Or would they at least be safe enough until we returned? And what would they do if we never returned, or if we weren't able to find a way to get rid of the corruption and give the king his usable hearts again?

I was so roiled and muddled in my own head that I tripped over a log and almost sprawled full-length.

"Here," said the woman, giving me a plate of stew when I had settled myself. It was good stew, thick and brown, with a strong, gamey taste that made me think it must be venison. Coins of carrot bobbed to the surface.

"Thank you," I said.

"We gave a plate to the magic-worker as well. If he'll stoop so low as to eat peasant food."

"He loves peasant food," I said, shoveling the stew into my

mouth. I hadn't realized how hungry I was. I hadn't eaten prop-erly since before I was taken to the palace.

She gave me an odd look. "You seem to know him well."

"I have little choice," I explained. "I am bound to him, and he to me. A heart-harvesting spell gone wrong."

"Or so he says," she said.

I felt too full of stew and goodwill to argue.

"So why have you come to us from the Invisible Kingdom?" she asked. "We rarely get visitors from beyond the mist, and even more rarely do they survive the journey."

"We were told to seek the Weftwitch."

She raised her eyebrows. "And why do you need the Weft-witch?"

"You know of her?"

"First tell me why you seek her."

I explained as best I could about the mold that was destroy-ing the king's hearts and his plan to cull half the population to replace them. She watched me with an unreadable gaze.

"And you believe that if you repair the hearts, he will be content with what he has and return to the old ways?" she asked.

"Well, no," I said. "But it is all we could think to do. We couldn't stay, and I had to do something to help repair myself. And it would slow down his harvest. If he does what he is plan-ning to do, he'll destroy whole villages at once."

"Even if you succeed, you will still be enslaved to a king who picks your hearts like apples whenever he has the need."

"What choice do we have?" I said. "At least before the mold started destroying his hearts, it was peaceful, for the most part. They took bits and pieces of us—rarely a whole heart. We might have been trapped inside the kingdom, yes, but it's not a bad place. And there hasn't been a war in a century."

"No war?" She laughed and spat out a wad of chewed bay leaf from the stew. It splattered on the stone, looking like a fat bug someone had stepped on. "Girl, there is a war. There has been a war for a hundred years or more. You just don't know about it."

"There can't be," I said.

She snorted.

"I'm not an imbecile," I argued. "I may never have known war, but I know what one should look like. There would be soldiers, weapons, shortages of food. We have always lived in peace. We have always had plenty. Our boys grow to old men, get fat, and die without ever holding so much as a wooden play-sword."

"There are other kinds of wars," the headwoman said, "with a king such as yours." She heaved herself to her feet, sucking noisily at her teeth, and wandered over to the fire to give it a poke. "You will see."

"I don't understand," I said.

"Your king has been invading us for a hundred years," she said. "He doesn't need an army. He has his heart magic."

She took a packet of tobacco and some cigar papers from a pouch at her waist and started rolling.

"We used to be able travel back and forth," she began. "I have relatives in your kingdom. Or had. I don't know if they're still alive, or what happened to them. For more than a hundred years now, that barrier has stood, cutting cousins and friends and sweethearts off from one another. We would have almost forgotten you, if it weren't for the mist pushing ever outward."

"Pushing outward?"

She nodded. I listened in silence and growing horror as she spoke, and the comfortable fiction of my kingdom gave way to reality.

She told me that the mist pushed out further every year. Early on, before people knew to fear it, and when it was still moving quickly, it had swallowed any settlement in its path. Whole villages—men, women, and children—disappeared as the mist flowed over them and consumed them. Worse than consumed them: swallowed up their souls and made them part of itself.

The powerful and near-impenetrable heart magic that Sylvester had sensed came from all those people, eaten up and transformed into an army of ghosts, their hearts fuel for an endlessly growing, endlessly hungry spell.

Everyone who had lived near the mist picked up and moved, leaving their buildings and fields abandoned. It had slowed over the years, but King Darius's mist was still invading the neighboring kingdoms by increments, growing the size of his own realm and pushing back all others.

"Then why do you live like this, so close to the mist?" I asked. "If it's so dangerous?"

"We are charged with protecting the borders as best we can," she said. "We map its edges and record the speed of its movements, along with any unusual behavior. We have magic-workers of our own, who are sometimes able to stall it for a time. Every few months, we have to pick up sticks and move our settlement farther in, so that we can keep our people safe while still fulfilling our duty."

"And who is this Weftwitch? Is she one of your magic-workers?"

"Not really," she said. "But she is someone who has to live apart from us. You will see."

This sounded ominous.

"So, you will let us go to her?"

"Yes. She will know what to do with you."

We were allowed to take our carriage to the very edge of the Weftwitch's realm, which turned out to be a wood not far from the mist, with a guard of several men riding alongside.

Cornelius and I sat inside the carriage, but Sylvester was still in the cage. It had wheels, and two men on horseback pulled it behind them. None of them spoke to us.

"What do you make of all this?" I said to Cornelius.

"I'm not sure why they didn't throw you both into the mist as soon as they saw he was a magic-worker."

"They certainly don't have much reason to help us."

"Perhaps they think this Weftwitch will take care of their problem for them."

"Very reassuring, thank you."

The carriage stopped. I looked out of the window and saw that our guard had stopped us at the edge of a thick wood. Their horses seemed restless, snorting feathers of mist into the cold air and pawing at the frozen ground. The road continued, but from here on it was shadowed with trees.

"We're here," said one of the men, opening the carriage door.

"So, we go on without you?"

"Yes, but you won't be able to take this in with you. No magic can survive in there." He knocked his fist against the side of the carriage.

No magic could survive? What would that mean for Sylvester and Cornelius? I stepped down from the carriage, and Cornelius followed.

I stood, blowing on my hands to warm them as they opened Sylvester's cage and unbound him. He unfolded himself, his limbs stiff. The guards kept their distance from him, I noticed. Even the horses shifted away a little.

"Good luck," said one of the men, smiling a little. He pointed to where the path wound between the trees. "That way."

They left us. Cornelius stretched luxuriously and said, "I didn't know how hard it would be, not talking to anyone. I suppose I've gotten used to it."

"It was for the best," I said. "If they reacted that way to a magic-worker, I can't imagine they would have been too thrilled with a talking cat."

Sylvester rubbed at the faint rope marks on his wrists.

"Thank you for not . . . magicking anything," I said to him.

"It would not have helped," he said.

We stared at the wood—this supposed magic-less place— and it seemed to stare back at us. There was a sense of something watching and listening. Not something unfriendly, necessarily, but something that was assessing us and waiting to see if we would be friend or foe.

"I'm not going anywhere near it," said Cornelius. "What if it snatches my voice away, and I can't get it back?"

"Fair point," I agreed. "You can wait here for us."

"How long will you be?"

"How am I supposed to know that?" I said. "I have no idea what we're going to find in there."

"Fine." Cornelius sharpened his claws on a tree trunk, then settled himself neatly at its base.

"Ready?" I said to Sylvester, who looked a little apprehensive. He nodded.

"Right," I said, and stepped over an invisible boundary.

Even I, the most unmagical person you could ever hope to find—practically the opposite of a magical person, in fact— could feel the difference at once. The world became denser and thicker, and even a little dimmer, as if seen through a widow's veil.

Sylvester, apparently, felt the difference like a bag of rocks dropped on his head, judging by the way he reacted. He bent over double, his tall frame crumpling in the middle, and started gasping, hands pressed to his heart.

It looked a little like my heartsickness felt, I observed with quasi-scientific interest, and not a little malicious satisfaction.

"Help me," he gasped.

I had to admit, I was taking a little pleasure in his suffering after all he had inflicted on me, intentionally or not, but I went over to him anyway. I wasn't sure what to do, so I rested one hand on his shoulder in a show of sympathy. He leaned into me heavily, setting me off balance, and I ended up supporting his weight.

I braced for the flood of love and desire to rush through me, as it usually would, but nothing happened. I backed away from him, shocked, and he nearly fell over.

"What was that for?" he shouted, sounding almost like a normal person.

"Nothing," I whispered. "There's nothing."

"What?"

"I don't feel it," I said, more loudly. I stood up straight, letting my spine uncurl and my throat loosen to let in a long, clean ribbon of breath. I had not realized how tensely I had been holding myself. For *weeks*.

That terrible, wonderful, all-consuming love and obsession was gone, like a fever finally breaking. And, as in the aftermath of a fever, I felt light and cleansed and free, shivering a little as my skin accustomed itself again to covering just ordinary old Foss, and not a boiling, infesting passion that could barely be contained. The air, even in this strange, heavy place, tasted light.

Sylvester, on the other hand, looked terrible. His eyes had violet petals of fatigue beneath them, and the carved perfection of his cheekbones now looked somehow hollow. "You don't feel that?" he managed to say.

"The spell," I said. "The spell has gone. It can't survive here."

And, more—now that the overwhelming love and devotion of the spell was missing, I could truly feel the absence of half my heart. It was hollow and yearning, like an empty belly, but deeper, more profound: perhaps like the emptiness a mother feels after her babe has left her womb.

I had never felt it, not truly, and now there was no chance of reuniting my heart with itself, because we had turned it to ash and powder in coming here, and it was gone forever.

A terrible, yawning grief filled me, a grief so wide and high that it blotted out the sky, and I clutched at a tree trunk to steady myself.

"Foss," came Sylvester's voice from far away. "What is wrong?"

I felt as one bereaved. It was as if Da had died, or if I had lost my mother all over again. I pressed my forehead against the bark of the trunk and waited for the swimming, breathless sensation to pass. What a change from the effervescence of a few moments before!

"I'm fine," I managed to say.

"You do not look fine."

"Neither do you." I stared at him. "And neither do your *clothes*."

Sylvester struggled upright. The dark edges of his clothing had become smoky and indistinct, crawling about as if alive and looking for an escape. The buttons on his coat seemed to have grown legs and scuttled about like bugs. The effect was unsettling, I can tell you. His clothes were unknitting themselves before my eyes.

"They're made of magic," he said. "They're coming undone."

I realized then that my magic-made cloak had disappeared,

but luckily, I was wearing my own dress underneath, the one I had taken from Da's.

I felt at the pocket, and my few things were somehow there. I suppose the cloak had only been an illusion, after all, while those objects were real and so hadn't vanished.

Had they really been in the cloak pocket then, all along, or had they really been in my dress pocket, and the magic had made me think otherwise? It all made my head ache, as magic business tended to.

"I didn't think of it." I suddenly realized how lucky we had apparently been. "Your father made you using magic. This place could have . . . unmade you."

"There must be enough of a real person left in me, then," said Sylvester drily.

"Right, but your garments are having some trouble."

One of the bug buttons pinged itself off his coat and was swallowed into nothingness. His boots appeared to have turned into some kind of black, oily substance and were trying to climb up his legs. Sylvester himself looked gray-faced and exhausted.

"Perhaps you should get undressed," I suggested.

He looked at me sharply.

"I'm not under the spell right now, remember?" I said. "I have no desire for you to be naked for nakedness's sake. Your clothes just look like they're about to eat you. Or strangle you. They're hanging on by a thread in this place. Literally."

He looked down at his frantically unravelling clothing and sighed. "Fine."

He divested himself of his belt and the jars containing the hearts he had taken from the storeroom (which seemed to be surviving the new environment just fine, as I suppose they were not inherently magical in themselves without a magic-worker's hand to wield them), as well as some other mysterious substances, and then busied himself with trying to get free of his suddenly uncooperative garments. Some of them had become smoke, some liquid, and some appeared to have winking eyes and too many legs.

As he peeled off each item of clothing, it was snatched away from him as if by a high wind and dissipated in the air without a trace. Soon he was clad only in what had once been under-garments, but were now more like some sleek, predatory little animal coiling itself around his hips—a weasel maybe, or a pine marten.

"Can you turn around so I can get these off?" he asked.

"And stay turned around for the rest of the day, walking back-ward?" I said. "I'm going to have to look at you at some point."

"At least while I undress," he said.

"Fine," I said, and turned around, my heart beating a little faster. So, I wasn't caught up in the spell anymore, but I was still a woman. And despite his current sickly appearance, Sylvester was still the best-looking man I would probably ever have the pleasure of looking upon.

I heard rustling and the snapping of tiny teeth, and then silence. Either he had freed himself from his undergarments-turned-attackers, or they had eaten him.

"Can I turn around?" I asked.

A pause. Then, "I suppose so," he said irritably.

An idea occurred to me. "Here." I hitched up my skirt and untied my petticoat, wriggling out of it and letting it fall to the ground. I held it out behind me without turning. "Fashion yourself something out of this."

My heart was beating fast, but it could not be the spell. The spell was gone. I felt the fabric slip from my fingers, and I let my arm fall back to my side. When the sounds of rustling stopped from behind me, I said, "Ready?"

He sighed. "Yes."

I turned and couldn't help snorting out a laugh before I clapped my hand over my mouth. "Sorry," I giggled.

He had made himself a sort of garment out of the petticoat, wrapping it around his torso and between his legs, but it barely reached the middle of his thighs. The rest of his legs were bare, as well as his feet, and his shoulders and arms poked out above the swathe of fabric. It looked rather like a diaper you would pin on a baby.

His head, perched on top of the whole concoction, looked both embarrassed and disgruntled, and he was altogether about as comfortable as a wet cat.

"What was I supposed to do?" he huffed. "There's no way not to look ridiculous."

"I like you looking ridiculous," I said. "Just don't bruise your pretty white feet on these pebbles."

We picked our way down the stony path. Sylvester was green-faced and struggling in the magic-less air, and, for a change, it was I who seemed the stronger of the two of us.

I was enjoying the new lightness of my body and spirit without the weight of the spell, and so I was practically skipping along. I slowed my pace to match his, though, and he leaned on my shoulder when he needed to.

It was odd, touching him without that overwhelming mess of emotions. I didn't feel *nothing*. I felt a warmth and some fluttering in my belly, but they were normal feelings that I would expect to have, being so close to someone who looked like him.

He let out a long breath of air—not quite a sigh, but not quite a normal breath either.

"What's wrong?"

"You will laugh," he said, "after what happened to my clothes."

"I won't," I said. "Well, I might. But tell me anyway."

"I was wondering, maybe hoping, even," he said, "that this

place would leech all the magic out of me and perhaps . . . return me to my original state."

I stared at him, but he kept his face turned resolutely ahead.

"Back to being . . . human? Fully human?"

"Yes. As I said, it was just a curiosity."

"A hope."

"Perhaps."

"Maybe you—the original you—and the magic are too entwined now," I mused. "Like the House and the old building beneath it."

"That seems likely," he said. "I hoped it were not so. That there was enough left of . . . the boy . . . to stand when the rest of me fell."

"Well," I said, "I can certainly understand that feeling, but I have to say that I would miss the whole Sylvester, even if the part of him that fell away was the magic part."

I realized to my surprise that this was true—that it had to be true, because I was temporarily released from the spell and therefore speaking truly, from my real self, and not from the ensorcelled version.

I *would* miss him if he were gone or changed irreparably. I *liked* him. That was a revelation and a half, I'll tell you.

"Thank you," he said, sounding as startled as I was and about as embarrassed as I was, too. I kept my face set and downward-facing and trudged on ahead of him, stolid old Foss, without turning to look at him again.

I had expected a witch's cottage, something all points and corners, with birds nesting in the nooks and spiders spinning in the crannies, and possibly even a pair of chicken legs growing out from underneath, but the house at the end of the path was instead a solid, housewifely sort of house. It had a well-swept yard that concealed no eldritch tangles of herbs, but instead a well-ordered vegetable garden and a couple of very attractive, if a little old-fashioned, flower beds.

"Is this it?" asked Sylvester.

"It must be," I said. "There's no one else around for miles."

"I could be better attired," he grumbled, picking at the threads of my petticoat he wore wrapped around him.

"From the sounds of it, this lady is none too keen on the magic-workers. I doubt she'd like you any better if you were in your fancy clobber."

"I could at least be wearing *trousers*."

I had to stifle a chuckle. I enjoyed seeing him at a disadvantage.

"Better let me ring the doorbell, then," I said. "Just in case she takes one look at you and gets the broom to shoo you away."

"Very funny," he said.

We did walk up the path with a fair bit of trepidation, though, not sure what to expect. Would she turn us away at once, before hearing us out? As far as I knew, she was my one and only hope to getting my heart back hale and (pardon the pun) hearty.

If this failed, what then? Sylvester, Cornelius, and I would either have to creep back to our kingdom and brave the king's wrath, or live out our lives in exile.

The closer we got, the more impressed I was with the cottage. It appeared freshly painted, and the front step, although bowed in the middle and worn shiny with years of use, was spotless. The door was painted red, with a large iron knocker near the top. Someone took great care of the place.

"Ready?" I said to Sylvester, letting my hand hover over the knocker.

He nodded.

I knocked, and I heard its hollow *clock-clock* sound echo through the cottage. Something squawked, a bird of some kind, and then I heard footsteps, and a voice that was probably telling the squawking thing to be quiet.

The door opened, and an attractive, round-cheeked, middle-aged woman stood wiping her hands on a red apron and looking at us with a brightly inquiring look. I had never seen anyone less witchlike.

"Yes?" she said.

I was taken a little aback, I have to say. It was clear that very few people came out here, but the woman was looking at us with her head cocked a little to one side and a polite smile on her face, as if she was used to fending off door-to-door salespeople and traveling preachers every morning when she was in the midst of her baking.

Add to that, Sylvester and I weren't the most usual-looking people. Especially if you took into account his odd manner of dress.

She was still waiting for a reply, and so I stumbled out, "Er, we were told to talk to you. About a spell. Are you the Weftwitch?"

"I am," she said. Her bright eyes flicked past me to Sylvester.

"Feeling a bit queasy, are we?" she said to him, and chuckled. "My little forest doesn't usually agree with your kind."

Sylvester did still look pretty green.

"I don't usually see anyone accompanying them, though," she said to me, looking me up and down. "No, you're something quite different altogether."

"I'm not a magic-worker, if that's what you mean," I said.

"Indeed not," she agreed, her small, shrewd eyes piercing me. "Well, I suppose you had better come inside."

She clapped her hands together, releasing a small puff of flour from beneath her nails, and nudged at something at foot level. I saw an extremely fat and extremely well-feathered hen hop back with an offended rattle of wings.

"Sorry," she said. "Come in."

I stepped over the threshold, which, if the old stories were true, meant that I was under the witch's power now. I didn't feel like I was under anyone's power, however.

The cottage looked like any other cozy, well-kept house back in my village and made me feel at home—even down to the chickens that swarmed around my feet and huffed along to keep up with my stride.

Sylvester followed more cautiously, picking his way through the birds with his bare feet, wrinkling his nose when one of them brushed up against his legs.

"They're just chickens," said the woman. "They won't bite."

Sylvester hissed through his teeth as one of them investigated his toes.

"They will give you a hell of a peck, I'll say that," added the woman.

We were in her kitchen. A large iron stove took up almost half the room, with dozens of mysterious drawers and knobs and whistling, wheezing parts.

A large orange cat was asleep on part of it, his tail and one leg hanging down dangerously close to a little window through which showed an open flame. His tail twitched lazily back and forth, like the pendulum of a clock, narrowly escaping singeing each time. I wondered what Cornelius would have made of him.

What little was left of the kitchen after the stove had filled it up contained a kitchen table with four chairs pulled up to it, and washed flagstones, and a very ordinary collection of household objects in one corner: brooms, buckets, a dustpan and brush, a roll of netting, and assorted walking sticks. Nothing that seemed at all magical or exceptional.

The tea the Weftwitch poured for us was just tea, and didn't bubble or turn green or melt a hole in the rough pottery cups. Her cottage stayed solid on its foundations and didn't shimmer, or shiver, or show any signs of life at all.

I sat in one of the chairs and accepted a cup, and Sylvester sat on the very edge of another, folding himself awkwardly into something that resembled a human sitting on a chair.

Without his throne to lounge in, he looked a little lost, and ridiculously too tall and lanky for the little room. Being half-naked didn't help.

In this terribly ordinary place, however, he looked even more extraordinary than he usually did—his cheekbones more dramatically slanted, his eyes more piercingly gray blue, and his whole being so strange, so unnaturally beautiful, that even the cat half-asleep on the stove twitched an eye open to stare.

The witch woman, however, didn't seem intimidated. She pushed another cup of tea over to him, and the sugar bowl.

"These magic folks," she said to me. "Mad about sugar, all of them. Anything sweet. It's the magic, you see. Makes everything taste just a little sour. Something to do with how it reacts with the body . . . coats the tongue somewhat."

Sylvester gave a grudging "Thank you," and I noticed that he spooned about six heaps of sugar into his tea.

"How do you know?" I asked. "Do you have magic-workers in your kingdom?"

She snorted. "Like him? No, we wouldn't stand for it. Not anymore. Not that sort. Poor thing."

I couldn't imagine why anyone would call Sylvester a poor thing. Even dressed as oddly as he was, he looked lordly, and nowhere near an object of pity.

"We have our own type of magic-workers here. Not in the way you understand them," she continued.

"We saw a boy, in the settlement," I said. "He had magic, a little . . ."

"Yes, no one has more than a little." She sipped her tea. "Your king saw to that."

"What?" I said sharply. "How?"

"Our kingdoms used to be one and the same," she explained. "A very long time ago. Did you know that? No, of course not. Your king has an unnaturally long life, as you may know, because of his . . . practices." She sipped her tea.

"He was prince over both our lands, once, but craved more power. He saw that some children were born with something—a spark, a brightness—that could be turned to magic. It happened a few times in every generation. People knew about it but did not trouble themselves overly. For the most part, the children used it for childish pursuits—magicking themselves odd little toys, starting fires, playing pranks."

I shot a glance at Sylvester.

"Your king, however, saw the potential for great power. He had a similar spark, and started experimenting on himself and these others to see exactly what could be achieved. He did this in secret for a while, but you can imagine that people did not take kindly to it when it was found out—particularly as the children he took for these purposes were never seen again.

"His own father, our king, did not take kindly to it either. He disowned his son, and would have banished him, but when he announced the banishment in front of his council, Prince Darius murdered his father in a rage. The rest of the royal family sought to capture and punish him, but Darius took his magic and his new knowledge, and split the kingdom in two, walling one half off from the other. Us, and you. The Invisible Kingdom." She paused to take another sip.

"Over the last century, the boundary between us has grown stronger, almost too strong for us to penetrate, and we knew little about what was happening there. Occasionally someone wandered through without being entirely consumed, but

349

usually the mist had stolen both their wits and their health, and they didn't last long."

This was all astonishing to hear. "And King Darius is still trying to expand the kingdom," I said. "And pushing into yours."

"More and more each year. If no one tries to stop him, he will swallow us completely. And not just us, but other nations too. Yes, there is a whole world out there, beyond your borders. That's why I'm here and why I do the work that I do, to resist it."

I glared at Sylvester. "Did you know any of this?"

"I had suspicions," admitted Sylvester. "I found it odd that the kingdom was closed in on itself, reliant on our magic. But no, I did not know. And I'm ashamed to say I didn't care much before . . ." He flushed.

"Before? Before what?"

"Before you," he finished simply.

I stared at him. The Weftwitch swallowed the last of her tea, swirled the dregs around, then stared at the leaves. "Hmmm. Interesting. Now, you and I will take a walk, and leave your magic friend here to amuse himself for a few minutes. We need to talk."

I looked over at Sylvester, who shrugged, nearly dislodging his makeshift garment.

"Don't get into any trouble while I'm gone," I said, standing up.

"Sweet boy," said the Weftwitch. "For a magic-worker."

I swear he blushed.

The Weftwitch led me outside to her garden and stooped to pull up a few weeds. "Would you mind?" she said, gesturing at the neighboring bed. "My back."

I knelt in the grass and pulled weeds of my own. The earth

was dark and bitter as coffee, the plants indecently green and full of juice. This was a healthy place, and I felt healthy in it.

"You are like me," she said conversationally.

"A witch?" I said, startled. She honked out a laugh.

"Dear child. No. The opposite of a witch, in fact. I have no magic."

"But . . ."

"No, what I have is the opposite of magic," she said. "A resistance to magic so strong that it can almost *seem* magical."

"I don't understand," I said.

"Oh, believe me, neither did I, before I figured it out," she said. "Confused me to no end, at first. We use magic differently here than you do in your kingdom, and it's not confined to just one special group. Lots of people have magic of one kind or another, even if it's as small as getting a kettle to boil a wee bit faster." She moved to another bed, and I followed.

"You need people who are resistant to magic, too, to balance it out. That's why they call me the Weftwitch—warp and weft, do you see, like weaving cloth? Both are necessary." She straightened up, stretching her back, before continuing to weed.

"Those with no magic, or a resistance to it, are celebrated here as the most powerful. Being the Weftwitch is a great honor. I work with the magic-workers to help them control their magic, give it limits. You have seen yourself how wild it can run without someone like me to contain it. It is its own sort of power."

I thought back to how I had quashed Sylvester's disastrous spell in the House, how I had helped him open the door to the chamber where Millie was prisoner. I suppose I could see how the presence of resistance, control, could keep balance in the complicated system that magic seemed to be.

"But real magic needs hearts," I said. "We were always told . . ."

"Oh, that's what they *tell* you," she said. "They wouldn't want you thinking that everyone had a bit of magic in them, oh no. You have to be some special, fancy royal person to have magic, is what they'd have you think. But you do not need hearts to perform magic. There are other ways."

"Well yes, but only for small things. Not for big, grand magicks, like the sorceresses do."

She snorted. "Not so. Heart magic is powerful, yes, but not the only powerful kind."

I blinked. "So, they don't have to use hearts at all?"

"For their kind of magic, they do," she explained, "But it's a dark, consuming kind. And it's greedy. Stealing the magic from other people—well, let me put it this way. If you train a dog with kindness, it'll do what you tell it and be loyal. If you train a dog with beatings and the like, it might do what you say, but it also might turn on you, given the opportunity."

". . . And magic is the dog?"

"It is. Fair comparison, too. It comes when you call. It obeys, most of the time. But it has teeth."

I had known that the magic Sylvester and the other magic-workers did was wrong somehow, unnatural. What I was having more trouble wrapping my head around was the fact that everyone could have a little magic in them, and that it could be a gentle, natural thing, with no blood or sacrifice necessary.

"So, they're not just taking hearts," I said. "They're taking whatever magicks someone has inside them?"

"Yes," the Weftwitch said. "Which is contained in the heart, I suppose, or part of it. Someone's magic is all bound up with the rest of them, though, and you can't take it out without doing damage."

"And some people have more than others."

"Right," she said. "And some have none. Everyone called me

a wet blanket when I was a child. I spoiled the fun whenever I turned up. If I were in a house, the kettle wouldn't boil, the bread wouldn't rise, and the hens wouldn't lay."

She sighed, then continued, "I thought I was just bad luck for the longest time, until I figured that something about me stopped magic from working. Even everyday things like water boiling and dough rising take a tiny spark of magic, and I sucked away every little spark I could without realizing it."

I thought back on my life in the village.

"I don't remember things like that happening," I said. "Although I rarely went into anyone's house but our own. I certainly never had the best of luck, but I kept house for my da and me right enough and worked in the shop." I thought harder. "I always thought I was cursed, and that's why I never seemed to do that well when it came to other people."

"Cursed?"

"Because my mother died when I was born. That hardly ever happens, and when it does, it means there is something wrong with the child. Or that's what we believe, at least."

"I've never heard anything so ridiculous," said the Weftwitch. "Utter nonsense. That's what comes from letting heart magic run wild—everyone relies on magic and forgets common sense."

She shook her head. "Even the most basic knowledge of human anatomy and medicine will tell you that your mother's death could have been for any one of a number of reasons. It happens here all the time, because we're not living under your so-called 'protections.' It is always a tragedy, but no one is *wrong* for it, and there is certainly no one to blame."

I let out a long breath. "I thought it was what made me different."

"Well, I don't know about that, but the amount of magic resistance you have is certainly unusual, and it would probably have given you some trouble as a young one without someone there to guide you. Here, a young woman like you would be apprenticed to someone like me, to learn how to use her gift. Because it is a gift, my dear, and not a curse."

"Then why did Sylvester—or some part of him—pick me out of all that crowd, if I were resistant to magic?" I asked. "Surely I'd be the last person he'd seek out to harvest."

She tapped her index finger against her bottom lip, frowning in thought. "Accident. Or fate, if you believe in that sort of thing. Either way, it was good luck for us."

"And can you indeed repair the hearts? I was told . . ."

But she was already shaking her head. "I am sorry, my dear."

I sagged. "Then there is no hope. We thought—we were told—that you could repair all the hearts, and those whose hearts had been taken."

"No," she said. "But I might be able to help you keep it from happening to anyone else."

She was looking at me with a strangely bright, direct look that made me want to dart my own eyes away. "What do you mean?" I asked, still reeling from the news that I was going to live out the rest of my life with half a heart.

I thought I had hardened myself to the possibility that I would never be whole again, but I suppose some part of me had held out hope that Basil's promises were genuine. When I thought about it, though, it seemed absurd.

"Have you wondered about the corruption, at all? Where it came from?"

"You know about that?" I asked, startled.

"Dear child, I helped create it. All of us here have been working on it for a long time. We needed something to slow the spread of your kingdom, and to stop your king in his tracks. It has taken us decades, but we finally came up with a concoction that would cause his store of hearts to sicken and slipped it through the mist whenever we were able.

"As I said, some are able to get through the mist without being consumed, and they were willing to make that sacrifice, despite them not surviving long on the other side. We got enough of the corruption through to take hold of the king's store."

"You made it?" I said, unbelieving. "But it just made things worse! The king is just going to harvest more hearts! It won't stop him! All you have done is doomed all the ordinary, non-magic people in our kingdom!"

"Perhaps not," she said. "It is *very* fortunate that you should have come here. You see, spreading the disease in your kingdom was only half the plan. The other half was to rid us of the king and his *children*"—she snorted—"altogether."

I stared at her.

"We had hoped that the corruption we created would work on them, too, but it wasn't strong enough. Luckily, since then, we have been able to create one even more powerful, that will work beautifully."

She looked at me carefully. "The trouble is, we need to get it through the mist, and the weak points we used before have been much harder to breach since the king realized he was under attack and tightened up his wards against us. We managed to get a few letters through, hoping to reach those who had already been caught in the magic-workers' spell, and tempt one through to help us take this new corruption back."

"The map," I realized. "Basil had a map with your name on it."

"That's it," she said. "We thought we may have to wait a decade or more before someone from the Invisible Kingdom made it through to us, if they made it at all. They had a better chance of getting back into their own kingdom afterward, and taking our new concoction with them, as the king would not be looking for one of his own people."

"You tricked them?" I said. "The Snagged?" I saw them fall in my mind's eye again—Basil, Nat, Em, all of them, tempted by a false promise of hope and healing, and rage rose in my gullet.

"It was the only way," said the Weftwitch. "And it worked, didn't it?"

She looked at me with her small, bright eyes.

"Wait . . . You want *us* to take it back?"

She spread her hands. "What could be more perfect? You want the king gone as much as we do."

"I don't even know if we *can* get back," I said. "Not without . . ." I broke off. I didn't want to tell her how we had bought our way in. "Why can't you take it?" I said instead. "You said magic doesn't touch you."

"Ah, but the king knows about me and has set particular wards to warn him of my approach if I dare to try. I would have tried, if there was no alternative, but"—she spread her hands—"here you are."

"And even if we do get it through . . . This new mold, or whatever it is, will infect the king and all his children?"

"Yes."

"Then what about Sylvester?" I asked.

She hesitated. For the first time, a shadow crossed her face. "Well," she said carefully, "he is a magic-worker."

"You yourself called him a sweet boy," I reminded her.

She laughed a little. "He's not the worst of them," she said. "But you have to remember, he's not really a person at all. Not as we understand it. He is a *made* thing, like a music box or a marionette. A toy for the king, fashioned out of the remains of a boy who will never come back to life, not as he was."

"But just because he is a made thing does not mean he should be unmade," I protested. "And he is helping me."

"Yes," she said gently, in a tone as soft as if she were telling a child that their beloved pet lamb had to be sacrificed for the family pot. "He has been helpful, I know. He is unusual. Perhaps because he is the only male magic-worker who has survived the king's process of creation—perhaps there was a fault in his making. It is to our advantage."

It felt wrong, to be discussing my sorcerer as if he were little more than one of the sharp-edged little animals that Da used to fold out of the butcher paper, to be crumpled and thrown away at day's end.

But he was a toy for the king, as she had said. And a dangerous one, at that. All the same, was it right to use him as a toy for our own game?

"I understand your feelings," she said. "You have been bound to him for a time."

"But I am not bound to him here," I said, "And I still don't feel right about using him in this way, knowing that he will die along with the others."

"Of course," she said, spreading her hands. "And if there were another way, we would do that."

"But there isn't," I said, letting my voice trail off so it was more like a question.

"But there isn't," she agreed. "Look, even if you do not take it, we will eventually find another way to get it there. And this way, you have a chance to save your family and friends before the king's great harvest."

I couldn't think of what to say.

"Do you have some small object I could borrow?" she asked. "Some trinket?"

"Um. . ." I rummaged through my pockets and came up with the little raven seal. "This?"

"Perfect." She enfolded it in her hand; her fingernails were caked with earth. "I will enclose a seed of the disease in this seal. Then all you have to do is will it, whenever you are ready, and it will come out. Or you can keep it sealed"—she chuckled at her own pun—"forever. Entirely up to you. Although, as I have said, we will find another way in eventually."

CHAPTER 21

What was left of my heart was troubled as we walked back to the cottage, but I tried to meet Sylvester's eyes without giving away the confusion I felt. It helped that he looked so ridiculous, and it was hard to do anything but smile.

"She can't help us with the hearts," I told him instead. "You were right. No one can fix them."

He unfolded himself from the chair. "I am sorry. I suspected it might be so."

"I am sorry, too," said the Weftwitch.

"We might still be able to stop my father, though," said Sylvester. "I have to try, at least. Knowing what I know now."

The Weftwitch raised her eyebrows. "Bold," was all she said.

"You said my father managed to defy his," Sylvester said to the Weftwitch. "Perhaps it runs in the family."

"You are welcome to stay here for a time, until you decide," offered the Weftwitch. She flicked her eyes to me, and I saw her fist was still closed about the seal.

"No," I said. "We have to go. The king is probably already

riding out. If we have any chance of stopping the harvest, we need to be quick."

"Very well," she said. "Let me make a few preparations, and I will pack you some victuals for the road."

She sent us on our way with a basket of fresh rolls, ham, cheese, and hard-boiled eggs, a skin of ale, and the little seal, which she slipped into my pocket without Sylvester noticing. It might have been my imagination, but it felt heavier and warm to the touch.

We said our farewells and started out toward the edge of the forest again. I imagined Cornelius curled up at the base of a tree, waiting for us, and resolved to save him some of the ham.

"Let us stop for a while," said Sylvester when we were perhaps halfway back. He had perked up considerably at the Weftwitch's cottage after the tea and the sugar, but now he looked very green about the gills again.

"All right. Maybe getting some food into you will help," I said.

We found a clearing and gathered some sticks for a small fire. Sylvester couldn't light one with magic, of course, but we managed all the same.

It was an oddly convivial little meal that we had there as the sun set and our little fire burned. We talked. I laughed, and so did he. I was surprised to find that I enjoyed his company, even without the spell, and that he seemed to enjoy mine.

"Are you feeling better?" I asked.

"Yes. I think food helps," he said. "It is like your meals, back home. Perhaps eating proper human food is what turned me into a proper human."

"Oh, so you're a proper human now?" I said, laughing.

"I feel like one, at least."

360

He stayed smiling and held my eyes, and his smile did not waver. I felt a spreading warmth, starting in what was left of my heart and moving through me and sinking into me like butter into hot toast.

I wondered if it was the spell descending again—but that was impossible. We were still in the Weftwitch's forest. I found that I wanted to reach over and touch the sharp lines of his cheekbone and jaw, see how his black curls would look against the pale skin of my breast.

Did I *actually* love him now, even without the magic?

That was a startling thought. I glared internally at the butterflies in my stomach and my quickening heartbeat, searching them for any sign of enchantment. I scoured them with my most clinical gaze, daring them to show any kind of magical sparkle. I doused them with my most wet-blanket, cold-water-pouring cynicism.

They were still there.

And what's more, he was still smiling at me. Even wrapped up in my comically too-small petticoat, he was inhumanly beautiful, and he had not dropped his gaze from mine. The moment stretched itself out like a yawning cat, long and luxurious, and the flattering firelight softened any chance of embarrassment or awkwardness.

Well, almost. I twisted my hands in my skirt. I wished I could forget myself even for a moment, and just enjoy the night and the firelight, without being painfully aware of how I looked from the outside.

"I remember the first time I saw you," he said, unexpectedly. "When you turned up at the House, out of nowhere, telling me you had come to be my housekeeper."

I felt myself cringe a little. "I was a fool," I said. "I didn't want to tell you I had been snagged."

"You were so sure of yourself."

"No, I wasn't!"

"Well, you seemed so," he insisted. "You spoke with such certainty. You seemed so strong. I wouldn't have dared turn you down. You are always so strong."

I remembered that girl, exhausted and heartsick, standing in front of the handsome sorcerer and trying to find any way possible to stay in his presence.

"Stop," I blurted. "I know how you see me."

"No, you don't."

"Of course I do!" I gestured at him. "Look at you. Everything about you is perfect."

"No, it isn't," he said, but I wasn't listening.

"You don't know what it's like," I said wildly. "To feel like you've always been wrong. That you shouldn't be here at all."

"Don't I?" he said drily.

"You can have anything, anyone you want. You can literally snap your fingers and *have* it, when you're out of this forest. You have no idea what it is like to be someone like me—none! You and your sisters think of us as servants, as crops to be harvested at your convenience." He had listened to me with his eyes turned down a little, allowing me to have my rant without interruption. He raised them to my face now.

"I'm sorry," he said.

That took the wind out of my sails. "What?"

"You are right about us. That we treat you like things and not people. It is what we were made to do. And you are right that we shouldn't exist. If it helps, we had no say in it."

"I know that," I said unwillingly.

"But you are wrong about some things too," he continued. "I do not think you are ugly. I do not know what you mean by that. I must see things differently from you, I think. Perhaps it is because I am not quite human, as you have said. I don't see the incredible beauty that you describe in me and my sisters, because I can also see the wrongness in us that you have talked about."

He paused and stared at the fire, before looking back at me. "I see it in myself like a sickness, moving under the skin. And I see the rightness in you. You belong in the world, Foss. You are right to take up space in it, and move through it, and leave your mark on it. There is nothing about you that should be other than it is."

I was flabbergasted. This was the longest speech I had ever heard from him concerning me—or anything.

"I don't understand what beauty is for you; but perhaps you can believe me when I say that *rightness*, that is beauty for me."

I didn't know what to say. No one had ever spoken to me like this, nothing near it. I couldn't believe that the sorcerer looked at me and saw something different from everybody else. And I could not believe the way he was looking at me now.

Neither of us was under a spell, for the moment, and we were in firelight, and his eyes glowed with ghostly light. I wondered if I was dreaming. It was so like dreams I had back at the House when I had been fully in his thrall and longing for him to enter my bedchamber at night.

"Am I dreaming?" I asked, just to clear it up.

"No," he said.

"Are you sure?"

"As sure as anyone can be about someone else's dream."

When he reached for me, I had to fight the urge to make a joke or say something about how much of a mess I was, or how marked the contrast was between his smooth white hand and the redness of my cheek as he rested his palm against it.

It took all of my strength to swallow the words and let him touch me without comment. He looked at me as if my face were wine, and he were thirst.

I could not meet his gaze, not even when he placed that

same smooth hand beneath my chin and tipped my mouth up to meet his.

His mouth was warm and soft, and tasted of magic: metal and spice. We bumped teeth for a moment before we found our rhythm, and I felt his smile against mine.

One of my hands gripped the grass at my side, while the other snaked into the waves of his black hair, smooth and lithe as water, just as I had imagined them, and his into my red locks, and I felt them tingle against my scalp.

Everything about me awoke. The woodsmoke was at once sharper, a blue-tinged scent, and the earth under my fist became as rough and sweet as sugar against my skin.

He pushed the stubborn curls back from my forehead and tucked them behind my ears, all without ceasing to kiss me, and I let my plump, work-roughened hands move over his skin also.

We clung together for a long time before we parted, and when we did, I felt the loss of his body against mine like a death. I would have died right on the spot, I think, had he not immediately taken my hands again and moved them to the buttons of my dress, showing me what he wanted.

I undressed myself, slowly, and with reluctance, peeling the layers off like you'd pick the skin off a stubborn orange. I was not accustomed to being naked, nor did I find it comfortable. When it was absolutely necessary, I did it as quickly as possible, leaping in and out of the bathtub as swiftly as I could and looking at as little of myself as I could possibly manage.

Occasionally I would glare at my knees, rising to the surface of the bath like two potatoes bobbing in a pot, or at my hands, red and stinging as I washed them free of the butchering blood, but for the most part, I avoided seeing any part of what I bound into place with buttons and belts every morning.

I had certainly never undressed before anyone else, as I was doing now. I felt like a babe learning about laces and fastenings for the first time—my fingers fumbled and slipped, until he put his hands over mine, gently, and stopped them.

I thought for a moment that he was stopping me altogether, I and flushed with shame—had I read it all wrong? Was the spell on me again, somehow, clouding my judgment?—but he took over the undoing for me, carefully taking apart all the fastenings of my clothing, his fingers working with grace and even reverence, as if he were undressing a goddess rather than my lumpen self.

Under his fingers, I felt myself softening and opening, forgetting my embarrassment as my body sprang to life everywhere he touched.

When he unwrapped himself from his makeshift garment and was fully naked, I could barely look at him for the beauty of it—his narrow hips, the length of his thighs, as smooth as if someone had carved them from cold butter.

I recoiled from him and did not meet his eyes. I did not want to see what was in them. Scorn would not have surprised me, nor disgust, although I imagined he would have tried to hide those for my sake. Kindness would have broken me, as would pity.

"What is the matter?" he asked.

"I am ashamed," I said.

"You should not be," he said.

He took my face in his long hands, closing it in like the frame around his old oil painting. I dreaded to think what I must look like, so encircled, and I pressed my eyes tighter shut. He stilled, however, and stayed unmoving for so long that, unwilling, my eyes started to open of their own accord.

I saw none of what I had feared. He looked back at me, open-faced, and, once again, there needed to be a new word for looking that didn't just mean eyes pointed in a direction, because this new look, like the very first, reached down into my gut, turned me inside out, and made me someone different and surprising.

I had thought, before this, all the times I had imagined this, that his being so well formed would look laughable beside my poor body, a body that I had been told so often with words and with glances was ugly, pitiable, even disgusting. But now I found that nothing of the sort was true.

When I reached for him and touched the smooth, white plane of his stomach, he shivered. I could not believe that I—I, Foss! Foss Butcher!—could produce such an effect. It made me feel more powerful than the king himself, knowing that I could touch Sylvester and make him tremble with wanting me.

"Wait," I said, as his hands traveled the length of my legs.

He paused.

"Just . . ." I said weakly.

"You are beautiful," he said, and pressed his mouth to the inside of my ankle, then my knee, leaving bright flowers of sensation wherever he kissed.

"I have never done this before," I confessed.

"Nor I," he said, and did not stop.

I finally saw what my body could be for, other than a clumsy sack for bundling up my innards. It responded so sweetly, so neatly, that it was hard to remember how ugly I had always felt. How ugly I thought the world had always found me.

I had experienced pleasure before, of course, at my own hand, but comparing that to this was like comparing a lone flute to the whole orchestra playing together, singing and strumming and drumming and all. And no edge of shame or anger to it either, as there had been on my own, when I knew that the things I was picturing would never really happen to me.

Even inside my own head, when I had imagined myself receiving pleasure, I had pictured myself as different—smaller, prettier, a different person altogether. There was no need for that now. I was myself only, and wholly myself, and he was himself, and we were together, traveling upward together in excited discovery toward some new, sweet landing place that would leave us both breathless.

My imaginings of it had all been exterior, from the outside looking in, which is perhaps why I had been so nervous about the real thing.

I had not expected the startling *interiority* of it. It was like the House, opening new rooms inside me in unexpected places. Inside me were whole worlds, it turned out, that people like Aron and his friends had never imagined.

I felt dizzy standing on the edge of my known self and looking into that vastness, seeing all the pinpricks of light that were little points of pleasure, placed all along every limb and nerve. The sorcerer worked a kind of magic in me, bringing all those separate lights together into one.

I was still not sure if he was entirely human, but all that meant was that we were discovering this together, how skin yielded to skin and opened, and I felt for the first time that I was made right, fit for my purpose, entirely well designed and engineered.

My hair was damp at the temples, and so was his. I was not aware of myself as ugly or beautiful, nor him. We were two creatures differently formed—unusually formed, maybe—but one no more wrong than the other.

I laughed, to feel myself so free.

CHAPTER 22

I woke in the morning feeling both comfortable and excruciatingly uncomfortable all at once. The discomfort came from the hard, cold ground that seemed to have fused the bones of my hips together, and the prickle of sharp grass against any patch of exposed skin—of which there was rather a lot more than usual, for me.

The fire had long died, and all that was left was a brave, orange smolder, like a half-open eye in the soapy mess of the ashes. The smolder and I stared at each other as I came back to consciousness, and took stock of my surroundings and inventory of my body, making sure that all bits were present and accounted for.

The comfort that I felt, despite the cold and the aches from sleeping outside, came from Sylvester. His long, smooth body was wrapped around mine as neatly as if I were a parcel of herbs and he the string that tied it.

I felt the rise and fall of his chest against my spine, and the warm curl of his hips against my buttocks—and something else that made me blush to think about.

He had drawn my petticoat up over us in the night, but it

had slipped down and now covered only the lower parts of our legs, leaving the rest exposed. I reddened, despite myself, and squirmed a little, and felt him huff out a breath against the nape of my neck as my movement made him stir before settling back into sleep.

Every inch of my skin, every ounce of my flesh, felt a delicious kind of surprise. The night before, I had awakened to myself in a new and unexpected way, and I felt as new as a fresh-born foal struggling to its feet.

I had seen inside myself, to my warmth and litheness and the intelligence of my lips and limbs, which had known exactly what to do without prompting, as wisely formed as any creature of the woods.

But it was morning now, and, despite myself, I felt that new knowledge retreating. I had been magical in the night and was no more; he was magical always.

We had been warm and laughing by the flattering fire. Looking down at my skin, exposed and with goose pimples, I could see every blemish, every hair, every vein, every pimple and dimple and roll. Would the sorcerer regret it, this morning, seeing me in this unforgiving gray light?

My bladder woke up and protested. I wiggled myself out of the sorcerer's embrace as slowly as I could, managing miraculously to extricate myself without waking him. I stood, my cold bones creaking, and looked back at him.

He was perfect, of course. His skin was completely smooth and unblemished, hairless even, featureless, and pale as bone. His hair was tousled, like mine, but where mine had turned into a bird's nest at the back, complete with twigs and leaves, his was merely artfully disheveled.

I made my way through the underbrush as quietly as I could to a secluded spot and squatted to relieve myself. When I had finished, I dressed myself as best I could with my chilly fingers, struggling a bit with the buttoning. It was a relief to feel the warm flannel against my skin, but also a sorrow to muffle the new, singing awareness of my naked skin.

I sank my hands into my pockets to warm them as I walked back to our little camp, and my fingers closed about the little raven seal. I froze. Was it my imagination, or did it feel denser, heavier? I remembered the Weftwitch's words and let go of the seal.

What if I willed it to work by accident, thinking of the king and the sorceresses in anger, and unwittingly destroyed Sylvester as well? Perhaps it would be best to throw it into the woods now and be done with it, as I certainly didn't ever plan to use it.

Or did I?

The thought startled me. Of course I didn't plan to use it, I told myself. Using it would mean annihilating Sylvester along with the rest of his so-called family. It was all or none, as the Weftwitch had said.

The little spell—or rather the enormous spell, contained in a tiny package—would kill all the users of heart magic, and there was no way around it. Sylvester was one of them. I couldn't spare him and eliminate the rest. I wasn't too keen on murdering the lot of them either, truth be told, despite how hateful they all were. It was so big, so grave an act.

I heard Sylvester sigh and yawn behind me, and I put my thoughts to one side. I brushed myself down and smoothed my hair as best I could, which wasn't much, and turned.

I was prepared for discomfort. I was prepared for embarrassment on his part, even shame, seeing me in the cold light.

What I was not prepared for was the smile that followed his yawn, an open, unfettered smile that turned his otherworldly beauty into something warmer and more human. I realized how seldom I had seen him smile or laugh before.

"Good morning," he said, without a shadow of awkwardness.

"Good morning," I replied, the words catching in my throat a little. I coughed, to cover it up. The sorcerer yawned again and stretched like Cornelius, seemingly completely unembarrassed by his nakedness. Of course, if I looked like him, I'd have been unembarrassed by my nakedness too. When he had finished his lengthy and luxurious stretch, he reached a hand to me.

"Aren't you cold?" I asked, keeping my voice level.

"I am never cold," he said, and smiled.

We stared at each other for a long moment. I did not take his hand, and after a few beats, he dropped it.

"We had better go," I said, a little gruffly. "Cornelius will be waiting."

"And so is my father," he said with a sigh. He rested his elbows on his knees and stared into space, his mouth set in a tight line. "Who knows how many hearts he has harvested by now."

"And who knows how many he has harvested while we sat here dallying this morning."

"I'm not sure how much use I would be, even if I were there right now. Me alone, against my father and all my sisters."

"Not just you," I said. "For all the good I'll do. But we need to get back. Even if it is a hopeless case. We need to try." Without thinking, I put my hand in my pocket and touched the little seal again, then flinched away as if it had burned me.

"Very well," he said, and stood, exposing his full glory. I had to avert my eyes, so I didn't turn into a beetroot. "Let us go."

We retraced our steps through the woods, back to the very edge where we had entered. We walked side by side, the sorcerer with his long stride and me with my usual small steps.

After a few moments, I felt something brush my hand. I looked down and saw the sorcerer's hand, palm up, welcoming, hinting. I put mine into it, and we walked that way, hand in hand, until we reached the edge of the forest. I dared not look at him, or speak, but our hands held their own kind of conversation.

The path ended just ahead, and there were our carriage and the magical horses, steaming a little in the cold.

It might have been my imagination, but I could almost see the air at the edge of the wood shimmering a little, like a mirage. *Magic.* Not heart magic but magic all the same. I halted and let Sylvester's hand drop.

"What is wrong?" asked Sylvester. He had a spring in his step, eager to get out of this forest that must have felt deadening and wrong to him, hobbling his powers. Probably also eager to get some proper clothes back on, to be fair.

"Just wait a moment," I said. I took a deep breath, trying to impress the taste of nonmagical air on my memory. I remembered the firelight, and the cold earth on my bare skin, and the tart, mineral smell of the ashes. Everything that I was leaving behind as I rejoined the world and rejoined the spell that had been lifted so briefly.

"All right," I said finally. "We can go."

We stepped out of the shadow of the trees, and I felt the spell settle on me again, like a bridle on a broken horse. It weighed down my butterfly-light spirit from the morning and turned it sickly, artificial, coated stickily with the false love and adoration that the heart magic created. I backed up in horror, colliding with a tree and setting its leaves to shivering.

"What is it?" asked Sylvester. Magical fabric swirled around him in ribbons of gleaming black, settling itself into a fine suit of clothes. A frothy cravat coiled itself round his neck, pinned with a single black stone at the hollow of his throat; and a pair

372

of tall, gleaming boots flowed up his shapely legs like oil before hardening.

He was the sorcerer again, remote and worship-worthy. I grasped for the genuine love I had felt for him inside myself, as you grasp for the tail end of a dream upon waking, but I felt it slithering away from me and disappearing, swallowed up by the heart magic.

Sylvester reached for me and pulled me toward him. I felt the terrible pull of the spell, the longing, and the real me was all mixed up in it somehow too, making a queasy hodgepodge of sensation that set both my stomach and my head to roiling.

I was drawn to him and repulsed at the same time. As his lips parted, I saw both the smile of a lover and the grimace of a monster.

"Don't touch me!" I cried, hands raised, warding him off, and stepped out of his arms.

"Foss . . ."

He took a step toward me. I backed away farther.

"What is it?" He stopped, one arm still outstretched.

"We can't," I said. I felt the spell swirling in me, thick and sweet as honey, turning my head and befuddling my senses.

"But why . . ."

"The spell," I said. "Now that we are no longer in the Weft-witch's wood, I am under your spell again. Snagged. Hooked. And with only half a heart left, if that."

He let his arm drop to his side as he thought about this. "But in the forest, when you were not ensorcelled by any magicks—you came to me then."

"I did."

"So that was not the spellbinding. That was just . . . us."

"I know." I swallowed hard, as childish tears rose in my throat. I plopped myself down onto a handy stump and dropped my head into my hands. "You have no idea how much

I want to," I said, my voice muffled through my fingers. "But that's the problem."

"Why?" he said. Was he being intentionally dense? But when I peeked at him, he looked concerned and puzzled, that was all.

"Because now it's all muddled up," I explained. "What I feel, me, Foss, is tangled with the spell that's *making* me feel things, all over again, and I can't tell where one ends and the other begins. If we . . . did anything now, it would be all snarled up, don't you see? It would be tainted."

"Tainted," he repeated, turning the word over in his mouth. It sounded oddly clean and distinct, the way he said it.

"Do you see?"

"Yes, I see," he said.

We looked at each other helplessly. How I wanted to leap at him, to let him kiss me, as he had the night before, and more! I felt weary, a hundred years old.

If I could not be free of this spell until one or the other of us died, Sylvester and I would never again be free to embrace as we had in the Weftwitch's wood. Unless, that is, we decided to damn the world, damn Da and all the population of our kingdom, and live together in selfish bliss in the forest.

I could train under the Weftwitch, as she had said happened with people like me. Sylvester would be safe from his doom. The corruption could not touch me there.

I imagined it: a cottage in the woods. Sylvester waiting there, perhaps tending the garden or the chickens, while I went to the villages for the odds and ends we needed. Cornelius curled up by the fire. Yes, all right, it was hard to picture Sylvester tending chickens, but we could deal with that later.

Maybe there would even be a way to bring Da across the border to live with us. Maybe he could open a new butcher's shop. And then all three of us would be free of the magic-workers and their terrible, voracious, insatiable appetites.

I wished it were possible. I wished it with all my heart. I didn't even *like* them, any of the other villagers with whom I'd grown up. I didn't even like people in general, really.

But I couldn't do it. I would never be happy, knowing that Da had been harvested and was dead, or worse. And knowing that we had doomed our kingdom to a slow death—half of it to heartsickness, the other half to the spreading corruption that would curse the crops, the livestock, and the water, and then finally dissolve the king's walls and let in the war. Sylvester would never agree to it, either. At least, I hoped he would not.

Thinking of living here, abandoning the kingdom to its fate, gave me the same skin-crawling sense of wrongness that I'd had when I had first seen Sylvester's magic in person.

The king's magic-workers weren't right. They were a creeping sickness on the world, like the mold that blighted their store of hearts, and I could not leave my kingdom, unnaturally warped and bespelled as it was, to suffer any longer under their rule.

"There you are," said Cornelius, pouring himself down from a tree like black ink and reassembling himself at the bottom. "I was beginning to think you'd never come out."

"We have learned a great deal," said Sylvester, and I knew he meant more than just what the Weftwitch had told us.

I held out my arms, desperate for comfort, and, to my surprise, Cornelius jumped into them. He touched my nose with his, feather-light.

"Did she fix your heart?" he asked.

"No," I said. "She doesn't know how. I don't think anyone does. She sent the message to the Snagged so they would help her spread the corruption. That's all."

"Then what was the point of all this?" said Cornelius. Reasonably.

Well, I couldn't tell him that she'd armed me with enough magic to fell all the sorceresses and the king—and Sylvester—at once.

"We just need to go back," I said. "Even if we can't repair the hearts, we can try to stop the king from taking more."

Sylvester nodded. I had been a little afraid he would argue with me, but Cornelius was the one who objected.

"Why can't we stay here?" he said. "It sounds like we're going to our doom."

Well, yes. It was hard to deny.

"You can stay here, Cornelius," I said. "I am sure you could find a home with a warm fire and plenty of bacon. I wouldn't blame you for it."

"Well, of course I'm coming with you," said Cornelius, giving his whiskers a quick wash. "But that doesn't mean I don't think it's a terrible idea."

"I agree that we cannot abandon the kingdom," said the sorcerer, "but I do not know how we are supposed to return to it. Did the Weftwitch give you any ideas?"

"She said there are weaker points in the mist, but that was it."

I had pinned so many of my hopes on the Weftwitch, thinking that she would mend my heart and send me back with the recipe for repairing all the rest, and she had been so very different from what I had imagined.

She had provided me with a way to defeat the magic-workers, it was true, but not with a way of getting back to the kingdom and using it.

They could sneak messages or objects through, she had said, but travelers lost their lives, or their senses, even if they did successfully make it through.

There were weak points through which her self-sacrificing messengers had forced themselves, but she had said they didn't survive long on the other side.

"The Weftwitch said they have their own manner of mag-icks here," I added out loud. "Magicks that don't use hearts. We've seen it."

"It won't work," said Sylvester with finality.

"Why?" I was annoyed that he wouldn't even entertain the thought.

"The barrier was created with heart magic. The Weftwitch is right—it is an evil magic, but it is powerful. The most power-ful. A spell cast with heart magic can only be undone with the same, as you can only unlock a door with the key made for it."

"Then how are we to get back?" I cried. "If you cannot use heart magic?"

"I do not know," he said.

"We didn't even have enough to get us through the first time without using mine," I said, folding my arms tightly over my chest.

"We are not using yours."

"I wasn't planning to volunteer, thank you very much," I snapped. "I'm not so much under your spell that I'm prepared to throw away the last piece of my heart I have left."

At the mention of the spell, his eyes dropped to the ground. I felt a pang and spoke more gently. "You're the one with the magic. You must be able to think of a way."

He sighed. "If we get back to the border, and I'm able to study the mist and the weak spots . . . maybe I will find one."

We found another escort waiting for us a little way out of the forest—I suppose the Weftwitch had arranged it for us somehow. They eyed us warily still, but less so than the day before.

She must have given us her seal of approval, or at least assured them that we posed no threat, because there was no traveling cage for the sorcerer this time. They didn't even bind his hands. They allowed all three of us to sit in the carriage and merely trotted alongside, not even looking in the windows.

Sylvester and I kept a decorous distance on opposite seats, arranging our knees so that they wouldn't brush each other. Cornelius jumped onto my lap and looked from one to the other of us. I suppose his cat senses told him something of what had been going on, but he made no comment.

Sylvester and I avoided one another's gazes until we got back to the encampment, and then exchanged one quick look before we stepped down from the carriage—a sort of bracing, a summoning of our resources, ready for the next challenge.

The headwoman took us back to the border. If you squinted a little, it could have looked like a forest of silver-barked winter trees, stripped of leaves, stark and tall.

But they were not trees. The endless, relentless mist shimmered and seemed to bend a little with the brisk wind, but it remained just as sinister and unbroken as ever. On the other side of that line was our kingdom, with all its beauties and terrors. With its pulsing heart magic.

The headwoman fell back a little so she could whisper in my ear.

"I hear that you might rid us of the king and his spawn for good," she said to me quietly. "All our magic-workers have been working on this spell for a century. If you can get it through ..."

"I don't know yet if we are able to," I said. "We will try."

"But *you* are able to." She raised her eyebrows meaningfully. I pressed my lips together. The Weftwitch had been altogether too free with her information, I felt.

"I'm not sure yet if I'm going to use it," I said. "We might be able to defeat them without a measure so ... drastic."

She snorted. "*Drastic* is all that will work," she said. "You think your sorcerer would be able to defeat all the magic-workers in the kingdom?"

"Maybe," I said defensively.

"The king would never create a child capable of defeating

him," she said with finality, "however many hearts that child might wield."

"I'm not ready to give up on him yet," I said.

She shrugged. "Whether you are ready or not," she said, "you will have to use it."

I was not ready for that conversation. "Can you show us the weak points in the border?"

We had caught up to Sylvester, who was almost at the mist. It swirled greasily. This close, I could see the faintest outlines of bare trees just inside it. Where it met the living grass on which we stood, the blades had turned yellow and limp.

"All souls taken by your king," said the headwoman. "Whether consumed by the mist itself, or stolen for him by the magic-workers. Always hungry. Never at rest."

"Taken by the magic-workers?"

"Oh yes. When their hearts are used up, and they can live no longer, some die, and their souls make their way here. Others are drawn to the mist by the king's magic and walk into it willingly while they still live. Either way, this is where they all end up. You have to admire the king for it, in a way—finding a way to use them even after their deaths."

I stared at the mist. So Dav was in there somewhere, and Colin. I did not know what happened to us after we died, but I was pretty sure we weren't meant to be trapped in a ravenous spell for all eternity. I had thought the Snagged would at least be free after their deaths, however tragic, but it seemed there was no chance of escaping the king—as long as he and the magic-workers lived.

I supposed I would end up in there too, if we failed.

The headwoman led us a little away along the edge of the mist and then scuffed at the earth with her foot, revealing a line of white chalk under the loose gravel and dead leaves.

"Here's one spot," she said. "It's a big one, relatively speaking.

I don't know how much luck you'll have, but you're welcome to try."

Sylvester stared at the mist, pacing up and down, reaching out a hand to almost touch it at intervals. It reminded me of the way a man would look at a horse for sale, examining its teeth, running his hands down each leg, feeling for the strength of its back. I suppose he was analyzing the spell again, looking for any chink that he might be able to use to prize it open.

It was almost like watching a dance as well, I decided, one with intricate movements and endless possibilities for missteps. His cloak billowed out behind him as he marched up and down, swirling dramatically every so often as he turned.

After a long time, he sank to the ground and sat cross-legged, staring straight ahead with his jaw set. Cornelius and I exchanged glances, and I ventured to walk over to him.

"Well?" I asked.

"Nothing," he said. "I can find no way to make an opening large enough for us."

I thought quickly. "What about one large enough for Cornelius? Maybe he could carry something through, something you imbue with enough magic to . . ."

"And then what? What is a cat, even a talking cat, going to do with it on the other side? He cannot cast a spell. Only I can do that."

If I gave him the little seal, I thought. *Maybe Cornelius could carry it through, and maybe he could will it to . . .*

No. I couldn't do that to Cornelius, put him in that kind of danger alone. Although the idea of keeping Sylvester in the Other Kingdom had an appeal. Perhaps the barrier would keep him safe from the seal, while the rest of the magic-workers died on the other side of it. Even if just Cornelius and I went through, and Sylvester stayed . . . I could use the seal, and perhaps he would be all right.

"What are you thinking?" he said.

"Nothing," I said. "I can't think of anything."

"Nor I." He sighed. He twisted his hands in a sudden, violent motion, and a fireball appeared between them. He juggled it between his palms, frowning. "And it's harder for me here. My magic doesn't work as well. Even for trivial things such as this."

"So, what we need," I said slowly, "is a vast store of heart magic for you to access. Enough that it overcomes the difficulty of using your magic here at all and is strong enough to break down the border, at least temporarily."

"Well, no such magic store exists, convenient as it would be."

"The House," I said.

"What?"

"The House. The whole thing is heart magic. And it has a life of its own. Growing, changing . . . spreading. It's enormous. Room after room. All heart magic. And it's part of you." I looked at Sylvester. "If it's part of you, can you still . . . feel it, from here? Can you use it to pull us through?"

Sylvester looked thoughtful. He balanced the fireball on his index finger and spun it. "That's not a bad idea," he said. "I suppose it is a store of magic, of sorts. Although it is a little . . . unpredictable."

"It's the best plan we have," I said. "And the only one. We can at least try."

So, try we did. Or rather, Sylvester did, standing very straight with his arms at his sides and eyes closed at the edge of the mist, as Cornelius and I hovered anxiously about him.

The mist shimmered and swayed. It may have been my imagination, but there seemed a new alertness about it, as if it was craning to see what we were doing.

Sylvester pressed his hands together, and an eye-aching blackness appeared between his palms. He drew them apart slowly, forming the blackness into a long tablet, and placed it on the ground like a tiny obelisk. He stepped back, and so did we.

There was an odd resonance to it, a hum, like a tuning fork just struck. It looked like it longed to be bigger. It was unsettling to look at it for too long, honestly—you started to feel like you might fall into the density of its blackness and keep on falling.

Sylvester made an odd gesture, and the sense of pressure and resonance grew stronger. I half expected it to pop open like one of those trick snakes the sprouts bought from the traveling peddlers, but instead it swallowed us up into blackness, arcing overhead and blotting out the sky so that we stood surrounded by warm, uncomfortably fleshlike darkness that seemed to be very faintly breathing.

There was no sign yet of our own kingdom, but I imagined I could somehow still feel its presence—a bristling menace at the edge of my consciousness. Cornelius had dug his claws into the skin of my shoulder, but I only noticed that once the world stilled around us, and I could catch my breath.

"Sorry," Cornelius said, and released my shoulder as gently as he could.

"It's all right." If I'd had claws, I would have stuck them out too. I could tell that this was the House, even though there was nothing remotely House-like about the long, dark throat in which we found ourselves. It still felt familiar.

I suppose it had either tucked the kitchen and throne room and bedchambers away inside itself somewhere, or re-formed them into some other shape, as was its wont. The floor moved ever so slightly under my feet, so slightly that I would have thought I had imagined it, if it weren't for Cornelius hissing, just a little, under his breath.

"It's ... different," I said, which didn't begin to cover it.

"It can take many forms," said Sylvester, "as you have seen."

"Well, I wish it had taken on a less unsettling one," I muttered.

The black tunnel stretched ahead, illuminated by a dim light that seemed to come from everywhere at once.

"Did it work?" I asked. "Will it take us back to the city?"

"I'm not sure," said Sylvester, comfortingly.

"And how will we know when we're past the mist?" I pressed.

"Distance doesn't have the same meaning here," replied Sylvester.

"So, we won't know?"

"I don't think so." He placed one white palm against the wall of the tunnel. It seemed to move slightly under his hand. "Follow me."

Sylvester led the way, and Cornelius and I trailed behind him, hoping that the House wouldn't dare swallow up its own master. I let one hand fall into the pocket where I kept the little seal and turned it over in my fingers, for comfort. I imagined that it had an odd, acidic tingle against my skin—but that could just have been my fancy. Cornelius growled softly in my ear.

"I know, I don't like it either," I said.

The House creaked and groaned around us. I imagined it as a beleaguered boat on a rough sea, the sea being the strange other space that it occupied, outside of what we thought of as distance and time. It felt like the House's boundaries were putting up a fight against whatever was outside, and that they might be losing, but Sylvester continued to stride ahead with the appearance of confidence, and so we followed.

"What will happen to us if the House collapses?" I tried to make it sound as if I was just idly curious.

"I don't know," said Sylvester over his shoulder.

"Would we be trapped in the House, or what's left of it? Or would we end up outside in whatever's out there?"

"I told you, I don't know," said Sylvester.

Either way sounded horrendous. Or what if it spat us out right into the mist? I tried to slow my thoughts. It was so dark; that was the problem. There was nothing to distract me but blackness and more blackness. I tried to concentrate on the sorcerer's lean silhouette ahead.

"Is it just me," I muttered to Cornelius so that only he could hear me, "or is the tunnel narrowing?"

I felt the flicker of his tail against my nape. "It's not just you," he said. "It's definitely getting tighter."

"That can't be good," I said.

"Keep going," said Sylvester—and was I imagining it, or was there a thread of anxiety in his voice?

My ears made a popping sound, and I felt pressure inside my skull. The blackness around us grew heavy and foreboding, like big-bellied storm clouds gathering before a downpour. I imagined I could feel the substance of the House pressing back against it, but something Outside was trying to push its way in. I pictured it slicing into the House somehow from the outside, cutting through its layers of heart magic to find us, pink and vulnerable as baby rabbits in a burrow when the plough comes.

Sylvester started walking faster, and I struggled to keep up with him. The pressure in my head was painful, and it was starting to affect my vision as well. The walls pressed in.

"Not much further," said Sylvester, in a voice that was probably meant to be comforting.

A sudden, blinding flash, something like lightning, tore open the dark—and it stayed open, hanging like cut cloth, opening to a sharply painful white nothingness that reminded me of teeth. More and more of the blackness behind us was shredded. The floor pulsed underfoot, forcing us forward faster and faster.

Sylvester reached back and grabbed my hand, and we

ran, keeping just in front of the terrible light and tearing. The House shuddered and bumped us along, keeping us always just far enough ahead.

I felt sorry for all the times I had been impatient or irritated with it, because without the House's help, we could never have run fast enough to escape.

I tried to keep pace with Sylvester, but I was holding him back. I released his hand, and, reaching up to where Cornelius had coiled around my neck, I hurled him at Sylvester. He hooked his claws into the sorcerer's cape, more from surprise than any sense of self-preservation.

"What are you doing?" demanded Sylvester, turning.

"I can't keep up with you," I panted. "You and Cornelius need to run ahead."

"Don't be ridiculous," said Sylvester, grabbing my hand again. I tried to wrest it from him, but his grip was too firm. "We are *all* going to reach the city."

We stumbled along, far slower than I would have liked, while the House fell piece by piece into the void behind us. The tunnel became narrower and narrower, until we could no longer stand straight, but had to stoop, almost bent in half, in order to fit.

We would never move fast enough like this, I thought, but again the House convulsed, and pushed us farther along itself, like a snake swallowing a mouse and working it down its long throat. Its movements seemed more labored now, though, and weaker. We didn't have too long.

"There!" said Sylvester, pointing ahead. I saw a sliver of light, little more than a fingernail. By now we were almost crawling. The press of the blackness around us was sickening, fleshlike and heavy and entangling, but it was better than the bright snapping and tearing behind us.

We pushed our way through, like babies struggling to be

born, using our feet and hands to push the darkness aside, and nudging our way toward the light as best we could.

There was little to no resistance to provide handholds or footholds as we pushed, just malleable black that gave way like bread being kneaded, and it felt almost impossible to make progress.

Sylvester was almost through, wiggling himself through the tiny gap, when my leg cramped horribly and stopped me from moving forward. I called to Sylvester for help, but his upper body was already on the other side, and I suppose sound might have been distorted or altogether muffled out there, because he did not respond.

I struggled but could not get enough purchase with one leg to move. Then I felt a furry nudging and Cornelius pushing with all his might. He could easily have followed the sorcerer through the exit, hanging onto him with his feline agility, but instead he had made his way behind me and was trying to help.

"Cornelius, you silly ass!" I cried. "Get out of there!"

It was helping, though. He pushed me enough that I could get my hands on the odd, amorphous opening and start to pull myself through. Sylvester was on the other side, and he grasped my arms at the elbows and started to pull.

"Come on, Cornelius!" I yelled behind me. "I'm fine now, you can come out."

I felt him scrabble at my back, trying to climb, and then he was gone. I fell out of the hole and into the Other House so suddenly that the sorcerer couldn't support my weight, and I staggered. I turned round immediately to see Cornelius struggling to follow. His head and one paw were out.

"Cornelius!" I cried.

He mewed, a kittenish noise. His ears lay flat on his skull, and his eyes were wide as platters. His throat moved as if he were trying to speak, but no sound came out. He seemed to be making progress, and then suddenly, he was sucked backward, as if something had grabbed his back paws and yanked.

"Cornelius, hold on!" I shouted. "Sylvester, do something!"

Before he could move, however, I thrust my arm into the swallowing black. It felt like plunging into the mouth of a great black leech that was intent on sucking the skin and flesh right off my bones. I did my best to ignore the pain and fished around for Cornelius in the dying maw of the House.

At first, I felt nothing but that terrible suction, and then my fingers touched softness. I thrust my arm in all the way to the armpit, hoping my shoulder wouldn't dislocate with the terrible pressure, and was able to grasp skin and fur in my fist.

"I've got him!" I cried. "Help me!"

I didn't even know if Cornelius was still alive in that black and airless space, but I pulled as hard as I could, so hard that I felt my elbow pop, and Sylvester held me under the arms and pulled in turn.

Together, we had just enough force to prize open the rapidly closing hole enough for Cornelius's limp, furry body to squeeze through. The pressure was so great that I worried he might be crushed by it, or at least have broken bones, but there was no way of telling until we had him safe.

Sylvester and I stumbled backward as I clutched Cornelius's body to my chest, and we fell together in a tangle on the dusty boards of the Other House as the magical House swallowed itself, like a snake eating its own tail, and disappeared into itself with a sudden, convulsive movement that felt like the world turning itself inside out for a moment.

The air seemed to rush toward it, then out again, a giant creature taking its last breath. Then it was just me, Sylvester, and Cornelius, flat on the floor, while the Other House creaked and groaned around us, and the spiders clung to their webs, wondering what on earth had just happened.

I was wondering the same and was scared to look down at the little bundle in my arms, fearing the worst. I was so worried, in fact, that I didn't realize I was lying right on top of Sylvester until he stirred under me, and then I jumped off him like a water droplet off a hot stove.

"Cornelius?"

His eyes were closed. I felt him gently for any damage, but he seemed to be intact. I held one fingertip to his dry little nose and felt a huff of warmth as he breathed.

"He's alive," I said to Sylvester. "But I don't know if he's injured."

"Let me," said the sorcerer. He got to his feet and came to me, taking the little cat gently from my arms and cradling him. He looked so small. His paws hung limply, looking naked and vulnerable.

Sylvester bent his head, his silky hair falling forward in a graceful swathe, and blew out a long, shimmering ribbon of breath that wound around Cornelius's body before dissipating.

Cornelius stirred and twitched. I had to clasp my hands to keep from reaching out to him as I watched and waited. After a second, a sliver of yellow eye showed, then two, and his ears flickered.

"Cornelius?" I said gently.

"Foss," he said. His voice was rough. He licked his dry nose, showing a sharp point of a tooth.

"Are you all right?"

"I think so." He stretched out his back paws experimentally and only then realized he was in the arms of the sorcerer. He started a little, but I heard the beginning rumbles of a purr.

"Cornelius." I reached out my hand and stroked him under the chin. His eyes closed to little slits of pleasure. "Thank you."

"I have not had a chance to examine him fully," said Sylvester, "but he may have been hurt internally. Cats are good at hiding such things."

"I feel fine," said Cornelius.

I cupped the cat's little head in my palm, my heart swelling with love and rage. "He had better be all right, or . . ." I realized what a ridiculous statement that was. "Well, he had just better be all right, that's all."

Sylvester released Cornelius gently, near the ground, and the cat started washing himself vigorously. He made a face and spluttered some loose fur from his tongue. "Tastes funny," he said.

"Like magic?"

"And ash." He shook himself vigorously. He seemed to be returning rapidly to his old self. "Now what?"

"We're in the Other House," I said. "We need to get out into the city, and then find the king and the sorceresses. With any luck, they haven't yet ridden out."

"I had no idea this place was still here, underneath," said the sorcerer, looking around at the wood and plaster.

"Not for much longer," said Cornelius.

He wasn't wrong. The place was creaking and cracking like a ship in a high storm. The final demise of the House seemed to have sucked the last bit of strength from its beams and buttresses, and I had the feeling that if we didn't hurry, we'd be buried under them. It seemed as if the vines were the only things holding it up.

"Yes," said Sylvester, shaking his head a little as if to clear it. "Come."

He reached out his hand to me, and after a moment, I took it. Even after all that excitement, it was cool and dry in mine. I fought the urge to take mine back and wipe it on my skirt.

We ran. I did my best to keep up with the sorcerer's long

stride, but it was a struggle, especially after having to push my way through the tunnel. I wasn't sure how much more my body would put up with. The cracking, occasional crash, and shower of dust gave my feet the added fuel they needed, though.

Even the vines were dying, shriveling and browning as we ran, then snapping underfoot, dry and parched. We made it out into the street and kept running, hearing the sounds of destruction behind us, until we were far enough that it felt safe to turn and look.

I looked at the place where the House had been and saw the Other House—the dusty, ramshackle old mansion—back where it belonged.

Like a tree that had been long colonized by twisting vines, it looked brittle and dead. Cornelius and I exchanged glances, remembering our first time fighting through the vines and cobwebs.

As I watched, it started to collapse into itself as an ordinary, rickety building collapses, creaking and crashing and sending up puffs of elderly dust.

The magic of the House had been supporting it in some way, I suppose, even while it had been shoved into that magical void, and with that support gone, the old building could no longer stand.

Even the twisted vines, so full of juice and malice, fell with it. I could smell their sap as they snapped. We stood and watched as it disintegrated—the sorcerer's House and the old mansion it had inhabited, both now gone forever.

CHAPTER 23

When the final rumbles from the two Houses' destruction had ceased, and the dust had settled, we finally had the time and leisure to look about us.

We were in the city—but I couldn't believe it was the same city. Perhaps we had somehow slipped through the complicated bonds between the House and the Other House into one of the distortions of space and time that Sylvester liked to talk about.

Not only was menace so strong in the air that you could almost smell it, but the streets were deserted, and all the windows and doors I could see were either shuttered tight or boarded up. The barricades showed signs of haste—the boards were mismatched, as if torn from different pieces of furniture or floorboards, and the nails that I could see were haphazardly set. The whole place felt as uninhabited as the ghost town that we had stumbled into across the border.

"What happened here?" I wondered, turning slowly around. This quiet was unnatural. More than that, there was tension thrumming in the air that even my nonmagical self could feel.

"I'm feeling a bit dizzy," said Cornelius. I gathered him into my arms, where he felt smaller than usual. I ran my hand over his fur, feeling for any injury.

"I don't think I'm hurt," he said. "I just feel odd."

"I'm not surprised, after nearly being swallowed back there," I said, and kept him cradled in my arms as we walked.

"There are people here. I can feel them," Sylvester said. "They are inside. They are afraid."

His voice echoed oddly off the buildings—the silence was that thick, with not even the scurry and squeak of a rat to break it.

I made a decision. I went to the nearest door and pounded on it, loud enough to wake the dead.

"What are you doing?" said Sylvester.

I banged my fists even harder. "Open up!" I yelled "I'm not going to stop!"

Finally, the door opened a sliver. I saw two frightened eyes and a slice of a nose.

"What's going on here?" I demanded. "Where is everyone?"

"The king . . ." said the eyes and nose in a wavering voice. They looked beyond me and saw Sylvester. The eyes widened in horror and panic, and the person would have slammed the door if I hadn't seen that coming and jammed my foot in the way, between some of the hastily nailed boards. "I thought they were all gone!" they gasped.

"The magic-workers? Where did they go?" I demanded.

"They rode out. All of them. The king, and the ladies . . . so splendid. Like a parade. Everyone came out and cheered." It was an old woman, I realized, and one who was clearly very frightened. "We'd never seen anything like it. The king told us there was an army on the border, that they were going to stop the army. He told us not to be afraid, but to stay inside and bar the doors until he returned."

Clever. We all grew up knowing that the king and his sorceresses protected us from war and invasion. If rumors of their vast harvest this time made it to the city and more central villages, the king could claim the people had merely been casualties of this supposed war.

And by couching the harvest as a parade to certain victory, they would have the kingdom's people lining the streets throwing flowers and waving flags, cheering on their own destruction.

The old woman's eyes kept drifting to Sylvester, and I saw the familiar look of awe and longing on her wrinkled face. Even now, as she huddled terrified in her house, she was caught up by his beauty and glamor, a rabbit mesmerized by a snake. The fact that I loved the snake didn't make me any less sympathetic to the rabbit.

"How long have they been gone?" I asked. I had to ask her twice, because she was so busy staring at Sylvester.

"Since yesterday," she said. "We haven't heard a thing. Do *you* know anything?"

This last was directed at Sylvester.

"Uh . . ." He was at a loss for words. "No. But . . . stay inside. Keep waiting for news."

"And keep your door locked," I said to her—uselessly, because, of course, the king and sorceresses were already gone, and even if they weren't, a wooden door wouldn't present much of an obstacle.

I had to say something, though, to assuage the terrible rage and helplessness I felt. She didn't need telling twice, but shot back into her burrow quick as winking, with only one more quick glance at the sorcerer.

"They moved swiftly," said Sylvester.

"We knew they would," I said. "And now we have to catch up. Who knows how many hearts they've harvested already?"

"And our visit to the Weftwitch armed us with nothing more than knowledge."

My conscience prickled as I thought of the seal. "We have to go to the palace," I said quickly, smothering my guilt. "We need some kind of weapon against the king. Your magic against him and all your sisters . . . Even if you were the most powerful sorcerer in the world, we would have no chance."

Sylvester nodded. "There may yet be usable hearts. Unless my father took them all with him."

"Let's hope he didn't," I said grimly. Cornelius was half-asleep in my arms. I stroked his head. "Maybe you should stay here," I told him. "Find a safe spot and wait for us."

"Nonsense," he squeaked. "I'm coming with you."

"I can get us up to the palace," said Sylvester. "Just. But we will need to use the carriage for the rest of the journey. It will take several hours to catch up to my father."

"Then we need to go now," I said.

There was a queasy lurch in my stomach as Sylvester re-arranged reality around us, but after the nightmare we'd just been through with the House, it felt like a pleasant evening stroll.

Like the rest of the city, the palace was abandoned. I suppose a skeleton staff probably continued working inside, as a place like that needed a lot of daily maintenance.

"No guards at the gate," I remarked. "That's lucky."

Sylvester shook his head. "It means the king has set wards that negate the need for guards." He stood with a wide stance, the same look of concentration on his face that he'd had when he faced down the mist. "I can feel them. Like a net cast over the place."

"Can you get through?"

"I think so." He turned to look at me, his hair sparkling with the first evening dew. He held out his hand. "With help."

"What?" I almost dropped Cornelius, who mewed in protest.

"This bond between us," he said. "I have been thinking on it for a long time. When my mistake met your heart, it formed a

394

connection that I still don't fully understand, but which seems to work on my magic in a similar way that the House did—only better."

"What?"

"You must have noticed how your touch has helped me when I am casting. When you managed to calm the chaos I caused in the House with the spell book. When you helped me open the door to the chamber where Millie was imprisoned. You diffuse the wild magic that could spill out and cause damage, but you also help me focus what remains."

I just gaped at him.

"With the House gone, there is no way to siphon off any excess magic I might produce," he continued. "From here on, all of it will pour into any spell I cast. That could be disastrous, especially when I am using the hearts."

"Right, we don't want to blow the place up," I conceded, remembering all the times he had nearly burned down the House. "Fine." I took his hand. "But I don't think . . ."

As soon as I touched his skin, an iridescent membrane shimmered into being before the doors of the palace.

"There it is," said Sylvester softly. He exhaled, and the membrane popped like a bubble. I imagined I heard a similar, smaller pop from inside his cloak as another of our store of hearts winked out of existence. I hated that we had to use them, but what choice did we have?

Even though the wards were gone, we walked into the palace with caution. Cornelius protested that he was well able to walk on his own four paws, thank you very much, but I continued to carry him.

Besides my concern about his well-being, his warm weight was comforting. The place still gave me the creeps.

Sylvester knew the way to the storage room, which I was

grateful for, since I hadn't been in my best frame of mind the last time I was here.

The corruption had clearly spread rapidly since we left. Almost every jar contained a heart speckled with green and black, furred with mold.

We walked quietly between the rows, with no sound but the faint clink and slosh as we lifted down those which seemed least affected. I tried not to look at the board to which I had been strapped, nor at the telltale stain on the floor where the jars had smashed.

Finally, we had gathered as many of the relatively good hearts as we could find, and Sylvester stashed them in his seemingly infinitely capacious pockets until even they ran out of room.

"Right, let's go," he said, when we had finished.

"Stop," I said. "There's one more thing."

He read it in my face. "Foss . . . It's too late. And if we interrupt the transformation before it is complete . . . I don't know if she would even survive. We can come back later, when all this is over, and I can study her then, mayhap find a way to . . ."

"There will probably *be* no later," I argued.

"Foss . . ."

"No, I'm being realistic. Of course we're going to try, but what chance do we stand, really? And if the king gets rid of us both, he'll just come back here and continue on his merry way. Millie will spend another few years floating in that godsforsaken tank, and then pop out as half a monster, just as you did."

"Thank you," he said, with heavy sarcasm.

"You know what I mean. Maybe she'll be more like you, but more likely not. And honestly, she might be better off dead than turning into that."

He huffed out a frustrated breath.

"Sylvester. Please." I touched his arm, lightly. He looked

down at my hand where it rested on the velvet of his sleeve and sighed.

"Fine. Let us go, then."

It seemed the king hadn't been too concerned that anyone would come for Millie, as the locks on the chamber with the transformation tank weren't even fastened. I suppose that, to him, it would be impossible to imagine that anyone would want this unwanted child, especially in her in-between state.

I knew what I was walking into this time, and it was still a shock. She hovered in that honey-gold liquid, pinned and preserved like a specimen. Her heart, now fully blackened, still floated just a little away from the rest of her.

"How do we get her out without hurting her?" I asked.

Sylvester placed his hands against the glass, or crystal, or whatever the tank was made of.

"I'm not sure exactly how it works," he admitted. "I do know that the heart is taken out of us and replaced with something else, and that our original hearts wither and die. But I don't know if she can survive without it attached to her yet."

The thread connecting her to her heart was something like an umbilical cord then, passing something from the organ to her. Something she must still need.

"I think I can get her out," Sylvester finally said, still touching the glass with questing fingers, like a blind man reading a face. I knew he was examining the spell as best he could, trying to see it like one of the fiery cats' cradles with which he liked to play. "But I can't do anything about her heart. The new one inside her may have grown enough to sustain her . . ."

"Or it might not have," I finished. I chewed on my lip.

"It's up to you." He turned to look at me, his eyes bright silver in the eerie light emanating from the tank.

"Do it," I decided.

Sylvester nodded. He reached out a hand for me again. I hesitated.

"Are you sure?" I asked. "This seems like a delicate process."

"All the more reason."

I gently placed Cornelius on the ground and touched Sylvester's hand, lightly at first, then laced his fingers with mine. He waited for me to nod and then pressed his other hand against the glass of the tank. I really hoped it wouldn't explode. Cornelius crouched beneath the shelter of my skirt, just in case.

The tank shattered. The liquid inside flooded out, so much more of it than I had expected, and it was sticky and warm around my ankles. Cornelius leaped up onto my shoulder and shook himself.

The threads holding Millie up snapped, one by one, and she slithered out of the tank and onto the floor. The rush of the liquid had been enough to carry her over the worst of the shattered glass, so she only had a few scratches that I could see. The black heart, dragged behind her, looked deflated and soggy. I fought down the urge to vomit.

Sylvester let go of my hand and knelt next to Millie's body. He removed each pin gently and bloodlessly, then took the cord attaching her to her heart and pulled it apart between his hands. It stretched out for a second, long and sinewy, and then snapped with a sound that nearly turned my stomach again. We both stared down at her.

For a moment, I could see nothing—and then I saw the faint pulse at her throat, and the surge of her chest. I let out a long breath of relief.

"We'll have to bring her with us," said Sylvester. With a

flicker of his fingers, he bundled her up in warm, black clothing, making her skin look even more bloodless against it.

"I can carry her. You worry about the hearts."

I hefted Millie up so that her lolling head rested on my
shoulder and my arms were curved around her back and under
her knees.

The liquid from the tank had left her skin slick and a little
tacky to the touch, and my hands struggled to find purchase, but
eventually I had her more or less secure. She was a substantial
weight despite her diminutive size. Only the almost impercep-
tible shiver of her eyelashes and the occasional puff of breath
against my shoulder reassured me that she was still alive.

Quick as winking, Sylvester magicked us outside again,
near where the House had been. The fact that we had so many
more hearts to use now, despite the corruption slowly dissolv-
ing them, made me feel a lot better about facing the king. We
would not be entirely helpless—and perhaps I wouldn't have to
use the Weftwitch's seal after all.

"We'll need the carriage," I said.

"Foss . . ." Sylvester began, but then out of nowhere came
the sour, old-penny smell of copper, twanging and blue-
tinged in the air—don't ask me how a smell *smelled* blue and
smelled like a twanging sound, but it did—and the air around
us seemed to knot up tight and tense like a horse's haunches
before a leap.

I gasped and collapsed against the brick of the old woman's
house, barely holding onto Millie. The sorcerer was just as un-
prepared as I was, and he crumpled with a faint "*oh*," as if he
were mildly surprised, falling to the cobblestones.

"Sylvester!" I let Millie down, then knelt beside the sorcerer
and cupped his face in my hands. "What happened? What's
wrong?"

Cornelius mewed from my shoulder.

"My father . . ."

The sorcerer's breathing was shallow, his lips already bluish. I tore open his shirt, feeling the shock of the spell when my skin touched his, but pushing it aside so that I could feel across his torso and find his heart. His pulse was faint and thready. The veins on his chest stood out dark and angry, and all his muscles were tensed.

"It's a spell," he managed. "Weaker because cast from far away, but still potent. I had my protections in place, but they must have slipped for a moment . . ."

"Your father did this?"

"He must have been waiting . . . for us to get back."

"Is he going to try again?"

"I've put the protection spells back up, but . . ."

His eyes were milky, streaked with dark veins.

"Sylvester. *Sylvester*. But what? What do I do?"

His eyes flickered. I wanted to shake him and embrace him all at once. "*Sylvester!*" I hissed again.

"They will hold," he said, as if every word was a great effort.

"What can I do? How can I help you?"

"Pocket," he said.

"What?"

"The carriage . . . in my pocket."

"Are you delirious?"

He shook his head violently from side to side, eyes closed. "*Pocket*," he repeated.

I rummaged through the pockets of his cloak. There seemed to be an infinite amount of them, and my fingers brushed against textures I didn't recognize or want to investigate too closely. At one point, I could have sworn that my hand disappeared into one pocket and poked out of another.

It was a wildly disorganized manner of storing one's

magical items, and I made a mental note to talk to Sylvester about this later, when he wasn't about to die. Finally, I felt something that thrummed with the texture of "carriage" under my fingertips. I grasped it and pulled it out, keeping it concealed in my fist.

It was an uncomfortable sort of thing to hold, smooth but somehow complicated, and felt impatient in my hand. Somewhere inside it, the horses were stamping on the ground, ready to run.

I shook Sylvester until his eyes opened. "What do I do?" I hissed.

"Throw it," he managed to say.

I threw it onto the cobbles, where it exploded. From a tablet the size of a snuffbox, it burst open and became, once again, a full, heavily ornamented carriage and two horses with steaming nostrils and restless, stamping hooves.

"We have to go," said Sylvester, struggling to hold himself up on one elbow.

"You're no match for your father in this state!"

"I'm no match for him in any state," he said with the ghost of a smile. "But we have to try."

Cornelius hopped up into the carriage, and I hauled Sylvester up to follow. He was heavy, but I could just about manage it. I bumped him up the carriage steps in an undignified manner, arranging him on one of the seats before checking his pulse. It was steady, but soft.

"Leave it," said Sylvester. "I'm fine."

"Of course you're not," I said. The success of our mission seemed more and more unlikely with every passing moment. I went back for Millie and did the same with her, arranging her against the opposite door so that her head was propped up, and spreading one of the heavy furs over her. "How are you holding up?" I asked Sylvester.

"I'm fighting it," he said, panting a little. "But we have to go."

"Go where? We don't know where they are yet! They could be anywhere in the kingdom."

"No," he said, his breath still coming raggedly. "One good thing . . . about the spell. It's like an arrow shot at me . . . from far away . . . with a rope trailing behind. I can follow it back . . . see where it came from."

"You can tell where he is?"

"By holding on to his spell, yes. I can trace it back." He closed his eyes. "I'm so sorry, Foss."

"Why are you . . ." But then I realized.

Da.

CHAPTER 24

Of course.

The king was in *my* village. Of course he would go there. He knew I would follow. He knew I would do anything to stop him from hurting my da, the bastard, even if it meant letting him chop me up and use my heart to cure all the rest. Angry tears burned my eyes, but I scraped them away with the back of my hand. There was no time.

The horses surged forward. They seemed even faster than before, as if their muscles had been waiting in that strange limbo and itching to gallop again.

We sped across country as fast as they could carry us, which, as it turns out, was blindingly fast. I couldn't look out the window at the moonlit landscape streaking past or I would have been sick, so I kept my eyes determinedly turned downward. Sylvester did look better, with some color returning to his cheeks, but he still seemed weak.

"Can you use even a little heart magic to heal yourself?" I kept asking him. "Just a pinch. Just a sliver. Or however you measure it."

"No," he kept saying. "We can't afford to use up even a little more. I need everything I have."

Would he still be able to fight the king in this state? We were already badly outmatched by the king and his small army of sorceresses, and what had to be a burgeoning supply of new hearts.

My thoughts went round and round like one of Cornelius's mice. Speaking of Cornelius, he was curled up small as an ink-blot, and his frantic purr told me he was still in pain.

I felt so helpless—the only one in the carriage unharmed and completely unable to help the others. Completely unable to speed our journey, also. I longed for Sylvester's power, to whip the magical horses into even more of a frenzy, but all I could do was sit there and hope we would reach the village in time.

Despite myself, I dipped in and out of a restless, involuntary sleep, like someone bobbing for apples in a barrel. I didn't want to sleep—I couldn't afford to sleep—but my body disagreed.

Whenever I woke, I first grabbed Sylvester's wrist to feel for the throbbing of his pulse and then Millie's. I don't know what manner of heart the king had installed in his "children" after removing theirs, but it appeared to beat strongly and regularly in both.

Millie remained unconscious. Sylvester slept too, for the most part, breathing shallowly through his mouth. Occasionally, his breath would be silent, and then I would panic and wonder if he had died while I dozed. When I was feeling for his pulse for perhaps the twentieth time, he woke and took my hand.

"Foss," he said gently. "I am all right."

"You don't know that," I said.

Still holding my hand, he pressed both his and mine against

my chest, where what was left of my own heart ticked away rapidly. "Strong as ever," he said.

"What does that have to do with anything?" I whispered.

"I am bound to you as much as you are to me," said Sylvester. "I don't think I, or my sisters, ever fully understood heart magic, even though we practiced it. I don't think even my father fully understands it."

"What do you mean?" I asked.

"We saw it as harvesting. Taking what was ours by rights, as a farmer pulls potatoes from the ground. It affected those whose hearts, or part of them, were taken, but we believed— we, the magic-workers—that it affected us not at all. But we were wrong. It is not like picking crops at all. When we take a heart, something of ourselves is left behind in its place. That is what keeps the heartsick alive, I believe, until that little piece of magic runs out."

"But the sorceresses take hundreds of hearts, piece by piece," I pointed out.

"Yes, and hundreds of pieces of themselves are left behind," said Sylvester. "It gives them power, but it also leeches something away. Some . . . human essence. I have felt it coming back, with you. And because you have a resistance to the magic, and it takes effect on you so much more slowly, more and more of me has become tangled up with you as the spell endures."

I wasn't sure what to make of this. "So, what does that mean?"

"I can only guess. I doubt any such bond has been tried for as long as ours. But I believe that while you are hale and hearty, you sustain me also."

"I don't want to test that theory. I'd rather we both stayed alive as long as possible. All four of us, in fact."

"We are tougher than we look," said Sylvester. The talk seemed to have tired him. He let his head fall back and his mouth drop open again in sleep, the involuntary kind that pulls you under when your body needs the healing. Even as he relaxed into slumber, though, his hand held fast to mine.

I stayed awake and thought and thought. I was starting to form a plan of my own—one that Cornelius and Sylvester certainly wouldn't like, but perhaps the only one that could save us *and* halt the king's destruction . . . without using the seal to kill Sylvester along with the rest of his family. Which now included Millie. Possibly she was far enough along in her transformation that the spell would kill her too.

The king needed my heart to stop the corruption. Even with his supply of new hearts, after his barbaric ride through the kingdom, he still needed it. The new hearts would be infected by the Other Kingdom's corruption just as surely as the old ones, and apparently, I held the key to curing them.

If I bargained myself in exchange for the king ceasing to harvest—at least for now—then I could figure out how to escape him later. I knew I had the strength for it; I had proven that to myself over and over these past weeks. It was Da, Sylvester, and Cornelius—and now Millie—for whom I worried.

We reached my village as morning was beginning to gray the sky. It seemed deserted, unnaturally so, as the city had been. On a regular morning, a village such as this, surrounded by farms and full of those who needed to rise early to work and perform their chores, would already be bustling.

I hoped that the seemingly dead streets were due to the villagers still hiding successfully in the woods and not due to any more sinister reason—and I hoped above all that Da was all right. I had barely allowed myself to think about him, but now all my love and worry came back in a rush.

I looked around at my companions. Millie still slept, of course, concerningly pale and blue about the lips, but the infinitesimal rise and fall of her chest reassured me that she was still alive.

Cornelius woke and stretched. I could see he was a little stiff still, but otherwise he seemed back to his normal self.

I nudged Sylvester, who appeared to be sleeping as deeply as Millie. For a moment I panicked, thinking he would not wake up, but he opened his eyes at last, as if it were a great effort.

"We're here," I said gently.

His eyes stayed soft and unfocused with sleep for a minute, then cleared and hardened as he remembered where we were. What we were attempting to do.

"I hope the villagers made it to the forest," said Sylvester, echoing my earlier thoughts.

"Do you think they would still be safe there?" I asked.

"No, but it might slow my father down a little," said Sylvester.

The horses' hooves rang loud and tinny on the cobblestones. We rounded the corner that opened up to the village square and realized at once that our hopes had been in vain.

It was crowded with people who stood unnaturally silent and still, pale around the lips, and ringed with the ornate magicworkers' carriages, with a shimmering row of yellow-gray mist behind those, providing a shifting, sinister backdrop to it all.

It could have been a theater performance, so carefully arranged was it, and I had the feeling that was exactly what it was meant to be—a stage set for our final meeting with the king, planned and orchestrated entirely by him.

He had known exactly when we would be coming, it seemed. We were already at a disadvantage, and the irony of facing the king in the place where I had met Sylvester for the first time was not lost on me.

"It is no matter," Sylvester said to me quietly, seeing the worry on my face. "We knew we would have to meet him, after all. If he is expecting us, that changes nothing. And remember—he'll want to keep you alive. You are useful to him."

"Very comforting, thank you."

I recognized villagers I knew, and some that I didn't, but I could not see Da among them, no matter how I squinted. They were clearly enchanted—either that, or had been harvested already, because they had the glazed and passive look of the thralls.

I suspected, though, that the king would have left them untouched for our arrival, all the better to manipulate us. I suppose I was grateful I still had some usefulness to him, but the idea of those old hands getting anywhere near me again made my skin crawl.

As our carriage pulled up and halted, the sorceresses stepped down from their own carriages one by one. The array was quite dazzling. The initial impression was one of Beauty with a capital letter; Beauty times eleven; Beauty beyond comprehension.

It made you want to drop your gaze. It made you feel unworthy. And, as I knew, it made you long to uproot your whole life and follow them to destruction.

The final and most spectacular carriage, of course, held King Darius. Half a dozen footmen scurried to open the door and help him down the stairs. He cut an impressive figure, I had to admit, crown and all, despite his ugliness.

He gave a grisly grin. But worse than the gaudy line of sorceresses, worse than the wizened figure of the king in his puce robes that made his skin more corpselike than ever, were the carts hitched behind each of the carriages.

They were ornate, too—the magic-workers never missed a chance to spangle anything over with jewels and curlicues—but stacked high with jars full of that golden preserving liquid, and hearts.

I could only imagine the sound as they traveled—the jars

knocking against each other, sloshing that liquid about, and sending the hearts flapping and slapping against the glass sides. It turned my stomach.

Sylvester was even paler than usual; he might as well have been a pen-and-ink drawing for all the color on him. Cornelius stood with his back paws on the seat and his front paws on the carriage windowsill, staring out, while his fur stood like the bristles of a brush along his back.

"You stay in here, Cornelius, and watch Millie," I said. "You can slip away unnoticed if you need to. I doubt the king knows about you."

"We'll see," said Cornelius grimly.

As we stepped out, we were able to look more closely at the assembled crowd. My whole village was there, but it wasn't the only one.

There were hundreds of people, bespelled and harried from their homes for the harvest, travel-weary, dusty, and swaying on their feet in the square where we had once all stood and marveled at the sorceresses' carriages as a pretty novelty and distraction from our daily lives—once a danger that brought us a pleasant thrill now and then, and little more.

I imagined that line of people snaking all the way back to the city—those who were unable to keep up with the unnatural speed of the magic-workers' procession, but felt the irresistible desire to follow them anyway, to keep pace with those carts loaded with their clinking stock of jars and their obscene contents.

"Sylvester!" cried the king in a voice that carried unnaturally far. He did not seem at all surprised to see us. In fact, I could see the twitch of a smile at the corner of his thin lips.

The crowd stayed completely still and silent. I could feel my heart pulsing in my throat. Sylvester took my hand, and together, we walked toward the assembly.

Sylvester had never looked more regal: his hair falling in its dark waves across his white forehead, his gray-blue eyes unnaturally light and gleaming. All the magic-workers seemed like actors in a play, and the rest of us were merely the audience lucky enough to gaze upon them. Only I knew that his teeth were gritted in pain.

"Father," said Sylvester, and his voice had the same unnatural volume as the king's. Everyone in every corner of the village could hear him, I was sure. We walked just far enough forward that everyone could see us clearly and stopped.

"That was a clever trick, putting us all to sleep," said the king. "I didn't think you had it in you."

"You have never understood my powers," said Sylvester.

"True, I suppose," said the king. "You have never been consistent. Not like your sisters."

"Which is why you always preferred them."

"Preferred? No. I had a foolish desire for a son, despite my dislike for my own father. I made so many failed attempts! And it transpires that you are one of them, despite my initial hope. A problem easily solved, fortunately."

"Perhaps because you killed your own father," said Sylvester without expression. "That could lead to some trouble with sons."

"You think I have a guilty conscience?" asked the king, smiling.

Sylvester shrugged. "It's possible."

"Ah, yes. They are still angry about that then, over there?"

"I think they are angrier that you are invading their borders year after year."

"So you know all about my younger days, now," said the king. " You and your little housekeeper. And armed with this knowledge, you have come here to do . . . what, exactly?"

"To stop you."

"Do you really think I would create a child capable of defeating me? I *made* you. I know exactly what you can do."

"No, you don't. That has always frightened you about me. I see that now."

"Frightened?" The king bared his teeth. "You do have odd fancies, Sylvester. Speaking of which. I still need the girl if we are to fight the corruption. And that's what you want, after all, isn't it?"

"What?" said Sylvester. "No. Of course I don't."

"I'm surprised. I thought your new, self-sacrificing nature would see the benefit of giving up your little housekeeper for the sake of saving a thousand others. If I stop the heart rot, we need harvest no more."

"No."

"Perhaps this will help." The king gestured to one of the footmen. He opened the king's carriage door and hauled Da out from within. I made an involuntary movement forward, but Sylvester held me back. Da was bound at the wrists but seemed unharmed. He tried to smile at me, and what was left of my heart twisted in my breast.

"Let him go!" I cried.

"Gladly," said the king. "I will exchange the father for the daughter. A fair trade. Or rather, I shall trade the father and *all* these fine people for the daughter. Really, you are getting the better end of the bargain, even though her sort is rare."

"Father," said Sylvester, "you cannot harvest all these people, and you cannot have Foss. Perhaps it is good that the hearts have become infected. It is time to try a different way."

The king snorted. "You have been of age for only a few months. You do not understand."

"But I do," said Sylvester. "You don't need hearts for magic. I know that now."

"To help a cow with its milking and a hen its laying? No. But for anything more than that, we need them. How long do you think this kingdom would last without us protecting its borders with heart magic? Keeping invading armies at bay?"

"The only invading army is you," said Sylvester quietly.

"That was what they told you? You don't think they covet our wealth? Our prosperity? Our crops grow lush and our livestock plump under my protection, and the kingdom is happy and thriving. For a hundred years, they have seen no war, no famine. Babies are born healthy and hale."

"Not anymore."

"And whose doing is that?" argued the king. "Any harm that has come to this kingdom has come from beyond our borders. Before the corruption spread, we took so few hearts. Snippets, here and there. Rarely whole hearts. A small sacrifice. If anyone is to blame for this harvest, it must be your friends over there."

"It is not right, however few you take," said Sylvester. "I have learned that, too.

"You have only the faintest inkling of just how powerful hearts are—and what I can do with them. You don't care if your subjects are happy, or peaceful. All you want is the power their hearts give you and to push the borders ever outward. You want more, more, more. Always." Sylvester shook his head.

"And again, I say, so? What does it matter if all I want from them is their hearts? Most of them will live their whole lives with their heart intact. They will never know about the world beyond their borders."

"They are cattle," said Sylvester.

The king shrugged. "Maybe. But if the cattle are content . . ."

I looked around at the assembled crowd, bespelled into stillness. The mothers, the housewives, the greengrocers, the apothecaries, the doctors, the barkeeps, the wenches, the lawmen, the children, the farmers, the laborers, the drunks, the schoolteachers, the blacksmiths, the pretty girls, the plain girls.

I felt such a hatred for the king at that moment that I almost felt like a sorceress myself, with the power to reduce someone to a burning heap of ash.

"Camilla," said the king to one of the sorceresses, and even in the midst of the horror I thought, *Of course she has a name like Camilla.* "Show them how gentle we are. Show them that they will not die. It is giving up a small thing, a very little thing, in exchange for peace and prosperity. Show them."

The sorceress chose, of all people, Aron. Aron of the "Toad Wine." There were many times I had fantasized about getting some sort of revenge for how he had treated me, but I would never have wished this upon him.

She just had to smile at him, and he moved toward her as if in a dream—I knew how that felt—and, when he reached her, allowed her to stroke his cheek and ruffle his hair, in a sisterly manner, while he swayed under her touch.

Then, as the whole village watched, she reached her hand into his chest, and he arched his back, and his head tipped back, mouth open like the big lunk he was, and his feet seemed to rise from the ground. She released him, and he collapsed. Only for a moment, though, and then he struggled to his feet, dazed and dead eyed. The sorceress held up his heart to show the crowd—crimson and glistening—before dropping it into a jar at her waist.

"See?" said the king. "It does not kill you."

After that horror show, I don't think anyone cared. Aron was so obviously empty, so obviously doomed. You could feel the fear, like a wind passing through us all, even though they were bespelled. None of the villagers had ever seen a whole heart taken at once.

"You have no idea how much study and experimentation it took," the king went on conversationally. "I started with animals, of course. Small ones. Then worked my way up. I found power my father could never have dreamed of."

"Then face me with your own magic," challenged Sylvester. "No hearts."

"Why on earth would I do that? This isn't a fairy tale, boy."

Sylvester made a sudden gesture as if to hurl one of his fireballs at his father but instead he staggered. I caught him as he started to wilt, ignoring the sorcerous tingle in the air and the overpowering scent of hot metal that magic seemed to bring with it. His eyes lost their unnaturally bright light and faded to their usual gray blue.

"I'm sorry," he said, leaning on me heavily.

"You have nothing to be sorry for," I said. "You tried."

He flicked his gaze upward to where his father still stood, arms upraised.

"Let my da go!" I cried, hatred turning my voice hoarse. "You can have my heart. I will come willingly. Just let my da go, and let Sylvester live."

"Foss . . ." protested Sylvester, but it was an effort for him to speak.

"You have to release him first," I shouted.

"With pleasure," said the king, and with a flick of his wrist, Da's bonds were gone, which is what I had hoped would happen.

Da rushed over to us, seeing me buckling under the sorcerer's weight, and threw Sylvester's other arm over his shoulders. We were both so much shorter than him that, even in that tense moment, I was aware of how comical it must look—two squat stakes propping up a willow tree.

The king turned away, back to his daughters, brushing his

hands briskly together like a man appreciating a hard job well completed.

"Come on, girl," he said to me over his shoulder. "That was the bargain."

"Let me say goodbye, at least," I snapped at him. "One more minute is no skin off your nose."

Sylvester released me and stood, swaying a little. Da kept one hand on his shoulder, to steady him.

"There must be something else we can try," Da whispered urgently.

Sylvester shook his head. "I am too weak," he said. "I am sorry. And even if I could fight him without the advantage of surprise . . . I have only a handful of hearts left, all near corrupted, and he has half a kingdom's worth. It was a fool's hope to begin with, but we had to try. Without a good heart, I'm no better than a hedge-witch telling fortunes."

I squeezed my eyes tight shut. Despite the heartsickness, my pain and exhaustion, I had traveled across two kingdoms, murdered a magic-worker—as Cornelius had pointed out—won the heart of a sorcerer, and, overall, done more than I had ever thought was possible . . . And it still was not enough in this last, crucial moment.

"Sylvester," I pleaded. "We have to try. Please. Just one more time. Use all the hearts we have. We have managed impossible things together before."

"I don't have the strength," he said.

"Yes, you *do*," I snapped. I grabbed both his hands in mine. "You said our connection is powerful. Use it. Use whatever we have left. We have to try, even just once."

He looked at me with those strange, light eyes and nodded.

"What are you doing?" asked the king, but it was too late, because Sylvester had already begun to weave a spell. It wrapped around us like ivy. I felt the power of all the hearts we had salvaged start to glow and burn in my veins. I looked up at Sylvester, and he looked back at me with his usual cool, blank stare.

"I . . . I love you."

"I love you, too," he said, and smiled. Then he reached for me, embraced me, and I felt the coiling magic flow away from me and into him. Whatever was pulling at me, tugging at me, using the power left in my poor heart, reversed itself and started flowing back toward him. I tried to clutch at it as you would clutch at a rope slipping through your fingers, but it squirmed beneath my touch and wriggled free.

"Sylvester. No." This wasn't the plan. "What are you doing?"

"We're not meant to be here, Foss," he said. "Any of us. But you are."

The words died in my mouth. Sylvester's eyes were wider and darker than I had ever seen them.

He kissed me, a fierce kiss with *goodbye* spoken silently in every second of it, and then he pulled away, and I saw that he was clutching something in his fist. I thought at first that it might be one of his magical toys, but it was too small.

Dread came over me. I felt for the seal in my pocket—its familiar smooth sides and carved top. It wasn't there.

"Sylvester, you idiot!" I yelled. He smiled a wide, heartbreaking smile, just for me.

"I heard you talking with the Weftwitch. I know what this is. I know what I have to do."

"No! No, I was never going to use it! *Sylvester! Don't you dare!*"

"I know you never would," he said. "Which is why I must."

His gaze reached out across the small distance between us, as it had the very first time we met, and like that first time, I felt it pierce me like a thorn and open me like a flower.

It was already too late, I knew. Sylvester had whispered his intentions to the seal, and its terrible, inexorable work had begun. The Weftwitch's magic was sure and swift. Terrible pressure built in the air around us, and the sky turned black as a bruise. The Other Kingdom's revenge was powerful.

The crowd swayed like so many ears of corn. The king staggered, his face fixed in a grimace of rage and confusion.

Sylvester floated a little way off the ground, his cloak swirling around, the seal in his open palm blooming like a black rose as its poisonous magic spread to encompass us all.

Well. I should have been terrified, but instead, all I felt was a great, boiling annoyance at him and his ridiculous desire to sacrifice himself.

That annoyance rose up in me, all tangled with love—both the bespelled love and the real—and then that in turn tangled with the powerful magic of the seal and Sylvester's own wild, erratic powers, until we were both knitted together again, even more strongly than before.

My own feet rose off the ground until I was right opposite him, staring into his perfect face and his startled eyes.

"Foss . . . ? What are you . . . ?"

This time I kissed him, putting all of that mess of power, anger, and longing into it, even as I felt the Other Kingdom's spell start to drain his power away, unmaking him from the inside out.

Live, you idiot, live, I thought as forcefully as I could. It was working. It had to work. I would not let him go. He kissed me back, finally, and I felt his smile. When we broke apart, I tore my gaze away from him to look down and watch the Other Kingdom's spell work its devastating power on the magic-workers.

Sylvester's sisters dropped, one by one, like a line of elegant dominoes, to lie beautifully pale and disheveled on the stones.

A poisonous mist the king had summoned blew away like dandelion fluff, just as light and just as harmless.

And then I watched the king double over, as comically jerky as a marionette, and then try to right himself, and then fall to the ground as suddenly and heavily as if a giant palm had flattened him there.

Somewhere else in the kingdom, I imagined a great storeroom full of hearts was crumbling too, or perhaps finally succumbing to the mold, as the king's last protections fell away. I hoped the vicious mist was melting, slowly opening our borders, welcoming us back to the wider world, and freeing all the souls trapped within.

The seal had worked like a charm, it seemed, and no one but Sylvester and I—and Da—knew what had happened. We lowered to the ground again as the magic unspooled around us, snatched away by the wind like leaves blown from a tree.

I almost laughed in relief and waited for him to laugh with me—but I knew the moment he died, the very moment, because his lips grew still and lifeless as wax against mine. He slumped to the ground. Da rushed over, and as he did, I felt the sorcerer's spell lift off me—for good this time, and with none of the joy and lightness I had felt in the Weftwitch's wood. He had done it—the noble, maddening, ridiculous fool—given his own heart in exchange for what remained of mine.

The dregs of the enchantment passed through me like a swift fever, burning me up and turning my bowels to water, and then it was gone, leaving me weak and bereft.

I was free, but I did not feel free. "Sylvester, you bastard!" I yelled through a raw throat—or tried to yell. My voice was hoarse and cracked and drowned out by someone else's shout: "They're dead! They're all dead!"

The crowd, freed from the spell, surged forward, parting

around me and Da where we crouched next to Sylvester's body as if we were a rock in a rushing stream.

They ignored the king—who in death had seemed to shrivel and pale even further, curling up on himself like a corn husk left in the sun—and rushed to the corpses of the women.

As the last of the magic-workers' spells passed, the villagers touched the sorceresses' smooth cheeks and closed the lids over their still-shining eyes; let their silken hair trickle through their fingers, soft as water; fingered the fine clothing tentatively, hushed and awed by bodices and skirts that were worth more than our entire village put together.

I saw people slip rings from dead fingers, and snip locks of hair and swatches of rich fabric. There was an odd worshipfulness to the way they touched them, and a greed, a hunger, an impossible desire to consume the beauty that lay lifeless before them.

There was grief, too, and I understood it. There is sorrow whenever a lovely thing dies, no matter how dangerous it may have been in life.

My grief was of a more specific, personal kind: my own precious sorcerer lay dead. I shielded him from those who would have prodded and poked him as they were doing to the others, snarling at them like a dog. Da rested his big hand on my head, stroking my hair as he had done when I was a sprout.

"It is better this way, sweetheart," he said. "Whatever world we have without them will be better, even if it is hard for a little while."

I only realized Cornelius was on my shoulder when he licked the tears from my cheeks. He was kneading my neck with a frantic, urgent rhythm, trying to provide what comfort he could. I reached up to touch him.

"I'm sorry, Foss," he said.

"You can still talk!" I felt a surge of excitement. If the House's spell still held, did that mean . . . ?

"Yes. But he's dead, Foss. I'm sorry. Look, the carriages are all still here, and the horses. It looks like some spells go on even after the ones who cast them die."

My small hope faded. "And Millie?" I asked, my voice cracking.

"She is alive. Asleep, but alive. I suppose she hadn't turned into one of them yet."

Such a small relief, but it was something to hold on to as the grief threatened to overtake me entirely.

Gradually, the crowd dispersed. I had no sense of the passing of time, but it must have been an hour or more before the last straggler left, leaving the magic-workers' bodies where they had fallen.

There would be talk tomorrow, and commotion, but today had been so strange and so world-changing that I imagined most would sit in their front rooms, perhaps with a comforting cup of tea, staring into space.

The village felt very gray. I watched as Aron's parents helped what was left of him to his feet, their faces wet with tears, and led him home. He would have the dubious honor of being the last person harvested, then.

I wish we had been in time to save the hundreds of others the king had harvested that day. I wish that everyone knew what we had sacrificed. I knew they were shaken, for now, by the spectacle of it all and relieved to have survived.

Our kingdom had been made anew—freed—but thrown into chaos. There would be confusion and recriminations, some of them directed at me. I would have to talk and talk until I was sick of it, explaining.

I didn't want to face it all alone.

It started to rain.

"Foss . . ." said Da, touching me on the shoulder.

Once we were home, I knew Da would reluctantly leave me alone with my grief. He would light the fire, I knew, and fill the kettle, and start something roasting in the stove, because we were never short of good cuts of meat.

I wasn't ready for that. I wasn't ready for the next part of my life to begin.

"Go home, Da," I said. "I'll catch up. Take the carriage, and Millie. She can have my bed."

"Foss . . ."

"Cornelius, you go too. I'm all right. I promise. I just want a few minutes alone . . . with him. Before you take the body."

"All right," said Da. "I'll come back with the cart in a bit. We'll make sure he gets a proper burial." He looked over at the carriages and the carts full of jars. "We'll have to bury all those somewhere too. Somewhere respectful-like."

I watched Da toddle off toward home, Cornelius in his arms, and then I stared down at Sylvester's body.

He was quite unchanged. I stared for a long time. I do not know how long. The rain was so light now that the droplets seemed almost to hover in the air. A light mist of water draped around my shoulders like a shawl. It was comforting.

We had been bound together for weeks now, the sorcerer and I, closer than any two sweethearts before. Who else could say that their beloved had their heart and really, truly mean it? A piece of my heart had lived in him, somehow, and had changed him. And he had changed me.

Cornelius wandered back after a while—an hour perhaps, although it was difficult to judge how much time had passed— picking his way through the wet grass and shaking off each paw with fastidious care. He settled himself by my feet and washed himself—a pointless exercise, as the misty rain kept on falling.

"Are you going to come home?" he said at last.

"Eventually," I said. "I'm thinking."

"I didn't think he would do something like that."

"He was very brave."

"So were you," said the little cat.

"I know," I sighed. "For what good it did."

We stared at the sorcerer's body for a while. I thought for a moment that I saw his chest rise and fall, but it was an illusion of the still-falling rain that shimmered in the air.

"I'm going back again," said Cornelius. "Will you be all right?"

"Yes," I replied. "I won't be long."

He licked my wrist, a tiny, rough burst of affection, and trotted off, back toward the house. I kept staring at the sorcerer. Part of me was dead right along with him, I thought. Part of my heart lay there, waiting to be buried, and another part of it had dissolved to dust. What was left?

A bubble of a thought rose in my head, so delicate that I was afraid to look at it directly for fear of bursting it. I let it float there, gently, and then I let it come to rest. It whispered a question:

If my heart had melded with his, if our bond had changed him as much as it had changed me, if we were muddled and mixed-up together, as he had said . . . Was there enough humanity in him now to survive?

The magic-workers had been destroyed, yes, and whatever part of Sylvester had been created by the king was destroyed also. But that didn't mean *all* of him had been destroyed.

I placed my hand against Sylvester's breast. I felt the full brokenness of my poor, depleted, bisected heart, piecemeal in my chest, too deep and dark for tears. My heart was broken, all right, and I would have to drag it around with me for all of my days. Unless . . .

My hand tingled and grew hot. Beneath my palm, Sylvester's

skin began to warm, but he lay still, and there was no answering heartbeat to my touch.

I remembered what I had said to him, all those weeks ago, about how, in the old stories, a kiss would break the spell, and I leaned forward to press my rain-wet lips to his. His were heartbreakingly warm and soft, but there was still no movement. No breath.

"Live, damn you! Live!" I shouted into his face. I dug my hands into the earth and uprooted great handfuls of grass, then threw the clods as far and as hard as I could. Then I sank back, my feet in a puddle and my muddy hands over my eyes, sobbing so hard that the snot ran as freely as the tears. I'm sure it was a lovely sight.

And he stirred.

And he opened his eyes.

"Foss," he said.

I couldn't have looked any less romantic, wet, gaping like a frog and wiping my nose on my sleeve, but he was staring at me like I had hung the stars, as he sat upright and ran his hands through his hair.

I could hardly believe he was really back. The flush of life returned to his skin—and was it my imagination, or was his face a little less perfect than before? Still beautiful, but not inhumanly so.

The otherworldly quality seemed to be gone. His nose was a little crooked, as if it had been broken a long time ago and improperly set. There was a smattering of freckles across his nose and cheekbones that I had never noticed before—and the spell had made me memorize every detail of his face.

He held his hands palms up in front of his face and stared at them.

"You're alive," I said stupidly.

"It would appear so," he said. He turned his hands over to examine their backs. "I feel . . . different."

"You look different," I said. He took my hand, and even his skin felt more human—warmer, slightly damp against mine.

"Are they dead?" he asked.

"Yes," I said. "It worked." The wide smile spreading across my face was almost painful.

"Millie?"

"She lived. We did it. She's all right."

"Are you still under the spell?" he asked.

"No." I took a quick inventory of myself, to make sure. "No, I felt it disappear when you . . . died. Or whatever happened to you. And it hasn't come back."

"So does that mean . . ." He did not finish his sentence but instead leaned toward me, hesitantly, and I made up the distance between us and kissed him. He tasted of rain and simple human sweat, and he was warmer than he had been before.

When we parted, he smiled at me. One of his front teeth was very slightly crooked. He was no longer my sorcerer—he was just . . .

"Sylvester," I said.

"How long was I . . . asleep?" he said.

I remembered what he had done and hit him as hard as I could manage on his arm. "Why did you do that? You could have *told* me."

He touched his arm where my punch had landed with a kind of wonder, as if he had never felt pain before. "I couldn't tell you," he said. "You wouldn't have let me do it."

"You're an idiot. You couldn't have done it without me."

"I know that now."

"You *died*."

I glared at him, then burst into tears again. I felt his arms around my shoulders and the warmth of him against my me as he pulled me close.

It was such a relief to have him here, to have him here to be furious with. He let me cry myself out, then waited as I very unromantically blew my nose.

"What will the world look like now?" he wondered.

"Well, for one thing, there's no king," I said. "Unless you're the king now that your father's dead. I'm not sure how the people will feel about another magic-worker being in charge, though."

"I don't want to be king," he said quickly. "And I don't think I'm a magic-worker anymore."

I saw a familiar shape wading through the puddles toward us: Da, with Cornelius on his shoulder.

"We'd better go tell him that you survived, despite your best attempts," I said.

"And that you are all stuck with me now."

"So it appears," I said, and he smiled and kissed me again for a long time.

As Cornelius had pointed out, many spells do not end when the magic-worker who had created them dies, as paintings do not disappear when the artists are no more.

The king's barrier still shimmers around the kingdom, but without its steady diet of hearts, it has started to gradually dissolve and disappear, freeing a few of the trapped souls at a time as it disintegrates.

One day, all of them will be released, free to float off to wherever souls were meant to go before the king trapped them in his magical web. It gives me comfort to know that Dav and Colin and the rest of the Snagged will be at peace at last.

We were able to send messages through not long after the king's death, to tell the Weftwitch and the rest of them what had happened. And now with the mist dissipated enough, many distant cousins were finally able to reunite after a century apart.

The kingdoms could be one again within my lifetime, perhaps. I still have some resentment toward the Weftwitch for her manipulation of the Snagged—and of me—but I understand her reasons.

I have promised that I will visit her, so that she can teach me more of what it means to be like us, and how I can put my particular magic-resisting skill to use as we rebuild.

We no longer had the relentlessly healthy crops and livestock that had seduced us into accepting the sorceresses' rule, but we did well enough.

Most babies were born healthy, but not all, and death of the mother or offspring during childbirth became, not commonplace, but accepted. I never heard a peep again about being wrong or cursed in some way, once our kingdom learned the normal way of things again.

Millie stayed with us. We do not know yet what kind of abilities she has, since her transformation into a sorceress was interrupted, but we do not trouble her with questions.

She has very little memory of the time before, which is a blessing, and she is very occupied with the important business of being a child. She has my old room in Da's house and is the great joy of his days—although he continues to hint at the possibility of more children in the future, giving Sylvester a wink that makes me blush every time.

Cornelius still has his voice, which he uses often and loudly. He still mews like a normal cat when fish is in the offing, but at all other times, he considers normal cat noises beneath him, and prides himself on his grasp of the human language and improved accent.

He and Da get along famously and often snooze together in the armchair in front of the fire, purrs and snores merging to become one contented, rumbling sound.

I work in the shop more and more now, as Da grays and grows more stooped, but I smile more than I used to, and the villagers curtsy or tip their hats to me as they would to a fine lady, despite my bloodied apron and the mobcap over my hair.

After a while of refusing to try, Sylvester found he could still create his little toys of flame and light, and he amuses the village sprouts with them, but performs few other spells. And magic seems to be creeping back into our kingdom—the natural, joyful kind.

Some of the new babies have grown into toddlers with little charms and magicks of their own. This startled their parents to no end at first, but it is quickly becoming usual. We are amazingly adaptable, it turns out.

We have all the jars of hearts that the king took in a big shed behind our house, and we work daily to see if there is a way to return them fully to their owners across the kingdom.

At least one or two of the Snagged trickle in to see us every day. Everyone in the village knows about the Snagged now, from that terrible day of harvest, and treats them well, offering them shelter and food for as long as they need it.

Sylvester has fashioned a sort of pendant that holds a piece of heart, and he devised a charm that allows it to connect again to its previous owner—taking inspiration from the magic-workers' transformation process, in reverse—which serves to keep the Snagged alive and hearty while we work on a larger cure.

As for Sylvester and me, we wake together in the new room Da built on the back of the house, behind the shop, and we sleep together in a tangle of rough blankets at the end of each day, Cornelius snoring at our feet.

I look at the road to my future spread before me, and I no longer see it pockmarked and rutted with barrenness and the ravages of solitude.

Instead, I see my life stretching ahead, as rich and complex as any woman's, even the most beautiful, because I know my strength now, and my worth, and nothing ahead can daunt me after what I have already overcome.

I might even stand before the holy man one day, with a basket of corn and wildflowers over my arm, and say the sacred words. And our children will grow to adulthood hearing tales of beautiful women who plucked hearts like apples and stole them away. But they will only be stories, and there will be no more need for fear.

Acknowledgments

First of all, a huge thanks to my agent, Sam Farkas of the Jill Grinberg Literary Agency, without whom this book quite literally wouldn't exist. She took a chance on the whimsical little novella that I submitted to her when I was sleep-deprived and hormonal with a newborn, and helped me to shape it into the fully fleshed-out story that became *A Harvest of Hearts*. Having Sam believe in me, my writing, and this book was such an immense gift.

Wrestling a book into shape is something like trying to fold a fitted sheet, if the sheet is the size of a football stadium and you're doing it blindfolded while wearing oven mitts and attempting to hum "The Star-Spangled Banner" at the same time. I was lucky enough to work with two absolutely top-notch editors and wonderful human beings—Diana Pho of Erewhon in the USA, and Ajebowale Roberts of Harper Voyager in the UK. Both of them gave such insightful and constructive notes. I'm honored to have two such inspiring women working to make this book the best it can be.

Thank you to the whole team at Erewhon and Kensington for their enthusiasm and passion for this book and all the others on their list. It is an honor to be one of their authors, and they give me hope for the future of traditional publishing. Thank you particularly to Viengsamai Fetters and the ebullient Marty Cahill for their encouragement and hard work.

I am very grateful to Theophina Gabriel, who provided

a sensitivity reading. The book deals heavily with matters of appearance—reality and illusion, perceptions of beauty and ugliness. Theophina's thoughtful comments helped to make sure I approached these themes in a conscious and responsible way.

On a personal note, thank you to friends who provide endless support and encouragement—my best friends Kelley Martin and Ally Mullord, my honorary brothers, Justin and Jason Scalise, and my group chat gurus Leah Fernandez and Layna Alberga, with whom I've been in a constant and wonderful running commentary for over five years.

And of course my family in the States and in New Zealand, particularly my husband, Kenny, and my daughter, Lyra, the great joys of my life.

Thanks also to my cats—Momo, Monty, Maggie, Babs, and Molly—who were no help at all but who are pleasingly furry and appreciated nonetheless. Except for whichever one of them peed on my laptop that time.